HARD PREJUDICE

A DAN RENO NOVEL

DAVE STANTON

LaSalle Davis Books

Cover art by *Steve Whan*

ISBN: 0989603148
ISBN 13: 9780989603140
Library of Congress Control Number: 2014922810
LaSallee Davis Books, San Jose, CA

For the hardcore rock n' rollers:

*Steve Ertzner, Jerry Kisling, Ernie Salle, and
Steve Whan*

1

BY ALL ACCOUNTS, ALEX Newman's life began in unfortunate circumstances and went downhill from there. Raised in lower-middleclass white suburbia, he dropped out of high school after his alcoholic parents divorced, and embarked on a career as a small-time crook. His record was littered with shoplifting and petty theft collars, and along the way he'd developed a particular fondness for rock cocaine. Now, at age thirty-four, he was a full-time addict. I'd learned of Alex Newman when his bail bondsman contacted me. Newman had skipped on a breaking and entering charge after his mother scraped together a five-thousand-dollar bond. Good son that he was, Newman flew the coop the minute he was released from lockup.

It didn't take long to find him. He lived in an oversized camper shell bolted to the bed of a rust-bucket Toyota pickup. A dealer he'd burned for fifty bucks put me onto him, said he'd probably be parked in one of a few out-of-the-way places.

I spotted his rickety contraption sitting on the dirt shoulder of a dead-end road under a cluster of oak trees that partially hid the camper. Beyond the trees, the terrain dropped into a rock-strewn gully that led into the forest. Five thousand feet up, the pine-studded peaks of the Sierra Nevadas were resplendent in the midday sun.

The camper's windows were taped over with cardboard. I got out of my rig and walked around the vehicle. No one was in the cab, but I could hear a faint tinkling of music from the camper. I went to the back door and jerked the handle. It was locked.

"Alex Newman, open up," I said. When nothing happened I pounded the door with the meat of my fist. "Open up, or I'll bust it in." I waited for a minute in the pleasant shade, until it became clear he hoped I'd just go away. It was a bad strategy but probably the best option he had.

As I returned to my truck for a crowbar, I heard scuffling and turned to see a man climbing from the gulley. Dirt coated the fronts of his blue jeans, his hollow cheeks were two weeks unshaven, and his long black hair looked stiff with grease. About six feet and a bony 160.

I ignored him and started back to the Toyota with the crowbar.

"What you think you're doing?" he asked, his eyes wide and dilated. No doubt whacked on meth or coke.

"You friends with Alex Newman?"

"Damn right I am."

"Stand back, please." I swung the weighted end of the bar and punched a big crease in the aluminum door.

"Hey, you can't—" he started, then the words became strangled in his throat. He froze for a moment, and I could almost hear his brain synapses misfiring. In his condition, any decision would likely be the wrong one. He confirmed it by coming up behind me and launching a roundhouse punch that was both ill-timed and weak. I blocked it and cracked him in the nose with my elbow. His eyes went dull, and he sat down hard and held his dirt-caked fingers to his face. I pulled a plastic tie from my pocket, shoved him facedown into the ground, and cinched his hands behind him. "You prick, you lousy bastard," he moaned.

I left him lying in the dirt and swung the crowbar into the door again.

"Last chance, Alex. Open the goddamned door." I waited a few seconds, then jammed the bar into the slot along the frame and jerked hard. The lock mechanism snapped, and the door flew open. "Fuck you!" a shirtless man rasped, his head big over his scrawny white torso. Crouching, he thrust a lit blowtorch at my face.

I dodged the blue flame and swung the crowbar. It banged into the canister with a loud ping, and the torch fell from Newman's hands. He scrambled back, but I reached forward, snatched him by his greasy hair, and yanked him out of the camper. His knees hit the ground hard, and he tried to get up and run, but before he could I kicked him in the ribs, the blow just enough to take his wind. He fell on his side and stared up at me with pleading eyes.

"Party's over," I said, and slapped a pair of cuffs on his wrists. I looked into the camper, where his crack pipe lay smoldering amid a slew of beer bottles, porno magazines, and dirty ashtrays. Propped against one of the bottles was a syringe.

"Let's go," I said. I pulled Alex Newman to his feet and pushed him toward my truck. When we got there, I sat him in the front seat and chained his wrists to a D-link installed in the passenger seat floor. Hunched over, he looked up at me. "I was gonna clean up. I was gonna get a job."

"Tell it to the judge," I said, watching the skinny, long-haired dude stagger to his feet and jog off, his hands cinched behind him. I shut my truck door, called 911, and asked South Lake Tahoe PD to send a tow truck. Then I called the bail bondsman and told him I'd recovered his fugitive. Alex Newman didn't have much to say after that. I suppose he knew the routine.

• • •

The parking lot was packed when we arrived at the police complex. I parked in a red zone and led Newman to the side door for booking. While I waited for the jailer, my eyes wandered out the window to the courthouse across the street, where there was some sort of commotion. At least a hundred people were assembled on the lawn, holding signs, their voices a low rumble.

Once I'd signed the prerequisite paperwork and they took Newman away, I walked out toward the courthouse. A van from the local television station had pulled up, and a woman with a shoulder-mounted camera was filming the gathering. I stopped on the sidewalk at the edge of the throng. The crowd included men and women of mixed ages. In front of me, a group of younger guys wore deck shoes and polo shirts tucked in their jeans, and two who were probably related had tan faces framed by tousled blond hair. One turned, and his profile made me think of country clubs and sports cars.

How bizarre, I thought. South Lake Tahoe is not a large town—and not a place where I'd ever seen an organized protest. People visited here for the casinos and to ski or hike or go boating on the lake. The permanent residents made a living catering to tourism, for the most part. The most controversial local issues usually involved nature preservation, which rarely resulted in serious debate.

The front doors to the courthouse building swung open, and two lawyer types in dark suits stepped out, followed by a young black man flanked by a pair of uniformed officers. The volume rose to a shouting level as the crowd pressed forward, their signs thrust in the air.

"You're a rapist!" a woman's voice near the front of the pack yelled, and everyone began screaming and waving their fists and signs. And then a loud male voice shouted, "We're gonna take you down!" I felt the remark reverberate through the crowd, and the hostile energy shifted to high gear.

The mob began closing in on the five men, who were trying to follow a path to two squad cars waiting at the curb.

The young black man was tall, his hair razor cut close to the scalp, his dark face shiny in the sunlight. He wore a red necktie, and a blue tattoo crawled up from beneath the collar of his dress shirt. His eyes were half-lidded and his gait was jaunty, and though his face was an island of black in a sea of white, he surveyed the threatening horde with seeming indifference. No doubt he was from an inner-city ghetto, I surmised. Probably split his time between dealing drugs and performing gymnastics on a basketball court. Sure, it was a racial stereotype. But being politically correct isn't a big priority in my job.

A balding man in slacks rushed at the suspect but was intercepted by a cop. The black man smirked and widened his eyes in mock fear. In a second three more guys from the crowd leaped forward, and the cops pulled their billy clubs. In a panic, the lawyers tried to run, but one was shoved to the ground. A young man from the crowd took a billy club to the head, and blood streamed into his eyes. He swung wildly and hit one of the cops flush in the mouth.

From the courthouse entrance, Sheriff Marcus Grier and two deputies burst from the doors and sprinted into the melee. They started pulling and pushing their way through the mass of humanity, but, as if by plan, a cluster of about forty people surrounded the cops and closed in until the officers could no longer move. I saw Grier's face one moment, his mouth wide in a silent shout, and then he was gone.

"Shit," I said. Grier was my friend and a decent guy. Of course, he sometimes was an asshole, but what cop isn't? I fought my way to where the crowd had pinned the policemen down, and started throwing people aside. A woman clawed at my face, and someone punched me in the kidneys. I saw Grier again and made eye contact, and I'd almost reached him when five helmeted officers stormed into the mob. Within a minute the protesters disbursed, and I saw the tall suspect duck into a squad car along with the suits. The car took off with a screech, and the cops scanned the remaining people, uncertain whom, if anyone, to arrest.

Grier put his smashed cap back on his head and blew out his breath.

"I know people are pissed, but I didn't expect this," he huffed. "What the hell are you doing here?"

"Not much, besides coming to your rescue."

"Don't overrate yourself."

"I'm good at that, I'm told."

"Go help her," Grier said to one of his deputies, pointing to an overweight woman with mussed makeup sitting on the grass and holding her ankle. As soon as the deputy left, a pretty, fortyish lady in tight jeans and jogging shoes walked to where we stood and pointed a red fingernail in Grier's face.

"Where's the justice?" she said. "That's what I want to know." She stomped her foot like a petulant child, her large breasts bouncing under her top. "Where's the goddamned justice?"

Grier straightened his collar and crossed his arms below where a button had been torn from his shirt. Behind his back, fellow cops sometimes referred to him as a black Pillsbury Doughboy. Grier battled his weight on a daily basis, but his natural physique would not be denied its puffiness. His arms were too thick for his shirt and looked ready to blow out the seams, and his gun belt rested on a thick paunch that rose from his crotch. His ass was like a medicine ball, and his cap sat high on his jumbo-sized head. We weighed about the same, and I was five inches taller than him.

"Yeah, I know, you're just like all the other dipshits running our fucked up court system," the lady went on, her eyes ablaze. She waved her arm, and the large diamonds on her fingers flashed like glittery weapons.

"I'm sorry you feel that way, ma'am," Grier said.

She pulled her blond hair away from her face. "I'll convey that to Lindsey Addison. I'll let her know the whole fucking South Lake Tahoe Police Department is really *sorry*."

"Blame the courts, not the police," I said, and instantly wished I hadn't.

"Who are you?" she snapped.

"Dan Reno, private investigations." I tried for a smile and handed her a business card.

She looked at my card for a brief moment, then folded it lengthwise and thrust it at me. "Tell you what, Dan. Stick it up your ass."

• • •

The next morning I woke late to an empty house. I had driven Candi, my live-in girlfriend, to the airport in Reno the night before. She was off to visit her folks in Texas for two weeks. I walked to my kitchen in sweats and a T-shirt and started a pot of coffee. Candi had moved in almost a year ago, and people were starting to ask if we planned to get married.

When the coffee was ready, I poured a cup and went out to my deck to read the paper. Candi had given my modest home a makeover—new furniture, paintings, and such—but I preferred the scenery outdoors, especially on a warm, sunny morning. I pulled my picnic table out of the shade cast by the huge pine tree in my yard. The grass surrounding the tree glistened silver in the early sun, which was already high over the mountains that rose from the alpine meadow behind my back fence.

Before I could take a sip, I heard my cell ring in the house. I set my cup down with a sigh and went back inside.

"Investigations."

"Yes, Dan Reno, please," a woman's voice said.

"You got him."

"My name's Cassie Longfellow. I work for Ryan Addison." She paused for a long moment, long enough for me to sense she anticipated a certain type of response. Like, *Oh my God, you mean* the *Ryan Addison?*

Instead, I said, "Who?"

"Ryan Addison. The actor."

"Oh, right," I said. Grier had mentioned him the day before. "Wasn't he in some movies?"

"Mr. Addison's been in many movies, as well as a leading TV series."

"He was in one of those reality shows, right?"

She gave a little gasp. "Absolutely not," she said, frost edging her voice.

"Sorry, I don't watch a lot of TV."

"Apparently not," she sneered, as if it was an insult. "Mr. Addison would like to meet with you this morning. Can you be here in an hour?"

"What for?"

"He'd like to discuss hiring you."

I walked back outside into the warmth of the sun and brushed my foot at a scattering of pine needles on the deck.

"Where?"

She gave me a local address. "Don't be late," she said.

•   •   •

The Internet hasn't revolutionized detective work by any stretch, but it's a convenient way to find information on people, especially those with a public persona. Sitting at the metal army surplus desk in my spare bedroom office, I Googled Ryan Addison, and the first hit provided a complete summary of his career, and then some.

He had spent his early acting years in supporting roles and B-class movies. Ten years ago, he played his first leading part in a film about a man struggling through a divorce, when his daughter is kidnapped for ransom.

The movie was a minor success and led to a role as an FBI agent breaking up a Wall Street Ponzi scheme. That role resulted in an Oscar nomination for best actor. After that he was in a sitcom I'd never heard of and also starred in a string of films, none of which I recognized, except for a pretty decent cowboy flick. I'd seen the movie and thought Addison played a convincing tough guy.

The summary also contained a long paragraph about Addison's personal life. He'd had three wives, and his divorces were scandalous messes, complete with public accusations of infidelity and sexual peccadilloes. Addison had apparently also developed a booze problem, which culminated in two drunk driving busts, the second photographed by paparazzi who followed him from a bar. The pictures of Addison grabbing his crotch and waving his middle finger during the arrest were published in leading gossip magazines. Rather than hurting his career, the incident gained him a cultlike notoriety. In his last two movies, he had played quirky, counterculture characters, and the critics had reacted favorably.

As for his family, Addison had a son and a daughter from his past marriages. His daughter, Lindsey, was the alleged victim in the rape trial that had resulted in the protest at the courthouse. Also notable was Ryan Addison's father, Troy Addison. He was an old-school actor who made the transition to politics in the 1990s. Now seventy-five, the senior Addison was a senator in Arizona.

I would have read more, but I still had to shower and shave. I did so in a hurry and put on a fresh pair of jeans and a blue, wrinkle-free shirt I favor because I hate ironing. Before leaving, I opened a can of food for Smokey, the fuzz ball cat Candi had brought home last winter. Then I backed out of my driveway and drove through the neighborhood out to Highway 50, the main drag of South Lake Tahoe. I turned right, toward the California-Nevada state line two miles east.

Ten minutes later I accelerated up a steep, curvy road, past a number of expensive vacation homes. At the end of a cul-de-sac was the most impressive of the bunch, a modern Tudor in dark wood, probably five thousand square feet, with a massive river-rock chimney presiding over its peaked roofs. I drove down a long driveway columned by fifty-foot Italian cypress and parked near a stone walkway leading to the front door.

As I walked toward the tiered porch, I paused to take in the expansive view from the top of the hill. The entirety of Lake Tahoe dominated the valley, twenty-two miles north to south and twelve miles wide, the water a deep, sparkling blue. There were only a few wispy clouds in the sky, and I could see clear across the lake to Tahoe City, where streaks of snow still clung to the granite peaks above the town.

"Ahem," a voice said. I turned to see a young woman standing in the doorway.

"I'm here to see Ryan Addison," I said.

The woman wrinkled her nose. She was slender and wore her dark hair up. "Yes, I know. I called you."

I climbed the porch steps. "You don't look the part," she said.

"What part is that?" I asked.

"I thought detectives wore suits."

"You ever try chasing a guy in a suit?"

"Is that what you do? Chase guys?"

"Sometimes."

She glanced away with a bored roll of the eyes and a curled lip, as if I'd said something stupid or mundane. Her expression looked practiced and was probably something she'd developed to let the noncelebrity class know their place. I guess she thought that was an important part of her job.

"Follow me, please," she said.

I did so without comment. She wore a dress and heels and had no ass to speak of. We walked down a marble floor hallway to a tall, paneled door. She knocked twice and pushed the door open just enough to stick her head in.

"The private investigator," she said.

"Well, let him in, goddammit."

She gave me a final, dubious glance, then opened the door wider.

"Dan Reno?" the man said. He sat on the edge of an elaborate hardwood desk, his hands crossed in his lap, as if posing for a photographer. One leg was straight and the other was bent at the knee to reveal an ankle-high suede boot. His beige pants were of a thin material, bunched tight around his crotch.

"It's Reno, as in no problemo."

"No problemo, huh? All right, Dan! I like you already." He hopped off the desk, grabbed a chair on wheels, and pushed it my direction. The room was lined with bookshelves and a large window offered a view of a forested canyon. He walked behind me to where Cassie was still standing and watching us. "Thanks, dear," he said, and closed the door on her. Then he turned and offered his hand.

"I'm Ryan Addison." He was a shade under six feet and wore an untucked denim shirt that didn't hide the barrel-like thickness of his torso. His blond hair was without a hint of gray and fell over his ears onto his tanned neck. Around his blue eyes, the skin was taut, but elsewhere it was grainy, as if his square features had been blasted with sand. I had not checked his date of birth, but I'm pretty good at guessing age. I pegged Addison at fifty-five.

We shook, and his hand was rough and dry and almost as big as mine. He gave a good squeeze and held his eyes on mine for a long moment, then he squeezed harder. I didn't quite know what to make of that, other than to guess he wanted to impress me with his physical strength, even if he was nearly twenty years my senior.

I sat, and he went behind his desk and scooted forward in a leather executive's chair.

"My daughter's name is Lindsey. I take it you've heard about the results of her trial," he said.

"I was at the courthouse yesterday. I heard the man accused of raping her was found not guilty."

His eyes flashed and locked onto mine. "It was a travesty of justice," he said, his upper lip raised to show his teeth. "The evidence was overwhelming. I'd like to hire you to look into it."

"What's there to look into? The jury declared the man innocent."

"I don't give a shit what the jury said. My daughter was brutally raped." He stood and peered down at me. "Listen to this," he said. "There were three things that happened during the trial. First, an eyewitness changed her mind on stand and said she didn't see a thing. Then a second witness disappeared and is still missing. And third, the DNA test results, which proved the son of a bitch was guilty, vanished. The DNA was in police custody, then it was gone. What do you think of that?"

"It sounds like the witnesses were coerced, and someone was paid off to lose the DNA," I said.

Addison threw up his arms as if pleading to the heavens. "Thank you. Thank you!" He came out from behind the desk, his face dark with a crazed intensity. "I want you to find out who is protecting this rapist—and why. I want you to bust it wide open, and I want to see justice done."

I looked past him at the rows of books covering the wall behind the desk. They looked like collector's sets, probably unread.

"Mr. Addison, no matter what I uncover, it's unlikely the defendant would be made to stand trial again. I'm not sure—

I stopped in midsentence when the door flew open and a young woman burst into the room. She had a freckled nose, round eyes, and a mouth smudged with lipstick. Black stretch pants clung tightly to the curve of her hips, and under her pink T-shirt a sports bra flattened her breasts into a band of flesh around her chest.

"I was raped!" she shrieked. "That fucking nigger did it and laughed at me!"

"Lindsey, honey," Addison said, rushing to the woman. "Please, you mustn't—"

"It was like getting fucked by a gorilla! I can't wash the stink off of me. His thing was black as wet rubber and like something on a horse!"

His face pooled with color, Addison tried pushing his daughter out the door, but she grabbed the frame. "Rudy!" Addison yelled.

"He fucked my ass and tore up my insides, and I can't even go to the goddamn bathroom anymore!" Her face was flushed red, and her voice had hit a hysterical pitch.

"Rudy, get over here!" Addison dropped his shoulder and tried to push his daughter through the door, but she held fast.

"Give me a gun, and I'll kill that nigger! I swear I'll shoot his dick off!"

A young fellow, one I thought I'd seen at the courthouse, came from behind Lindsey, peeled her fingers from the doorframe, and pulled her out of the room. Before Addison shut the door, I caught a glimpse of his lady assistant, her smug demeanor gone, replaced with an astonished and mortified expression.

Fumbling with the doorknob, Addison locked it, then walked with slumped shoulders back behind his desk. We listened to Lindsey's screams and sobs become faint. Addison sat and placed his hands on his temples. After a long pause, he said, "I'm sorry you had to see that."

"I can come back later if you like."

When he looked up, his face was slack beneath his fallen eyes. "No, that's okay," he mumbled. "We have her in therapy. The shrink said she's suffering from an unusual form of posttraumatic disorder. She has a compulsion to shout out in public, as if publicizing her experience will help her deal with it. It's like a temporary case of Tourette's syndrome."

"I see."

"It's quite awkward, you understand." He paused and then sighed. "I didn't raise my daughter to be a racist. I've never heard language out of her like that. But I can understand her anger at that black man. Can you?"

"Yes. But there's plenty of assholes of every race, white included."

His faced jumped, and his lips tightened over his teeth. "You know that from experience, huh?"

"That's right."

"I believe you. But somehow, it's not much of a comfort." His expression shifted again, and his eyes looked brittle as puddles of thin ice.

"How long ago did the attack happen?" I asked.

"Two months, now." He straightened in his chair and blew out his breath. "Let's talk specifics. I want to hire you, effective today."

"You're asking me to look into something that could involve police corruption. I'm not sure what I can do for you. It's a damn uncertain thing."

"I know it is. Uncover what's going on and bring me justice, and I'll double your pay."

I raised my eyebrows.

"Bend the law, break it, I don't care. I'll pay you to do whatever it takes."

"Breaking the law is not part of what I do," I said.

Addison smiled. "You're a lousy liar."

"Excuse me?"

"I've seen your résumé, Dan, and you have a hell of a track record."

"Says who?"

"I'm connected in Washington."

"Your father the senator, huh?"

"He's very unhappy about what happened to his granddaughter. I'll leave it at that. Anyway, I read your FBI file last night. Impressive stuff."

I shifted my weight in the chair and rubbed a spot on my jaw. I was aware the FBI had compiled a dossier on me. But I'd never seen it.

"You've killed nine men."

I was silent for a moment before I said, "Self-defense is no crime."

"It beats the alternative, right?"

"That's true."

"You'll take the job?" he asked.

I stared at Addison, who seemed to have fully recovered from the embarrassment of his daughter's outburst. I stood and walked over to the single window in the room. My relationship with the South Lake Tahoe PD was something I managed carefully. Marcus Grier was the top cop in town, and he cut me a fair amount of slack. This dated back to three years ago, when I'd been responsible for the demise of a corrupt elected official who'd fired him. After Grier was rehired, he knew he owed me. But I didn't take his latitude for granted. Our relationship had a certain balance to it. An attempt by me to uncover corruption in his department could easily screw up a good thing. It would be much more difficult to make a living in Tahoe if I put myself on Grier's shit list.

Still, though, it was hard to pass on the offer of a double rate. Especially given that my phone wasn't exactly ringing off the hook with work offers. South Lake Tahoe is not a big city, and if I passed on this job, I might wait a month or two before my next shot at a payday.

"Let me sweeten the pot for you," Addison said. He pushed his chair back from the desk and sat with his legs crossed. "Duante Tucker is the name of the scumbag who raped Lindsey." He pulled open a drawer and set a four-inch thick folder on the desk. "These are the trial transcripts, complete with all the prosecution's interviews and so on."

I came back to Addison's desk. "How'd you get this?"

"It was brought to me by courier this morning. Tim Cook, the DA, was plenty pissed about giving it up, but pressure was applied."

"Your old man?"

Addison nodded, then uncrossed his legs and fixed me with a deliberate stare. "Take this case. And if Duante Tucker ends up dead, I'll pay you a hundred grand." He reached into the same drawer from which he'd produced the trial folder and placed four bundles of fresh bills on the desk. "Cash," he said.

"You think I'm a hit man?"

"Not at all, Dan. You're a licensed private investigator and bounty hunter. But criminals have a tendency to wind up dead when you're involved. Your record speaks for itself. It's simple as that."

I shook my head. "We need to get something straight. I provide a legitimate service. I don't operate outside the law. If you think I'm some kind of rogue agent, you're wrong."

Addison raised his hands in a placating gesture. "I understand completely. I'm simply offering to hire you for the purposes we discussed. Legit and aboveboard."

"Then put your cash away."

"As you like." He returned the packets of crisp notes inside his desk.

"I accept your offer, then," I said, watching him shut the drawer. "Excluding the part about killing anyone. I'll bring a contract back this afternoon. I expect to be paid weekly for my time, including expenses."

"Excellent." He rose and shook my hand. "By the way, this home belongs to Sam Aldon, who produced my last film. He's been gracious enough to offer it to my family and me for the summer. I'll be either here or at my home in Beverly Hills for the next two months. In early October I'm leaving for Europe to begin a new film."

"And?"

"I hope to have this matter resolved well before then."

"I understand."

"Good." We began walking toward the door, then he stopped. "Oh, there's one more thing I forgot to mention. I've also hired another person to work on this. Because Duante Tucker lives in San Jose, I felt it would help to have an investigator based there involved. I understand he's someone you know."

"Who's that?"

"Cody Gibbons."

I tried to keep my face blank, but felt my brow crease.

2

I'D BECOME FRIENDS WITH Cody Gibbons when we attended high school in San Jose. Shortly after we met, his father kicked him out of their house. At fifteen, Cody forged his way on his own, working odd jobs, sometimes living on the streets, sometimes renting a room. As teenagers we often worked together at different jobs through a temporary agency, usually hard, bust-ass labor. Though he hadn't yet reached his eventual six feet five and three hundred pounds, Cody had tremendous physical strength. We once took a gig loading freezer cars with boxes of meat. The job was simple: lug and stack hundred-pound boxes all day long. I was a wrestler and a middle linebacker in high school, and I thought I was pretty tough. I tried to keep up with Cody. It was an ego thing, and I finally conceded it was pointless. Five o'clock in the afternoon, and he was still carrying a box under each arm, tossing them as if they were weightless.

Cody never missed school, but sometimes wore the same clothes for days on end. Occasionally my mother would do his laundry and insist he stay for dinner. She asked me if he had enough money, and how he survived. I couldn't give a good answer. At times he would show up with a roll of bills in his pocket. That he was involved in shady endeavors I had no doubt, but I never asked him about it.

During our senior year, Cody was the star defensive end on our football team. The coaches tried to harness and direct his reckless aggression, with limited success. At half time of the final game of the year, our head coach chewed him out for committing a meaningless penalty. Cody picked the man up by his neck and groin and tossed him into a garbage bin. Despite the incident, Cody was offered an athletic scholarship by a university in Utah.

After graduating with a degree in criminal justice and missing the NFL draft, Cody returned to San Jose to take a job with San Jose PD. Back then I was employed in my first job as an investigator, and in the process of drinking myself out of the job and a marriage. I'd convinced myself that closing bars was a natural and allowable response to the guilt I felt for killing a man. Looking back, I think that was mostly an excuse. More likely, I was irresponsible and self-destructive and just plain liked to drink. Regardless, Cody stuck with me during those wild, bleak times, and despite his own bibulous tendencies, he made it clear he'd not let me drown in my sorrows, be they legitimate or otherwise.

For seven years Cody lasted as a San Jose cop—seven years of insubordination and irreverence and accusations of excessive force. But in the end, what got him fired was his unwillingness to take dirty money. That's where he drew his ethical line, and that was unacceptable to his fellow cops and the precinct captain. To punctuate the end of his career, Cody had an affair with the captain's wife, who hated her husband so much she begged Cody to set up a camera and film them getting it on, and then distribute CDs around the squad room.

Cody's subsequent career as a private investigator was once described by a local judge as "letting a rabid dog off the leash." Cody took cases most investigators shied away from, and he mined the niche into a good living. His name became well known within criminal circles. On two occasions the mafia tried to kill him, and the ensuing mayhem convinced local mobsters to focus their energies elsewhere. When gangbangers recognized him on the streets, they tended to disperse. Even Mexican drug cartel members operating in California viewed him with trepidation.

The effect of Cody's antics on San Jose's law enforcement community was polarizing. Some officials wanted him jailed. Others saw him as a convenient ally, a shortcut around a cumbersome and often ineffective court system. Whether friend or enemy, Cody knew exactly where he stood. That was his strength; he had an uncanny knack for knowing what he could get away with.

As for my dealings with Cody, he had saved my life at least twice. He did his best work with a double-barreled shotgun or a large-bore revolver, but he could be more creative when the situation called for it. Last winter he blew up the home of a white supremacist who had kidnapped and nearly killed me. The man was the leader of a skinhead biker gang, and he and five of his cohorts were in the house when the C-4 went off. Their bodies had to be identified by dental records.

• • •

I spent the rest of the morning at home, reading through the trial papers. There was too much information to process in a single sitting. I took a break for lunch and then lifted weights in my garage, sets of upright rows, bench presses, and curls with a hundred-pound bar. Just as I finished the final reps, my phone rang. I wasn't surprised to see the name on the screen.

"Hello, Cody."

"Dirty Double-Crossin' Dan,'" he said. The nickname was based on his claim that I once left a bar with a woman he was hitting on, sneaking out while he was in the men's room. Whether or not that actually happened, I don't recall. The supposed event was more than ten years ago, during a long night of drinking.

"What's going on, man?" I said.

"Women trouble, that's what."

"Again? Not you."

"I'm serious, I think I need to file a restraining order. I'm in bed last night, early, like the good citizen I am. About three in the morning I wake up, and someone's in my bedroom. There is no creepier feeling, let me tell you. The alarm bells start going off in my head, and I grab my piece from where I've been keeping it under the pillow. Then she flips the light on. It's this nutty broad I went out with a couple times."

"Sounds like she just couldn't get enough of your romantic charms."

"Yeah, right. So she starts taking her clothes off, like she's ready for a romp in the hay, and there I am, staring at her down the barrel of my .357."

"Let me guess, the gun turned her on."

"Who knows with her? She's a head case, sneaking into my house like that. So I tell her she's got to split, and she starts ranting and raving about how we were good together. And I'm telling her, wait a minute, lady, you basically told me to go have sex with myself on our last date. Then she starts going off on tangents, making no sense at all. I finally had to call nine-one-one."

"You always seem to attract the psychos," I said.

"Yeah, it must be a special skill I have. Anyway, I thought it would be perfect timing to blow Dodge for a while. What you got planned this afternoon?"

"Where are you?"

"Placerville. I just stopped at Jimboys for some tacos. I figured I'd drive up, and we'd strategize on the Addison case. Can you believe he hired both of us?"

I left my garage and walked out to the picnic bench. It was a warm, quiet day, and the air was fragrant with pine and the sweet scent of wildflowers growing in the meadow. "Ryan Addison said he saw my résumé," I said. "My FBI file, actually."

"Yeah, that's his shtick. He said the same thing to me."

"It sounds like he'd like to see Duante Tucker dead."

"I'd probably feel the same if my daughter was raped."

"Yeah, but would you hire someone to kill the rapist?"

"I don't know. Why?"

"Addison offered me a hundred grand if Tucker ends up dead. He put the cash on his desk."

"No shit, huh? He didn't say anything like that to me."

"Probably didn't want to do it on the phone," I said. "You haven't met him, have you?"

"No."

"I think he considers us good candidates to kill Tucker. I told him to forget it."

"He's a Hollywood celebrity, Dirt. He probably thinks money can buy anything. I'll see you in a couple hours, all right?"

• • •

After we hung up, I spent another couple hours going through the files Addison provided. When I was done, I not only understood the events of the trial and the reported crime, but also why an outraged group of Lindsey's friends and family had rioted outside the courthouse.

Two months ago, Lindsey Addison had flown to Reno from Los Angeles with two girlfriends. It was mid-April, and the ski resorts were still open after an abundant snow season. Lindsey and her friends rented a car and drove from Reno to South Lake Tahoe, where they checked into expensive rooms on the top floor of Pistol Pete's Casino Hotel. They snowboarded for two days at the ski resort in town, and on the evening of the second day, they went to a popular dance club across the street from Pistol Pete's. Around eleven, Lindsey's friends decided to leave with two men they had met. At eleven thirty, Lindsey exited the dance club alone, with the intention of returning to her hotel room. But she never made it out of the dark parking lot. She claimed she was struck on the head from behind and wrestled into a vehicle.

Witness number one was a man named Leo Rosen. He was an aspiring screenwriter, and it was revealed that he not only knew Lindsey Addison, but was in fact smitten with her. Rosen conceded that he traveled to South Lake Tahoe on his own after learning Lindsey would be there. He hoped this might lead to a romantic situation. Instead, Rosen was still working up the gumption to approach Lindsey when he followed her out of the nightclub and witnessed the kidnapping.

Rosen was able to get the license plate of the vehicle, a dark-colored, late-model GMC Yukon SUV. He also provided a brief description of the assailant: a black male, six feet three inches. Rosen called the police and reported the incident. South Lake Tahoe PD put out an APB on the vehicle, and also for the owner, a thirty-four-year-old San Jose resident named Lennox Suggs.

Hands tied behind her back and woozy from the blow to the head, Lindsey was driven to a building near the lake that served as a storage facility for a company that rented assorted recreational gear to tourists. There, she was beaten and forced onto a rubber blow-up mattress, where she was raped repeatedly over a two-hour period. She claimed there was only one assailant; it was not a gang rape.

When the rapist was done, he tied Lindsey's hands to a metal shelving unit and left her, naked and bleeding, in the cold room. She was found at dawn the next morning, shivering and incoherent, by an employee of the rental company.

The medical exam included pictures of Lindsey's battered face. Both eyes were swollen shut, and her upper lip was split. In one photo, her lip was pulled back to reveal a missing tooth and bloody gums. The rape kit mentioned extensive trauma to her vagina and rectum, including a laceration in her colon that was likely caused by a foreign object. The medical report said it might necessitate a colostomy while it healed.

San Jose PD immediately arrested Lennox Suggs, a paroled felon, but released him after confirming he'd been in Southern California during the attack. Suggs claimed he had not lent his vehicle to anyone, but when detectives questioned Suggs's roommate, Duante Tucker, he became the primary suspect. He was arrested when witness number two, Lindsey's friend Amber Meline, identified Tucker as a man she'd seen outside the nightclub.

Before Tucker's attorney could intervene, Tucker's DNA was appropriated from a water glass and found to be a match for hair and fluid samples on Lindsey's body. With this DNA evidence, the case should have been a slam dunk. Tucker was transported to South Lake Tahoe, where he was held without bail.

Tim Cook, the prosecuting DA from Tahoe, went to trial with all the good cards in his hand. Representing Tucker, to everyone's surprise, was Darrian Bannon, an attorney with a national reputation as an advocate for underprivileged black clients. Bannon had done some widely respected work in the south on cases with heavy racial overtones.

The case began smoothly for the prosecution but began unraveling the second day, when Amber Meline would not identify Duante Tucker while on the stand. This in itself was minor, but when Tim Cook called his second witness, Leo Rosen was nowhere to be found. Without Rosen's testimony, the vehicle used to abduct Lindsey could not be put at the scene.

But the real bomb dropped on day three, when the all the DNA evidence, including samples taken from the Yukon SUV, vanished from the evidence locker. The lack of witness testimony could have been overcome. But without the DNA evidence, the judge had no choice but to dismiss the charges.

• • •

By the time I heard Cody pull up half an hour later, I'd filled two pages with scrawled notes and questions. But they all seemed subordinate to the central issue, which was, how did the DNA disappear, and who was behind it?

Cody parked his red, diesel-powered Dodge pickup in my driveway and climbed out of the cab. He wore faded blue jeans and a brand of running shoe he claimed was easiest to find in size fourteen. His untucked shirt was short-sleeved and had Western-cut pockets and snaps instead of buttons. He had trimmed his unruly beard back for the summer, but his hairstyle hadn't changed; the thatch-like, straw-colored disarray covering his head looked impervious to comb or brush.

"Hey, buddy," I said, from the corner of the deck near the driveway.

"Beer?" Cody walked behind his rig and opened the tailgate.

"I'm fresh out," I said. If I hadn't been so deep into the trial transcripts, I might have done the hospitable thing and picked up a case or two of Budweiser. Cody could make six-packs disappear in minutes.

"I figured as much. Come grab this for me, would you?"

I went around and saw a large plastic cooler in the truck bed. I grabbed it by the handles and lugged it up onto the deck. It had to be close to eighty pounds.

"What's in here, bricks?"

"More like a king's ransom." Cody opened the cooler, and it was packed with ice and beer, and in the corner was a bottle of tequila and margarita mix. He grabbed a beer and lobbed it my way. I caught the wet can and tossed it back to him.

"No alcohol for me until happy hour."

"Mr. Discipline," he said with a wistful frown. He dropped the beer in the cooler and closed it. "Have you read through the case file yet? Addison told me he gave it to you."

"Yeah, I went through it."

"Fill me in, then."

We sat at the picnic bench, looking out over the yard. My lawn had been infiltrated by native grasses and cloverleaf, and a series of gopher mounds had erupted near the fence line. Cody lit a cigarette and squinted out at the mountains while I recounted what I'd learned from the transcripts.

"We need to find out who had access to that evidence locker," he said when I'd finished.

"Right."

"How's your amigo, Marcus Grier, doing?"

"Just peachy."

"Why don't you give him a ring-a-ding, tell him we need to talk?"

"I'm sure he'll be overjoyed."

Cody laughed and clapped me on the shoulder. "That's life in the big leagues, Dirt." When I didn't say anything, he added, "Just use your diplomatic skills." Then he stood and looked around. "Where's your old lady?"

"Texas for two weeks, visiting her family."

"Ho. I booked a room at Pistol Pete's."

"Cancel it. You can bunk here."

He stretched and smiled broadly. "Just like old times."

While Cody grabbed his bag from his rig, I dialed Marcus Grier's office. The on-duty receptionist said he wasn't in his office. I paused for a second, then called Grier's cell number. He had told me not to use it unless it was urgent.

"What's up?" Grier said in the distracted tone he liked to use to let me know he was busy.

"Hello, Marcus," I said. "Can we meet this afternoon?"

"What for, if that's not too much to ask?"

"Ryan Addison hired me to look into his daughter's rape."

Grier was silent for a long moment, then he said, "Really."

"Yeah," I said, "and…"

The line went silent, as if Grier was waiting for the other shoe to drop. And who was I to disappoint him? "He also hired Cody Gibbons," I said.

"You're kidding, right?" he said, his deep voice rising.

"Nope."

I heard him breathing. "Well, ain't that a kick in the pants."

"Can we meet at five?" I asked.

"Forget it. I've got too much going on."

"Work with us here, Marcus. It will be best for everybody."

"Is that some kind of threat?"

"No, it's not a threat. Come on, Marcus."

"What's Addison expect you to do?"

"He believes Duante Tucker raped his daughter," I said. "From what I understand, it would have been an open-and-shut case if the DNA hadn't disappeared."

"You didn't answer my question."

"Addison wants justice. It's as simple as that. He's hired me for that purpose."

"He expects you to fix our judicial system, huh?"

"Do you believe Duante Tucker was innocent? What if it was your daughter he raped?"

"All right, that's enough," Grier said. "I'll meet you. But don't push me, understand?"

"Zeke's at five?"

"Fine," he said, and hung up.

"How'd it go?" Cody had been in the house and had come out to hear the end of the conversation.

"About like I thought it would." Marcus Grier had a wife and two daughters, one twelve and the other fourteen. I'd been to his place for dinner, and his wife was a friendly, jovial woman, his daughters well-mannered and talkative. Grier was always in a hurry to get home and hated working late. After meeting his family, I understood why. I felt a twinge of guilt at mentioning rape and Grier's daughter in the same sentence. But he needed to be reminded that I was on his side, working against the bad guys. Putting a rapist behind bars was something Grier would surely want to see happen. At least I hoped it was that simple.

• • •

Zeke's Pit sat on a plot of land along Highway 50, about a mile from my house. The Folk Victorian structure was originally built in the late 1800s. It was designed to be a lakefront vacation home, but once the highway evolved into a commercial thoroughfare, the building became host to a variety of businesses. It was a speakeasy during prohibition, then a gambling parlor, and later a bordello. For a brief period in the 1950s, it was headquarters for the local police department. After that, new owners reconfigured the downstairs interior into two large rooms, one a dining area and the other a bar. Since then it had always been a restaurant and saloon.

Zeke's Pit was run by Zak Pappas, who inherited the business from his father. I invested a chunk of cash in the joint a year ago, after Zak fried his circuits on cocaine and shut the restaurant down. After he came out of rehab he was flat broke, and I was looking for a place to hide some tainted cash from the IRS. I floated the money to Zak based on two conditions: one, he stay sober, and two, he return Zeke's to its previous status as the best Old West–style BBQ joint in the region.

Cody and I arrived a few minutes before five. I parked my Nissan pickup near the huge, old-growth pine in the center of the parking lot. The tree trunk was scarred by the bumpers of innumerable bar patrons, the bark battered and scraped away. My truck looked at home next to it; the paint on the front quarter panel was badly scratched, and the metal was uneven where I'd pulled a dent by hand.

We went through the old doors and across the floorboards to the forty-foot mahogany bar. A handful of patrons sat watching a baseball game on the TV in the corner. Sunlight filtered in through the slatted window shades in front of the room, and motes danced in shafts of light over the cocktail tables.

Cody motioned to the bartender. "What are you drinking?" he asked me.

"Nothing, until we get done with Grier."

Cody sighed, tapped his fingers on the bar, and turned his disinterested eyes to the ballgame.

"Get a drink if you want," I said.

"No. I'll wait."

I ordered a coffee and sipped it while we sat at the bar. At 5:15, Grier arrived, and we went to one of the larger lounge tables.

"Well, well, Mr. Gibbons," Grier said.

"Hello there, sheriff."

"How's the arm?"

Cody pulled back his shirt sleeve to show a long scar across the meat of his shoulder. He'd been shot during a case we worked last year.

"It looks healed," Grier said with a shrug. "So, Ryan Addison hired *both* of you to investigate his daughter's rape? How does that work?"

"Duante Tucker lives in San Jose," I said. "So does Cody."

Grier straightened in his chair and removed his cap. "How convenient."

"What do you think about the case, Marcus?" I said.

"It's always disappointing when we can't get a conviction."

"Hey, sheriff, you want a beer?" said Cody.

I cut my eyes to Cody, but Grier said, "Yeah, I do."

Cody immediately went to the bar. Grier leaned forward, and a beam of sunlight fell across his shaved head like a diagonal laser.

"Do you have any ideas on who took the DNA?" I asked.

"Nothing definite," he said, the slash of silver light bisecting his face. "We're conducting an internal investigation."

"Who had a key? Guy Hanson, right?"

"Yeah, Hanson was in charge of the locker."

"You think someone bought him off?"

Grier eyes me warily. "It's possible. But Hanson's worked for the department over twenty years. He's never been involved in any of the past corruption. It's hard to imagine he'd take money for this, especially because he'd be the first suspect we'd look at."

"Maybe someone has something on him. Like, give me the key and keep your mouth shut, or else."

"It's possible. We're not ruling anything out."

"Who else would have had access to a key?" I asked.

"Just me. I keep a spare locked in a safe."

"Hmm. Is that trouble for you?"

"Probably. El Dorado County Internal Affairs is getting involved."

Cody came back to the table with a pitcher of beer and three mugs.

"So the spotlight's on you and Hanson," I said.

"Yeah, but it's not that cut and dried," Grier replied. "Hanson admitted that he sometimes left his keys in his unlocked drawer. He said he didn't like to always be carrying a big set of keys on him."

"So anyone could have made a copy."

"Pretty much."

"Any idea on motivation?"

"Nothing more than the obvious—someone was motivated to see Tucker get off." Grier's lips were downturned, and deep creases split his jowls.

"Hey, sheriff, have a beer, man. You look like you could use one." Cody pushed a mug across the table.

"Listen, Dan," Grier said. "I've told you more than I should have. I did that because I trust you. In return, I want you to keep me posted on everything you find out in your investigation."

I nodded. "Fair enough."

"And one more thing—don't go trying to interview any cops. If you interfere in our internal investigation, that's a big problem."

"Understood."

"As for you, Mr. Gibbons," Grier said after nearly draining his beer in one pull, "leave your hell-raising habits in San Jose. I've got enough problems without you flouting the law."

"Best behavior, scout's honor," Cody said, saluting with two fingers.

Grier shook his head and finished his beer. "Goodnight, men. Be in touch."

• • •

When the pitcher was empty, we went out back to the beer garden. Three empty rows of picnic benches baked under the late afternoon sun. Pennants advertising sports teams and liquor hung overhead from a cord strung between pines just outside the fences. In the corner, a black, split-barrel barbeque rested on a trailer. Cody lit a cigarette and moved out of the sun into a shaded area.

"I need to swing by Addison's place and have him sign my contract," he said. "He's expecting me."

"Okay."

"I want to interview Lindsey, if she's there. Is that Tourette's thing for real?"

"I guess. I don't know why she'd fake it. I think we should track down the two witnesses. Seems they were both discouraged from testifying."

"What are their names again?"

"Amber Meline was one of the women with Lindsey. Leo Rosen is the guy who had a thing for Lindsey and came up to Tahoe by himself, hoping to hit on her."

"That didn't pan out too well for him," Cody said.

"No, it didn't. They're both from Southern Cal. But Rosen went off the air during the trial, and no one could find him."

Cody flicked his cigarette out onto the hard dirt. "Let's go visit Addison."

We walked around the side of the building to my truck. The traffic on Highway 50 was thickening as tourists began heading out for dinner. The congestion got worse as we made our way to where the casinos rose at the state line. Once we crossed into Nevada, I turned east toward the mountain range and found the winding road that led to the fancy home where the Addisons were staying. We drove up the grade, past houses with balconies looking over the sloping mountainside, until we reached the end of the street.

"About what I'd expect," Cody said, eyeballing Addison's place as we parked and walked down the path to the front porch. He rang the chimes, and after a minute, the young woman who was Ryan Addison's assistant opened the door. She wasn't wearing glasses like when we'd met earlier, and she'd let her dark hair down. Instead of her prior conservative skirt, she wore shorts, which revealed thin but quite shapely legs.

"Hello, there." Cody said.

"Hi, I'm Cassie. You must be Cody Gibbons." She smiled and looked up at him. "Please come in. I'll let Mr. Addison know you're here."

"Thank you, Cassie," Cody said. She stared at him with bright eyes and continued to smile. After a moment she stood aside so we could enter the house.

"Afternoon, Cassie," I said.

She shifted her gaze to me for an instant. "Yes, hello," she said, her tone flat as yesterday's pancakes. Apparently, Cody had made a favorable first impression on her, and I had not. For what reason, I didn't know, and I didn't bother to speculate.

She asked us to wait in the foyer, where we stood beneath a chandelier hanging from the twenty-foot ceiling. She reappeared quickly and led us through the house and outside to a massive redwood deck overlooking a swimming pool a level below.

Ryan Addison sat under an umbrella in a chaise lounge near the deck railing. A stack of magazines and a cocktail glass rested on a table beside him. He'd changed into a turquoise shirt and cream-colored shorts, and his eyes were hidden behind dark glasses.

"Hi, Dan. Cody Gibbons, I assume?" he said.

"That's me," Cody said. "I've got my paperwork for you to sign here, Mr. Addison."

Addison swung his legs off the cushion and planted his bare feet on the ground.

"Call me Ryan. Christ, you could fill a doorway." The scent of pot smoke wafted from him. "You played ball, right?"

"College," Cody replied.

"I played myself, back in the day. Strictly a scrub. Third string running back."

When neither Cody nor I responded, Addison took a hit off his drink. "Those were good times, back then. All about team work. Speaking of which, have you two got started yet?" He removed his sunglasses and stood.

"We met with South Lake PD," I said. "They're investigating the disappearance of the DNA."

"That's reassuring, given that they were incompetent enough to lose it in the first place." Addison took the papers from Cody's hand and shuffled the pages.

"We want to talk to the two witnesses who wouldn't support the prosecution," I said. "We'd like to talk to Lindsey about them first."

Addison's eyes snapped onto mine. "She's having a good afternoon. Her first in a long time. I'd really hate to interrupt that."

"We just want to ask about her relationship with the witnesses," Cody said. "Very routine. Nothing about the crime itself."

Addison sighed and walked over to the railing. On the far side of the pool, a few people I'd not noticed before sat partially obscured under a cabana. It looked like they were playing a board game.

"All right, come with me." Addison led us down a set of redwood stairs to the pool. We waited while he went to the cabana, and after a minute he returned with his daughter.

Lindsey Addison looked much different than the distraught woman I'd seen in the morning. She wore capri pants, low heels, and a sleeveless V-neck shirt. Much of her makeup had been removed, and her hair was nicely styled to frame her face. Unlike earlier, her countenance was not angry or combative. Instead, she looked reserved and calm and maybe just a little sad.

"Lindsey, this is Dan and Cody. They'd like to ask you a few brief questions about Amber and Leo Rosen."

"Okay," Lindsey said. We stood in a circle by the side of the pool.

"Thanks for taking a few minutes, Lindsey," I said. "Did you speak with Amber or Leo during the trial?"

"I talked to Amber. She said she thought she recognized Duante Tucker, but when she saw him in the courtroom, she wasn't sure anymore."

"Did she mention if anyone tried to discourage her from recognizing him?" Cody said.

"She didn't say anything like that."

"How about Leo Rosen?" I said. "Have you spoken with him since the attack?"

"He left me a couple messages when I was in the hospital. I called him back when I got out. I left him a voice mail, but he never called again."

"How well did you know him?" Cody asked.

"Just barely. I'd see him at parties occasionally. He once tried to talk to me about a role in a script he was writing. I really didn't pay him much attention."

"Do you have any idea where he is now?"

"No," she replied. "The attorney, Tim Cook, said he disappeared. But Leo had told me he lives in Santa Monica."

We were quiet for a moment. "Is that all?" Lindsey said.

"Yeah, I think so," I said.

"Thank you…for whatever you can do." She gave us a small, forced smile, and walked back toward the cabana.

"Why don't you guys have a seat for a few minutes," Addison said, pointing to a couple chairs under the deck. "I'll look over these papers and sign them." We nodded and he turned and went up the stairs.

"Let's go back to Zeke's after this and get some Texas brisket," Cody said. "Then I want to spend tonight reading the DA's transcripts."

"Okay."

Cody started to say something, but stopped when we saw a woman with long blond hair and high heels strut toward us. When she got closer I recognized her as the lady I'd spoken to briefly during the fracas at the courthouse. The one who suggested I do something anatomically improbable with my business card.

"So you're the badasses Ryan hired." She stood with one hand on her hip and the other pointed at us accusingly.

"Yes, ma'am, that's us," I said.

"Cody Gibbons, at your service." Cody stood before I did and took her hand while gazing at her breasts, which were large and barely encumbered by a skimpy bikini top.

"Keep your eyes to yourself," she sneered. "I'm not flattered by lechery." I tried unsuccessfully to suppress a chuckle. Her pink hot pants were skin-tight and so sheer that the folds of her labia were visible. She looked like she'd wandered off the set of a porno movie, maybe one where middle-aged women serviced horny teenagers.

"That poor girl," she said, pointing at the cabana, "was traumatized beyond anything you'll ever know. Do you understand that?"

We nodded, but she smirked.

"Ryan said you two are the best. From the looks of you, I'd say he's mistaken. I doubt young, dumb, and full of cum has what it takes to get the job done."

Cody and I exchanged curious glances. She gave us a final, withering stare, then turned and pranced off, just as we heard footsteps coming down the stairs.

"Ah, I see you met Ramona, my girlfriend," Addison said. He held his hand out as if to fend off our compliments. "Yes, I know, I'm a lucky man."

"Indeed," Cody said.

"I've signed your contract. It looks fine."

"Good."

"I'd invite you to stay for a drink, but I know you have work to do."

"Yup," I said, and began for the stairs before Cody could say otherwise.

"Cassie will show you out, then," Addison said. When we reached the deck, I saw her waiting by the sliding door. She led us through the house, but when we went out the front door, she stopped Cody on the porch. I took a few steps down the path leading to the driveway, then stopped to look back. Cassie had her hand on Cody's wrist. She shot me a dismissive glance.

"Run along, this is private," she said.

"Run along?" I shook my head, walked to my truck, and waited in the driver's seat for a couple minutes until Cody climbed into the cab.

"What the hell was that about?" I asked.

"She has an idea for a movie and said I'd be perfect for a part," he replied.

"No kidding, huh? And I thought she was just a meager assistant."

"Everyone's got to start somewhere."

"She's got some attitude," I said. "What'd you say to her?"

"She wants to have dinner tomorrow night and talk about it. I said okay."

"Hell, maybe she's your type."

"What's that supposed to mean?"

"I don't know. Except I've never met a bigger bunch of head cases. Everyone in that house seems to have a few screws loose. Like Lindsey. What was your impression of her?"

"Composed. Dealing with her situation pretty well, it seemed."

"Right. But this morning she was seriously losing it, I mean coming apart at the seams. A few hours later, she's mature and polite. And then Addison's broad, Ramona, shows up looking like a streetwalker and starts teeing off on us."

"That was the flimsiest bra I'd ever seen. Her knockers were one false move from falling out."

"And she rips into you for staring. And then she goes off on that young, dumb, and full of cum bullshit. What was that about?"

"You got me," he said.

"And let's not forget the patriarch of the loony bin, Addison, and his hundred-grand offer."

"He reeked like he just strolled out of an Amsterdam hash bar," Cody said. "But what's wrong with Cassie?"

"Nothing, except she's treated me like a walking case of gonorrhea."

"Come on, you're overreacting. She's kind of cute, don't you think?"

"The place is a freaking nut house, is what I think." I started my truck and turned down the driveway. "Sigmund Freud would have had a field day with these people."

3

WHEN I GOT OUT of bed the next morning, Cody was still asleep in my guest room, snoring like a freight train. We'd spent the night drinking coffee and reading through the trial folder, trying to absorb the entirety of the contents. The cooler full of beer and tequila that Cody referred to as a king's ransom remained untouched. I'd retired at midnight, but when I woke briefly at two in the morning, Cody was still sitting under a lamp in my living room with a yellow highlighter, the papers splayed about the couch and coffee table.

At 8:30 I called Tim Cook, the assistant district attorney, and left him a message letting him know I'd been hired by Ryan Addison. I suspected Cook would view that dimly, but I was betting it would motivate him to talk to me.

I'd never met Cook in person, but based on what I'd heard, he was not a balls-to-the-wall prosecutor. Rather, he'd spent most of his career trying small-time crimes. On the occasion something more significant was at stake, the head DA from El Dorado County usually got involved. But Cook had handled Lindsey Addison's case on his own. I assumed this was because the DNA evidence made a guilty verdict almost a foregone conclusion.

Cook called me back at nine sharp. "Dan Reno, Tim Cook here," he said.

"Hi, Tim."

"I can't say I'm surprised Addison hired you," he said.

"Why's that?"

"He's pretty unhappy with the outcome of the trial."

"I think that's an understatement. Do you have time this morning, Tim? I'd like to come by."

"Here? I don't think that's a good idea."

"Where, then?"

"Hold, please." I heard muffled voices, then he came back on with a sigh. "Tell you what. Meet me in twenty minutes in the parking lot behind Carrows."

I threw on a button-down shirt and a sports coat. Cook was a suit and tie guy, and I thought the meeting would go better if I dressed smartly. A little mirroring sometimes helps.

As I drove down 50, I considered the history of corrupt cops on both sides of the border. A bad sheriff from Placerville, the seat of El Dorado County, had died a few years back, the victim of a mob hit. His cronies had been prosecuted or resigned and fled the area. Then last winter, a chief detective from Silverado County in Nevada was stabbed to death by his estranged son. The detective had been taking dirty money from a variety of sources.

Did the demise of a handful of crooked law officers suggest the local police agencies were now free of corruption? Obviously not. Drug rings and escort services still flourished around Lake Tahoe, mostly unimpeded by the police. The pool of payoff money from these enterprises is like rainwater coming down off a mountain. The water flows in streams large and small, taking the path of least resistance. Whether a trickle or a torrent, the water finds its way.

On the California side of the border, South Lake Tahoe's economy is intrinsically attached to the casinos across the state line. Much of South

Lake's tourism is directly attributable to the Nevada gaming houses, where gamblers cram the aisles and feed their paychecks to the slot machines. Those who win typically pour their money back into the local economy, at restaurants, gift shops, or maybe on a call girl or a bindle of cocaine. After all, people come here to party.

But while threads of vice and graft are no doubt woven into the region's fabric, the acquittal of Duante Tucker was something of a different magnitude. The rape was egregious and horrifying. And the heinous nature of the crime had been revealed to the public. I thought, or at least hoped, that someone within the police department would come forth and identify who stole the DNA. Especially if the person had been at the trial, or had seen the pictures from the court files.

Maybe the case will resolve itself sooner rather than later, I thought, as I pulled into the diner where Tim Cook had said to meet him. Then I could collect my pay for time spent and be done with Ryan Addison and his circle of nut cases.

I spotted Cook standing beside a Chevy Blazer parked along a split-rail fence separating the back parking lot from a large field of vacant grassland. The Blazer's paint was a faded white and showed signs of rust along the running boards. Next to it, Cook, in a blue business suit, presented an incongruous image. The suit fit tightly on his slim frame. His face was equally narrow, the nose caved in on the sides. A dark, neatly trimmed mustache looked painted above his upper lip. The mustache was the type that had gone out of style a long time ago, probably before he was born.

We shook hands when I stepped out of my truck. Cook's grip was bony, and dandruff coated the shoulders of his pinstriped suit coat, which had a polyester sheen to it. Regardless of the material, it was in dire need of a cleaning. A crusty ketchup stain overlapped a smear of mustard on one lapel.

"I'm glad you called instead of snooping around behind my back," he said. "But I've only got a couple minutes, so let's get to it."

"Right. I've just got a few questions. I understand your witnesses bailed, and the DNA vanished. Any idea what happened?"

"You got this from the case file I sent Addison?"

"That's right."

Cook put one hand in a pocket and sucked his cheeks in. "Duante Tucker is nothing but a ghetto thug, as far as I know. I don't know who would be motivated to see him go free. We're putting every member of South Lake PD on a polygraph. Someone stole that evidence, and we'll get to the bottom of it."

"What about his attorney, Darrian Bannon?"

"What about him?"

"He's got a national reputation. What's he doing defending Duante Tucker?"

"He claimed he took the case pro bono. Said Tucker was just another example of a poor, disadvantaged black man being persecuted by white society."

"Doesn't make sense," I said. "The DNA evidence should have been irrefutable, right? How did Bannon think he could win? And even if he did, how could he paint Tucker as a victim? It doesn't match Bannon's style."

"He said he would prove Tucker's rights were violated, both during the arrest and during the collection of the evidence. But it was all by the book. We conferred with San Jose PD. Everything they did and everything we did was spot on. No holes."

"Do you think Bannon might have some ulterior motivation?" I asked.

"It's not something we consider a primary line of inquiry," he replied.

"What do you consider primary?"

"Our internal security. We'll find out who took the DNA."

"What about investigating Duante Tucker?"

"He lives in San Jose. We'll leave that to SJPD."

"I see."

"Is there anything else?" he asked.

"Nope," I said.

"One more thing, then, before I go. Whatever you do, don't embarrass the department. We've got enough issues as it is."

I shrugged. "Do my best."

"Let me make this a little more direct. You've been involved in a number of shootings and deaths since you've worked here. As district attorney, I've looked at each incident and decided no charges were warranted. But there's been plenty of gray area, and some in my department who disagreed with me. Am I making myself clear?"

"You're a guy I want to keep on my side."

"Exactly. So proceed with caution."

"Understood."

"Good," he said. He climbed into his rig and hit the starter, and the motor turned over a dozen times before it fired and choked a cloud of white smoke into the morning air. He glanced at where I stood, and I gave him the thumbs up. He grimaced and drove away.

I headed out to 50 and stopped at the Safeway to pick up eggs, bacon, a box of donuts, frozen hash browns, orange juice, and a loaf of bread. I don't usually eat a big breakfast—haven't since my hard-drinking days—but Cody was a different story. I figured he would want to head out to a restaurant as soon as he woke up. It would save time to have food at the house.

When I got home, Cody was sitting outside at my picnic table in camouflage print shorts, flip-flops, and a gray Utah State T-shirt. A lit cigarette smoked in the ashtray, and he held a cup of steaming coffee. His eyes were closed, his face tilted back to take in the sun. He opened one eye. "Where you been?" he asked.

"I just had a chat with Tim Cook." I set the bag of groceries on the table.

"What'd he have to say?"

"South Lake PD is giving polygraphs to everyone who may have had access to the key to the evidence locker."

"Interesting. What else?"

"We talked about why Darrian Bannon would represent Tucker. Cook said Bannon took the case pro bono. Bannon was going to declare the DNA inadmissible."

Cody opened his other eye and dragged off his cigarette. "Based on what?"

"Procedural technicalities. But Cook said that both San Jose PD and South Lake did everything by the book."

"Bannon's involvement doesn't jive," Cody said. "I spent some time researching him last night. He markets himself as a defender of the down-trodden, but he's really just a money-grubbing maggot. There's nothing charitable about him. He'd only take a pro bono case if he thought the publicity would pay off."

"I was beginning to get that impression."

"He graduated top of his class at Columbia, and he's made a shitload of money in the last ten years. He's considered one of the five top African-American attorneys in the US. But his personal life's a train wreck. He's still paying off two expensive divorces, and the bank foreclosed on his mansion near Atlanta. I don't think this dude is in a position to do anything for free."

"So how could Duante Tucker afford him?"

Cody leaned forward, stamped out his butt, and swigged the rest of his coffee. "We need to look into Bannon. He's moved to SoCal. Got an office in El Segundo."

"I think first we should go find out what Duante Tucker is up to. That's the most obvious starting point." I picked up the grocery bag, and Cody followed me inside.

"What's cookin'?" he said.

"The works." I turned on the griddle atop my stove, cracked eggs, and laid out strips of bacon. Then I microwaved the potatoes until they were thawed and added them to the griddle.

"Tucker was a juvie gangbanger in Compton," I said. "He moved to San Jose three years ago."

"Right. But he has no reported gang affiliation in San Jose. No job, either."

I pushed the eggs aside to make room for more bacon. "So what's he do for money?"

"That's what we're gonna find out, partner."

"You ready to head to San Jose?" I asked.

"Not yet," he replied. "There're things we shook look into here first, don't you think?"

I turned away from the sizzling griddle. "I think looking into Duante Tucker should be our first priority."

"Yeah, but we're here. So let's do our due diligence. We can drive to San Jose tomorrow morning."

I looked at Cody out of the corner of my eye. "I'd hate for you to miss your date with Cassie, the uppity assistant."

"She wasn't uppity to me," Cody said with a smile. He reached over the counter and grabbed the coffee pot. "She reminds me a little of my ex-wife."

"And you want to go to dinner with her?"

"She also reminds me of this nymphomaniac I knew once."

"All women remind you of nymphomaniacs. Get a plate, the grub's ready."

Cody walked around the counter to the griddle. "Hmm. Looks like your cooking's improved," he said. "You go first."

"It's all for you," I said. "I already ate."

"Ho. My lucky day."

Cody piled his plate, and I opened my notebook PC on the kitchen table. "I'm a little curious about Tim Cook," I said. "His suit looked like he bought it from the bargain rack at K-mart, and he was driving a beat-to-shit Blazer."

"The white-trash-mobile of Tahoe." Cody sat and forked a huge bite of scrambled eggs into his mouth.

"An assistant DA should make a pretty good living," I said. "But he looks like he's on welfare."

"You think Cook threw his own case?"

"It's a stretch. But if he's hard up for dough, who knows? He might have been desperate. I'd like to see his bank records, see if he recently ran into a pot of money."

Cody put down his fork. "I've got a guy at the IRS who does favors for me now and then. But I don't want to use him unless we really like Cook for this. The guy could lose his job."

"Don't call him. I'm just thinking out loud. I'll ask Grier about Cook."

"How about the shyster? Did Bannon leave town yet?"

"Don't know. We can find out."

"First thing I want to do is go to the crime scene," Cody said, wiping his mouth. "I always start that way."

"All right. Eat up, and let's go."

• • •

Fifteen minutes later we pulled into the parking lot in front of Caesars. The recession had taken its toll on the casino-hotel, and a new ownership group had bought the property and announced they would rename it. A wall constructed of oversized cinder blocks rose ten stories above the parking lot on the far side. The mortar had decayed, and streaks of grime stained the façade from top to bottom. On top of the wall, the large neon sign advertising loose slots and video poker had become partially detached from its metal frame, and leaned crookedly against the roof.

I parked in a spot near where Lindsey Addison said Duante Tucker had abducted her. The half-full parking lot was large, perhaps the size of a football field. Cody and I stood and looked toward the main entrance. Inside was the VooDoo Lounge and Night Club, where Lindsey and her friends had partied the night she was raped.

"No lights out here. Must have been pitch black," Cody said.

"She would have walked this line," I said, pointing to the main entrance, then across the street to Pistol Pete's. "But she only made it about this far." We began walking toward the building, where bell boys and valet drivers moved about in the circular drive. I briefly questioned a pair standing at a podium on a concrete island near the glass doors. I didn't expect to learn anything, but you never know. But neither of them had worked that night.

Inside the casino, the clatter and pinging of the slots was quiet as elevator music. In a business that never closes, dawn through noon is the lull period. We followed a carpeted path to a dark hallway that led to the Voodoo Lounge. The doors to the establishment were locked, as I suspected they would be.

"All right," I said. We turned and headed back toward the exit. I walked slowly, trying to imagine a boisterous, drunken crowd of twenty-something-year-old partiers. I imagined Lindsey walking in my footsteps. Her friends had left with two men they'd met, leaving Lindsey alone and vulnerable. I wondered if Lindsey felt dejected she didn't find a man that night. She was a reasonably attractive woman of twenty-three, and during ski season, Lake Tahoe is a boy's town; single women have to fight off the men. She must have gotten plenty of attention. Maybe she just didn't find anyone who interested her.

And then I thought of the smitten Leo Rosen, lurking in the shadows, following Lindsey and trying to summon the courage to speak to her. His best opportunity would have been after her friends left. Lindsey abandoned, and Leo to the rescue. But she stayed at the club for half an hour by herself, and Leo never spoke to her. He must have been going crazy, not having the balls to take advantage of the situation. Or maybe there was something else going on.

Suppose Lindsey had offended Leo by blowing him off when they'd met before in Southern California. What if Leo was angry enough to arrange Lindsey's rape? The going rate for murder for hire is only about ten grand. Leo could have hired a rapist for less. It was hard to imagine, though. I thought back to two women I'd been infatuated with, one when I was a teenager and another a few years later. Infatuation is a powerful thing, all consuming, more intense than love. Your perspective—hell, every trivial thought—becomes centered on your object of desire. It's a high that can last for weeks or even months. And when it's over, the humiliation and hurt can last even longer. But I never felt any inclination to harm the females I fell for. I realized the folly was solely my doing.

But who knows what was going on in Leo's head? People do all sorts of crazy shit when they're in love—or when they think they are. One thing though: Leo had been the one who called the cops and reported the license plate of the GMC SUV. I suppose that could have been spur-of-the-moment remorse on his part, but it put him at huge risk for incrimination. The prospect of prison has a way of sobering even the most emotionally wrought individuals. Unless Leo had completely lost his mind, he wouldn't risk that.

We walked out into the sunshine. It was a stretch to think Leo was behind the rape. For now, I was just mentally throwing theories against the wall to see what stuck. Leo hiring a rapist didn't stick, at least not very well, but I still wanted to talk to him.

I shared my thoughts with Cody as we headed back to my truck. He grunted and peered out past the highway. We could see a swath of the lake between Pistol Pete's and a smaller casino. The water was silver with the sun's reflection, like some sort of cosmic mirage.

I drove us east on Highway 50 a couple miles deeper into Nevada, past a campground to a road that led through a stretch of forest to the lake. I stopped at a small parking lot right on the shoreline. A short trail led to a fifty-foot dock. A windowless, rectangular building sat at the edge of the lot, its wood siding painted a tan color. It was a prefab unit, a doublewide trailer. We walked to a large door on the broad side. It was locked by a pair of deadbolts.

We looked around the building and knocked on the door. There were a couple cars in the lot, but no one was around. A breeze whispering through the pines was barely discernable from the faint whoosh of cars on the highway. The only other sound was the water lapping at the shore.

"What a perfect spot for a rape," Cody said.

I pointed to the metal cylinders set in the wood. "Those deadbolts must be new."

"Tucker supposedly broke in by cutting a padlock with bolt cutters."

"Here comes someone," I said, pointing to where a motorized dinghy was approaching from up the shoreline. It was towing another dinghy stacked with kayaks.

We walked across the dusty lot to the dock, kicking at pebbles and raising little clouds of dirt. Typically, after the snow melts every year, rains come and wash away the dirt and gravel left on the pavement. That hadn't happened this year. The sun was hot and bright in May, and the snow melted quickly and it never rained.

We stood on the dock and watched the boat slow until a man stepped into a few inches of water and looped a rope around a piling. Then he waded back to the second dinghy, removed a kayak, and splashed ashore.

Cody and I intercepted him as he hiked across the parking lot toward the building.

"Hey, buddy," I said. He reached the big door and set down the kayak.

"Can I help you?" He had crew-cut blond hair and the type of suntan that comes from working outdoors.

"Private investigators," I said. "We're looking into the rape that occurred here in April."

"Oh, man," he said, taking off his sunglasses. "That was ugly, man. And I heard the sick freak got off."

"Can we take a look inside?" Cody said.

He hesitated, then smiled. "Help me lug the rest of these kayaks?"

We followed him back to the water and waited for him to pull the remaining five plastic boats ashore. Cody lifted one on each shoulder as if he'd been doing it all his life. I tried the same technique and decided it was easier holding them low, as if carrying suitcases. The crew-cut man hauled the last one.

When we got to the building, he unlocked the deadbolts, slid the door open, and hit the lights. The floor was concrete, and the walls were lined with steel racks holding bicycles and canoes and assorted boating gear. In the back were snowboards and skis. The room was dank and smelled of mildewed lake water and melted snow. Directly opposite the door was a workbench, above which hung a pegboard full of tools.

There wasn't much room to move around. I assumed the rape must have occurred in front of the workbench.

"I found her right here, tied to this frame," the man said.

"You found her?" I looked at the man. His eyes were a lazy blue, and he was about thirty.

"Yeah. Scared the shit out of me. It was like something out of a horror movie. I opened the door, and she was bloody and shaking, and I jumped. I mean, literally, I jumped. Freaked me out."

"You must have noticed the lock was cut, right?" Cody said.

"Yeah. We used to just have a chain and padlock, and I thought somebody ripped us off. But I never expected to see anyone inside."

"What'd you do?" I said.

"I called nine-one-one and got her a blanket from my car. She was naked, and it was cold, man. I cut the rope she was tied with, and in a few minutes the cops showed."

"What happened then?"

"Well, they called an ambulance, and then more cops came. It was dawn, just getting light."

Cody was looking over the assortment of tools hanging on the wall. "Was anything missing?"

"Any tools?" the man said.

"Anything," Cody said. "Did the rapist take anything?"

"Well, just one thing. You probably already know this. The screwdriver."

"What about it?" I said.

"The twelve-inch screwdriver. It used to go there." He pointed at an empty spot on the pegboard. "But we haven't got around to replacing it."

"He took it?" Cody asked.

The man looked down. "No. Not exactly."

"What then?"

"The police took it. For evidence."

"Evidence? How so?" I said.

He coughed and scratched his nose. "He stuck it up her ass, man. That's how I found her. With a bloody screwdriver stuck in her."

• • •

We didn't say much as we drove away. Cody's brow was pinched into a V, and he sat looking out the passenger window. He lit a cigarette, took two drags, and threw it out onto the asphalt.

"I don't remember anything about a screwdriver in the trial folder," I said.

"They said something about a foreign object," Cody said, still staring away. "But I didn't see anything specific about what Tucker did with it."

"Now we know."

Cody turned back toward the windshield. His jaw was clenched, and crow's feet spread from his eyes. "This guy, Tucker," he said. "I'd like to meet him, have a philosophical conversation."

I stopped at the light before Caesars. "I hear you. But stomping his shit into the tar won't solve anything."

"Unless we beat the truth out of him. Is it noon yet?"

"No, why?" I said.

"I need a fucking drink."

I stared at the traffic light impatiently. Cody's version of philosophical conversation usually meant broken bones. I also knew that, in his case, alcohol and anger were a dangerous combination.

"We'll get him. But let's go one step at a time."

"Always the voice of reason, huh?" His eyes were like slits.

"I try."

"He beat the shit out of her, raped her, sodomized her, then impaled her. This guy's a walking plague. He needs to be in a cage, at a minimum. And that's going easy on him."

I met Cody's glare and nodded. He'd worked his share of rape cases as a San Jose cop, and I knew he recognized that while the injury to Lindsey's body was bad, it was only part of the damage Duante Tucker inflicted. The body would heal and be whole again. But the mental trauma was a different story. The attack might leave no permanent physical scars, but it had robbed Lindsey of a piece of her humanity. That was something she would never recover. The degradation would always be with her.

I wondered if a psychologist or sociologist had ever created a hierarchy of sadistic behavior. It would be a complex job, detailing degrees of pain and suffering and the potential motivation for each act. At the bottom of the chart might be common assholes like abusive bosses, casual racists, and bullies. Another tier could include wife-beaters or punks who beat up homeless people or gays. Move up the ladder, and you get contract killers and gangbangers. At the top of the heap would be a special class, not those who killed for financial gain or revenge or as the result of some dispute, but a different breed: those who take a perverse pleasure in hearing their victims scream and beg while their mental and physical beings are violated and ultimately damaged beyond repair. Unfortunately, there're more of them out there than most people know. Duante Tucker was a prime example.

"Call Darrian Bannon's office," I said to Cody. "Let's see if he's returned yet."

I steered into Pistol Pete's and parked while he worked his mobile device. When it started ringing, he turned on the speaker.

"Darrian Bannon law offices," a woman answered.

"Is Mr. Bannon in?" I said, speaking into Cody's phone.

"Not at this time. May I take a message?"

"Yes. Do you know when to expect him?"

"He's traveling the remainder of the week. He should be in Monday. Who's calling?"

"My name is Charles Ulysses Farley. I was vice-president at a large corporation, and I just got fired. My boss is a bigot, and I think my termination was racially motivated. I've heard Mr. Bannon specializes in this type of case."

"Absolutely, sir," said the woman. "How may Mr. Bannon reach you?"

"Well, I'm in South Lake Tahoe now, with my family."

"Oh, really? Let me have your number. Mr. Bannon may be able to meet you there."

"You mean he's up here?"

"I can't guarantee it, but he might be available. Your number, please?"

I gave her a phony number and hung up. "Sounds like Bannon is still in town," I said. "There're only four or five places I think he'd stay. Let's start here."

We got out of my truck and headed to Pistol Pete's hotel entrance.

"You're still using that Chuck U. Farley bit, huh?" Cody said.

"Gotta do something for kicks."

We went into the lobby, where a huge metal sculpture of a cowboy riding a rearing horse dominated the circular room. Pistol Pete's, once run by the mafia, had been sold last year to a major casino conglomerate, after the previous owner and his top manager vanished. Since then, the hotel had become one of South Lake Tahoe's most expensive and fashionable destinations.

There was a short line at the registration desk. Various pieces of Old West memorabilia were mounted on the blue walls—saddles, six-shooters, cowboy hats, and the like.

"Let me handle this," Cody said when a clerk became free. She was a young Asian woman with silky black hair and skin so perfect she could have been mistaken for a porcelain doll.

"How are you?" Cody said.

"I'm fine, thank you."

"I'm glad to hear that."

"I'm glad to hear you're glad to hear that," she said with a giggle.

Cody laughed in return, then said, "Could you do me a favor and call the room of Mr. Darrian Bannon?"

"Of course." She pecked at her keyboard and studied her screen. "Gee, I don't see his name."

"Maybe he checked out yesterday."

She hit a few more keys and frowned. "I'm sorry, he's not coming up."

"No worries, dear," Cody said. "Have a nice day, okay?"

We headed to the doors. "Let's walk over to Caesars," I said.

"What's the plan if we find the shyster?" Cody asked, once we were outside.

"Feel him out. See what he has to say."

"Really? Since when did you become such an optimist?"

"What have we got to lose?"

"In case you forgot," Cody said, "the guy's a lawyer. The attorney-client privilege applies even after the case is done. Unless we give him a damn good reason, he ain't gonna tell us shit."

"I know that," I said. "Look, let's try to be chummy with the dude. Hell, maybe buy him a drink or two. You never know what we might learn."

"The other option is get him alone, put him in a headlock, and threaten to snap his neck."

"Goddammit, Cody," I began, but when I looked at his mug, he was smiling.

"I'm just kidding, Dirt," he said. "Seriously, I'm good here. Let's do it your way. Chill out and have a drink."

I looked at my watch. "At least it's noon."

•　•　•

We crossed the street to Caesars, struck out, and had the same result at Harvey's and the Embassy Suites in California. The last place on my list was Harrah's. We waited for the light and hoofed it across the crosswalk at the state line.

"Why don't you call Grier and ask about Tim Cook?" Cody said as we walked the long stretch of sidewalk alongside the black glass facade of Harrah's casino.

"All right." I dialed the number for South Lake PD and asked the receptionist if Grier was in. To my mild surprise, she transferred me to his desk.

"Yes, what is it?" Grier answered, around a mouthful of food.

"Hey, Marcus. You asked me to keep you posted on my progress."

"Go ahead."

"I met with Tim Cook. What do you think of him?"

"What do you mean, what do I think of him? Is this your idea of an update?"

"He drives a junker, and his suit looks like a giveaway from a homeless shelter."

"So what?" he said.

"Is he broke?"

"Dan, his wife had terminal cancer and passed away about four months ago. Cook spent every dime he had caring for her after his insurance ran out. Yes, I'd say he's broke, and probably in debt, too."

"You think he's desperate enough to take a payoff to make the DNA disappear?"

"Cook? I don't think so."

"Why not?"

"Because I know the guy, and he's handled his situation with dignity."

"Cook said everyone who might have had access to the key to the evidence locker will be given a polygraph."

"He told you that?" asked Grier.

"Yeah," I said. "Look, I feel bad for the guy, but…"

"What?"

"Make sure Cook gets hooked up too, huh?"

"Thanks for the advice. Should I tell him it was your idea?"

"I'll talk to you later, Marcus."

"I can't wait," he said.

We went into Harrah's and through the casino to the hotel registration desk. Cody asked the attendant, a young Hispanic man, to dial Darrian Bannon's room. He checked his computer, then looked up.

"Whom should I say is calling?"

"Timothy Leary."

We waited while the clerk held the phone to his ear, until he said, "I'm sorry, he's not picking up."

"Thanks anyway." I began walking back toward the casino floor.

"You want to wander around?" Cody said.

"Yeah. Maybe we'll get lucky." I'd seen Bannon's picture on the Internet. While his hair and facial features were clearly those of a black man, his skin was the color of coffee diluted with too much cream. High yellow, people from the south used to call it. At some point, white blood had become comingled in Bannon's gene pool. It may have been the result of a white slave owner having congress with a female slave. There was no law against a master raping his slaves, and the most attractive females were usually victimized. It was a common practice before the Civil War.

The casino was picking up with the after-lunch crowd, and new card tables were opening. We walked by row after row of slots and scanned the tables, looking for a face matching Bannon's. We checked the sports book, the coffee shop, and another set of tables and slots at the opposite end of the casino. The place was nowhere near capacity, but there were still hundreds of people milling about. After twenty minutes, I said, "I'm starving. Let's get some chow."

"Let's hit the cantina downstairs," Cody said.

In the middle of the casino, an escalator led down to an underground walkway that connected Harrah's to Harvey's, which was on the other side of Highway 50. We took the escalator, but instead of following the underpass, we went the opposite direction to a cavelike Mexican restaurant.

The dining room was hidden behind a bar that serviced a dozen cocktail tables and a stage where live music played at night. The lighting was dim, the lamps tinted red. Half the tables were taken by people eating appetizers and sucking on margaritas or beers.

Sitting at a corner table was a couple, the man with his back to us. The woman had long, brown hair and milky white skin, and she wore a low-cut, aqua-green dress. A barbed wire tattoo circled her arm below her bare shoulder. She sat with her legs crossed, one high-heeled foot dangling under the table, and she was not wearing a bra—her nipples were pointy against the sheer material.

Cody and I sat a few tables away. I went to the bar and asked for a glass of water. When I turned, I got a good look at the man. He was clean-shaven, and his eyes looked puffy beneath his gold-rimmed spectacles. He wore khaki pants and tennis shoes and a purple knit shirt. Five-foot-ten, a soft one-ninety. Forty years old. A plate of prawns sat on the table. The man drank from a cocktail glass—vodka or gin or maybe silver tequila. The woman lowered her lips to dual straws and took a long sip from a blue concoction in a hurricane glass.

I came back to our table. Cody was reading the menu.

"It's Bannon," I said.

"That his wife?"

"I don't think he's married."

"Girlfriend?"

"Could be. Or she's a pro."

Cody lowered the menu and shifted his eyes to the woman. "She doesn't look like she's done it for free for a long time."

I started to reply, but stopped as a waitress arrived.

"Hi, beautiful," Cody said. "I'd like a Bud draught, and I'd also like to buy a round for that cute couple over there."

"Okay. And for you, sir?" she asked me.

"A diet Coke. And some fish tacos."

"Bring some nachos, too," Cody said.

We waited a minute for the waitress to deliver the drinks to Bannon's table. When she pointed to us, Bannon turned and looked over. I smiled and waved. His eyes moved from me to Cody. After a moment he nodded and turned back to the woman. She cast a disinterested glance our way and shared a few hushed words with Bannon. Then she wiped her hands on a napkin, took a final sip off her drink, and stood and walked out of the lounge.

Bannon turned again toward us. He made no gesture, and his face was void of expression. I got up and went to his table.

"I'm sorry. Do I know you?" Bannon said.

"No. Sorry if we created any issue for you and your lady, there."

"Don't worry about it. Are you South Lake PD?"

"Nope."

"Do we look like cops?" Cody said, walking over with his beer.

Bannon looked from Cody to me. "Christ, you're not journalists, are you?"

"Wrong again."

"To what do I owe the pleasure, then?"

"Actually, we'd like to have a drink with you," Cody said. "If you're okay with that."

"Have a seat if you like," Bannon said. We'd been standing over him. I knew if we stood there long enough, he'd either stand or tell us to sit. I took his lady's seat, and Cody pulled up a chair from another table.

"So, what's on your mind?" Bannon said, folding his hands in front of him.

"We'd like to chat with you about your recent case."

Bannon pulled on his ear and pressed his lips together. "Sorry to disappoint you, gentlemen. That's something I'm not at liberty to discuss."

"What a surprise," I said, smiling. Cody waved his empty beer glass at the waitress.

"It's a matter of professional ethics. Anyway, it's been nice meeting you," Bannon said, looking at his watch. "But I do need to be going."

"Let me guess," Cody said. "That babe is waiting for you in your room. What does a piece of tail like that run, about five hundred an hour?"

The insult didn't register on Bannon's smooth face. "I wouldn't know," he said.

"Mr. Bannon," I said, "I've heard you claim to have taken Duante Tucker's case pro bono. Is that correct?"

"Yes."

"I'm sure you're aware, the IRS would take a dim view if you were in fact paid under the table."

Bannon forced a smile, his pink gums high above his small teeth. "I'm really not sure why you'd say something like that. And I really don't have the time to listen to your insinuations."

"Why did you take Duante Tucker's case?" Cody asked.

"It's my way of giving back to the community."

Cody barked a laugh. "I'm sure greater society is thrilled Duante Tucker is back on the streets."

Bannon stood, but my chair was blocking his only exit route. "The witnesses were scared off, and someone stole the DNA evidence," I said. "If not for that, you'd never have gotten him off."

"Those were external factors I had no control over. Now, if you'll excuse me."

I made no effort to move. "Maybe you had no control over those factors, but I bet you know who was behind it. Am I right, Mr. Bannon?"

Pinned between the wall and me, Bannon was trapped. He stood with his pants leg nearly touching my shoulder.

"Absolutely not. Further, I resent this intrusion on my day. I'm leaving now. Please move."

"Sit down, counselor," Cody said.

"I beg your pardon?"

"Sit down and finish the drink I bought you."

"This is ridiculous. I'm calling nine-one-one." He reached for the cell phone clipped to his belt.

"No, you're not." Cody stood and glared down at Bannon. "I doubt the local cops think much of you. I also think you give up certain rights when you throw in with a shitbag like Duante Tucker."

Bannon's complexion became paler, and he opened his mouth as if gulping air. "My client was entitled by law to fair representation," he recited. "And that is all I have to say to you."

"Wrong," Cody said. "You've got a lot more to say. But it's no problem, old buddy. I'm sure we'll talk again soon." Cody winked and picked up Bannon's untouched drink.

I stood and moved my chair so the attorney could escape. "Enjoy your stay," I said.

Bannon didn't reply and hurried out of the restaurant. Once he was gone, our waitress came to the table. "Is everything okay here?" she asked.

"Right as rain," Cody said.

"He left without paying his bill."

"His name is Darrian Bannon, and he's staying at Harrah's," I said. "Charge it to his room."

• • •

It was midafternoon when we got back to my place. Cody changed into his camouflage print shorts and went out to the deck. When I came outside, he was sitting in a plastic lounge chair facing the sun, shirtless and wearing sunglasses and a baseball cap. His jumbo cooler was next to the lounge chair. He took a swig from a can of beer and set it on the lid. "Now, this is the life," he said.

I sat at the picnic bench and rubbed my jaw. "You pleased how our meeting with Bannon went?"

"Sure, why not?"

"The only thing we accomplished was putting him on alert."

"I figured that would happen. But I thought it went great." He finished his beer, crushed the can in his fist, and grabbed another from the cooler.

"How's that?"

"Bannon's shittin' scared. The money trail might lead through him. One way or another, he knows something."

"Right, and since we leaned on him, he'll be extra cautious."

"I hope he takes it one step further." Cody hit off his new beer and belched. "You know how it works. Make 'em think you're getting close, and the rats come out of their holes."

"That's one way of looking at it." I stared at Cody's massive white frame. His chest looked like iron plates had been inserted under the skin, and his arms were shaped like cannons. He picked up a tube of sunscreen and smeared some on his nose. I stepped off the deck onto the lawn. "I'm gonna jog down the trail. Be back in a little while."

On the other side of my back fence, a dirt path followed a stream through the meadow. I took off down the trail toward the mountains, the sun beating down on my neck, dry grass brushing my shins as my feet pounded the loose dirt. I went across a makeshift bridge over the stream, and soon I was in the woods.

My mind wandered, like it always did when I ran, and I thought about my father. He had been a district attorney but left the job for private practice. He specialized in fraud cases, defending his clients against a variety of scams, some perpetuated by large corporations. He was relentless when he thought he was right, and he wouldn't take a case unless he felt that way. As an attorney, he'd made plenty of friends and a fair number of enemies. Eventually one of his enemies, a recently paroled piece of white trash, caught up with the old man and ambushed him with a twelve-gauge outside his office. One shot, point blank.

I had problems after that, angry, confused, my teenage years a series of brawls and disciplinary issues. I didn't know how to deal with a world where a psychotic miscreant could rob a family of a loved one and then simply return to a prison that offered him a more comfortable life than he would otherwise have. Things got so bad that my mother sent me to a shrink, who made pointless comments and grew visibly uncomfortable at some of the things I said. I stopped going after two sessions. A school counselor thought sports might provide an outlet for my aggression, so I joined the high school football team. But it wasn't until I tried out for wrestling that things changed for the better.

Wrestling. One-on-one combat. Strength, speed, stamina, technique. Factor in guts, perseverance, and, as important as anything, the ability to endure pain. And if those attributes aren't enough, then you'd better get plumb dog mad. Because sometimes you have to get mad to win. And I hated losing.

A competitive wrestler's exercise regimen is grueling. The workouts last for hours, and if you haven't puked, you haven't pushed yourself hard enough. And that means you'll probably get your ass kicked in the ring.

My workouts these days are candy-assed compared to what I did when I wrestled in college. Nowadays, I might hit the weights for an hour, then jog three miles. And, once a week, I hang out at Rex's Gym in Nevada. Rex is an ex-karate champion, and a crew of cage fighters train at his place. I participate as a sparring partner, sometimes with pads, sometimes without. In return for the bruises and occasional cuts, I stay up on the latest in submission holds and striking techniques.

After a mile the path steepened. The grade increased for another half mile until the trail became narrow and rocks and ledges made jogging impossible. I stopped in a shady area a hundred feet below the base of a waterfall that gushed with snow melt. A fine mist hit my face when I looked up at the torrent breaking over the granite cliff. I lowered myself to pushup position and drank from the stream. Then I headed back home, where Cody Gibbons lay in a lounge chair, drinking beers and catching rays as if he didn't have a care in the world.

4

B Y NINE O'CLOCK THE next morning Cody and I were on the road, heading west toward San Jose. It's a four-hour drive, up over Echo Summit at 7,300 feet, then down fifty miles of winding two-lane through the El Dorado National Forest, until the road widens in the foothills above Placerville. After that it's mundane freeway driving through the low lands of Sacramento, past towns with names like Davis and Dixon, until the interstate veers south toward Santa Clara County. An hour later you come off a hill, and a large, densely built valley appears. Silicon Valley, some out-of-towners still call it. Home to many of the world's top technology companies. Mostly orchard land before the computer boom, but now every acre is fully developed. A million dollars buys what would be considered a modest home in most parts of the United States. Despite the expensive real estate, immigrants still flock here. Those with a college background come for engineering or marketing jobs. Those without the education work in service professions or as laborers. Almost two million people live in the valley, and despite the lingering recession, that equates to a lot of jobs.

At the heart of the valley is San Jose. It's a sprawling city, but to me it still feels like a podunk town. A small collection of modest high-rises marks the downtown, while the rest of the city fans out in a blend of residential neighborhoods, shopping centers, and business parks. Ask people what's special about San Jose, and they'll tell you two things: first, the jobs, and second, the climate can't be beat. As for the city's personality, it's like that of a quiet, unremarkable child in the shadow of a more rambunctious and interesting sibling. San Francisco, fifty miles north, is what most people think of as the heart of Northern California. San Jose, despite its emergence as an economic powerhouse, is an afterthought. I know this, because I lived in San Jose most of my life.

While Cody had been out to dinner with Ryan Addison's assistant the night before, I'd logged onto a subscription site and compiled a profile on Duante Tucker. He was twenty-five years old, and in his public record were two incidents of juvenile assault. As an adult he'd been arrested twice, once for aggravated assault and once for dealing. Both arrests occurred in the ghettos near Los Angeles, and neither resulted in a conviction. Except for the recent incident in Tahoe, Tucker's record was clean for the three years he'd reportedly lived in San Jose.

There was no mention of Tucker's mother among his relatives, but I found names for his father and sister. Shanice Tucker was three years younger than Duante. She'd been convicted for prostitution when she was eighteen, but other than that there was no information available on her. No current address or employer listed.

The public record for the father, Lamar Tucker, was more extensive. Lamar Tucker had owned real estate in and around Compton and had a lengthy criminal record that included a mayhem charge. There was no detail as to the charge, but he had been convicted for that and other violent offenses. Whether or not he was still in prison, I couldn't tell.

I called Cody's cell as I followed him on the freeway west of Sacramento. We'd not had time to speak this morning because I was anxious to get on the road. He'd woken late and I'd rushed him out of the house.

"How'd your date with Miss Charming go last night?" I asked.

"Not bad, I guess," he said. "She's a weird one."

"How so?"

"Her grand idea is to write a screenplay based on Lindsey's rape. She's offering me a part in the movie if I tell her the details from our investigation."

I laughed. "That's the most ridiculous thing I ever heard."

"Yeah, I admit it's a little farfetched."

"So, what'd you tell her?"

"I said I'm not an actor, and besides, I'm not sure if I want my handsome mug splashed all over the silver screen. She got kind of pouty and bitchy when I told her that, and then she cuddled up and pulled out the heavy artillery."

"Meaning?"

"She said she gives life-changing blow jobs, and she'll prove it to me once I deliver the goods."

"Now, that's raw ambition. It piqued your interest, I take it?"

"Wouldn't it peak yours?"

"Not from her," I said.

"Well, you're married, or you might as well be, so who cares?"

"Not me, that's for sure."

We hung up, and I called Candi. She didn't pick up, but I knew she'd ring back when she saw I called. It was two hours later where she was visiting her folks in Houston, and I imagined she might be sitting down to lunch. Her father was a lawman, and Candi had grown up on a ranch before spending her teenage years in the Houston suburbs. She was vivacious and smart and had an hourglass figure that still drove me to distraction. She also understood my work and was more tolerant than any woman I'd ever met. Still, she wouldn't be thrilled I was working with Cody again. She liked him, but was wary of his ways, as any sane person would be. But she knew he'd saved my life before and would not hesitate to do so again. If it ever came to that.

• • •

Cody's office was on the second floor of an older building in downtown San Jose. The building was in San Pedro Square, the city's hotspot for dining and nightlife. We walked down an alley and up a rickety flight of stairs. His small office was above a Mexican restaurant, and the aroma of tortillas and seasoned meats permeated the room.

Cody opened the shades, and sunlight burst through the hazy darkness. He picked up the phone on his scarred oak desk and asked someone to bring us a couple specials.

"You're gonna love this. They make the best burritos in town," he said.

"When did you move here?"

"A few months ago. The Sanchez family gave me cheap rent after I helped them out with a little trouble."

"What kind of trouble?" I asked.

"A biker took a liking to Tina, the daughter. She wasn't interested, but he wouldn't get the message. So I helped with the communication."

"You spoke his language, huh?"

"I suppose you could say that. I kicked him in the balls so hard they're probably still stuck in his throat."

"Nice," I said. I looked from the scuffed floor to the wood-paneled walls, which were covered with framed Forty-Niner and Oakland Raider pictures. Behind the desk, Cody's bounty hunter and private investigator's license hung beneath a Schlitz Malt Liquor mirror. I lowered myself into a folding metal chair, and said, "Where do you want to start with Tucker?"

"We've got an address. Let's spin on by after lunch."

"Incognito, right? I want to tail him for a day or two."

Before Cody could reply, there was a knock on the door. I opened it to see a boy about ten years old, holding two Styrofoam containers. He had a shock of black hair and skinny brown arms.

"Hey, Pedro. *Qué pasa*, little man?"

"Not much, Mr. Cody." He set the containers on the desk, and Cody handed him a twenty.

"Keep the change, okay, buddy?"

"Okay." He smiled, and we heard him run down the stairs.

"If we're gonna do surveillance, we better use my rig," Cody said, opening one of the containers.

"Your *red* truck?" I said.

"No, not my red truck. What do you think I am, some kind of jackass?"

"What, then?"

"I never told you about the hellfire hooptie, did I?"

"Not that I remember."

"Ah. Well, today's your lucky day."

• • •

After we finished eating, I followed Cody to his home a few miles southwest, near the border of San Jose and Los Gatos. He had bought the place a decade ago, when he was married, and when the marriage ended, he managed to keep it. Almost half the homes in the neighborhood had since been rebuilt into two-story mini-mansions of various styles. The other half, which included Cody's, were cookie-cutter, three-bed-two-bath houses built in the late 1940s, during the postwar prosperity.

I parked on the street and walked behind Cody's pickup as it crunched down a long tar-and-gravel driveway that led to an oversized garage in the rear of his lot. The garage door opened, and he pulled in next to a maroon sedan. He got in the car and backed it out into the sun.

I looked at the vehicle and shrugged. It was an older-model Toyota four-door. One of the rims didn't match the others, and someone had keyed the faded paint along the rear quarter panel.

"What do you think?" Cody said.

I walked around the car. The front bumper was badly scuffed on one side.

"It's the kind of ride you buy for a thousand bucks when you can't afford anything better," I said.

"Exactly, my friend." He came behind me and clasped his hand on top of my shoulder. "A 1988 Toyota Camry. Mundane. Nondescript. And dig the ugly color. You see this ride parked at the curb, your eyes glaze over, and you look away. It's the perfect undercover car."

I raised my eyebrows. "Is it reliable?"

"Funny you should ask. Check it out." He popped the hood to reveal a gleaming engine.

"New motor?"

"New, and supercharged. Four hundred fifty horses, baby. All the running gear is completely redone. Tranny, brakes, suspension. This thing is so goddamned fast I almost killed myself when I first drove it. I had to take two weekends of racing school at Sears Point before I felt comfortable."

"I always thought you were a pretty good driver," I said.

"No. This is totally different. You'll see. Come on, let's go."

Cody climbed into the driver's seat, which must have been lowered, because instead of his head nearly touching the ceiling, he looked like a man of average height. I got in and buckled my seat belt, and we backed down the driveway.

"It doesn't feel like anything special," I said as we rolled down his street. The engine was quiet and smooth, like an ordinary car. Cody shifted the manual transmission into second gear, and we turned out of his neighborhood onto the main thoroughfare. We stopped at a traffic signal.

"See any cops around?" he said. We were first in line at the light.

"No."

When the light turned green, Cody mashed the accelerator and we launched off the line with a neck-snapping jerk. We were doing forty by the time we crossed the intersection, and Cody hit second with his foot on the floor. The freeway on-ramp was coming up on the right. He snapped the gearshift into third, and I looked over and saw the speedometer moving past eighty.

"Cody," I said. The on-ramp looked tight, and we were approaching it at a suicidal speed. I reached up and clutched the chicken bar above the passenger door. He grabbed fourth gear, and we catapulted forward. I felt the muscles in my legs tighten as I pushed back in the seat. If we missed the turn—and that was becoming a near certainty—we would fly off a dip into a thick stand of maple trees.

At the last possible instant, Cody downshifted, hit the brakes hard, then accelerated through the sweeping turn. The tires howled and slid, but Cody counter-steered and stayed on the gas. The Camry came out of the turn at a hundred before Cody eased up.

I exhaled. "I hope you don't do that on a regular basis."

"Please don't wet your pants in my car," he said. "That's one of my rules."

We drove along 280, heading south, and took the 101 interchange. After a couple miles, we exited onto Tully Road and headed into east San Jose.

Like any metropolis, Santa Clara County has a variety of socioeconomic zones. West and central San Jose, despite patches of slummy areas, cater mostly to a solid middleclass. South San Jose offers less expensive real estate and can be a little rough around the edges. The same holds true for north San Jose. Santa Clara County's wealthy typically reside outside of San Jose, in posh communities along the mountains, like Los Gatos, Saratoga, and Cupertino.

As for the valley's poor, east San Jose has long been their domain. When I grew up, I remember an east side populated evenly by blacks and Mexicans. When the population exploded with the computer boom, the racial demographic changed. Today, the poor part of town is dominated by Mexican and Vietnamese families. African Americans have become a small minority.

"Hang a left here," I said, looking at my GPS. We turned onto a street where the houses had tar roofs and were separated by chain link fences. I rolled down the window. Ninety degrees of dry heat hit my face. I pointed, and Cody turned down a narrow lane that was crisscrossed overhead with telephone wires. Most of the yards were hard-packed dirt, and some served as parking spaces for junkers, or shiny rides probably bought with drug money. Gang graffiti coated every suitable surface, and the windows were braced with iron security bars.

"Next right," I said as we approached a corner where a squad of young Asians gave us the deadeye. In the driveway of the corner house were two gleaming Japanese coupes with aftermarket rims and spoilers. Two men wrenched under the hood of one.

"I got a faster rice burner than you," Cody muttered.

Duante Tucker's street was semipaved and lined with vehicles. I watched the street numbers until we came to a white stucco house with a blue door. A black GMC Yukon sat in the driveway.

We neared the end of the street. "Turn around and find somewhere to park," I said.

"You sure that's the car?"

I reached to the rear seat and took a folder from my bag as Cody hung a U-turn and drove slowly by the house.

"Yeah. Registered to the roommate, Lennox Suggs. It's the one Tucker drove to Tahoe."

We drove to the opposite end of the street and turned around again, looking for somewhere to park that offered a view of the house Duante Tucker reportedly rented with Lennox Suggs. But the street was packed with cars, and there wasn't a single spot open.

"Shit," Cody said.

"What about here?" On the opposite side of the street, three houses from Tucker's address, a flat-roofed home had a 'For Rent' sign in the front window. The yard was waist-high in dead weeds, and two-by-fours were nailed across the door.

Cody slowed and backed into the driveway, until we could just see around a work van parked in the neighbor's driveway.

"Not bad," I said, and lowered the window. From our position we had a decent view of Tucker's residence.

We sat in silence for five minutes. The hope is always to get quick action on a surveillance. It rarely happens.

An hour passed. The car was hot, and my back was stuck to my shirt. There was no shade to be had, and nothing stirred at the Tucker house. It looked like a blanket had been hung inside the single window facing the street. The paint on the door was peeling, and rusty streaks stained the stucco below a gutter that hung limply from the roofline. It was quiet, and the air smelled of dust and motor oil, and when a warm breeze rattled the weeds, I caught a whiff of raw sewage.

"I wonder if that dump has air conditioning," Cody said.

"I doubt it."

"You think they're sitting in there watching TV?"

"Maybe. They probably have fans," I said.

"I'd like to get in there and bug the place." Cody looked at me. A drop of sweat ran down along his sideburn.

"We should probably figure out if anyone's home first."

"Got any ideas?"

"We got company," I said. Two of them, walking diagonally at us from the other side of the street. Pants baggy and low on the hips, white T-shirts, chains dangling from belt loops, and red bandanas covering their heads. *Cholos.*

"What's up, homes?" The first man stood a couple feet from my window. I couldn't see his face.

"*Nada*," I said.

"You looking for something, man?" he said. His Chicano barrio accent was a gravelly whine, thick with menace and intimidation.

"Nope."

He dropped to a crouch, and his face suddenly appeared. He had a stringy mustache and a busted nose that hadn't healed right.

"You look like cops," he said with a smirk. "You the heat?"

I looked in his dark eyes. One was half-lidded, but the other was wide open. "Not us," I said.

"Then you better get gone, pronto. You get what I'm saying?"

"This your turf?"

"*Simone*. And you're on it."

"Hey," Cody said. "This your turf, what's up with the spades that live over there?"

The Latino cut his eyes at Tucker's place, and when he responded, a hint of passivity replaced the aggression in his voice. "It's a free country, homes. Besides, it's only one *negro*, and I got no beef with him." He grunted at the other Latino, and they turned without further comment and walked back the way they'd come.

"What do you make of that?" I said.

"He sure adjusted his attitude quick."

"Like he respects Tucker. Or Lennox Suggs. Or both."

Cody lit a cigarette and blew a stream of smoke out the window. "He said only one *negro*."

I stared at the house, my face squinted against the sun. The *cholos* had headed the opposite direction and the street was quiet.

"I'm gonna go knock on the door," I said. "Be back in a minute."

I strode across the street and along the cracked, uneven sidewalk, paused at the black GMC, then quick-stepped up to the door and rapped twice with my knuckles. Instantly the stillness was interrupted by loud barking. I darted back around the GMC and behind a panel-bed truck parked on the street just as two pit bulls rushed at the chain link fence securing the side yard.

The dogs barked, gnashed their teeth, and stood on their hind legs pawing the fence. Through the truck's rickety slats, I saw a man I recognized as Lennox Suggs open the door. His head was shaved except for a faint strip down the middle. He was shirtless, and the bulging muscles beneath his jailhouse tats rippled in the sunlight. Six-two and 220 pounds of serious body building. Probably a habit he brought home from prison.

Lennox Suggs stepped off the porch and glared right and left, the white of his eyes flashing under his brow. He walked over to the dogs and calmed them, then came back to the front door.

"Fuck you," he huffed after a moment, and went back inside. The dogs retreated behind the house. I waited another minute and saw the blanket covering the window move aside. Suggs watched his yard for five, ten seconds, then the blanket fell back to its original position. I hustled down the street and crossed over to the Camry.

"Lennox Suggs?" Cody asked.

"Yeah."

"He's a walking advertisement for the failure of our justice system. Did you read his jacket?"

"Yeah," I said. "He's had a busy life."

"Apparently three strikes doesn't apply to him. He's spent most of his adulthood in the joint."

"The gangbanger said only one person lives there," I said. "Looks like it's Suggs."

"I thought Tucker and Suggs were roomies."

"Maybe Tucker moved."

"We want to bug the place, we'll have to deal with those dogs," Cody said.

Our conversation stopped when the front door opened again. This time Suggs was wearing sunglasses and a white shirt open at the collar. A silver chain circled his neck and rested against his dark skin. He climbed into the GMC and backed out of the driveway.

"Follow him?" Cody said. "Or you want to creep the dump?"

"We don't know the house is empty, and those pit bulls would alert the whole neighborhood. Let's tail him."

We hunched low as Suggs drove past us, then we pulled out half a block behind him. At that distance, we followed the SUV out to the main thoroughfare and toward the freeway.

"How much energy you want to invest on this guy?" Cody said.

"Hell, Tucker borrowed his wheels. They must be close. Let's see where Suggs takes us."

"I'd rather follow Tucker." Cody accelerated through a light and followed the SUV onto 101.

"You want to turn around and go back and hope he shows his face?" I asked.

"Not now."

Suggs stayed to the right and merged onto 280. Two miles later, he exited onto Guadalupe Parkway.

"He's taking us downtown," I said.

"Looks like it," Cody replied as Suggs took the first turnoff onto Saint James Street. The GMC went around the block on one-way streets, passed within a stone's throw of Cody's office, then pulled into a driveway at a black glass high-rise that looked brand-new.

"What's this building?" I said. Cody parked on the street and we watched Suggs stop at a drive-up kiosk in front of a copper-colored metal door blocking the entrance to a parking garage.

"The Skyscape condos. Been here less than a year. Luxury apartments for yuppies."

Suggs's finger jabbed at the kiosk keypad, and the door slid open horizontally. He drove into the garage and the door closed.

I got out of the car and stared up at the building. The sun reflected off the dark glass in sharp bursts. Small balconies rose in a column up the side of the structure, which was about thirty stories high.

Cody climbed out of the Camry and leaned on the roof across from me.

"From the slums to this place, huh?" he said. He adjusted his sunglasses and looked up and down the street.

"Why don't you wait here?" I said. "I'll go inside and have a look."

"All right."

"Call me if Suggs comes back out." He nodded, and I went across the street to opaque glass doors that I assumed accessed a lobby, but they were locked. Next to the doors, instructions said to punch in a resident's code or 0 for the sales office. I hit 0 on a keypad inset in the concrete wall, and a moment later the door clicked open.

The lobby was decorated in stainless steel and blond wood. The lack of color created a sterile, modernistic look. The woman sitting behind a concierge counter added to the effect. Short black hair, silver crosses dangling from her ears, green shadow above her eyes, and a thin-lipped smile.

"May I help you?" There was a pair of security cameras mounted high on the wall behind the counter.

I stuck my hands in my pockets and looked past her to an elevator in a hallway. "Yeah, I'm thinking about renting a place here. Can I ask you a couple questions?"

"Sure, but you should really talk with our sales office."

"Right. So, if I lived here, and wanted to have guests, how would they get in?"

"You'd give them your access code. They could come in the front here and go up the elevator. Or, they could use the code to go into the garage and take the elevator from there. We have plenty of visitor parking."

"Gotcha. Do you have units for rent?"

"I think we do. Let me get you a salesperson." She picked up her phone, and after a moment, a man in tan slacks and a black button-down shirt appeared from an adjacent room. He walked across the lobby to greet me, a broad smile on his face.

"Welcome to Skyscape. You're interested in renting?" His brown hair was styled in a wave, and he had a silver stud in one ear.

"I'm thinking about it," I replied.

"Most of our homes are occupied by owners, but we do have a few for rent. Would you like to take a tour?"

"Sure."

We walked to the elevator. "Skyscape opened just six months ago, and we're nearly sold out. We offer everything from studios to three-bedroom, two-level homes with balconies. Every unit offers great views from floor to ceiling windows. We are the tallest building in San Jose."

The elevator dinged, and we stepped in. "There are three homes available for rent. A one-bedroom with balcony on the fourteenth floor, a two-bedroom on the sixteenth, and a three-bedroom on the twentieth. What price range are you looking for?"

"Two grand a month, give or take."

He hit the button for the fourteenth floor. "A one-bedroom would be in that range."

"This is kind of new for San Jose, isn't it?" I said. "I mean, high-rise city living."

"Yes, but San Jose is changing. Are you from here?"

"No. Out of town. Thinking of relocating."

"Downtown San Jose is booming. New restaurants and night clubs are opening all the time. The San Jose Sharks hockey team sells out every game, and we think we'll have a major league baseball team soon."

"What kind of people live in this place?" I asked.

"We have quite a notable ownership, actually. Some top technology executives own our penthouse units, and other affluent members of the community live here too."

The elevator stopped and I followed the man down a hall to a door marked 1401. He unlocked a door knob and a dead bolt, and then he tapped a code on a keypad next to the doorframe.

"Quite a bit of security, isn't it?" I said.

"Oh, we take security very seriously. Every unit is protected this way—traditional locks plus electronic. We've never had an incident of theft."

"How about security cameras?"

"We have cameras covering the lobby and the garage elevator. So we know who is entering the building. Basically, thieves don't bother us."

We went inside. The place was furnished and the decor looked staged, like something out of an interior design magazine. The kitchen and living room were large, but the single bedroom was small. He showed me the bathroom, then we returned to the living room, where he opened a glass door and stepped out onto the balcony.

"It's a little smoggy today, but most of the time the view of the mountains is spectacular." We stood looking over the southwest half of the valley. The street grids and buildings stretched without pause before ending miles away at the base of the Santa Cruz Mountains, which ran from just south of

San Francisco all the way around the western flank of Santa Clara County. I had spent years exploring the three-thousand-foot-tall range, hiking and riding dirt trails, rock climbing, and occasionally bringing a date to an inspirational spot.

I looked up at the subfloor of the balcony above. To the side, a six-foot-wide column of flat gray concrete rose to the top of the building. Next to it was a vertical row of black windows.

"Very nice," I said. "What if there's a fire?"

"This building has an iron frame. The whole thing is mostly steel and concrete. And we have smoke-activated sprinklers in every room and in the hallways too."

"That's good," I said absently. "Let's go." I followed him off the balcony back into the bedroom. When I closed the balcony door, the latch didn't fully engage. I took a moment and pulled the handle until it clicked shut. There was no lock on the door.

"Would you like to look at another unit? A larger one?"

"Maybe. How about stairs?"

"Of course. We have stairs at the end of each hallway. For emergency purposes. I mean, they're not for people to exercise on. We had one owner who wanted to do that. But we discourage it."

"You can get a good workout running stairs," I said, as we went out to the hallway and back to the elevator.

"Well, you look in great shape," he said. He had a loose smile on his face, and it occurred to me he was gay.

"How about a gym or a swimming pool?" I asked.

"Yes, on the twenty-eighth floor. Our fitness center is on our rooftop."

"Let's go check it out."

"Certainly."

We took the elevator up, then hiked a flight of stairs to a carpeted lobby with vending machines offering energy drinks and protein bars. I followed him through a doorway into a large, mirrored room lined with stationary bikes, treadmills, and elliptical machines, all facing glass walls looking out over the valley. The center of the room was occupied by racks of free weights and a variety of weight machines.

"Not bad," I said.

"Access is free for both owners and renters."

"And the pool?"

"Right this way." We went through a hallway and out a door. A burst of sunlight hit my eyes as we walked onto the white roof. A sparkling turquoise pool lay in the center, surrounded by lounge chairs. Off to the side was a small building—a restroom or perhaps a changing room.

"Sometimes we have resident parties up here. Set up a portable bar, appetizers, that sort of thing."

I shaded my eyes and looked around. Two tanned blond women in bikinis reclined in the sun. Another two sat sipping drinks at a table under an umbrella. Beyond the pool, a gold-painted, waist-high fence ran a foot or two inside the edge of the roof line. A taller fence, made of three horizontal, six-inch thick black tubes, was erected on the outer boundary. The fence was visible from the street, and I assumed it served nothing but a decorative purpose, as the gaps between the tubes were wide enough for anyone to slip between and fall to their death, if that's what they chose to do.

"What do you think?" the man asked.

"Pretty nice. Let's head back down. You got some brochures you can give me?"

"Sure. But just so you know, the available units will go quick."

"I'll keep that in mind."

• • •

"What took so long?" Cody asked when I got back to his car. He was leaning against a wall in the shade of a building on the opposite side of the street.

"I told them I was looking for a place to rent and took the sales tour."

"Did you find out who Suggs is visiting?"

"How the hell would I do that?"

"I don't know. You usually find a way. What are those papers?"

I looked at the sheets I held. "Prices of units for sale. Frequently asked questions. Concierge services."

"No map of the place?"

"No, why?"

"Because Suggs is hanging out up there on the sixteenth floor. He just had a smoke on the balcony with some dude. Take a look, I got a picture." Cody handed me his cell phone. On the small screen, I could barely make out two black men, one in a white shirt.

"You're sure it's Suggs?" I said.

"Yeah. Zoom in, you can see the chain on his neck."

I handed him the phone back. "You counted sixteen balconies up?"

"No, fourteen. It doesn't look like the balconies start until the third floor."

I put on my sunglasses and peered up at the rectangular shapes of the facing. "We need to figure out the address for that unit."

"Right."

"They said there was a unit for rent on the sixteenth floor. I suppose I could go back in."

"You want me to go instead?" Cody said.

I shook my head. "No, they've already seen me. You might as well stay off the radar."

"Suits me."

I went back into the building and approached the woman at the concierge counter.

"Could I talk to that salesman I was with?"

"You mean Gerald," she said.

"Yeah."

She lifted the phone, and the salesman promptly appeared in the lobby.

"Back so soon?" he said.

"You mentioned a two-bedroom on the sixteenth floor. Can I take a look?"

"Of course."

We rode the elevator to the sixteenth floor, and I followed him to unit 1608. The interior looked identical to the unit I'd seen previous, modern and sleek.

"Is there a balcony?" I asked.

"No, not on this one. Only the end units have them."

"I see." We spent a minute going from room to room, then went back out to the hallway. I started toward the elevator, past 1607 and 1606.

"The balcony units are this way?" I asked.

"Yes, but there's none available on this floor."

"I know." I walked by the elevator and continued down the hall.

"Sir?"

"I just wanted to get a sense of where the stairs are. I don't always trust elevators."

"Oh. Well, the stairway is there at the end." I kept walking and he followed until we stood at 1602, which was directly across from a door that opened to the stairwell.

"Okay," I said, opening the door and glancing down the stairs. "So, 1602 is a balcony unit?"

"Yes."

"Do you have any balcony units available on the lower floors? Lower than the fourteenth?"

"Oh, no. Those units are all sold out."

"Nothing on the second floor?"

"Actually, our units start on the third floor."

"I see." We walked back to the elevator and headed down to the lobby.

"Would you like to fill out a rental application?" he asked.

"I'll take one with me," I said.

• • •

"What's the scoop?" Cody said, when I came back out. He was sitting on a brick flower bed down the street from his car. Rows of purple and yellow flowers stretched behind him.

I pointed up at the building. "That one should be 1602."

"We can look at a reverse directory, find out who lives there."

I checked my watch. It was 3:30. I sat next to Cody and watched the parking lot door slide open. A couple in a blue Jaguar convertible drove out and turned down the street. The metal door closed with a soft clang, and I looked back up at the balcony. An elderly lady came around the corner walking two toy poodles, one black and one white. A jet taking off from the airport a mile away thundered upward, its gritty blast a smudge on the blue sky.

Twenty minutes went by until the garage door opened again. We saw the GMC Yukon before the door was half opened, and we were in the Camry by the time it pulled onto the street. As it turned, I caught a brief glimpse of a man in the passenger seat.

"Duante Tucker," I said. Cody started the engine and pulled from the curb.

"You sure?" he asked.

"It's him.

We tailed them around the corner and onto Guadalupe Parkway. They headed south for a mile, then got on 880, one of San Jose's three main arteries. The rush hour traffic was picking up, and by the time we reached Brokaw Road, it was stop and go.

"You miss the traffic?" Cody said.

"Yeah. Kind of makes me homesick."

The freeway narrowed to three lanes, and we crawled along. The black GMC stayed in the fast lane a football field ahead.

"Some of these poor bastards spend three hours every day doing this," Cody said, gesturing at the gridlock. "Commuting in from Livermore or Tracy."

A big rig merged in front of us and we lost sight of the GMC until Cody maneuvered to the left and from there the flow picked up to forty miles an hour. Then the traffic cleared and we hit seventy until it slowed again. Twenty minutes later we were in a corridor known as the East Bay. We exited in Fremont, a growing city with a heavy population of Chinese and Indian immigrants.

The GMC drove five minutes down Mowry Boulevard and bounced into a small shopping square. An auto parts store, a Jack-in-the-Box, a liquor store, a barbershop. Three other businesses I couldn't identify because their signage was in a different language.

"Hindi," I said.

"What?"

"That writing is Hindi. It's what they speak in India."

"You can recognize it?" Cody asked, eyebrows raised.

"That's right."

'Where'd you learn that?"

"I'm worldly."

"My ass."

The SUV parked at the end of a retail strip, across from Abdul's Mediterranean Cuisine. Beneath the sign on the window was a block of foreign writing different from the others.

We parked and watched Duante Tucker and Lennox Suggs walk from their vehicle to the restaurant. Suggs's legs were bowed, and he held his arms far from his body, as if necessitated by his thick musculature. Tucker had an aggressive bounce to his step, his eyes half-lidded, his puffed lips set in a grimace.

They swung open the door and disappeared into the eatery. We were thirty yards away in a diagonal direction.

"What's that writing?" Cody said. "It doesn't look like Hindi."

"I don't know. Arabic, I think."

"You know what? I'm getting hungry." He unbuckled his seatbelt. "You want anything?"

"What do they have?"

"Like the sign says, Mediterranean food. Hang tight." He got out of the Camry and strode toward the restaurant.

After he went in, I pointed my cell phone at Abdul's Mediterranean Cuisine and took a couple snapshots. I waited a minute, watching occasional patrons of the various stores come and go. Then I slid from the car into the late afternoon sun and, as discreetly as I could, took pictures of every car and license plate in the immediate area.

I returned to the Camry and five minutes later, Cody strolled out of Abdul's holding a white plastic bag.

"How'd it go?"

"Had a beer and ordered some shish kabobs. Try one."

"What about Tucker and Suggs?"

"Never saw them. They must have gone into the back."

"Really," I said, my eyes glued to the front of the place.

"It does seem strange, don't it? Check it out—I got a picture of the dude who served me." He handed me his phone. The image on the screen was of a man with a scraggly beard, wire-rimmed glasses, and a white turban.

"What do you think?" Cody asked.

"I think I'd like to know who they're talking to in the back room, and why."

"No, I mean what do you think of this scroungy-looking douchebag?" He held his phone up so I could again look at the picture.

"I don't know. What am I supposed to think?"

"Let's play a little free association, okay, Dirt? What's your immediate impression of this guy? Don't think, just answer."

"All right," I said. "He looks like the Taliban."

"Right. A terrorist. Exactly the same thing occurred to me."

"Come on. You could probably say the majority of Arabs remind you of terrorists. But only a tiny percentage are."

"Well, that was certainly a politically correct response."

I turned and looked at Cody. "I'm not trying to be politically correct. I'm just stating a fact."

"Very proud of you. But here's our situation. Two ghetto thugs who'd probably slit their own mothers' throats for a hundred bucks drive through rush hour traffic to a dumpy strip mall and go straight to the back room of an Arab restaurant. Now, call me suspicious, but I start drawing conclusions."

"Like what?"

"Like it's not a social call. So it's business. It's about money. And whoever was behind the disappearance of Tucker's DNA probably laid out plenty of money to make it happen. So, somehow, there's a connection."

"Okay, fine. But what does that have to do with terrorism?"

"What's the most common crime Arabs are involved in?"

"Here in the US? None, that I know of."

"You never heard of nine-eleven?"

"That was an isolated incident."

"Wrong answer. Since nine-eleven, there's been over twenty planned large-scale jihadist attacks busted by the FBI before they could strike. Terrorist cells are active in almost every state. The FBI and CIA are all over it."

"I didn't know you were such an expert. But based on that, you assume every turban-wearing Mideasterner is a terrorist?"

"Nope. Only the ones meeting with known criminals."

I shrugged. "Who knows? Maybe they're plotting to blow up the Golden Gate Bridge." I took a foil-wrapped shish kabob from the bag Cody had set on the center console and pulled a square of chicken off a stick with my teeth. It was tough and stringy and tasted stale.

"Anything's possible," he said. "There they are."

Tucker and Suggs came out of the restaurant and headed toward their ride. In Tucker's hand was a plastic to-go bag. A middle-aged white couple had just parked next to the SUV, and when they saw the two black men approaching, they walked out of their way to give them a wide berth.

Tucker glared at the couple as if to let them know their trepidation was justified. Either that or maybe it was just raw hatred on his part. I didn't know much about Tucker except that he had a ghetto upbringing and had viciously raped a white woman. Was that enough to assume he hated whites? Maybe he hated blacks too, and Arabs and everyone else. What was definitely clear was that, like all rapists, he hated women.

I watched the two men. They were nearly the same height, but Suggs was about thirty pounds heavier. Tucker, despite his slighter build, struck me as the more physically dangerous of the two. He wore a tank top, his long arms rippled with veins, and his hands were freakishly large. For a moment I imagined how terrified Lindsey Addison must have been, tied up and alone with him.

Suggs said something, and Tucker responded, and I could see an angry tension in Tucker's frame. Suggs had no reaction other than a brief curl of his lip. They climbed into the GMC and drove toward the boulevard. We waited until they'd merged into traffic, then we followed them back in the direction of the freeway.

"Exactly the kind of guys you don't want to meet in a dark alley," I muttered. "My mom used to say that."

We stopped at a light, three cars behind the GMC. "She's speaking for the law-abiding, white middleclass,"

Cody said. "What scares the common citizen is that lowlifes like these would rob and kill you, and they really don't give a shit if they go to prison."

"Not far from the truth."

"Fuckin' A. Life's cheap for their kind."

"They learn it in the ghettos. Crime is the only way out."

"That's bullshit." Cody accelerated onto the freeway. "There's all sort of cases where ghetto blacks became successful members of society."

"But most don't."

The traffic ground to a stop. "Crap," he said. "We're gonna be crawling all the way back. Give me one of those shish kabobs, would you?"

I unwrapped the tin foil and handed him a skewer. He took a bite and made a face. "This sucks. Seriously." He lowered his window and flipped the shish kabob out onto the freeway. "Fuckin' dog food."

"Hard to imagine they would have driven up here just for takeout," I said.

"Excellent deduction, Dr. Watson."

• • •

Young whites in BMWs and Porsches. Chinese businessmen in older Mercedes sedans. Mexicans in work trucks, Indians in Pontiacs and liberals in hybrid cars. A freeway packed with workers heading home, a sign of a recovering economy. Unemployment rates falling and technology companies growing again. The newspapers said all signs indicated the great recession was over. 2013 promised to be the beginning of a new prosperity.

It took forty-five minutes to get back to downtown San Jose. Suggs took the Saint James exit and followed the one-way streets to the front of the Skyscape building. Cody slowed, and from the corner we saw the GMC stop. Tucker got out and went into the front lobby. He was not carrying the white bag he held when he left Abdul's Mediterranean Cuisine.

Suggs drove off, and we followed him back onto the freeway for another fifteen minutes, until he got off on Tully Road. I assumed he'd head straight back to his house, but instead he turned into a Del Taco drive-through. We drove past it and parked in the strip mall lot next door, facing the busy street, ready to pull out as soon as Suggs appeared from the drive-through.

"Something else must be in that to-go bag," I said.

"Like heroin."

"How do you figure?"

"The Taliban and al-Qaida are into heroin big time. Afghanistan is by far the world's largest producer of opium. Their economy would collapse without it."

"So I've heard," I said. "You think our boys just scored, huh?

"Maybe. There's been a lot of brown flake on the streets lately."

Theories. In any investigation, theories are natural and necessary, and when they're right, they can provide a direct path to solving a case. But you have to be careful. Following a wrong theory can blind you to the true motivations at play, and in the process, drain your time and energy. Best to keep an open mind until you really know what you're dealing with.

I moved the windshield visor to the passenger side to shield my face from the sun's glare. Cody lit a cigarette and sat with his arm hanging out the window. We had worked plenty of cases together, and I'd learned to not discount his instincts, despite my skeptical tendencies. His experience as a cop couldn't be underestimated, but I believed what made Cody a great investigator were the teenage years he spent scraping to survive. He didn't speak much of those days, but every so often, usually when we were drinking, he'd bring up an incident or two. Like the time he tried to steal a safe from a bar. He broke into the bar in the predawn, but was surprised to find the safe weighed at least two hundred pounds. Regardless, he dead-lifted it to his chest and tried to shove it through the window he'd broken, but it wouldn't fit. So instead he took twenty bottles of liquor and sold them at our high school for lunch money.

There were darker episodes after that, things he'd only recently told me. In our senior year, he had found work with the Scarpa family, whose involvement in organized crime was well-known. His financial problems vanished, he bought a new wardrobe and moved into his own apartment. The day after we graduated from high school, he left town and hitchhiked to Utah. I thought it was because he'd broken up with his girlfriend, but I later learned he'd bashed in a car windshield with the face of one of the Scarpa boys.

•　•　•

The black SUV rolled by, and I caught a glimpse of Suggs drinking from a straw. We had to wait for a number of cars, and by the time we merged into the lane I couldn't see his vehicle.

"Get over to the left," I said. "He's probably headed home."

We made a yellow light, and Cody cut into the left lane. "There he is," he said. Suggs was waiting in the turn lane at the next signal.

The light turned green, and we hung back and gave him some distance. When he turned right into his neighborhood, we went straight and came around the block to approach his house from the opposite direction. Suggs had parked in the driveway, and we saw him going in the front door.

Cody found a spot two houses down, behind a lowered Chevy Impala with chrome rims. It was almost six o'clock, but the sun was still high and it was about eighty degrees.

"Tucker's chillin' at the high-rise, and Suggs is back at the shithole," Cody said. "You got any theories?"

"Tucker's unemployed and doesn't own a car. Someone's taking care of him."

"Like who?"

"Pull up that picture you took of Suggs on the balcony."

He worked his phone, then held it low so we could both see the screen. The picture had been taken at too far a distance to make out much other than two black men, one in a white shirt.

"Can you zoom in any more?"

"Yeah, but it doesn't help. The resolution's too grainy."

I looked back toward Suggs's house. "We have the address. We'll find out who lives there tomorrow."

A fly buzzed into the car. At the far end of the street, two fat women were having a conversation that seemed to be escalating into an argument.

"How long you want to wait here?" Cody said.

"I don't know. Until something happens."

"I could use a bite."

"Have a shish kabob."

Half an hour passed. Cars came and went, and residents appeared on shaded porches and took places on ratty couches or metal chairs. Teenagers began congregating on the corner, first in twos or threes, then the groups grew larger.

"We're gonna get made, we stay here much longer," Cody said.

"Yeah, it's time to boogie," I said. Then I paused and pointed down the street. "I think that's the bent-nose *cholo* we met before."

Cody started his car. "Hold up a second," I said. The *cholo* and two younger gangbangers came up the opposite side of the street, but before reaching us, they stopped in front of Suggs's house. Bent Nose walked up to the door, and the pit bulls raced from the back and jumped at the cyclone fencing. The front door opened, and Bent Nose went inside, leaving the other two Latinos waiting on the sidewalk. The dogs barked and snapped and rolled their eyes.

Five minutes later Bent Nose stepped out the doorway, his hands deep in the pockets of his baggy jeans. He nodded at his underlings, and they walked back the way they'd come.

"Drug buy," Cody said. "Let's roll."

We hung a U-turn, and when we slowed at the corner a group of Mexican teenagers looked at us expectantly. Cody pulled over to the curb.

"What are you doing?" I asked.

He rolled down the window, and two brown-faced youngsters approached.

"Whatchu looking' for, man?"

"How about a twenty bag of H?" Cody held a twenty-dollar bill between his fingers. In a second the bill was gone, and in Cody's palm rested a small, tied-off ball of black plastic.

"*Gracias*," Cody said, and hit the gas.

●　　●　　●

Our next stop was a place Cody described as "one of the only decent bars left in San Jose." It was a stand-alone building, the sole structure on a street running next to the last remaining orchard in the valley. For years, both the city and private real estate developers had been trying to convince the owner of the seven-acre parcel to sell out. The land was worth tens of millions. It belonged to an eighty-eight-year-old man with no surviving family members. He had rejected all offers and had made public that his will specified the orchard be granted to an organization that would preserve it after he died.

When I was a kid, the bar had been called Gerhard's Garden Room. It was a hardcore biker hangout, and the ABC eventually revoked its liquor license and forced the owners to sell out. A retired narco officer named Ed Schneider had bought the place and run it for the last fifteen years. It had been one of my favorite haunts back when I thought there was something noble and romantic about swilling whiskey until I blacked out.

The interior was as I remembered, fuzzy as those memories were. Ceiling fans turned lazily above the scarred tables. Dim yellow lights were set in the soffit over the bar. The room was square and lined with dart boards, neon beer signs, a jukebox, and an unlit pinball machine. The barstools were occupied by men huddled over drinks.

"Kitchen still open?" I asked Cody.

"Best burgers in town," he said.

We waited for the bartender. She was a tall woman with sandy hair, tight shorts, and a T-shirt that looked as if the collar had been cut low with a pair of scissors. When she finished pouring drinks, she came to our end of the bar.

"Hi, Cody," she said, smiling. Her face was peppered with freckles, her breasts long, her fingers yellow with nicotine. "Who's your friend?"

"My partner, Dirty Dan. Dan, Lana."

She looked at me with dancing eyes that plainly suggested she might be available for some backroom fun if I was inclined. "Hi, Dirty Dan. I didn't know Cody had such good-looking friends."

"He doesn't. It's an optical illusion," I said, but felt my face growing red. I also felt an electric jolt in my groin and a nostalgic yearning over certain transgressions in my past.

"Forget it, Lana. He's in a committed relationship," Cody said. "Did I say that right?"

"So?" Lana smiled and put a finger on her lips.

"How about some grub?" Cody motioned at a whiteboard behind the bar. "Double cheeseburger for me and a basket of fries."

"Single burger, no cheese," I said. "Coleslaw, no fries."

"And a pitcher of Bud," Cody added.

She scrawled our order on a pad and stepped away with a wink and a swing of her hips.

"I got to take a leak," Cody said, and walked off toward the back reaches of the room. I went to a table near the dartboards and dialed Candi's number.

"Hi there," she said. "I'm sorry I missed your calls."

"I'm sorry I missed yours. How's Houston?"

"Hot and dusty. Do you miss me?"

"Yeah," I said.

"What are you up to? Behaving yourself, I hope?"

"Yes, doll. Actually, I'm in San Jose with Cody. We're working a case together."

"A case? With Cody?"

"Uh-huh. Have you heard of Ryan Addison, the actor?"

"I think so. Why?"

"His daughter was attacked. He's hired Cody and me to look into it."

"Oh. Both of you?"

"It's nothing to worry about," I said. "Very routine stuff. How are your parents?"

"They're doing fine. They insist you come next time."

"I promise I will."

"Dan?" she said.

"Yes?"

"Be safe. Promise me that."

"I promise."

We hung up as Cody came back with the pitcher and took a seat. "Your old lady?"

"Yeah."

"Everything copacetic?" he asked.

"Sure."

"That's good to hear."

A woman's laughter erupted from the bar, and we turned to look. In the light I caught a certain wistfulness on Cody's profile. It took a long moment to pass, and I wondered about his quiet nights alone in his house or the hungover mornings waking up with someone like Lana. I wondered how long he would immerse himself in wild women and wanton violence as a salve to the emptiness in his heart. We were alike in many ways, except that my father had been taken from me, while his willingly abandoned him. But when my old man died, my mother was there for me. Cody's was not—she was as absent as his father, and I knew for a fact that Cody had not spoken to either of his parents since he was forced from their home as a teenager.

Cody's lone attempt at marriage had ended after two years, and his love life ever since been a parade of closing-time bimbos, strippers, assorted nut cases, and gold diggers. His stories were endlessly sordid, and he took great pleasure in the recounting, but behind it I always sensed an undercurrent of regret and sadness. This had become more pronounced in the year I had been seeing Candi.

I picked up my beer mug and my lip touched a coating of ice on the rim. A sip turned into a couple large swallows. I put the mug down and stood.

"What's up?" Cody asked.

"You still drink boilermakers?"

"No, but I like Shirley Temples."

I went to the bar and asked Lana for two shots of Jack Daniels. When I brought the shots to the table, Cody was grinning broadly. "What's the occasion?" he asked.

"I feel like a drink," I said.

"What a coincidence. So do I." He dropped the shot glass in his beer, drained it, and returned the mug to the table with a loud bang. "Not bad."

I followed his example and wiped my mouth. The booze hit my gut, and almost instantly I felt more relaxed.

"You got any Doggie Doze at your house?" I asked.

"I should. What's your thinking?"

"I'd love to bug the high-rise Tucker's at, or even Suggs's ride. But we need to find the path of least resistance."

"The bugs I use won't work in a car," he said. "They only work with a stationary transmitter nearby."

"I know—the vehicle bugs cost a fortune. And there's no way to get into that high-rise, at least no easy way. I think the best thing is to put those pit bulls asleep and bug Suggs's house."

Cody looked at me, and after a moment he said, "You mean tonight."

"Why wait? Suggs doesn't strike me as the type who'd sit around that shit pit all night long. I bet by dark he's gone. Maybe headed to a night club, on the prowl for a piece of ass. Or otherwise blessing the general population with his presence."

"Give you a shot and you're a man of action."

I poured a beer from the pitcher. "What else we got to do?"

Cody toasted me with his mug, then nodded toward the bar. "There's Pronto Schneider."

I looked and saw a heavyset man perched on a barstool in the corner behind the bar. He had white hair and gray stubble and sat with his arms crossed over his thick gut.

"Pronto?"

"Yeah," Cody said. "I started calling him that when his gout flared up and he was tending bar. All the boozers were pissed because he was so slow. Everyone kept telling him to hang up his cleats. But Schneider's a cheap bastard, and stubborn too. It wasn't until his regulars boycotted the place that he finally hired a couple bartenders. Now he's got a squad of floozies pouring drinks."

"Business is booming, I bet," I said.

"Never been better, he says. He sits there in the corner, counting his money."

I caught Schneider's eye, and after a moment, he blinked in recognition. Then he hefted his weight off his stool and shuffled over to where we sat.

"I haven't seen your face in here for a while," he said.

"Sobered up," I said. "Moved away."

"I hate it when my customers do that."

I smiled, and Cody leaned forward. "I hear heroin's getting popular again, Ed. Cutting into the cocaine trade. You hear anything like that?"

Schneider pulled at his ear, and his eyes narrowed. "Yeah, I see it. It's bad for business. People love boozing on coke. But not on heroin."

"It's that's noticeable, huh?" Cody said.

"Heroin's a downer. It's a substitute for alcohol. The cartels are even getting concerned."

"Coke sales are down?"

"That's the word out there," Schneider replied. "The heroin on the street is cheap and plentiful. And it's not the Colombian black tar the cartels bring in. It's all high grade, coming out of Afghanistan. And the Mexicans don't have any relationship with those camel jockeys."

"Who does?" I asked.

"The Afghans don't trust the West. Imagine that, huh? They operate mostly through Lebanese or Turk smugglers."

From his pocket Cody produced the small bag of heroin he'd bought on the corner of Suggs's street. He pulled it open with his fingernails. The powder was a dull tan color.

Schneider put on a pair of reading glasses and poked at the contents with a toothpick.

"What do you think?" Cody asked.

"I haven't seen junk like this since the eighties. You picked it up local?"

Cody nodded.

"You want to have it tested?"

"Not really," Cody said. "You think it's Afghan?"

"I'd bet on it."

We all stared silently at the coarse powder resting in the torn scrap of black plastic.

"Go flush it," Schneider said.

•   •   •

We hung out in the bar until well past dark. Cody bought a round for the house, and Schneider acknowledged it by ringing a bell mounted behind the bar, which prompted another patron to shoot the rail. After that, the middle-aged happy hour regulars began migrating out. A younger crowd filled their seats, and the room grew crowded. A short, buxom woman came on shift and began working the floor, tray in hand. We drank slow beers and carefully avoided the lure of whiskey. At 9:30 we left for Cody's house.

While Cody crushed pills and mixed the powder into two balls of raw hamburger, I changed into black clothes. When I was done, I saw he'd set a bag on his kitchen table. In the bag were self-adhering, nickel-sized discs, each capable of gathering and sending auditory activity in a twenty-foot radius. The bag also contained a transmitter, a device roughly the size of a tennis ball. Attached to it was a tapered plastic wedge, designed so the transmitter could be secured into the ground, typically hidden in bushes.

We decided to take my truck, as the modified Camry had already been seen in Suggs's neighborhood. My truck was older than Cody's red rig, the bronze paint less conspicuous.

It was a little past ten when we turned down the street where Suggs lived.

"No GMC," I said, eyeing the empty driveway in front of the dark house. I turned off my lights and backed into the driveway of the vacant house where we'd previously parked. A couple hundred yards away, several gangbangers were hanging out at the corner. There were no streetlights except for the one under which they stood.

I stretched rubber gloves over my hand, grabbed the small sack holding the hamburger balls, and took a final glance up and down the avenue.

Moving swiftly, I crossed the street and approached the chain link gate at Suggs's side yard. Barks erupted, and the two pit bulls raced from the back of the house. I tossed the first ball, and the nearest dog stopped; in a second, the meat was gone. I lobbed the second ball to the other dog with the same result and retreated to my truck. A couple more barks sounded, then it was quiet.

Cody was in my passenger seat, looking at a stop watch. After three minutes he said, "Your cell phone on?"

"Yeah."

"I'll ring if anyone's coming."

I nodded, went back across the street, and shook Suggs's metal gate. After a quiet pause, I scaled the fence and dropped to the other side. The side yard was packed dirt bordered by weeds and a scattering of trash. I looked over the fence into the neighboring yard. The windows were dark, and I could see the gate latch did not have a lock. An emergency exit route, if need be. When I came around into the backyard, I saw the dogs lying on a patch of dirt, dead asleep.

There was a small concrete patio under a corroded awning. At the foot of the patio was a sliding glass door. I switched on my flashlight and saw the door was bolt locked at the base. I moved to a bedroom window. It was reinforced with a mounted slide lock. A very basic design, and very effective.

On the far side of the house was another window. This one was not secured with a slide lock. I inserted a steel strip between the frames, gave a quick twist, and the catch released. I slid open the window, climbed up, and quietly stepped into the room. My flashlight panned the walls. It was a bedroom, unfurnished and vacant. There was no obvious place to hide a bug. I looked around for a minute until I found a nook behind a shelf next to the window.

I went down a hallway to the main room. A big, flat-screen TV was mounted on a wall above a cable box and DVD player. Against the opposite wall was a leather couch. I stuck a bug beneath the couch, pressing firmly against the frame. I looked around for a phone but didn't see one.

In the kitchen I found a good spot beneath the counter ledge, then I went back down the hall to the closed door of a second bedroom. It was not locked, and I stepped inside.

The room was neat, the bed made, a desk clear of clutter in one corner, a bookshelf in another. The books were a mix of old paperbacks and high-school textbooks. I removed a couple books on the lowest shelf, secured a bug against the shelf above, and replaced the books. I scanned the desk with my flashlight and pulled open a metal filing cabinet. The file folders contained bills, parole paperwork, and car insurance notices. I spent a few minutes rifling the files and found nothing interesting.

Before leaving I checked the closet. It was packed with clothes on hangers surrounding a three-foot iron safe bolted by L-joints to the floor and walls.

My cell beeped. It was Cody.

"Suggs is coming," he said. "Move."

"Shit."

I closed the door behind me and went into the empty bedroom and out the window. The dogs were still lying motionless in the dirt. I crept across the yard to the slatted fence and saw the flash of headlights in the driveway. I moved back and hopped the fence into the neighbor's yard. A few feet from me, an overgrown hedge lined the rear fence. I thrust the transmitter deep into the thicket until I felt it lodge firmly. Crouched low, I moved down the side yard to the gate. The headlights went dark, and I heard the engine shut off and the car door close. I waited until I heard the front door to the house open and shut. Then I went out the gate and hustled back to my truck, where Cody waited behind the wheel, headlights off, the motor idling.

We pulled out of the driveway and turned away from Suggs's house. From the passenger seat, I saw yellow light shining around the blanket in the front window.

"How long until those dogs wake up?" I asked.

"At least an hour."

"He's gonna be suspicious."

"Unless he's a dumbass."

"He'll probably think someone was trying to rip him off," I said.

"Good," Cody replied.

5

I USUALLY SLEEP LIKE a rock wherever I am, but when I woke at three a.m. in Cody's spare bedroom, my head was beset with a nightmarish swirl of voices and images. Lindsey Addison on a hospital bed, her legs spread and her face gruesomely distorted. Outside her door, Duante Tucker jabbed his finger at a doctor's chest. Marcus Grier's voice said he didn't want to get involved, and then a group of men in turbans and white robes appeared, and Tucker smirked and vanished.

I sat up and turned on the light. The room was stuffy, and I lay back down and tried unsuccessfully to fall asleep. After a few minutes, I took my notebook computer from its bag and went out and sat at the kitchen table.

The first site I tried provided no hits when I typed in the address for the Skyscape condominiums, unit 1602. I tried another site without luck, and finally went to one I subscribed to but didn't use often. This time, when I entered the address into the reverse directory, a name came up: Farid Insaf. I ran a public records search on the name, and it produced eight individuals.

Of the eight, three were elderly, one was deceased, and two had addresses in the eastern United States. The remaining two were slightly more promising. One was for a fifty-two-year-old man with a Texas address. The other was a forty-three-year-old in Seattle.

I spent another half hour typing the name into various databases. None of the responses identified anyone living in San Jose. The only thing of interest I found was a reference to the Muslim meaning of the name. Farid Insaf could be loosely translated to mean "unique justice." What did that mean, if anything? Probably nothing.

"Typical," I muttered. Public record sites are notoriously incomplete and outdated. But there are plenty of armchair private investigators who make a living selling public information to unsuspecting clients. Some of these investigators are ex-cops, some are wannabe cops who never made the grade, and some are enterprising college kids, unlicensed and advertising on the Internet. What do they all have in common? Lack of scruples, lack of competency, and laziness.

Bottom line, real detective work is a bitch. I once met a PI who dedicated twenty years to a cold case involving the murder of a friend's daughter. The investigator traveled all over the United States, even spent a month in Vietnam, interviewing people, following up on leads, digging through scraps of evidence. When he hit dead ends, he reset and started all over. Eventually he identified a strong suspect and closed in, intending to extract a confession by any means necessary. But when he broke into the suspect's house, he had a face-to-face encounter he didn't expect—the suspect had hung himself minutes before, the still-warm body swaying over an upended chair in the living room.

I turned off the lights and sat on Cody's couch in the darkness. The composite information we'd uncovered so far suggested Tucker was involved in drug dealing. That alone meant next to nothing. Drug dealing is probably the most common crime in the world. It's lucrative, easy to engage in, and pervades many other criminal activities. But factor in the possibility of Tucker buying heroin from Arabs, and you have something a bit more unusual.

Equally unusual was the concept of Tucker living in a fancy San Jose high-rise with a man who might be named Farid Insaf. What kind of person would house someone like Tucker? What could the motivation be? One obvious thought was there could be an Islamist connection between Farid Insaf and the Arabic restaurant that Tucker and Suggs visited. Something to consider.

I thought back to the attorney, Darrian Brandon. He claimed his reasons for representing Tucker were altruistic, which I didn't believe for a second. I wanted to ask Brandon if he knew Farid Insaf. Of course, the counselor wouldn't be inclined to answer. Unless leverage was applied. Maybe Cody's style of leverage.

An hour passed, and I returned to the bedroom. We needed to get to the bottom of Farid Insaf, if that was truly the name of Tucker's benefactor. But there were other angles as well. We'd never spoken to either of the reluctant witnesses. They both lived in Southern California. And so did Darrian Bannon. That was something that should be explored. With that thought in mind, I fell asleep.

·   ·   ·

I woke to a pounding on the door. "Rise and shine, Dirt." I looked at the clock. Eight a.m.

Cody handed me a cup of coffee when I walked into the kitchen. "You're always up early," he said. "Catching up on your beauty rest?"

"I was working in the middle of the night. I got a name for unit 1602. Farid Insaf."

"Huh? What the hell is that? Afghan? Pakistani?"

"Arabic. I think it comes from the Quran. It means unique justice."

He hooted a laugh. "Lovely. If his sense of justice means catering to ghetto thug rapists, yeah, I'd say it's unique."

I sipped at my coffee. "I ran a people search on the name. Found two possibles, one in Dallas and one in Seattle."

"Nothing in California, huh?"

"Nope."

"Balls," said Cody. "We want to find out about this dude, looks like we're gonna have to get creative."

"Like what?" I asked.

"That depends how many laws we want to break."

"How about none?"

"Maybe we could bribe someone at the Skyscape," Cody said. "Or con them."

"Pretty tough. And if it backfires, all we'll have accomplished is putting Insaf on alert."

Cody didn't respond, and I went to his refrigerator and poured some milk into the scalding tar in my cup. "You got anyone on the force you can run the name by?" I asked.

He grimaced. "Only as a last resort. Even then it's no sure thing."

"I got another idea, then. Let's go find the two witnesses, Leo Rosen and Amber Meline."

"They're from Southern Cal." Cody looked up at me from where he'd sat at the table.

"Right. And so is Darrian Bannon."

"So?"

"I want to have a follow-up conversation with Bannon. See if he knows Farid Insaf."

Cody smiled. "You do, huh?"

I nodded. "Why don't you check on flights to Los Angeles while I confirm a few things?"

• • •

At noon we took off from San Jose on an American Airlines regional jet. It was an hour-long flight to Los Angeles International Airport. I'd been able to verify that Bannon was in his office today, in El Segundo, only a mile or two from the airport. Also, I'd learned that Leo Rosen had resurfaced. He'd picked up when I called his number, and when I told him I was from FedEx and had been unable to deliver a package a week ago, he said he was at his Santa Monica address. As for Amber Meline, she didn't pick up her cell, but I had her address, also in Santa Monica.

I sat crammed next to the window, shoulder to shoulder with Cody, watching as the plane descended over the Angeles National Forrest and then down over Santa Clarita and Van Nuys. Coach seats are large enough to comfortably fit a narrow-shouldered, 150-pound man. Cody was about 300 and I was 215 or so. I tend toward claustrophobia and couldn't wait to get off the plane.

Twenty minutes later we walked through the terminal at LAX and took a shuttle bus to the rental car lots. I know people in Northern California who like to refer, with a certain disdain, to any destination in Southern Cal simply as "LA." Maybe there still exists some form of regional sibling rivalry between Northern and Southern Cal, but there's no doubt who is the bigger of the two; with over two hundred cities populated by twenty-two million residents in a 150-mile-long-by-50-mile-wide geography, SoCal dwarfs the San Francisco Bay Area.

We rented a full-sized sedan, a Ford Crown Vic. I entered Leo Rosen's address into my GPS and drove out to the 405. It was ninety-five outside, and heat waves rose in a low haze off the black asphalt. We headed north, and I knew a mountain range lay just beyond Santa Monica, but it was hidden behind a layer of orange-brown smog.

"I want to see what Leo Rosen has to say before we talk to Bannon," I said. I changed lanes and let a BMW pass. The surrounding traffic was flowing at eighty MPH. Another car came up close, and I accelerated hard and contributed a blast of exhaust to the local air pollution.

"Everyone's in a hurry," Cody said. "I love it down here."

"Why's that?" I asked.

"Life moves at a faster pace. And there's more variety of people. Check her out."

I looked to the left at a brunette in a yellow convertible Corvette. Her hair was tied in a ponytail, and her bikini top held obviously enhanced breasts that looked immune to gravity.

"We're in the capital of cosmetic surgery."

"And that's a bad thing?" Cody replied, staring past me and straining to get a better look at the woman in the convertible.

"I didn't say that."

"We should stick around tonight. Maybe hit a few clubs."

"I make a lousy wingman," I told him.

"Nonsense. You got rugged good looks but no lines. You're the perfect wingman."

"Gee, thanks."

We drove for another couple minutes until I took the ramp onto Interstate 10. A minute later the freeway terminated at the Pacific Coast Highway, which hugged the coastline for the length of California. I turned left and lowered my window. The smog seemed to have dissipated, and the air that rushed in was cool and tinged with a briny scent. After a half dozen blocks, I took another left onto Ocean Park Boulevard. Another couple turns, and we rolled down a narrow residential street shaded under a canopy of willow, birch, and cypress. Halfway down the street I pulled over in front of a house with two arched brick doorways.

We went through a picket gate and down a wet stone walkway splitting a water-soaked lawn. The house was a duplex. The door to the left was 1A. We went to 1B and knocked. Cody stood aside, and I bent at the knees, leveling my face with the peephole in the center of the door.

After a minute the door opened. The man in the doorway was less than average height, and his receding hairline was obvious, even though he'd arranged his curly black hair to fall over his high forehead. His nose was prominent, and his lips were pouty, like a woman's. He wore black designer shorts advertising a brand targeted at surfers—or those who identified with surfers. His beige shirt was the same brand, and around his neck was a string of bleached shells.

"Leo Rosen?" I said.

"Yes?" he said, his voice a nasal drone.

"Dan Reno, private investigations. We'd like to talk with you regarding Lindsey Addison."

He glanced up at Cody, who was standing behind me. After a pause, he said, "Who hired you?"

"The Addison family."

He crossed his arms, eyes downcast, and shook his head. "What do you want to know?"

"How come you wouldn't testify?" I asked.

"It wasn't in my best interest," he replied, measuring his words carefully.

"You care to elaborate on that?"

"Look, I feel sorry for Lindsey and all, but the trial's over."

"You don't give a shit about her," Cody said.

He blinked. "What? That's not true."

"Then what happened?" I said.

"I'm not at liberty to say."

I felt Cody's hand on my shoulder, and he pushed his way by me. "Listen up, Leo," Cody said. "We're considering motivations here, and we know you had a hard-on for Lindsey. So maybe you and Duante Tucker were planning on tag-teaming her, but you chickened out. Is that what happened, you twisted fuck?"

Leo blanched and stepped back as if Cody had spit in his face. "No," he stammered. "That's ridiculous."

"We get all sorts of ridiculous ideas when pukes like you start jacking us around." Cody took a step into the house.

"Hey, you can't—"

"Or maybe you hired Tucker to rape her when she wanted nothing to do with you," Cody went on. "Is that how you get your rocks off?"

"You're crazy! Mister, tell him he's crazy!" Leo shouted at me around Cody's towering mass.

"Let's go sit down, Leo," I said. "You'll feel a lot better when you get this off your chest."

"Okay. Okay, goddammit." We followed him inside to a glass-top dining table perched on wrought iron legs. "I had nothing to do with any of this. I'll tell you what happened. You just keep my name out of it. Deal?"

Cody and I sat across from him and nodded.

"Look, I liked Lindsey. I hoped maybe I might…get to know her, you know."

"Go on," I said.

"I knew she was going to Tahoe, so yeah, I went up there, hoping to hit on her. But I never even said a word to her."

"But you followed her to the nightclub," I said.

"Yeah, but that was it. It's not like I was stalking—I never even talked to her." He looked down, and I could see his face reddening.

"What happened at the nightclub?"

"Man, she was with her friends, and then those bimbos split with a couple dudes, and she was all alone." He looked up at us, and I could see the shame and regret taking hold on his face. "I wanted to go sit with her, but I get all tongue tied, and…I just couldn't make myself. If I had, maybe none of this would have happened."

"What happened next?"

"She left the place, and I followed her out, thinking maybe I might find a way to at least say hello. Maybe in the parking lot or something. I was probably thirty yards behind her when the man came out of nowhere. He hit her, and in a second she was in his car."

"What'd you do?" Cody asked.

"I ran to help her. But he was too fast. He took off just as I got there. But I got the license plate, and I also got a pretty good look at the guy."

"So you called nine-one-one," I said.

"Right."

"And then?"

"I flew back home the next day. When I landed, a cop from Nevada called, told me Lindsey was in the hospital, and I basically I told him what I just told you."

"Did you identify Duante Tucker?" I asked.

"Not until a week later. The cop called again and e-mailed pictures of twenty different black guys. I picked out Tucker. The cop told me I'd need to come back to Tahoe and testify at the trial. I said okay."

"So what happened?"

"About a week after that, I get a phone call. A voice tells me I better not even think of testifying. He says he and his crew are watching me, and I need to stop talking to the cops and disappear until the trial's over. He said if I don't, I'll be paid a visit by some gentlemen from South Central LA, and they'll make me the object of a bitch party. You know what that is?"

"I can guess. Did you get a phone number where he called from?"

"No. The caller ID said unknown. So, just so we're clear, a bitch party is prison slang for a gang rape. The man said they'll hurt me so bad I'll be begging to suck their dicks and swallow their jism just to make the pain stop."

"Did you tell the cops?" Cody asked.

"I told the man on the phone, hey, I'll be subpoenaed, they could arrest me if I don't show at the trial. And he said he doesn't give a shit, and the cops won't protect me when he and his boys with the horse dicks show up."

"So you didn't call the cops?"

"Listen, the next morning there's an envelope on my front porch. In it's a picture of a white man sucking a black dick while getting butt-fucked by some big black dude. The white guy's face is all bloody. There's a little note paper-clipped to the photo. It says, 'Could be you.'"

"You think about giving it to the police?" I asked.

"Yeah. For about two seconds. Then I packed my bags and took a vacation for six weeks. Spent most of that time south of the border, where my cell phone doesn't work. Burned through some savings, but I'm still alive. I was hoping I'd never hear about any of this again."

"Sorry to disappoint you," Cody said.

"Hey, I cooperated with you, I told you the truth. I'd love to see Tucker rot in prison. I'd love to see him suffer and regret every moment of his shitty life. But I got my own life to worry about."

I looked at Cody, and neither of us had a response for that. We stood, and as we headed for the door, I said, "You still infatuated with Lindsey?"

Leo's mouth opened, then he closed it and slowly shook his head. "No, I think I'm pretty much over her."

"Go figure," Cody said.

• • •

When we drove away, flecks of sunlight had penetrated the trees and danced on the pavement and across our windshield. The houses on the street were an eclectic mix of small haciendas, ivy-covered cottages, and neat bungalows. The scene could have been an idyllic slice of SoCal life, but my mind was on other things, namely, Leo Rosen's grim tale, which sat in my gut like a bad burrito.

"Did you believe him?" I said.

"Yeah," Cody said. "I don't think he made that up. What do you think?"

"I don't think he was lying. I also think he did the smart thing to cover his ass."

"Literally."

"I mean, I think the threat was probably real," I said. "And I doubt the local police would have put a twenty-four-hour surveillance on him."

"Not for all the weeks leading up to the trial, anyway." Cody was studying his mobile device. "Turn here. Amber Meline's address is a couple miles north."

"I got an idea," I said, slowing for a stop sign. "After we're done with Amber, let's take a spin by Tucker's old neighborhood."

"In Compton?"

"Right. Maybe we can find someone who knows him."

"In Compton?" he said again, eyebrows raised.

"Why not?" I asked.

"We're unarmed, for one."

"Well, we'll just have to stay out of trouble. Play it low-key."

Cody cast me a dubious glance. "Compton ain't a low-key kind of place. Couple crackers like us, we'll be about as welcome as Muhammad Ali at a Klan rally."

"That's why they pay us the big bucks."

"Isn't that one of my lines?"

"Probably."

We made our way north on the highway. To our left was the Pacific Ocean. The sea was a muted blue, and a thin line of clouds hung over the horizon. From the pallid sky, a flock of gulls descended to where the waves lapped at the shore. We turned onto a street that followed a bluff until we were a hundred feet or so above the beach.

"This is it," Cody said. I pulled over at the curb, and we walked past a hedge to a curved driveway that circled a tiered stone fountain. The house beyond looked like something out of Renaissance-era Italy. The front door was shaded under a deep portico supported by twenty-foot fluted columns. The roof above was terracotta, and colorful flowers grew around two small circular balconies on the upper floor. To the right, three cars were parked: a late-model Ferrari, a Porsche Carrera, and a Ford SUV.

We walked to the door and rang the bell. A minute passed before a lean man in his sixties answered. "Yes?" he said. He wore a black suit jacket and black pants. His hair was gray, and wire-rimmed spectacles rested low on his pinched nose.

"Is Amber Meline available?" I asked.

"Who may I say is calling?" he said, his voice a droll monotone.

"Dan Reno and Cody Gibbons, private investigations. This is regarding Lindsey Addison."

"Please wait," he said. It sounded as if gravity was pulling the words from his mouth. "I'll let her know." He closed the door quietly.

"I'll be goddamned," Cody said. "I think that's a butler."

"I didn't know they still existed," I said.

It took another five minutes for the butler to return. He wore an expression of resigned exasperation but simply said, "Miss Meline will see you now. This way, please."

The expansive interior of the house was dominated by a sweeping staircase that rose from the white marble floor. We followed the butler into an adjoining room, where a pool table and wet bar were bathed in sunlight pouring in from a pair of opened French doors. As soon as we stepped outside onto the flagstone patio, I heard a man's laugh and saw a small cluster of people, cocktail glasses in hand, gathered under a wide umbrella next to a swimming pool.

The group, four men and two women, didn't acknowledge us as we approached behind the butler. Two of the men wore jeans and T-shirts, and one had a large video camera resting on his shoulder. The other two men were clad in bathing trunks that revealed uniformly bronze skin and hairless chests. Their physiques were slim and well-proportioned but not necessarily athletic. Blond hair, blue eyes, small noses. They were twins.

The two women, both in bikinis, lay on lounge chairs. One had short, platinum hair and snakelike eyes. Fake boobs, thin waist, curvaceous hips. The other had long, dark hair, thick eyebrows, and a less abundant figure.

"Miss Meline, your guests."

"Hey, there," the brunette said, smacking her gum. "Private eyes, huh?" She turned her head to look up at us, her tanned legs stretched out before her.

"I'm Dan Reno, Miss Meline. Can we go somewhere else to talk?"

"No way," she giggled. "Whatever you got to say, say it here." She wore big sunglasses. Behind them, I imagined a drunken sheen in her eyes.

"Regarding your testimony at the trial, Miss Meline," I said.

"It wasn't much of a testimony, really."

"That's what I heard." I stood looking down at her. In the sunlight a faint trail of peach fuzz ran upward from her navel. "I also heard you'd previously identified Duante Tucker, but on the stand you changed your story."

She licked her lip and took a sip from her drink. "So what? I changed my mind."

"Hey," Cody said. "Is that thing on?" The man with the camera was pointing it at us.

"I'm just testing the lighting," the man said.

"If you want to keep it in working condition, point it somewhere else."

"No problem," he said and turned away.

I turned back to Amber Meline. "Did somebody influence you to change your mind?"

"What does it matter?" she said. "I didn't recognize the man. End of story."

"It matters a lot to the Addison family," I said.

"I'm sure they'll get over it."

"I'm surprised to hear you say that, Amber. I thought Lindsey was your friend."

"Acquaintance, more like," she replied.

"Excuse me," the platinum blonde interjected. Her pupils were tiny pricks of black, and her irises were speckled with yellow flecks. The bikini bra she wore clung wetly to her breasts, and her large brown nipples showed plainly through the thin material. "I hate to cut you short, but we have a schedule to keep," she said.

"What kind of schedule is that?" Cody asked.

"My boyfriend and me are filming a promotional piece," Amber said.

"To promote what?"

"My career."

"Which is…?" I asked.

"Amber will be starring on a reality show this fall," the platinum blonde said. "You ever watch reality TV?"

I shook my head. "Not often," Cody said.

"You've heard of Paris Hilton? Kim Kardashian?" the blonde asked.

"Who hasn't?" Cody said.

"How about Pamela Lee Anderson?"

"Sure. What's the point?"

"The general public considers them airheaded bimbos. But they're among the richest entertainers in the business today." She looked at her watch and sat up in her chair. "You know why? Because they understand marketing. They understand that sex sells."

"You know what all three of them have in common?" Amber added, her tipsy voice like a little girl's compared to the throaty tone of the blonde's. "They all made hot sex tapes with their boyfriends, and that's what launched them to stardom."

The blonde with the snake eyes stood and slipped her bare feet into a pair of heels. "Now, if you'll excuse us," she said, "we need to begin filming."

"Hey, I recognize you. You've been in movies yourself, right?" Cody said.

She nodded. "Don't get a hard on, big boy."

The butler approached, and the group began moving toward the house. "Which one is your boyfriend, Amber?" I asked.

The twins came to either side of her, and each hooked a thumb into her bikini bottom. "Both, today," she said.

· · ·

As we drove away from the posh mansion where Amber Meline lived, I tried not to question her actions regarding her testimony, or how she planned to supercharge her career. As to the former, I had no doubt she'd been threatened, probably by the same people who scared off Leo Rosen. It probably hadn't taken much to get her to clam up.

As for her movie-making plans, maybe a sex flick was what it would take to catapult her from anonymity to stardom. She didn't seem to have a problem with the concept. Maybe one day, every aspiring actress would do the same. Hollywood culture seemed to reward that sort of approach. But I doubted Lindsey Addison, given her recent frame of reference, would have been too entertained by her friend's behavior.

We drove inland toward the freeway, and within five minutes, the digital temperature gauge in our rental car moved from 79 degrees to 90.

When we got on the 405, the freeway was choked with cars. We crept along through a haze of smog so thick I could nearly taste it coming through the air conditioning vents.

"I can almost remember the name of that blonde," Cody said. "I think she used to be big time. She was in a lot of films."

"Looks like she's moved into directing and producing."

"I think she's still got a few good roles in her."

"I'm surprised you didn't ask her out," I said.

"Hmm. Maybe we should head back."

"You had your chance."

I forced my way into a different lane, and a pair of teenagers in a BMW shot us the bird. "I wonder if Lindsey's rape was simply a rape, or if maybe there was something more to it," I said.

"What are you talking about?"

"Maybe Tucker had dated Lindsey before. Maybe she has a thing for gangsta blacks. Maybe Lindsey shined him on, and Tucker was out for revenge."

Cody bit at his thumbnail. "That's from left field."

"Is it?" I countered. "Nothing would surprise me with these people. They seem to operate under a moral code from another planet."

"You're reaching. If Lindsey knew Tucker beforehand, she would have said so."

"I guess."

"Let's just keep asking questions. We'll get to the bottom of this." Cody lowered his window and spit a stream of saliva into the fumes.

We passed a fender bender blocking a lane and made time for a few miles before taking the 105 east. The freeway split the area commonly known as South Central LA. Watts, on the north side of the 105, was where the race riots in 1965 occurred. Twenty-seven years later, the black population rioted again. The riots of 1965 and 1992 were eerily similar, both brought on by the beating of a black man by the white police. I looked over as we passed a residential neighborhood next to the freeway. Barred windows, a chaos of telephone wires, graffiti, and spiked fencing. What's changed here in the twenty years since the last riot? Not much, except the Mexicans had encroached and now outnumbered the black population. If anything, the ghettos had become worse.

We took the exit for West 116th and headed south on Vermont, into Compton.

"California's version of a war zone," Cody said as we slowed at an intersection where a man slept on a bus stop bench. On the opposite corner, a young black woman rooted through a pile of rubbish strewn on the sidewalk.

"It has some redeeming qualities," I said.

"Like what?"

"Compton is where gangsta rap originated. Some of the top bands came from here."

"That's redeeming?"

"I always like to look at the bright side."

"Bright side, my ass," said Cody. "These slums are where the crack trade began back in the late eighties. Every square block is run by gangs. Bloods, Crips, the Varrios. The violent crime rate is off the charts."

"Don't sweat it," I said. "We're just here to ask a few questions."

"I'm not sweating it," Cody said, eyeballing a trio of men hanging out on a corner. "I just wish I had my piece on my side."

"You won't need it."

We turned and drove by a liquor store where a group of black gangbangers leaned against the facade. Down the street a pair of hookers motioned at us. We turned again onto a potholed road lined with telephone poles, lowriders, gas guzzlers, and various junkers. On one side of the road were small homes, some which looked abandoned. One of the homes was barricaded with plywood. Cars rested on their frames in the front yard, and the end of a sleeping bag hung from one of the car's open windows. Across the street an apartment building covered with graffiti advertised units available.

I slowed and found a parking spot. "This is the address I have for Tucker, before he moved to San Jose," I said.

"Let's hope our car is still here when we get back," Cody said. We got out and started up the street toward a rectangular opening in the apartment building's gray stucco walls. Behind a window I saw a curtain move and felt eyes on my back. From down the avenue, a hunchbacked man came our way, pushing a shopping cart. He stopped and rubbed furiously at his face as if being attacked by an invisible swarm of insects.

We went through the opening into a small concrete courtyard. A rusted washing machine sat near an empty flower box. From behind one of the doors, a loud argument erupted, and a woman shrieked with such agony that we paused. Then her voice resumed in a calm tone, and the argument seemed to end as abruptly as it started.

"Up there," I said, pointing to a second floor unit. "Two-twelve."

As we climbed the stairs, I saw a dark teenage face watching us from the courtyard entrance. The face disappeared in a blink, and we stepped onto the upper walkway and walked around garbage cans and discarded junk to apartment 212. I knocked on the door and waited. After a minute I knocked again.

When the door cracked open against three security chains, I was taken aback by the emaciated face that appeared. The eyes were rheumy, lifeless globules set in cavernous sockets, and the surrounding skin had a yellow pallor to it, blotched and papery, as if the slightest touch might cause it to fall from the bone. Below a flat nose, the lips were parted, the gums black and cratered with sores, the teeth little more than nubs. Growing thinly from the scalp was an afro that was neither black nor gray but instead a dull tan color. It was a black woman. As to her age, I couldn't guess.

"I'm sorry to bother you, ma'am," I said. "A teenager named Duante Tucker used to live in this apartment. Did you by chance know him?"

"Who?" she whispered.

"Duante Tucker."

"I don't know who that is."

"Okay," I said. The door closed. "Thanks anyway."

"Next," Cody said. We walked to 213 and knocked. No answer. We continued to 214, then 215. A middle-aged black man with a potbelly answered and wordlessly shut the door in our faces after I began talking.

"I detect a certain lack of manners in the neighborhood," Cody said.

We turned the corner, and after two more no answers, we came to the end unit. I could hear hip-hop coming from the front window. I rapped loudly on the door with my knuckles.

A smallish man with shiny black skin and a wide nose jerked the door open. He wore baggy parachute pants, the kind made popular by M. C. Hammer back in the early days of rap. Hanging from his scrawny torso was a black T-shirt displaying a red-green caricature of Bob Marley surrounded by pot leaves. The man's fingers clutched a can of King Cobra malt liquor.

"What da hell you want, mothafucka?" he asked over the thump of the music.

"I'm looking for Duante Tucker. Do you know him?"

"What? You blind or somethin'? Cain't you see you're interruptin' my day?"

"Sorry about that. I just have a few questions—"

"Questions?" His eyebrows danced on his forehead. "I might be able to carve out some time for you it's worth my while, you know what I'm sayin'? If you got the dime, I got the time." He snapped his fingers to the beat.

"How about turning the music down?"

"Hey, Lionel! Get yo' ass off da couch and pause that tape!"

In a moment the music stopped, and a black man nearly Cody's size appeared behind the smaller man. His features were small on his fleshy face, and his expressionless eyes considered us blankly.

"Dis Lionel. My name's P. W. Huggins. Y'all want info an' you willin' to pay, you came to da right place."

I narrowed my eyes. "All right," I said.

He stuck his head out the doorway and looked down the walk. "Then come on in and sit yo' ass."

Inside, it reeked of pot, stale food, and beer breath. The man who called himself P. W. Huggins pointed at two plastic lawn chairs next to a cable spool that served as a coffee table.

"Go on, sit. It's twenny bucks a question, so you best make 'um count. Now, y'all look like some bad mothafuckas, but lemme tell ya 'head a time, I seen Lionel bust up plenty a bad asses, and you don't want to fuck with him, no sir."

"No problem, P. W.," I said amicably. Cody and I sat while Lionel watched us from a couch that looked like it had spent some time outdoors.

"Ask away, then." P. W. hiked a foot up on the spool and leaned forward as if to show he was focused and our money would be well spent.

"Do know a man named Farid Insaf?" I said.

He jutted his hand forward, and I laid a twenty-dollar bill in his palm. In a swift motion, he stuffed it in his pocket.

"Nope," he said.

"P. W.," Cody said, a smile on his lips, "are you fucking with us?"

"Hell, no. It's twenny a question. I tole' you da rules. If you want me to make some shit up, I kin do that. But I don't know no one with a weird-ass name like that."

"All right," I said. "What do you know about Duante Tucker?"

"Quite a bit, I definitely know quite a bit." He shot his hand out again. I ignored it.

"Who did Tucker live with when he was here?"

"That I can tell you, my man. It was a no-count couple, name a Greeley. Foster parents to six or seven kids. They did it for the monthly checks state a California sent 'em. Lazy and worthless as hell, my opinion."

I passed over another twenty. "They still around?"

"Not that I know. They left one day, an' I never saw 'em again."

"Their names?" Cody asked.

"Nate. Nate and his fat bitch of a wife, Delores."

"How about Tucker's real parents? What do you know about Lamar Tucker?"

"Ah, Lamar Tucker. I know him from way back. You hit me with forty, and I'll tell ya all 'bout him."

I handed over two more twenties. "This better be good," Cody said.

"These goods is good, so listen and learn. I know dat bad nigger from more'n twenny years ago. He was high up in da Crips, a crack kingpin, made a lot a money sellin' da shit. Smart, too, but he was a angry mothafucka. Never met a man hated whitey like he did. I tell you, when Rodney King got his ass beat by LAPD in ninety-two, when they said those cops was innocent, Lamar Tucker was one of the first brothers to take to da street. Fifty-five people died in dat riot. Tucker killed at least two a dem. I saw it.

"Anyways, after dat shit calm down, Tucker goes back to sellin' hubba, an' he start buying houses an' shit. A liquor store, too. All here in South Central 'cause he had cash money, and people were sellin' cheap. Tucker was usin' real estate to hide his drug money from da tax man. I tole you he was one smart mothafucka. People from IRS came snoopin', but they din't find shit."

P. W. paused to take a swig from his can. "Some people thought Tucker might go mainstream, but I never thought dat, 'cause I knew the dude, and he was whacked, man, he had hate in his soul. Sure 'nuff, he start havin' trouble, an' Johnny Law start watchin' him close and bringin' him in for dis or dat. Then he took da big fall."

"What happened?"

"I don't like talkin' 'bout dis, man. It's some bad, scary-ass shit."

I gave him another twenty. "Keep talking."

He contemplated the bill as if it might be counterfeit, then he folded it carefully and slid it into his pocket.

"Awright. Dere was dis dirty white boy used to come around with his skinny-ass bitch. Dey be hangin' out an' smokin' hubba in dis one crackhouse, happened to be owned by Lamar Tucker. One day, dis white boy run outa money, an' he jonesin', so he offers his ole' lady up for some rock. So one a da local boys starts a fuckin' her real hard, and she din't like dat and starts cryin' and fightin'. And the white boy calls timeout, but he already got his rock, and about this time in come Lamar. Some shit gets said, and somethin' piss off Lamar, and next thing you know he declares she's a toss-up, which mean anyone can fuck her any which way, and she ain't got no say."

P. W. sat down on the spool and put his hands between his knees. The room became quiet except for the faint patter from a television show Lionel was watching.

"Go on," Cody said.

"Well, dey was tearin' her up real bad," P. W. said in a lowered voice. "And dey was holdin' down dat white boy, and he yellin' and kickin'. Then he said the wrong thing, and dat got Lamar's attention."

"What'd he say?"

P. W. shook his head. "He shouldn't said it. Damn fool. He called Lamar a nigger. Dat's what he did."

"What did Lamar do?"

"Understan', a white boy callin' Lamar Tucker a nigger, dat's askin' for trouble, bad trouble. Lamar found hisself a razor knife and cut up dat boy bad, carved his face, and before he done, he sliced off his ear, clean off."

"And he got arrested for it?" Cody asked.

"Yes, sir, he did. Threw the book at him is what I heard, an' he went to the big house. Dat was last I ever seen of Lamar Tucker."

Cody rested his chin on his fist and studied P. W. Higgins. "Let's get back to Duante Tucker. What do you know about him?"

"Well, he be livin' with dose worthless foster parents, and you could tell he didn't like 'em one bit. He was bangin' with da Crips from an early age. Word was, he been cappin' gangstas since he was fourteen. I believe it, too. Know why? You look in his eyes, you see his old man. Cold-blooded, pissed off, and not givin' a shit 'bout nothin' but hisself. Dem Tuckers is born killers."

"When was the last time you saw Duante?" I asked.

"Oh, been a few years now. Heard he moved out a da hood. Ain't seen him since. Ain't missed him, neither."

We stood, and I gave P. W. one more twenty. "Thanks for your time," I said.

"Right on, brother. You have yourself a fine day, hear?"

•   •   •

We left the apartment complex, and out on the sidewalk, I again saw the homeless man slapping at his face. Then I looked up the street and saw a group of young blacks standing around our rental car. One was bent at the waist, working on the window, while the rest stood watching.

"Hey!" Cody yelled. We strode vigorously toward the car. As we got closer, I could see they were teenagers, except for one man who was about thirty. His cheekbones were wide, and his jaw was unusually narrow, creating a triangular effect. A do-rag covered his head, and his long sideburns were shaved into sharp angles. He stared us down, his eyes half-lidded, his expression dead cold.

When we reached the car, the kid trying to jimmy the door straightened.

"Sorry to spoil your fun, fellas," Cody said.

"Hey, mon," the older man said. "Make it easy, hand over da keys." He spoke with a thick Jamaican accent; whether it was genuine or manufactured, I couldn't tell. He lifted the bottom of his shirt just enough to show a revolver stuck in the waistband of his jeans.

"LAPD, off duty," I said, flashing my PI badge. "Get lost, or we'll all go downtown." I moved to the driver's door and opened it. Cody went to the passenger door, and three of the gangbangers backed off. The rest stood their ground, eyeing us uncertainly.

Before they could reconsider, I started the car and took off, burning the tires and leaving them in a cloud of dust.

"Nice job," Cody said.

I looked in the rearview mirror. The gangbangers were flailing their arms and looked to be arguing. "Let's get the hell out of here before we get shot," I muttered. We turned a couple quick corners until we hit a traffic light, followed by a series of stop signs. The sun bore down relentlessly and revealed the stark detail of the poverty-stricken streets. Jobless men huddled in the shade of dusty alleys and clutched bottles in paper bags. Gangbangers massed on the corners and sold rock cocaine and meth. Garish streetwalkers, some likely transvestites, offered ten-dollar backseat blowjobs. Filth and despair seemed to ooze from every doorway and barred window. Behind it all, simmering like a rancid soup, was the threat of sudden gunfire and the realization that innocent women and children might die on any given day. Life in Compton, if nothing else, meant being in the wrong place at the wrong time. We continued in silence back to the 105.

As we took the ramp onto the freeway, Cody began speaking without preamble, as if a switch had been clicked in his head.

"I was dating this cougar a few weeks ago. She had a couple kids, eleven and fourteen. They live in the suburbs, and she was telling me that at their school, the races are all mixed. Asian, Hispanic, Indian—but the kids are all second-generation, right? So English is their native language, and for the most part they only know one culture—American. They all get along in total harmony, with no racial prejudice."

"It wasn't like that when we were in school."

"Hell, no, it wasn't. I think we had one black kid and two Japanese at Oakbrook. Everyone else was white bread. And life sucked for that black kid, and the Japanese got their share of prejudice, too."

"Yeah, but remember our senior year? The Chinese, the Taiwanese actually, started showing up."

"Right. They were from the wealthy class in Taiwan, here for the electronics business."

"Yeah, but I felt bad for them," I said. "They were quiet and educated and polite, but they were different. They were from a different culture, and they got a lot of shit for it."

"Some kids used to call them green-toothed pencil dicks," Cody said. "But it's changed now. Today's ethnic kids are second-generation, and they just blend in."

"Sounds like a positive thing."

"It is. Kind of like the sappy John Lennon song, 'Imagine.' But we're talking strictly a middleclass phenomenon. It doesn't apply to the lower class."

"Because it's all about money," I said.

"You got it." Cody turned toward me, and I saw a hard edge in his green eyes. "People tend to behave when they're comfortable. But when you're struggling, you band together with your own kind. Because there's power in numbers, and then it becomes an 'us against them' thing."

"So that's your social theory on gangs?" I said, hitting the brakes to avoid a motorcycle splitting lanes.

"When I was with the force," Cody said, ignoring my comment, "there was a lot of political pressure against racial profiling. All of us cops, regardless of our race, knew it was a joke. None of us ever hassled anybody strictly because of race. We profiled criminal types, which included blacks, Mexicans, Vietnamese, and also whites. So if I saw a bandana-wearing Latino covered in tattoos driving a lowrider, I might pay him a little extra attention. That was the extent of it. The ethnic community leaders tried to make it something else, which was bullshit. They were just pissed because more of their people were getting busted, and they didn't want to admit that it was because they were the ones committing the crimes."

"What about the time the UC Berkeley wide receiver got pulled over?"

"That was the biggest bullshit of them all," Cody said with a laugh. "He was going ninety in a Mustang that was illegally gifted to him by recruiters. He had a gram of blow in the ashtray and a joint tucked in his sock, plus he blew a one-point-two in the breathalyzer. Next thing you know, he's got a high-priced attorney claiming racial profiling."

"Did he get off?"

"I don't remember. I think his attorney pled him out on a lower charge."

"Speaking of attorneys," I said, exiting the freeway, "let's go see if Darrian Bannon is in."

• • •

At times I question certain things I do. There's a part of me that clings to the idea that my motivations and ethics are an extension of my late father's. I think he did what he believed was right and just and would bend the rules to accommodate his vision. But he died before I was old enough to understand the true nature of his professional behavior. Regardless, I thought he was a man of virtue and integrity. But those can be hazy terms.

In my life I've done much I regret, some of which will weigh on my conscience to the grave. I've drunk too much and cheated on a wife I loved and had a child out of wedlock whom I will probably never meet. I've beaten men unconscious in anger and killed in self-defense when it might have been avoidable. I've also, on two occasions, pocketed significant chunks of dirty money that otherwise would have ended up wasting away in the hands of the federal government.

I've photographed couples having illicit sex, planted illegal wiretaps, represented myself as a police officer, trespassed, vandalized, and even tortured individuals. I committed these crimes because it was required to bring evil men to justice, but also because this is my chosen profession, and I'm committed to doing what it takes to be successful. I'm not interested in failing.

Sometimes there are lines that must be crossed and rules that must be ignored. When Ryan Addison hired me, he called me a liar when I said I wouldn't break the law.

He was right.

• • •

The office building where Darrian Bannon practiced law was on an industrial street in El Segundo. The concrete marker in front of the two-story structure listed a dozen businesses. Darrian Bannon Legal was sandwiched between a digital editing service and a certified public accountant's office.

We opened a glass door and went down a white hallway to a door marked with the number eight. Cody put his hand on the knob.

"Hold on. How rough you want play it?" I asked. The words felt pointless as soon as they left my mouth.

"That depends on him." Cody opened the door, and inside was a desk where I assumed a receptionist would sit, but it was vacant. To the side I saw another door, half open. We went in and found Darrian Bannon at a file cabinet, his back to us. He wore a brown, pinstriped business suit that was a shade darker than his skin.

"Yes?" he said. His head was buried in the contents of a file.

"I got a question about your rates," Cody said.

Bannon turned, and the skin at the corner of his eyes pinched. "You two," he said.

"Sorry we didn't call first for an appointment," I said.

"What is it you want?" Bannon stood facing us. He put his hand in his pocket, then withdrew it.

"We've got questions about the Tucker case, counselor," Cody said. He picked up a paperweight shaped like a piece of abstract art from Bannon's desk and weighed it in his palm.

"We had this conversation before, when you accosted me in Tahoe. If you expect to come here and intimidate me, I think you'll find I'm not—"

I looked away for a moment, out a window stained with water streaks. In that instant Cody took two quick steps and pounced on Bannon, shoving him face down on the desk. Papers scattered, and a keyboard fell to the floor. Cody put his knee in the center of Bannon's back and fitted his hand around the attorney's neck, pinning his face against the desktop.

"You get to make an important decision today, asshole," Cody said. I closed the door and lowered the shades on the window.

"What?" Bannon hissed. His lips were pushed up and distorted over his small teeth.

"Who is Farid Insaf?" I said.

"Never heard that name." He had to force the words as Cody angled his body to push harder on Bannon's face.

"Who hired you to represent Tucker?" Cody said. "Who paid you?"

"You're crushing me," Bannon croaked.

"And I'm just getting warmed up," Cody said. "You get to decide how bad it gets."

"I took the case pro bono."

With his free hand Cody held the paper weight, which had two spiked metal edges. He put one of the spikes up to Bannon's eye. "Pro bono, my ass," he said. "Lie to me again, I'll take your eye out."

Bannon's tan skin flushed a deep red. His hands were balled into fists.

"I was paid a modest retainer. For expenses."

"By who?" I said.

"The caller never identified himself. He mailed me cash."

"How much?"

Bannon, his eye clenched shut, took a moment before answering. "Ten grand."

"A modest retainer, huh?" Cody said.

"That's right."

"You better come clean with a name," Cody said. "Who paid you?"

"I swear I never knew. The cash came in an unmarked box, no return address, local postmark. Can you let me up, please?"

Cody looked at me. I stepped around the desk to the file cabinet in the corner. In the top drawer were alphabetized folders. I opened the second drawer, then the third. Toward the back was a green folder titled TUCKER. I removed the file, then checked the bottom drawer, which was stacked with a mess of unorganized papers.

"Let's go," I said.

Cody pulled Bannon up and sat him in his chair.

"You can't take that," Bannon said, his necktie askew, his collar tight against his sweaty skin. His eyes were wide with fear and indignation.

"I'll mail it back, if you ask politely."

Bannon started to say something but thought better of it.

"You need to get some air freshener for this place," Cody said. "It smells like someone shit their pants."

• • •

The airport was two miles away. It was almost six p.m. and we'd booked the nine o'clock flight out. I was hoping we could get an earlier flight, but when we got to the terminal, the ticket agent said everything was full.

We went to wait in the security line. Waist-high poles and synthetic straps formed a serpentine pathway. There were probably a couple hundred people ahead of us. Parents with small children, businessmen, elderly folks. A wide mix of races, all waiting and shuffling forward with their luggage.

"The curse of Osama Bin Laden," Cody said. "Got to hand it to him, he screwed us pretty good."

There was a large group of college-aged guys ahead in the line. They were clean-shaven and wore jeans and T-shirts. One was Asian, and two were of Mideastern descent, with black hair and dark skin. The rest were white.

One said something that prompted the others to laugh. They joked back and forth as we proceeded toward the TSA agents checking boarding passes and IDs.

"We've shafted the Mideast pretty good too, for the last hundred years," I said.

Cody raised his eyebrows. "How so?"

"We use our military power and money to make sure the oil keeps coming. We buy the cooperation of sheiks and regimes who don't give a shit about the welfare of their people."

"And that's justification for killing three thousand innocent American civilians?"

"That's how they see it."

"Sounds like we're the scapegoat for their shitty state of affairs," Cody replied.

Cody's phone beeped, and after studying the screen, he said, "I just got an e-mail with an audio file."

"The bugs from Suggs's house?"

"Yeah. We'll listen to it when we get back."

We waited another twenty minutes before nearing the metal-detecting machines. I wondered if anyone had calculated the lost man hours and drop in productivity resulting from post-9/11 security measures. Then I saw TSA agents, followed by a pair of uniformed cops, converge around the two young Arabs who had just passed through one of the imaging booths.

A burst of raised voices caused everyone to look. One of the Arabs had his shirt pulled up and held a shoe. Four more policemen rushed to the scene, and words were shouted in a foreign language. The Arabs, eyes flashing, struggled and tried to resist when the police accosted them, and one went down, shocked with a jolt from a stun gun. The second wasn't as lucky. He ducked a baton, but another cop caught him alongside the head, and blood poured from a gash above his ear.

Within two minutes, the Arabs and the other men in their group were whisked off to back rooms. The crowd was abuzz, but quickly quieted while TSA personnel notified us that there would be an indeterminate delay before the security checkpoint reopened.

For a minute there was a confused pause, then the noise level resumed. Groans of despair were followed by the inevitable questions and conjectures. *They didn't look like terrorists. Maybe he just had a bag of pot in his crotch. It could have been an underwear bomb. Al-Qaida will never give up. We should nuke the whole region. Forty virgins—what a joke. Life means nothing to them. I'd kill myself too if I was one of those pieces of shit.*

After a while some folks sat and tried to get comfortable on the hard floor. Cody and I stood in stoic silence. I tried to shift my mind to the almost meditative state that I practiced during long hours of surveillance. When that failed, I removed half the papers from the inch-thick file I'd taken from Bannon's office and handed Cody the remainder.

An hour passed. Flights were missed, and I wondered if ours would be canceled. I was hungry, and my cursory reading of Bannon's file revealed nothing I didn't already know. Later I'd give it a more thorough examination.

We waited another hour before the checkpoint reopened. After we cleared the screening process, we went to our gate and saw our flight was not canceled, but was pushed back an hour. The nearest bar was jam-packed. We settled for cold sandwiches and bottled beer, which we consumed at an abandoned gate, where I stared out at the runways. The blinking lights set in the pavement stretched until they were swallowed by the black abyss of the night. I stared out and thought of explosions and war and atrocities, and then I thought of my home and my girlfriend and the surrounding mountains and the lake that was sometimes so blue it appeared from an alien world. I tried to hold those thoughts in my mind, and when that didn't work, I closed my eyes and tried to think of nothing.

6

WHEN I WOKE THE next morning in Cody's guest room, the previous day's events seemed as fuzzy as a whiskey dream. I went to the kitchen and started a pot of coffee, then began writing down and organizing the details of what we'd learned from the trip south. I started with Leo Rosen's claim he'd been threatened by an anonymous party, which prompted him to flee to Mexico during the trial. Next I noted Amber Meline's lack of testimony, which she did not elaborate upon. Then there was the input from P. W. Huggins, an obvious hustler whose comments may have been exaggerated or contrived, but I felt likely contained some elements of truth.

And then there was Darrian Bannon's file. If, from something buried in the papers, I learned who hired Bannon, that would steer us in the right direction. If not, we were still at ground zero, because nothing we'd discovered so far provided any clear path to answering the central question, the question we needed to keep at the core of our investigation. I looked up from where I sat on the couch, watching steam rise from the cup I held in both hands. "Who was behind the disappearance of the DNA evidence?" I said aloud.

"Talking to yourself again?" Cody said, lumbering around the corner in his boxer shorts.

I stood and flexed my shoulders. "We need to refocus. We need to know who Farid Insaf is, or whoever the person is at the high-rise."

"Can I have a cup of coffee first?"

"I think yesterday was mostly a waste of time."

"I don't." Cody poured himself a cup and began poking through his refrigerator.

"Based on what?" I asked.

"You know how it works, Dirt. Sometimes cases get solved in a circular path. Like spiraling in on the truth. Every data point brings us a little closer."

"Yeah, yeah. But I'm running low on patience."

"Hey, it was your idea to go to LA."

"Right, but now it's time to quit screwing around. I want to stake out that high-rise until we know who lives in 1602, and what his connection is to Tucker."

"Don't you think we ought to listen to the recording from Suggs's place first?"

I sighed, and said, "All right, fine."

• • •

The program Cody used downloaded everything the bugs recorded via cellular signal and generated audio files that we could play back on our PCs. We were able to skip over periods of silence, and the program even differentiated television noise from actual live voices. Updated files would be sent every twenty-four hours for seven days, which was the projected battery life of the bugs.

I sat with my PC on the coffee table, listening through earphones to the section from ten p.m. to ten yesterday morning. Cody replayed the portion from ten a.m. until the recording concluded after twelve hours. In this fashion, we were able to cover the entire twenty-four hours in less than two hours.

There were only two conversations Suggs had during my time frame. Shortly after he got home and found his dogs asleep, he'd called someone and discussed the possibility of a robbery attempt, but said his supply was secure in his safe, and he didn't see any indication anyone had broken into his house. After that, he had another phone conversation, presumably with a woman. After some references to their sexual relationship, Suggs said, "After this shit's done, we'll get away to an island somewhere."

Cody had started later than me, and while I waited for him to finish, I reread Bannon's case file. Most of the information I'd already seen in the trial transcripts. Still, I looked at every page carefully, hoping to find a reference that might reveal a clue to who hired Bannon. There was nothing even remotely helpful.

$$\bullet \quad \bullet \quad \bullet$$

By noon we were parked on the street outside the Skyscape condominium building. I sat in the passenger seat of Cody's Toyota holding my 35 mm camera, the long telephoto lens resting on my thigh. Cars passed in and out of the underground garage. Every now and then, people would appear on the balconies that stretched upward in a vertical column.

Across the street from the Skyscape was a long brick office building. I moved from the car into one of a few shady alcoves the building offered and pointed my camera up at the balcony for unit 1602. At full zoom I thought I'd be able to get a clear shot if anyone appeared.

Cody joined me, and we watched the balcony from the shadows.

"There was one phone conversation on the tape that was weird," Cody said, sitting on a shaded bench next to a dark doorway. "Suggs kept referring to 'the timing.' He said, when will we know the timing? Then he repeated it."

"Any idea who he was talking to?" I asked.

"No. He didn't use any names."

"It could mean anything," I said.

"He said it with emphasis. Like it was a big deal."

We continued staring up at the balcony. "He's got to take a smoke break sooner or later," I said.

"You're assuming anybody's home."

Two hours passed. While we waited, I aimed my camera at the garage entrance, where drivers had to punch in a series of numbers to enter. I was able to get three separate four-digit codes.

Finally, at about two o'clock, a figure appeared on the balcony. I knelt, pointed the camera upward, and started clicking away. After ten shots I paused to check the camera's LCD and saw a middle-aged black man smoking a cigarette. The display was too small to make out much detail, but the shots were in focus.

"These ought to blow up nicely." I handed the camera to Cody.

Cody looked at the pictures. "What would be nice is if he'd leave. Get his license plate, see where he goes. Maybe get him alone somewhere."

I pointed the camera back at the man on the balcony.

"If that's Farid Insaf, he must be a Muslim convert," I said.

"Think how much easier this would be if he didn't live in this freaking high-rise," Cody said.

"Be patient. It's all just billable hours, right?"

"You keep on using my lines."

"I'll try to work on some of my own."

"Check it out." Cody pointed at the garage. A tan Ford Taurus had pulled up. I zoomed in with the camera and saw a young black woman entering a code at the kiosk. The garage door opened, and I clicked a couple photos before she drove in.

I lowered the camera and I looked at Cody, and our eyes blinked almost simultaneously.

"How many black—"

"I got her code," I said. "Wait here." I handed him the camera and ran across the street to the Skyscape's lobby entrance.

After tapping in the code on the outside wall, I went inside and saw a teenage Asian kid working the reception desk.

"Good afternoon," he said. I nodded and went by him to the elevator in the hall, where I entered the code on the keypad.

A minute later a ding sounded and the elevator door opened. When I stepped inside, I experienced a brief moment of elation when I saw I had timed it perfectly; the black woman was there. Then I almost did a double take. Her heels put her at my eye level, and her profile was stunning. Green eyes, a perfectly tilted nose, exquisite cheekbones and jawline. But to simply say she was beautiful wouldn't be adequate. In a room full of gorgeous women, I had no doubt she would be the center of attention. I snuck a second glance at her and realized that what set her apart was a certain regal countenance, as if she belonged to a royal bloodline.

Her hair was done in cornrows, and I wasn't sure if that was an affront to her noble carriage or perhaps a cultural affirmation. The elevator started up, and it was then that I noticed her body was also extraordinary. She wore a tangerine-colored sleeveless blouse, her breasts high and conical, the nipples denting the material. Below her tapered waist, her designer jeans were tight against the sweep of her hips. Unable to resist the temptation, and hoping I wasn't too obvious, I took a step backward and saw her ass was heart shaped, pert and round, a perfect diamond of space visible between her legs.

The elevator stopped. We were on floor sixteen. *Of course*, I thought. I'd punched in her code. The elevator was probably programmed to go only to the floors indicated by the entered codes.

We got off, and she turned in the direction of 1602. I went the opposite way, stopped at a doorway, and watched her walk down the hall. I watched her all the way to 1602 and then, to my chagrin, noticed I was getting an erection.

She knocked on the door and I saw it open. I got a brief glance at the face of the man who answered. I was wondering if Duante Tucker was there, but it was the middle-aged man. His head was bald, and his jaw was hidden by a gray goatee that was squared off below the chin. Our eyes met for an instant, and I quickly looked away. I felt a pang of concern; I didn't want him to see my face. But I told myself he would expect any man to eyeball her, and he probably took little notice of me.

The door closed and I strode down the hall to where the stairwell was across from 1602. I hesitated for a second when I got there, then I opened the EXIT door and quickly descended the stairs to the garage.

The tan Taurus was parked in the visitor parking area. I took down the license plate, found a door next to the car gate, and went out into the sunshine.

"What's up?" Cody asked when I came across the street. I joined him in the shaded area where he sat.

"She went to 1602, all right. We rode the elevator up together."

"Nice. What do you think?"

I took the camera from Cody and aimed it up at the balcony. No one was there. "I'm trying to think the right way to describe her," I said. "Outrageously attractive would do it. But classy."

"Like a high-priced escort?"

"No. I don't think so. She seemed…too cultured. Maybe even a little haughty."

"Haughty, huh?"

"I don't know. We didn't talk, and I didn't hear her say a word. It was just an impression I got."

"I've met haughty hookers before," Cody said.

"I'm sure you have," I replied.

"You got any idea what she's doing up there?"

"Nope."

"You want to follow her when she leaves?"

"Absolutely," I said.

•   •   •

Twenty minutes later the Ford Taurus drove out of the parking lot, and we followed it down the street.

"Just enough time for a quick trick," Cody said.

"Don't rush to conclusions."

We tailed her to Guadalupe Parkway and then onto 101 North. It was a clear summer afternoon, the kind that attracts residents to Northern California. Comfortable for shorts and a T-shirt, or a business suit. When I lowered the window, the air that rushed in was crisp and hinted at an early fall. We stayed back three cars and followed the Ford off the Sunnyvale exit and to a restaurant right off the freeway. Behind the restaurant a hotel was tucked away, hidden by a tall row of eucalyptus trees.

The hotel belonged to a small chain priced to cater to budget-minded business travelers, but there was only a small sign to advertise its existence, and its location was invisible from the main boulevard. We hung back until the Taurus reached the end of a narrow road that terminated at a parking lot in front of the hotel rooms, which were arranged in an L-shaped configuration.

Once she parked, we pulled into a spot on the opposite side of the lot and watched her leave her car and walk toward the green painted doors on the first floor. I pointed my camera and zoomed in. From a hundred feet, I could make out the detail of a silver bracelet around her wrist.

"Let me see," Cody said. I handed him the camera.

"Yowza," he said. "Look at that body. A real African queen."

"Snap a couple shots before you get too distracted."

She reached one of the doors and knocked. The door opened almost immediately, and I glimpsed a white man with hair that looked too black. He had a thick torso, muscular but fat, and stood about six feet. He opened the door wide, and she went in.

"Well, fuck me," Cody said, and clicked a final picture.

"What?" I asked.

"That's Russ Landers."

"No way. You're sure?"

"There's no mistaking that asshole."

•   •   •

The controversy that ensued during Cody's termination as a San Jose cop had left him with a few cautious allies on the force, but far more sworn enemies. Chief among his adversaries had been his boss and the precinct captain, Russ Landers. According to Cody, Landers not only epitomized corruption but was in fact the squad's most egregious participant, back before Cody's accusations had resulted in a widespread investigation. The investigation resulted in the conviction of three cops, but somehow Landers had avoided the fallout.

The chief of police in San Jose had declared his department graft free after the arrest of the three officers. Meanwhile, Landers kept his job and his two-million-dollar home in Los Gatos. He'd also remarried after Cody had a brief affair with his soon-to-be ex-wife.

• • •

"You ever talk to Landers after you left the force?" I asked.

"Once or twice."

"How'd it go?"

"He suggested I leave the state, if I remember. Wait here for a minute."

"What are you doing?"

"Just sit tight." Cody got out of the Toyota and walked across the lot to the door where the black woman had entered. He stood near the front window, trying to peek though the drapes, and then pressed his ear against the glass. After a minute he strolled back to where I waited.

"Ole' Russ is having himself a hell of a time," he said.

"Yeah?"

"He's banging the hell out of her."

"Did you see anything?" I asked.

"No, but I heard the bed springs squeaking away, and I could even hear the son of a bitch panting. Then he says, 'Mama, you got the sweetest black ass I've ever seen.'"

"Wow."

"You still doubt she's for hire?"

"Guess not," I said.

We sat for a minute. A breeze blew a scattering of leaves across the pavement, and I noticed some cars were coated with yellow dust. From the nearby trees, a flock of birds cawed and took flight, and a white splat hit our windshield.

"So she's a call girl," I said. "You want to spend any more time here?"

He looked at me out of the corner of his eye. "Yeah, I do. I want to know who she is."

"You think it's more than a coincidence that Farid Insaf and Landers share the same hooker?" I asked.

"I'd say it's suspicious. Landers has the moral standards of a cockroach. I wouldn't put anything past him."

"We got her license plate."

"Yeah, but there's no guarantee the car's registered to her," Cody said. "So let's stick with her a while."

I grunted and tried to get comfortable in my seat. "I'd rather be back at the Skyscape."

"I doubt she'll be in there much longer."

Twenty minutes passed. I tried to imagine what connection Landers could possibly have to Farid Insaf or the Tucker case. Tucker and Suggs were dealing heroin, but it seemed small time. Landers probably wouldn't take a bribe unless it was worth the risk, as in thousands of dollars. That raised the potential that the heroin business could be bigger than I thought. Maybe Farid Insaf was behind it. Maybe he was connected to the Arabs who supplied Tucker and Suggs.

When I shared my thoughts with Cody, he shrugged. "Anything's possible," he said. His eyes remained fixed on the hotel room door.

"Could be Landers is just taking a freebie from a high-paid escort," I said.

"That's about his speed."

Yeah, and this is all speculative bullshit, I thought. Some investigations involved little more than a few interviews, and the facts revealed themselves as readily as a prostitute sheds her clothes. Quick, tidy, instant gratification—or damn near. But from the moment Ryan Addison hired me, I knew this case wouldn't resolve itself like that. We needed to keep probing, and eventually we'd get a breakthrough. "Work hard, get creative, make your own luck," an old boss of mine used to say.

Someone was seriously motivated to see Duante Tucker go free. But who, and why? What could be the motivation to keep a violent rapist out of jail?

The core reason for most crimes always boiled down to one of three issues: love, hate, or money. Who loved Tucker? A girlfriend? It seemed unlikely a man of his tendencies would have one. His family? That needed looking into. Where was his father, Lamar Tucker? Or his sister, whose name I couldn't remember?

As for hate, did someone hate Lindsey Addison, or the Addison family, enough to orchestrate Tucker's freedom? While possible, it seemed a stretch. If anyone had a real problem with the Addisons, there'd be far easier ways to cause them grief.

That left money. What value could Tucker provide that would be worth the risk and expense of threatening the witnesses and making the DNA disappear? At least we had a clue as to that; Tucker was involved in heroin trafficking, though it seemed to be street-level stuff. Could that be a prelude to a bigger score? Maybe the Arabs at the restaurant where Tucker and Suggs picked up a shipment were looking to move kilos rather than ounces.

The black woman emerged from the room after almost exactly a half hour.

"She does have a certain look, doesn't she?" Cody said. Her clothes were molded to her body, and she held her head high, as if she'd just completed an act of great dignity and importance. She walked to her car, strutting like a fashion model on a runway.

After exiting the lot, she drove west on the freeway and exited within a few miles. Five minutes later she parked in front of an apartment building in Sunnyvale, not far from where I lived when I was going to college.

The apartments were called the River Glen, even though there was no river nearby. Three white trellises stood along the sidewalk, and a sign offered a lease signing bonus. The paint on the wood siding was fresh, and the shrubbery was neatly trimmed. *Probably renovated recently*, I thought. Target tenants would be young professionals just starting on their path to the American dream.

From the corner, we watched her go to a door facing the street. She took her keys from her purse and let herself in. Cody pulled forward and I jotted down the apartment number. Then my cell rang. It was Candi.

"Hi, babe," I said.

"Hi. Are you still in San Jose?" she asked.

"Yes."

"Oh, darn it. I was hoping you could pick me up from the airport tonight."

"You're coming home early?"

"Yeah. I don't know why I planned two weeks here. It's too much. I'm going nuts with boredom."

"Did you already reschedule your flight?" I asked.

"I did. I'll be landing in Reno at ten tonight."

I looked at my watch. It was almost four o'clock. "I'll call you back in five minutes," I said.

Cody turned onto Lawrence Expressway and darted in front of some slow-moving traffic. "I heard," he said. "I'll take you back to your rig."

"What? I haven't decided anything."

"What's to decide? Candi's a good woman. You don't run into gals like her very often."

"That doesn't mean I should neglect my job just because her schedule changes," I said.

"You're not neglecting anything. I can hold down the fort here."

"We need to get back to the Skyscape, get—"

"I'll take care of it. Do the right thing, Dan. Go pick up your girlfriend. And work the local angle."

"I can drive back here tomorrow."

"Look," Cody said, sighing. "This ain't about being pussy-whipped, so don't even think that. It's about keeping your priorities straight. Take a couple days. Snoop around, talk to Marcus Grier or the DA, see what else you can find out."

Cody accelerated hard and blew through a light just as it turned red. Then he downshifted and veered onto the freeway ramp heading toward downtown San Jose. Ahead I could see the long flanks of the Diablo Range rising over the valley. Much of the terrain was barren, and the dirt hillsides rose steeply into a series of ravines and chasms. At the highest point I could see the white observatory on top of Mount Hamilton.

"All right," I said. "I'll be back in a couple days."

* * *

I wasted no time getting on the road, but I was too late; the northeast traffic on 680 was clogged with commuters heading home to where real estate was less expensive, in Livermore, Tracy, even as far out as Stockton. I crawled forward and looked out over the sea of cars. It was hard to imagine an existence that included three hours of stop-and-go traffic on a daily basis. But that's what these folks did, making the sacrifice to provide a better life for their families.

During my early career as an investigator in San Jose, I worked for three different outfits. I drank my way out of my first job, and my second ended when the bail bondsman who hired me was forced to close up shop. My third job was for a penny-pinching incompetent named Rick Wenger. That gig ended when I freelanced a case in South Lake Tahoe. The resulting payday allowed me to move to Tahoe and buy my home.

I don't think much about my history in San Jose anymore. But occasionally I take stock of certain episodes. Many of the regrettable things I can attribute to my immaturity and drunkenness and just plain selfishness. Over time, I've worked to address those issues. The violence, however, I view differently. It was always sudden, beyond my control, and disconnected from any decision-making process. I think back to when I rammed my truck into a Mexican cartel member or to the time I shot a child molester who was trying to slit my throat. I believe in my heart that these men deserved their fate, and the world is better off with them dead. At times, my conscience questions my logic, but I win those arguments.

But what I cannot account for is the way I treated Julia, my ex-wife. She was a bright woman with a sunny disposition and freckles that danced beneath her eyes when she smiled. It was shortly after we married that I first killed a man. I convinced myself that the rational, justifiable reaction to that was a full tilt drunk binge, one that lasted for weeks. Much of it I don't remember, but a few things are time-stamped in my brain, like damaged nerves that have scabbed over but won't fully heal. I remember having sex with a drunken woman in a kitchen next to a grill that reeked of grease. I remember when two wannabe bikers wrestled my wallet from me in a bar bathroom. And I remember, near the end of the binge, waking up in the sunlight, curled in the fetal position against the stucco wall of a seedy wino bar in San Jose called the Corners Club.

When I finally sobered up, Julia forgave me…then divorced me. I could hardly argue her decision. I knew I didn't deserve her. Eventually I realized that was a main issue behind my self-destructive behavior. She was too good for me, so I set out to prove it. Did a damn good job of it, too.

Some benefit did come from those days, though. I learned about myself. You probe the bottom of a toilet bowl, there's no place to go but up. I didn't drink for two years after the divorce, and when I started again, I never felt inclined to abuse the privilege. While that was certainly due to a lack of alcoholic tendency in my genes, I'd also experienced a catharsis of sorts. I'd hit my rock bottom and, having survived it, set out to live a better life. A reasonably sober life, a stable life, and a life I hoped might include another woman to love.

Previous to Candi, my only relationship in the four years since moving to Tahoe was a misguided affair with a much younger woman. Other than that, I'd spent long months celibate, save for the occasional fling. I was cautious when I met Candi, who lived out in Elko at the time. Because of the six-hour drive separating us, our relationship proceeded slowly at first. But when she left Elko and moved into my home, I never regretted it. Among other things, she brought a cheeriness to my life that I had long lacked. And also something else, something that once I recognized, I did not want to give up—she brought a sense of normalcy.

I sat at a dead stop and checked my mobile device. Candi's flight was still on time, but at this pace, I wouldn't be. The minutes ticked by, and finally the traffic eased past the 580 interchange. I drove at eighty for a while until I hit more gridlock outside of Concord. Crossed the Benicia Bridge, then slowed to a crawl again on 80.

It took three hours to drive the 125 miles to Sacramento and another half hour to clear the city traffic. Then Highway 80 opened up, the pavement wide and smooth, and I hauled ass through Rocklin and Auburn and into the Sierra foothills. The sun dipped behind a granite ridge, and the clouds turned purple and orange against the florescent sky. I drove hard, and by the time I cleared Donner Summit, it was full dark. My headlights swept over rows of pines that rose like black ghosts until the forest gave way to the sparse landscape of the high desert. I crossed over the Nevada border under a crescent moon and bombed down the straights, my speedometer bouncing off 100, my tires humming in anticipation.

7

WE'D GONE TO BED at midnight the night before but hadn't slept until two. When I woke in the morning, I opened my eyes to see Candi coming out of the bathroom nude, wisps of light hair in the triangle between her legs, her pink nipples high on her breasts. She slid under the covers and reached between my legs.

"You're not wore out from last night, are you?" she asked.

"I don't know," I admitted.

"Let's find out." She swung her leg on top of mine.

"Nymphomania is a treatable disease, you know."

"Oh, hush."

Fifteen minutes of heavy breathing later, I limped out to the kitchen. Candi made coffee, and we sat looking out the big window at the yard and the green meadow beyond. The sun cast a broad stripe across the table where we sat, and I stretched my forearms out to feel the heat.

"I'm going to start a new painting," she said. "I took a lot of neat pics, and I have an idea for a Texas ranch landscape."

"Cool, babe. I'll take you out to lunch later."

"It's a date." She went off to the room she'd converted to an art studio, and after a few minutes, I went to my truck and got my camera.

While downloading the photos I'd taken over the last two days, I updated the case report I owed Ryan Addison. I included my conjectures on possible relationships and motivations, but when I reread it, the words sounded like rambling guesswork. I reduced the paragraphs to bullet points, which at least lent a bit more structure to it. Then I spent thirty minutes detailing my hourly activity and expenses. At double rate, it was a good chunk of money. Maybe not to Ryan Addison, but to me it was.

I absently picked at a spot on my desk where the paint had chipped away from the metal surface. Addison was also paying Cody the same amount. For that kind of money, he should expect results.

I started going through the pictures on my computer monitor. I separated the blurred shots from the sharper images and blew up the best ones to full screen. There were a couple good shots of the black prostitute and one that showed Russ Lander's face in the doorway as she was leaving. She looked as good in the photos as in person. I lingered on her pictures and felt a pang of guilt, but she was a woman of extraordinary beauty and sex appeal, and I had a hard time taking my eyes off her.

But more interesting to me were the shots of the man on the balcony who seemed to be housing Duante Tucker. Two of the images, once I worked them over with photo enhancement software, were good, clear face shots. He was about fifty, with some discoloration on the skin below his heavily lidded eyes. Other than that he was handsome; straight nose, square cheekbones, the features even and well-proportioned.

I studied his mug for some time, then I compared it to Duante Tucker's face and also to Lennox Suggs's. Besides the skin color, there was no commonality with Suggs. But with Tucker, I did see similarity. The lips perhaps, and definitely the eyes. The same thick hoods and deep bottoms. Could the man be Lamar Tucker? If so, that would explain his son staying with him. I examined their faces again. Yes, I decided. This could definitely be father and son. And the man on my screen looked about the right age.

I dialed Sheriff Grier at his office, and a secretary told me he was on patrol. So I called his cell, even though I knew it would annoy him.

"Yeah?" he grunted after half a dozen rings.

"How you doing, Marcus?"

"What's up?"

"I've been in San Jose the last couple days."

"That's nice," he said. "What'd you find out?"

"Tucker's living in a fancy high-rise and is involved in heroin dealing."

He paused for a moment, then said, "How's that relate to the rape case?"

"Don't know yet. I could use your help on a couple things."

"I should have guessed."

"Lamar Tucker is Duante's father," I said. "He spent some time in prison, but I think Duante might be living with him now in San Jose. Can you pull his record?

"Anything else?" he asked.

"Did anything come of the polygraph tests all the cops were supposed to take?"

"Nothing positive so far. What else you got?"

"How about running a license plate?"

"Serves me right for asking. Give me the number."

I recited the tag number from the Ford the prostitute was driving. "Come by my office at five," he said.

We hung up, and I hiked a foot on my desk and thought about Lamar Tucker. According to what I heard in Compton, he'd been big in the drug trade and used the profits to buy local real estate, but then he was sent to prison. Maybe he'd been released and cashed out his investments and moved to San Jose to be with his son. Maybe he felt bad about not being there when Duante was growing up, assuming Lamar was imprisoned during that time.

Another angle was that Lamar Tucker might have big plans for Duante, big enough that Lamar financed the disappearance of the evidence. And what could those plans be? The obvious answer was drugs. Could be that Lamar was building something big in San Jose and was using his son as a front man, which meant Duante would take the fall if anything went wrong. The hustler in Compton had said Lamar was a coldhearted son of a bitch, so it wasn't much of a stretch to imagine he'd use his son to insulate him from the law.

I stared off, running all sorts of related what-ifs through my mind. Most of my thoughts just opened more unanswered questions, and the exercise began to feel pointless. On the other hand, you get enough ideas swimming around in your head, you might hit on one that makes a difference, once the right scrap of information comes along.

At one o'clock Candi asked if I was ready for lunch. I hadn't realized it was that late. I drove us to a restaurant that overlooked a sandy stretch of beach on the west side of the lake. It was a warm afternoon, and we sat on an outdoor deck under an umbrella. A family with two small children was on the beach, and the children were playing where the water lapped at the shore. Further out, a group of sailboats tacked toward the center of the lake.

"Tell me about your new case," Candi said.

I hesitated. I didn't want to hide anything from Candi. I didn't want to lie or misrepresent anything I was involved in. But I saw no reason to burden her with sordid details. Ten years ago, Candi's sister had been raped, and later committed suicide. The mere mention of rape would cast a pall over an otherwise pleasant afternoon.

"Do you not want to talk about it?" she asked.

"A man committed a violent crime but was found not guilty when the key evidence vanished from the police locker. The family of the victim hired me."

"Wow. They want you to turn up the evidence?"

"They want to know who took the evidence and why. They want the man to pay for his crime."

"So, they want you to make up for the incompetency of the police?"

"Not really. How about if we talk about it later? I'm really kind of burned out on it right now."

"Sure," she said, but I could see a flicker of hurt in her eyes.

I reached out and touched her hand. "There's some grim stuff involved, Candi. I just need a break. I really don't want to screw up our day by getting into it."

"I understand." She squeezed my fingers.

"Look at those sailboats," I said. "Have you ever been on one?"

She shook her head. "How's Cody doing?"

I continued gazing out at the lake for a moment, then turned back to her. "Pretty good."

"Is he behaving himself?"

"Yeah, he is. I think he makes a special effort when I'm around."

"That's good," she said. "It sounds like he respects you."

"Respects me?" I said, eyebrows raised. "I've been friends with Cody for twenty years. I've never questioned if he respects me or not."

"Yeah, but people change as they get older. Friendships aren't always forever. Actually, most aren't."

"I'm not sure what you're getting at."

"I'm just commenting," she said.

A waitress came to take our orders, and when she left, we were quiet for a minute. The sky was cloudless, and the surface of the lake was like glass. Two small birds landed within arm's reach on the railing and eyed us expectantly.

"Candi," I said, "Cody's my best friend, and I don't expect that will ever change. His personal life may be rough around the edges, and sometimes it seems like he's at war with himself, but he's the best friend a man could have."

She ran her nails through the hair on the side of my head, then patted it into place. "You're a loyal man. I think that's a great way to be."

"Thanks, babe."

"Just promise me you'll be safe and sane. Especially around Cody."

"That's always my intention."

"I just worry sometimes," she said.

"You really shouldn't. I've been doing this work for a long time. I know how to stay out of trouble."

She smiled, but there was a certain sadness behind her shiny eyes, as if my words were obviously disingenuous and uttered only as a clumsy attempt to appease her.

"I know my work is sometimes dangerous," I said, "but so are a lot of jobs. Hell, I know a tree trimmer who got zapped by a power line. And a fisherman who fell from his boat and drowned."

"I'll be fine, Dan. Don't forget, my dad was a cop. I can handle it. Just be careful out there."

"I promise I will."

• • •

When we got home, I lifted weights in the garage and then jogged a five-mile loop that rose and fell along the base of the foothills. My shirt quickly became soaked under my twenty-pound pack, and I had to keep wiping the sweat out of my eyes. By the time I got home, my body had that empty, cleansed feeling that comes after a good workout. The exercise had left me in a tranquil mental state, as if my subconscious had reached conclusions and was at peace. What conclusions those were, I didn't quite know, but when I got out of the shower I felt rejuvenated. I looked in the mirror, and my muscles were tight against the skin. I left the house just before five and drove to the police complex.

A young patrolman escorted me through the squad room to Marcus Grier's office. Grier sat behind his desk, peering intently at his monitor. His beefy shoulders hunched forward as he worked a mouse and tapped at his keyboard. Tiny curls of salt and pepper hair sprouted from his ears, and his eyebrows were pinched in concentration.

"Take a seat," he said, his eyes glued to the screen.

I sat and looked out his window. Cars were parked in the shade cast by a line of tall pines on the far side of the lot, leaving the spots nearer the building open. A Mexican couple left the police station and walked down the sidewalk, clinging to each other as if they were suffering from tremendous emotional strain and might collapse if separated. They climbed into a small car with a dented door and drove away.

After a minute, Grier said. "I got the lowdown on Lamar Tucker."

"Yeah?"

"Yeah." He rubbed at his mouth. "Tucker was one of the pioneers of the crack trade down in Watts, during the eighties and early nineties. He rose up in the Crips and supposedly made a lot of money. But then he got busted and sent up the river on a mayhem charge."

"I heard all that. I'm curious what he's been up to more recently. He's not still in prison, is he?"

"Nope."

"When did he get out?" I asked.

"He didn't," Grier replied. "He died in Corcoran State Prison."

My head jerked. "He did? When?"

"In 1996. He'd been there about a year before getting into it with the Aryan Brotherhood."

"They killed him?"

"Yeah, after he killed one of theirs."

"You're sure?"

"They caught him alone and beat him, broke his arms. Then they held his head to the cell bars, and a three-hundred-thirty-pound AB enforcer kicked his head through. The bars were five inches apart."

"That was the end for him, huh?" I said.

Grier nodded. "Massive head trauma. His skull broke apart. They had to scoop his brains up with a dustpan. You ought to see the pictures."

"Can you print them for me?"

He hit a few keys, and his printer began clicking and whirring.

"How's the internal investigation going?" I asked. My voice sounded distant to me, the words forced.

"A couple IA pricks from Sacramento showed up yesterday. They're running around like they own the place. A real barrel of laughs, these guys."

I crossed my arms and stared at the printer as it chugged out pages. "Shit," I said. "Lamar Tucker had money. I thought he might have been behind this."

"Not unless he's doing it from the grave." Grier looked at his watch.

"Farid Insaf," I said.

"What?"

"Duante Tucker is staying at a fancy high-rise condo in San Jose with a middle-aged black man I thought was Lamar Tucker. But Farid Insaf is the listed resident. I thought Lamar might have converted to Islam, changed his name."

"You were wrong."

"Can you run Farid Insaf through your system? I'm trying to figure out who he is. Maybe he has a record."

"Write down the address for me."

While Grier typed, I stood and paced a lap around his office, then I leaned against the wall and squinted out the window. I had assumed the man living at the Skyscape was the listed tenant, Farid Insaf. But there was no guarantee that was true. Farid Insaf may have bought or rented the unit, then subleased it out. Or he could just be letting a friend stay there.

Grier looked up after a minute. "What do you got?" I asked.

"There's no record of anyone named Farid Insaf in California. There's a few in other states, but none have criminal records except for minor traffic infractions."

I sighed and stared blankly at a smattering of papers tacked to a corkboard behind Grier's desk. "Did you run that license plate yet?" I said.

"No. I'll do it now, but I got to get going."

"You have any suspicions who took the DNA, Marcus?"

He glanced at me with bleak eyes. "There's a few cops around here I wouldn't trust as far as I could throw them. But they passed the polygraph, and we haven't found any indication of wrongdoing."

I stuck my thumbs in my belt loops. It was happy hour, and I suddenly craved a good belt of whiskey.

"Hey, look at this," Marcus said.

"What?"

"2006 Ford Taurus, registered to Shanice Tucker. Is she related?"

"Shanice? Jesus Christ, I think that's Duante's sister."

"I'll check," Grier said. "I'm sure it's in his file."

As Grier started clacking away again on his keyboard, my mobile phone beeped with a text message alert. It was from Cody. "What's shakin? Call me," it read.

"You're right, she's Duante's sister," Grier said. "Twenty-two years old. You saw her in San Jose?"

"You got a picture of her?" I asked. Grier nodded and motioned for me to come behind his desk. I looked and saw a driver's license blown up on his monitor.

"Yeah, she was in San Jose all right," I said.

"What's she up to?" he asked.

"That's a good question."

•   •   •

Grier wanted to split for home, so our conversation ended there. I drove away, fighting the urge to stop at Whiskey Dicks for a shot or two. The calm, relaxed state I'd felt before meeting Grier had vanished. I'd convinced myself earlier that Lamar Tucker was living at the Skyscape condos under the assumed name of Farid Insaf. But Lamar Tucker was dead. He had died when his son was just nine years old. If I had any doubt, all I had to do was look at the graphic pictures from the prison death report Grier had printed for me.

But the man at the Skyscape bore a family resemblance to Duante Tucker. Or did he? They all look the same, racists like to say. I stopped at a light on Highway 50 and flipped through the pages to a mugshot of Lamar Tucker from 1994. His heavily lidded eyes started back at me, hostile and threatening. His son had the same eyes, but what about the man at the Skyscape? Similar, but not quite the same.

And what about Shanice Tucker, the stunning vixen—what could she possibly have to do with all of this? Running around and performing tricks with, of all people, SJPD captain Russ Landers. Duante Tucker's little sister, her beauty such a contrast to the ugliness of her brother's acts.

I parked in my garage and went inside. Candi was sitting on the couch, one leg outstretched, surfing the channels.

"Ready for happy hour?" I asked. I walked to the kitchen and began mixing a double whiskey seven.

"Sure," she said.

When I came to the couch, she took a ceramic pipe from a Tupperware container and packed the bowl with s small bud of marijuana. She stood, lit up, then exhaled out an open window next to the front door. We have an even distribution of vice, Candi and I. She smokes, I drink. I find the arrangement convenient, especially when I've had a few and she drives. My DUIs are over ten years old, but I can't afford another.

I drained half my drink in a long pull. "I thought I was getting somewhere on my case this morning," I said. "But Marcus Grier just blew my theories out of the water."

"That's too bad. What do you do now?"

"Keep peeling the onion—come up with new theories."

"Nothing more specific?" she asked.

"I got to sleep on it, Candi." I finished my drink and headed to the kitchen for a refill. But before I got there, my cell rang. It was Cody.

"Is your old lady within earshot?" he said.

"Yeah."

"Well, go into your office. I got to tell you something."

"Like what?"

"You need to call me back when it's more convenient?"

"Hold on." I waved at Candi, went to my desk, and closed the door behind me.

"Go ahead," I said.

"Last night, after you left, I call this one lady I've been dating on and off, but it seems she's boogied on for greener pastures. So I head over to the Ready Room for a few pops. Then I drove over to Mulligan's, but the place was deadsville. A couple more drinks, and I get this idea, why not pay a visit to the African queen, do some recon?"

"You drove to her apartment?"

"Yeah," he said. "I sat out front for a while, and the light was on in the window, so I figure, why not? Maybe she's in a social mood, strike up a conversation, never know what I might learn. So I go knock on the door and she answers. She looks me over and says smooth as silk, 'May I help you?'"

"What did you say?"

"I said I was a friend of Russ Landers, and she didn't bat an eyelash. She just smiled and invited me in and asked if I wanted a drink. She was wearing this short terrycloth robe that barely covered her ass. I sat on the couch, and she brought me a beer, then she sits next to me with her legs curled under her. I asked her how long she's known Landers, and she says not long. Then I ask if she knows he's a cop, and she doesn't say anything, just smiles with her eyes—and you've heard of bedroom eyes, she takes it to the next level. I ask her if she knows anyone living at the Skyscape condos. 'Maybe I do,' she says, and her robe was falling open in front, and she starts running her fingernail along my thigh. And, Dirt, I shit you not, I thought my dong was gonna rip through my pants."

I took a deep breath. "And then what happened?"

"I asked her to tell me about Farid Insaf. And that threw her for a second. Then she says, what about him? I say, he's hanging out with a known rapist and killer, and I ask if she's aware of that. She shakes her head no, then she puts her leg over mine, and she's got nothing on under that robe. And then she whispers in my ear, 'You ready to party?'"

I squeezed my eyes shut and pinched the bridge of my nose. "Let me guess, by this time it was a rhetorical question."

"Yeah, pretty much, given she had already started groping my pole. We went at it right there on the couch, and whore or not, she was the most wild, exotic piece of ass I ever had."

"How much did it cost you?" I asked.

"Who cares how much?" he replied. "She cleaned out my wallet. But I'm going to expense it to Addison."

"Cody?" I said.

"Yeah?"

"You just banged Shanice Tucker. Duante's sister."

"Oh." The line went silent. "You're sure?"

"She's the registered owner of the tan Ford. Did you get any meaningful information out of her?"

He cleared his throat. "Not really. No."

"But now she knows you're interested in her brother and Farid Insaf."

"I suppose…yeah."

"I hope it was worth it," I said.

"Relax, man," he said. "I don't think it's a big deal."

I rubbed at my temples, hoping to stem the headache I felt coming on.

"There is one more thing," Cody said.

"What?"

"I snagged her cell phone before I left."

"You're kidding."

"Would I bullshit you?"

"Hmm," I said.

•   •   •

When I woke the next morning, I checked my computer and saw Cody had e-mailed me updated audio files from the bugs I planted at Lennox Suggs's house. While brewing a pot of coffee, I considered the prospect of spending a couple tedious hours on the tapes. Then I went to my desk and instead began a public records search for the address at the Skyscape condos.

I started with the Santa Clara County assessor website, then I tried the web address for the clerk/recorder. Next I went to the tax collector site, but it was closed for maintenance. For an hour I probed and prodded, trying different search criteria at a variety of public record portals. Finally I found a real estate link that revealed the parcel number for unit 1602 at the Skyscape. The unit was reported as sold six months ago. I went back to the assessor site and searched using the parcel number. It took another half hour for the Internet to cough up the detail I was looking for. Unit 1602 had been sold by a firm representing the Skyscape management group to another real estate company based in Denver.

The website for Clocker, Daniels, and Partners described a company that used investor money to acquire "commercial and residential properties in key growth segments and markets." I called their Denver phone number and asked to speak with someone regarding the unit at the Skyscape. The receptionist transferred me to a polite man who said that although his company did own the unit, they did not handle its leasing. For that, he referred me to the main phone number at the Skyscape.

I hung up and sat with my elbows on the desk. Why not extract information on the resident of 1602 from the people who worked on the ground floor at the Skyscape? It seemed simple enough. The most obvious ploy would be to flash a badge and claim to represent a police agency. But in doing so, I would be recorded on security cameras committing a felony—one the courts prosecute with unusual vigor.

A less risky option would be to bribe the receptionist or one of the sales agents, maybe offer $500 for a copy of the tenant file, which would include Farid Insaf's lease application. But I doubted a bribe would work, not in a situation where people would be risking their jobs, and not in a place that puts a priority on security. And if we tried and failed, Insaf would likely be alerted. I rolled my eyes. Given Cody's indiscretion, that might already be a moot point.

Of course, we could simply barge in and strong-arm the information. But that would definitely result in a police complaint. A safer approach might be to coerce one of the agents outside the building, follow him home, and tell him to provide the tenant file or else. That might work, but it could just as easily backfire and invite police attention. Despite his inclinations, I doubted Cody would want to risk it.

Blackmail was a thought that might hold some merit. Take some compromising photos, maybe of the Skyscape's gay sales associate in bed with a boyfriend. But I disliked blackmail as a general tactic. It was not only often sordid, but rarely went smoothly.

Another option was breaking and entering in the dead of night, when I assumed there would be no attendant at the main desk. If the building was less secure, that might be a tenable approach. But the Skyscape was full of security cameras and electronic locks and certainly had a modern alarm system. Breaking in would only be a last-ditch, desperation tactic—unless we could devise some way to do it and avoid detection.

I went out to the kitchen and had toast and more coffee with Candi, who sat on the couch with our furry gray cat snuggled in her lap. Streaks of sunlight were patterned across the carpet, and when I looked out the window, the sky was brilliant against the ridgeline. I walked out the front door and into the morning sunlight to a granite boulder just inside the fence line. When I first moved here, I'd found the big rock in the meadow and rolled it into my yard. I had some vague plan to plant flowers around it, but I never did. I sat on the rock and tossed the dregs of my coffee onto the dirt and rested my palms against the stone's coarse, heated surface. The smell and feel of the granite made me think of assembling my rock-climbing gear and trekking out beyond the meadow to where stone walls rose among the pines. But for now, I had desk work that needed to get done.

Back in front of my computer, I put on earphones and began playing the audio files from the last twelve hours at Lennox Suggs's house. I allotted two hours to review the files, but twenty minutes later I was done. There were no voice imprints, not even a grunt or a cough. Suggs must not have been home. Either that or the bugs had failed.

I flipped open the notebook I'd been using to record the details of the case. Scattered across the pages were various theories, suppositions, and hunches, along with addresses, names, license plate numbers, and interview summaries. My eyes roved over the pages, searching for an angle to pursue. I stopped when I saw "Abdul's Mediterranean Cuisine."

Fresh from the Skyscape title search, I was able to find the proprietor of the restaurant in just fifteen minutes. Being a commercial property, the data was far easier to access than that of a private residence. A year ago, a liquor license had been granted to Abdul Talwar for use at Abdul's Mediterranean Cuisine. I ran a public records search on Abdul Talwar, and apparently it was not a common name; there were many Talwars, but only one Abdul Talwar. A thirty-nine-year-old man, previous addresses in Pennsylvania and New Jersey, most recent address in Fremont, California. Four known relatives listed: a wife, a ten-year-old son, and two cousins, all living in Fremont.

We had suspected Duante Tucker and Lennox Suggs had bought heroin at Abdul's, an Arabic restaurant that served lousy food. It was hard to imagine the restaurant doing much legitimate business, although a liquor license wasn't cheap, so Abdul had to have made a significant investment in the place. If all their cuisine was as bad as the tasteless chicken kabob Cody had ordered, maybe Abdul—and maybe his cousins, too—were relying on drug money to stay afloat.

"So what?" I asked aloud, drumming my fingers on the desk. *So follow the money,* I said to myself.

I turned to a blank page in my notebook and wrote "Duante Tucker" in the middle of the sheet. In the surrounding spaces, I added the attorney, Darrian Bannon, then Farid Insaf, Lennox Suggs, Abdul Talwar, and Duante's sister, Shanice. I paused for a moment, then to the side, I wrote "South Lake Tahoe PD," and then I neatly printed "Russ Landers."

Criminals, all of them, including someone in South Lake Tahoe PD who took a bribe to dispose of the DNA. But what were the connections?

I picked up my cell to call Cody, but before I could enter his number, the phone rang in my hand.

"Investigations."

"Hey, No Problemo Reno, Ryan Addison here. I just took a look at your progress report."

"Yes?" In the background I could hear voices and music.

"Forgive me in advance, my man, but you seem to be burning a bunch of calories going nowhere."

"That's not true," I said.

"I mean, you *think* Duante Tucker is living with someone named Farid Insaf, but you don't have any clue who Insaf is?"

"It's a work in progress." A loud splash and a cheer erupted, and Addison said, "Hold on a second." The sound became muffled, but I could hear a voice yell, "Someone get her top!"

"Sorry about that," Addison said when he came back on the line. "We have some folks from the studio visiting, and we're having a barbeque. You're welcome to drop by if you like, rub elbows with some movie people."

"Thanks, but I'll pass," I said.

"Not in a social mood, huh?"

"Actually, I'm working, Mr. Addison. On your case."

"Well, how about Cody Gibbons? He's invited, too."

"He's in San Jose right now. I'll be headed back there shortly."

"That's too bad. Cassie will be disappointed. She has a thing for Gibbons, the lusty wench."

I looked at my watch. It was not yet eleven, and Addison sounded drunk.

"Is there anything else?" I asked.

"Yes," Addison said, and he must have changed locations, because the background noise ceased. When he spoke, his casual tone was gone, and his words sounded forced, as if he were speaking with his hand clutched to his throat.

"Every day Duante Tucker is free is like a saw blade cutting into the soul of my family," he said. "Lindsey is irreversibly fucked up. She was an innocent victim of a vicious psychopath, and she'll never be the same. Now, I hired you because you're the legitimate article, so don't deny it. I want Tucker to go down in flames. And I want him to suffer first, just like Lindsey did. That's why I'm paying you. Do you hear me?"

"My ears work fine."

"Good. Cassie is putting your check in the mail. I expect your next report will have a little more meat on the bone, right?"

"That's the goal."

"Well, don't just say it, do it."

"I should let you get back to your guests."

"Fine, then."

There was an awkward pause, then I said, "Good-bye, Mr. Addison."

"Adios," he replied.

I set the phone down and ran my hand through my hair. I really didn't know what to make of Ryan Addison and his surrounding cast of characters. They all seemed like actors practicing roles, one moment serious and contrite, the next animated, outraged, or even deranged. I suppose the ability to adopt varied personas is a valuable trait in the acting business, but to practice in real life situations? I shook my head.

At least Addison was consistent about one thing, though; he wanted Duante Tucker dead. And I didn't think that was an act.

• • •

By three o'clock I was on the road back to San Jose, after some unanticipated early afternoon bedroom activity with Candi. Before leaving the house, I checked the gear I kept locked in the steel toolbox bolted to my truck bed. Arranged in a shoebox atop my bullet proof vest were my 35 mm camera and a miniaturized camera, which was obsolete, given the picture-taking capability of smartphones. Next to the cameras lay my Beretta .40-cal pistol and two loaded eleven-round magazines. The Beretta was fifteen years old, but it was far from obsolete. It never jammed, the action was quick and smooth, and it was just as lethal as the day I bought it.

In a second shoebox were a pair of binoculars, a variety of listening devices that were mostly old and in need of replacement, and a collection of fake badges and face makeup, including glasses with noncorrective lenses and a kit for applying phony facial hair. Just before backing out of the garage, I placed my nylon climbing rope in the steel box, along with a rappelling device and a couple of carabiners.

As soon as I cleared Echo Summit and the cellular signal improved, I called Cody. "Got any plans tonight?" I asked.

"Plans? Yeah, I've been invited to audition for Dancing with the Stars."

"I didn't realize you were so popular."

"I'm not. I'm in a slump, man," he said.

"I thought you just had the wildest piece of ass of your life."

"I feel like a dumbass for that, I have to admit."

"Have you done anything with her phone yet?" I asked.

"No. It's password protected. I can't see call history, texts, nothing. I dropped it off yesterday to a guy who'll decrypt it."

"Good. Why don't you get some rest, take a nap if you can. I want to work tonight."

"What you got it mind?" he said.

"We haven't seen Farid Insaf leave the Skyscape during the day. So let's try after dark."

I heard him blow out his breath. "Did you hear anything interesting at Suggs's house?" he asked.

"No, not a goddamned thing. I don't think he was home."

"I got the same result. So, you want to pull an all-nighter?"

"You got any better ideas?"

• • •

When I came off the final rolling grade just north of Fremont, I could see a band of midsummer smog resting over the bowl of Silicon Valley. I made my way through the last of the rush hour traffic and met Cody at his office at seven thirty. We walked to an outdoor café and ate standing at the bar, then we drove to the Skyscape. The sun was just disappearing behind the Diablo Range when we pulled over at the curb. The day's heat had faded, and I could feel a cool breeze when I opened my window.

Cody got out of my truck, knelt behind the cab, and focused his binoculars up at the balcony for unit 1602. "All quiet," he said.

A few minutes went by, and the dusk turned to full dark. Unlike many of the other balconies, there was no light behind the glass doors at 1602. Over the next couple hours, we watched every car that came and went from the underground garage. There was a light over the steel garage gate, and it illuminated the faces of the drivers to the extent that we could easily discern if a face was black or otherwise. By midnight the trickle of cars ceased. We had not seen a single black person.

We sat in my truck. The light at 1602 hadn't come on since we'd arrived. "The man's a smoker," Cody said. "I don't think anyone's home."

"Maybe you're right."

"You want to stay longer?" he asked.

"Yeah."

"Why?"

"We need to be patient," I said.

Two hours passed. The street was quiet and without activity during that time. It was two thirty on a Thursday morning, but I was wide awake. I reached behind my seat and yanked my duffel bag onto my lap.

"What's up?" Cody said. He'd been dozing for the last half hour or so.

I pulled a black shirt over my head. "It's time for plan B."

"What you got in mind?"

"We're going to take the elevator from the garage to the top. Then I'm going to rappel down to the balcony of 1602."

"Are you fucking serious?"

"As a heart attack," I said.

"You got a rope?"

"Yeah. There's no lock on the balcony doors."

"You sure about that?"

"There wasn't in the rental unit I looked at. And the door latch on 1602 looks identical."

He shook his head. "You're nuts, man."

"Like you said, I don't think anyone's home." I got out of the truck, opened the lockbox behind the cab, and stepped into my climbing harness. Then I cinched my shoulder holster tight on my chest. Cody came out into the cool darkness and watched me gear up.

"What do you want me to do?" he asked.

"When we get to the top, I need you to watch and make sure I can get into 1602. I'll signal you if all's okay. Then pull the rope up and meet me back here."

"What if it's locked and you can't get in?"

"Then I'll have to climb back up."

Cody shook his head. "I realize you think you're a badass mountain man, but it's fourteen stories you'd have to climb."

I tied a double figure-eight knot and clipped a carabiner through the loop. "I know what I'm doing. How about grabbing me a few bugs and a transmitter?"

While Cody retrieved his bag from the cab, I put a small flashlight, a roll of duct tape, and my cell phone into a waist pack. Then I pulled a black beanie low over my ears and began attaching a phony goatee to my chin.

"Look up," Cody said. "You're making a mess of it." He put his big fingers on my face and pressed the fake whiskers into place.

"I've only got three bugs left," he said. He dropped them into my pack along with the tennis ball–sized transmitter.

"When we approach the elevator, we'll come in from the left," I said. "There's a camera aimed at the keypad. If we stay left of it, we should be out of range. Let's go."

We walked across the street to the kiosk in front of garage. I punched in the code I'd seen Shanice Tucker use to enter the premises. The garage door slid back smoothly, and we went in. The lighting was dim, and our sneakers squeaked against the polished concrete as we made our way to the elevator. I approached the elevator door from the left and reached out and tapped in Shanice's code. The door pinged and opened right away. We got in, and I pushed the button for the top floor, but I was fairly certain the elavator would allow us access only to the sixteenth. We began moving upward.

"What are you going to do if someone's home?" Cody said. "Shoot them?"

"I've got my stun gun in my pack. I'll use it if I have to."

"I've seen guys take a jolt and keep on coming."

"Not this stun gun. Not when it's turned on high."

We rode in silence until the elevator came to a stop.

"They got a security guard making the rounds?" Cody asked.

"Let's hope not."

Like I suspected, the door opened at the sixteenth floor, and we had to take the stairs the rest of the way. We silently climbed fourteen floors to a door that opened to the roof of the building. The only illumination came from a pulsing red light affixed to a thirty-foot pole on the far side of the building. When the light blinked, I could see the exercise machines facing out from the windows of the fitness center. There was a soft wind blowing, and the water in the swimming pool glittered with silver reflection.

"This way," I said. We walked along the edge of the pool, past the lounge chairs and tables and folded umbrellas to the two fences at the roofline. I stepped over the waist-high bar of the first fence and rested my hand on the cold steel of the outer fence. It was made of three large horizontal tubes, each about twelve inches in diameter. The posts were the same size and shape. I rapped on a tube with my knuckles. A hollow ring sounded.

With my arm hooked around a post, I leaned out and looked over the edge and saw I was about twenty feet left of the flat concrete portion beside the column of balconies. The surrounding rooftops below were dark. The street, three hundred feet beneath me, looked tiny. I walked ten paces left and looked again.

"Right here." I lifted the coil of rope off my shoulder.

"You sure about this, Dirt?"

I looped the end of the rope around the welded crease where the tubes intersected. The metal had a glossy finish. I looked up at Cody. His shaggy hair looked garish in the flashing light.

"Piece of cake, man. I'll flash you when I get to the balcony. Two flashes means pull the rope up and boogie."

Cody stared at me, his eyes like green marbles. "All right," he said.

I finished double-knotting the rope around the tubes and clipped my carabiners and rappelling device in place. Then I ducked between the tubes, pulled the rope taught, and began lowering myself over the side.

Once my feet were firmly planted on the wall, I checked the angle of the rope and saw that it might come in contact with the concrete edging of the roofline as I lowered myself. Too much of that could cause the rope to snap. If I had to climb up, I might be up shit creek.

I took a couple steps downward, then eased off my hold, lowered myself a foot or two, and jumped out and descended past the first balcony. I paused for a moment when I came back in contact with the wall and looked up. The sky was black except for a pulsing red glimmer off a low strip of clouds. I flexed my ankles, jumped again, and dropped another twelve feet past the second balcony. Pleased and a bit exhilarated, I pushed off harder and swooped past two more. The rope above quivered with tension.

I continued in this fashion, rappelling in twenty-five-foot increments. None of the balconies were lit, and the only sound was the whir of rope through the steel mechanism I held in my palm. It took perhaps a minute to count off the balconies to my destination.

When I reached 1602, I had to grip the wall and push myself a couple feet horizontally before I could grasp the balcony railing. Then I pulled myself close and put my foot on the concrete floor and stepped over, smooth and easy. I crouched low and stared through the dark glass doors. No light, no movement.

I eased opened my carabiner and let the rope fall free. My eyes straining, I peered at the door again. The door lever was stainless steel, and there was no keyhole. I touched the butt of my pistol where it rested on my chest and took my flashlight from my waist pack. My hand reached for the lever and slowly turned it. I pulled, and the door came open with barely a sound.

I removed a glove and used it to prop the door open, then reached over the balcony railing and blipped my flashlight twice. A moment later the rope began moving back up the side of the building.

I turned back to the door, eased it open, and stepped into the house. The interior was pitch-black. I stood still for thirty seconds, listening and waiting to see if my eyes would adjust. Aside from a faint hum from the ducts, it was dead silent. The only light source was natural illumination coming through the balcony doors and the windows. The moon was a sliver, and the light was next to nothing. I turned on my flashlight and pointed the thin beam of light to my left.

An old tube television sat on a pair of plastic milk crates. Across from it, a black coffee table and a couch and two folding chairs. The floor was concrete, same as the balcony. I crept across the room to the dinette. On the table, a dirty plate and a soda can. I peered down a hallway where the doors were closed, then moved into the kitchen.

The floor in the kitchen was also unfinished concrete. The counters were black granite, or perhaps a composite surface, and were covered with miscellaneous items. An empty microwave dinner box, a screwdriver, a blender, a fifth of vodka, a stack of napkins. In the corner, three postmarked envelopes. An electric bill, a water bill, and a solicitation from an interior design company. All addressed to Farid Insaf. The envelope for the electric bill had been opened. I removed the statement and photographed it.

The kitchen cabinets were occupied by a sparse collection of plastic plates and drinking glasses. Two of the cabinets were bare. I stuck a bug under the wood molding of one of them.

The cabinets beneath the counter were also randomly populated. A couple pots and pans and a stack of paper plates. I opened a third door. On the shelf was a semiautomatic pistol, an inexpensive, off-brand .32. Next to it sat a cardboard box that had once contained a DVD player. I pulled the box out. It was light. I held the flashlight in my teeth and opened the flaps. Resting on a bed of white Styrofoam were two rectangular bricks, each about three inches by a foot. They were coated in black plastic. Yellow block lettering was etched across each brick: Charge Demolition 112 with Taggant (1–1/4 lbs Comp C–4). More lettering followed—a coded or serial designation of some kind.

I took pictures with my cell, then slid the box back into the cabinet. Then I went to the couch and stuck a bug on the underlying wood frame. I peered around the room, looking for a suitable place to hide the transmitter. Between the living room and the kitchen, there weren't many options. No potted plants, no clutter of furniture or shelves. No closets, either. Finally I lay on my side, lifted the rear of the couch, and tried to wedge the transmitter into the frame. It didn't fit well, and when I lowered the couch, the transmitter was partially resting on the floor. But it wouldn't be detected unless someone moved the couch.

I walked to the hallway, where there were three doors. The one at the end was not fully closed. I assumed it was a bathroom. The other two would be bedrooms. Maybe a file cabinet was in one. Or a person. My hand moved to unzip my waist pack, where I could feel the weight of my stun gun.

I froze when I heard a faint squeak, then a rustle. I moved back, and just as I crouched behind the end of the kitchen peninsula, a bedroom door opened. A dark figure walked away from me toward the bathroom. He pushed the door open, hit the light switch, and began urinating loudly. Duante Tucker stood with his hands on his hips. He was naked, and the light fell over his shiny black skin. The cords in his neck were taut, and his back was tattooed. His ridged triceps muscles reminded me of a serrated blade.

He finished with a sigh, shook his phallus, and switched off the light. I gripped my stun gun and ducked deeper into the kitchen. Tucker's feet made no thump on the concrete floor. I waited for the sound of his bedroom door closing. A second went by. I looked up from my crouch, over the counter. And then the kitchen light came on.

Poised in a wrestler's stance, it should have been easy. I had the element of surprise on my side, and my stun gun was at the ready. I should have been able to zap Tucker into quick submission, hogtie and gag him, and search the rest of the house. As long as no one else was home.

But when Tucker came around the corner, he was quick, unbelievably quick. When I lunged at him, his bare foot shot out and kicked the stun gun from my hand. It went clattering behind me, and our eyes made the briefest of contact. The skin on his forehead was cranked tight on the bone, his nostrils flared, his eyelids pulled back as if in a windstorm. He raised his upper lip in a snarl, and I tried for my Beretta, but he swung down with a left, forcing me to raise my right arm to block. The blow glanced off the top of my head, and I swept my foot at his ankle, trying to trip him. He deftly hopped over my foot and kicked at my face. I dodged his foot but lost my balance and went to a knee. He came at me hard in a flurry of punches, his fists a blur. I dropped to my butt and aimed a kick at his crotch, and I hit him right above his large, hanging member, but it was not a disabling shot.

I was on my back now, and Tucker leapt on top of me, one hand going for my throat, the other punching at my face. I blocked a punch and got my right arm around his neck. I clenched him close, using all my strength. I felt his bare chest digging into where my pistol rested in my shoulder holster. He wedged his right hand toward the holster, but I grabbed his wrist with my free hand and wrapped my legs around his waist and pinned his body tightly against mine. He squirmed and flailed, and he was very strong, but he could not break my grip on his wrist. The most he could do was throw left-handed blows at my head and ribs. The punches were rapid, and his knuckles would leave bruises, but from his position he could not strike hard enough to force me to let go of his neck.

Sweat was beading on my forehead, and I could smell Tucker's deodorant. His close-shaved head was rough against my face. "You're gonna die, motherfucker," he hissed in my ear. I tried unsuccesfully to curl my wrist around his throat and and reach his thorax. He jerked his head, and from the corner of my eye I saw a kitchen towel hanging from the handle on the oven door. I released his wrist and snatched the towel, taking a quick punch to the head. I fed the towel to my right hand, then looped it around the back of his neck. He bucked and clawed at my holster, but before Tucker could figure out my intention, I brought my left hand around and cinched the towel around his throat. Then I pulled with both hands as hard as I could, my arms pounding with blood, my mind focused on a single thought: pull harder.

Twenty seconds of intense exertion, and his body went limp. Gasping for air, I pushed him off me and onto his back. His eyes had rolled back in his head. I yanked my automatic from its holster, stepped around his body, and pointed the barrel down the hallway. The second bedroom door remained closed. Tucker and I had made a considerable racket, banging and kicking against the kitchen cabinets. If someone was in the second bedroom, he would have heard us, unless he were one hell of a deep sleeper.

I turned Tucker onto his front and bound his wrists behind him with a plastic tie. My phony facial hair had come off and was plastered like a smashed insect against his shoulder. I peeled it free and stuffed it in my pocket, then checked for his pulse and found it. He'd regain consciousness in a minute, maybe less. I retrieved my stun gun, tied his ankles, and used a third tie to loop them to his wrists. Then I duct-taped his mouth and eyes and went down the hall to the unopened bedroom door. I was still breathing hard, and adrenalin pounded in my ears. I took a slow breath and turned the knob, but the door was locked.

I wiped at a thin trickle of blood on my cheek, then raised my leg and slammed the sole of my shoe into the door. The jamb splintered, and the door flew open with a loud crack. I found the light switch with a single swipe of my hand. A cot-sized bed in one corner, a small desk opposite. No one was in the room.

I started in the closet. Shirts and trousers neatly hung, the floor lined with a straight row of shoes. On the shelf above was a single wicker box. It contained a silver chain necklace, a couple men's rings, a rolled belt, and a pair of sunglasses. I returned the box to its place and went to the desk.

There was no computer or file cabinet, and there weren't any papers about. A letter opener, a stapler, a tape dispenser, and two pens were arranged on one side. A paper shredder to the right, perpendicular to the wall. I leaned forward and looked behind the paper shredder. In that space sat a metal box about the size of two shoe boxes attached side by side. A welded latch and hinges, and a combination lock. I lifted the box and pulled on the lock. Even if I had a screwdriver handy, it wouldn't be enough to break it.

I stuck Cody's final bug under the desk and glanced at the bed. The blanket was tucked under at the corners and folded in a sharp line at the pillow. A comforter folded in a perfect square lay at the foot of the mattress.

The remainder of the room was bare, save for a dresser with separate drawers for underwear, paired socks, and pressed T-shirts. Carrying the metal box by the lock, I went to the hall and back to the kitchen. Duante Tucker lay writhing on the floor. One elbow was bleeding, his buttocks were clenched, and the striated muscles in his shoulders were flexed and quivering against the constraints. When he heard me, he tried to yell, but the duct tape limited it to a muted garble. I turned the light off, unlocked the two bolts on the front door, and in two steps I was in the stairwell. I descended the sixteen floors rapidly and entered the dark garage. I saw no one, and thirty seconds later I climbed into my truck, where Cody eyed me expectantly.

8

"TROUBLE, SPIDERMAN?" CODY ASKED, starting the motor.

"Drive," I said. I flipped down the visor and checked my face in the mirror. My eye was beginning to swell, and there was a series of bloody scrapes on my cheek where Tucked had punched and clawed before I choked him unconscious.

We turned a corner and drove toward the ramp to the parkway. "Duante Tucker was there," I said.

Cody kept his eyes on the road. "What happened?"

"He was asleep, but got up to take a leak, then came into the kitchen. I meant to jolt him, but he kicked the stun gun out of my hand."

"Really?"

"Bastard is fast, I'll give him that."

"Then what?"

"We wrestled and I choked him out with a kitchen towel. Left him hogtied while I searched the place."

"Alive, I take it?" Cody asked.

"Yeah, alive. What, you think I would kill him?"

"If you had to. Would have been mighty convenient."

I looked over, but Cody's face was shadowed. Then we passed under a streetlight, and sharp angles of light cut across his profile. His eyes were still, his skin pale as a mannequin's.

"Sorry to disappoint you," I said.

"I'm not disappointed," he replied. "Would he have killed you if he had the chance?"

"Probably. But I was an armed intruder in his home. He would have been legally justified."

"In the old West, he would have already been lynched."

"Sounds like you were born a century too late."

"Maybe so, Dirt." We took the exit for Cody's home and turned onto his street. "Did you plant the bugs?" he asked.

"Yeah. And I got this." I lifted the metal box at my feet.

"Any idea what's in it?"

"Some decent intel, I hope."

• • •

I woke in Cody's guest room after three hours of sleep. Once I had a pot of coffee brewing, I went out to the detached garage and found a pair of bolt cutters hanging on the wall. I brought them inside, snipped the lock on the metal box, and sat on the couch with the box in my lap. Rappelling from the roof of the Skyscape and entering Farid Insaf's residence had been a risky gambit. The altercation with Duante Tucker raised the stakes. I was hoping the contents of the box would be a suitable payoff.

I pulled open the cover and saw an uneven stack of papers. The top sheet was a signed six-month lease for unit 1602 at the Skyscape. Farid Insaf's signature was scrawled at the bottom. I read over the details and found that he had paid up front for the six months. The due date for the next payment was forty-five days from now.

Beneath the lease were several receipts. Clothing, car repair, restaurants, stereo equipment. Nothing interesting except the fact that all were cash payments. No credit cards or checks.

A leather-bound album was underneath the receipts. It was half an inch thick and made a crackling sound when I opened it. It was a photo album; the pages were plastic sleeves. In the first sleeve was a team photograph of the 1977 National League Champion Los Angeles Dodgers. The pages that followed contained what looked to be a complete set of Dodgers baseball cards from that year. I recognized a few of the players—Dusty Baker, Steve Garvey, Reggie Smith, and the manager, Tommy Lasorda.

I set the album aside and looked through the thick colored paper stock at the bottom of the box. There was a promotional flyer for a 1978 Isaac Hayes concert in Anaheim, a brochure for a 1995 Cadillac Eldorado, and a Los Angeles Rams versus Dallas Cowboys game program, dated December 1981. That was it, except for a small black case that looked like it might contain a piece of jewelry.

Dust puffed from the case when I pried it open. Resting on a black cloth background was a gold heart-shaped medallion. Attached to it, a folded purple neckband. A raised bust of George Washington was on the front of the heart. I lifted it in my fingers. On the back, in raised letters, it read, "For Military Merit." Inscribed below that was a name: Lawrence Tucker.

I arranged the entire contents of the box in piles on Cody's coffee table. Sun had already cut through the morning overcast and was shining through the partially opened front window curtains. I held the medal in my hand and stared at the name. After a while, I put the medal down and began doing Internet searches. Then, despite two cups of tar coffee, I fell asleep on the couch.

It was almost noon when Cody woke me. I sat up and rubbed my eyes. "I'm starving," I said.

"I cooked some bacon and made you an omelet," he said, nodding toward the stove.

"How good of you. When did you learn how to cook?"

"Hell, I've spent more years as a bachelor then you."

"I don't remember you ever cooking a damn thing."

"That's because you refuse to recognize me as the Renaissance man I am."

"Ah. That explains it."

"What secrets did the box unlock?" Cody asked, eyeing the stacks of papers.

I handed him the black case. He squinted and fingered the medal. "Son of a bitch, a purple heart. Who's Lawrence Tucker?"

"My first guess would be Lamar Tucker's brother, using Farid Insaf as an alias."

"Do we even know if Lamar Tucker had a brother?"

"No, not yet."

"Okay, so who is *Lawrence* Tucker?"

I sat at Cody's table with a plate of chow. "Obviously ex-military."

"Be nice to have a look at his military record."

"I did a search earlier this morning. Found his serial number, but that's about it."

"How about that retired general you know?" Cody said, replacing the medal in the case.

"What about him?" I asked.

"Call him. He should have access to everything."

"Just like that, huh?"

"Why not?"

"You're assuming he would share classified information with me, just for the asking."

"You saw two slabs of military-grade C-four, Dirt. That stuff ain't commercially available. Send those pics to the general, tell him there's a national security risk at stake."

I swallowed a mouthful of Cody's cooking and looked up at him. "All right. Then let's go back to the Skyscape, see if anything's going on."

"You got any more surprises in store for me?"

"Not at the moment."

•   •   •

Retired three-star General Raymond Horvachek didn't sound displeased to hear from me, which was a pleasant surprise. I had investigated his daughter's death two winters ago, and although I'd delivered the closure he and his wife sought, it was no victory, not for them or for me. I doubted their anguish had receded much in the two years since we'd spoken, and I had no desire to revisit the matter. I imagined my voice might open a floodgate of grief.

But when I mentioned the C-4, the general became all business, as if invigorated with a sense of purpose and perhaps relieved at the distraction and a potential avenue for his energies. He confirmed Cody's suspicion that the C-4 I saw in Farid Insaf's home was almost certainly stolen, and its possession by a civilian was a crime. He also said he would have Lawrence Tucker's full military record in his hands by five o'clock today ("by seventeen hundred," he stated) and would call me later in the evening.

At two o'clock Cody and I drove off in his Toyota sedan. The sky was cloudless except for a light haze that hung low over the green mountains to the west. It was a comfortable eighty degrees outside, the high sun bathing the valley in warmth. We got on the freeway, and as we were nearing the exit for Guadalupe Parkway, I was thinking it would have been a fine day for a hike in the Santa Cruz Mountains. Then Cody said, "Check your mirror. I think we got a tail."

I turned down his passenger seat visor and flipped open the vanity mirror.

"Two cars back. Black SUV."

"I can't see them," I said.

He changed lanes. "How about now?"

"Yeah," I said. "Two black dudes. Looks like Suggs's GMC. Maybe they're headed to the Skyscape."

"Let's find out." We took the Guadalupe on-ramp, merged to the fast lane, and drove past the exit for the Skyscape.

"They're still on our ass," Cody said. "The driver is Suggs. But I don't recognize the passenger."

"Not Duante Tucker, huh?"

"No, doesn't look anything like him."

"How do you want to play it?"

"Let's find out what they want." Cody took the next exit, reversed direction, and got back on the parkway heading west toward Los Gatos. He drove at a leisurely pace, and the black GMC remained two cars behind us.

"What's the plan?" I asked.

"They want to talk, or whatever, we'll pick the place," he said.

"Like where?"

"Up in the hills."

We crossed over to Route 17, the freeway that leads over the grade to Santa Cruz. Within ten minutes we began navigating the sweeping curves heading into the mountains. We passed the sparkling waters of Lexington Reservoir on our left and the old Cats Tavern on the right. After that the forest became more dense, and the turns grew tighter. Just before we reached the summit, Cody turned off onto an auxiliary road, one that was seldom traveled—and only by the residents that lived in a few remote homes set back far off the track.

"They got to know we're onto them by now," I said.

"So what? They don't dig it, they can turn around."

"I don't think so. They're coming up quick."

"Oh, yeah?"

The road was shadowed by tall pines, and thick brush grew in tangled clumps between the trees We approached a mild bend, and Cody downshifted and hit the gas, taking us up to sixty, which was about as fast as any sane person would go on that particular stretch. We came to a corner, braked sharply, then eased around the turn and did not accelerate. We drove at twenty-five until I saw them approaching fast behind us.

"They're back," I said.

This time we were on a straightaway, and Cody mashed the gas pedal. We launched forward and hit ninety, then he slammed the brakes before a sharp right-hander. The Toyota squealed around the corner, all four tires drifting, and Cody gassed it hard again, then he cranked the wheel onto a steep side road. He drove for a couple hundred yards until we reached a dirt shoulder wide enough to execute a Y-turn. Then we drove back, and just as we approached the highway, we saw the GMC roar by.

"Let's see where they want to go." Cody worked the gear box and burned rubber, dirt and gravel spitting from the rear tires. We gained on the black SUV rapidly, right as we entered a series of corkscrew turns dropping into a gully. The road had been cut out of the hillside, a steep rock wall to our right, a sharp drop-off to the left. The Toyota's stiff suspension hugged the pavement, and in seconds we were on the bumper of the GMC.

"Take my piece out of the glove box, fire a shot over them," Cody said.

"What?"

"Let's see how serious these bad boys are. Fuck 'em if they can't take a joke."

"Bad idea," I said.

"Give me the gun, I'll do it." The SUV accelerated, its big tires howling as it lurched down the sustained right turns. Cody reached out with his paw and slapped me on the shoulder. "Come on." We drifted into the opposite lane.

"Keep your eyes on the road," I said. I opened the glove compartment and, under a stack of papers, found a Smith & Wesson short-barrel .32 automatic. A small gun, probably too small for Cody's hand, and not very accurate either, at least not past fifty feet. Someone had ground off the serial number and installed patterned grips designed to obliterate finger-prints. Cody had probably acquired the piece, untraceable and disposable, in a back alley somewhere. I pulled open the slide and saw a brass jacketed round in the chamber.

"Hurry up," he said. I could see Suggs's eyes, white against his black skin, flicking back and forth to his rear view mirror as we tailed them. For a moment I considered all the bad results that could come of this. Then I blew out my breath and stuck my arm out the window, the gun pointed up into the blue void looming over the trees on the ridge above us. Just before my finger tightened on the trigger, I saw the passenger's face in the side mirror, the dark features expressionless behind sunglasses.

The pistol bucked in my hand, sparks flashing from the barrel, the blast ear-splittingly loud. The SUV slammed its brakes, the tires skidding on the coarse pavement, then Suggs stepped on the gas and regained control. We followed at not more than ten feet from the rear doors. I could see the chassis straining against the springs as Suggs steered hard and tried to maintain speed. The roof almost scraped a rock ledge jutting from the wall as the vehicle leaned into the turn.

We came out of the corner onto a straight, sunny section. A stream ran along the road to our left, and a rolling meadow lay to the right. The GMC bolted forward, then abruptly stopped accelerating at about fifty MPH. Up ahead were more curves, the foliage deep in shadow.

For a few seconds we followed in silence. I held the pistol to the side of my seat. A pair of squirrels ran above us on a solitary telephone wire.

"They're not trying to…" I said, then paused when the SUV's rear doors flew open. The man who'd been in the passenger seat was sitting with his legs splayed before him, holding an assault rifle, probably an AR-15. He brought the rifle to his shoulder, but the doors swung back on him.

Cody hit the brakes and veered to the left. I leaned out my window and trained the automatic at the back of the SUV. The right side rear door opened, which blocked my view of the man. Cody swerved hard to the right and onto the dirt shoulder of the road, putting us out of the shooter's eyesight. We skidded, and plumes of gritty dust spewed from our tires. The SUV moved right, trying to bring us back into range. For a brief second I saw the man holding the rifle. His foot was extended to hold the door open, and he had us dead in his sights. If we moved left, back onto the pavement, it would make his shot that much easier.

A burst of shots rang out just as Cody steered further to the right, off the shoulder and into tall grass. A bullet punched through the door behind Cody and tore a hole in the back upholstery. I fired twice, but we were bouncing violently over rutted terrain, and my shots flew off into the forest. The meadow ended a hundred yards up ahead, where the paved road turned into the trees.

Our tires washed into soft dirt, and the Toyota slowed. Cody cranked the wheel and downshifted, and we banged over a ditch and onto the hard shoulder. I saw the rear door to the SUV close as it turned into the corner. We hit the asphalt skidding and fishtailed in pursuit.

In seconds we were approaching the back bumper. The road was serpentine, the turns coming quick. The SUV rocked at sharp angles with every turn of the wheel, its high center of gravity throwing it all over the road.

The rear door opened again, but the momentum of the vehicle caused it to slam shut. Then the window above the door exploded, the butt of the rifle knocking the glass from the frame. In a second the barrel was pointed at us. I extended my arm and shot into the window, but my angle was awkward, making it unlikely I'd hit the man.

I ducked low, waiting for the shooter to return fire, but at that moment the road turned sharply left, the corner tighter than the turns previous. When Suggs yanked the wheel, the sudden change in direction caused the GMC's suspension to overrebound, and the right tires lifted off the ground. The top-heavy vehicle tilted almost to the tipping point before Suggs hit the brakes. For a moment the SUV remained pitched diagonally, balanced on its left tires. Then it fell back onto all four wheels and careened to the right, toward a steep drop-off beyond the pavement.

I saw the front tires steer left, but it was too late. Skidding but still moving at about thirty-five MPH, the GMC plowed off the road and fell from sight, followed a second later by an earth-shaking crash. A dust cloud rose into the trees and a cascade of brown pine needles rained down from above.

We stopped at the SUVs skid marks, jumped out, and looked over the edge. Thirty feet down, the GMC had collided head on with a large redwood, the trunk at least four feet in diameter. The impact had thrust the SUV onto its nose, where it leaned precariously against the tree. The roof over the front seats looked smashed flat to the doors. We stared at the undercarriage of the black wreckage. The wheels were still spinning.

"Got a coat?" I asked. I went back to Cody's car and took my jacket and a pair of gloves from my bag.

"Why?"

"Poison oak down there."

"Shit. You go."

I pulled on the coat and stepped down into the dry mulch off the road. Leaves and sticks crackled as my boots sunk into six inches of loose ground cover. The grade was about forty-five degrees. I dug in my heels and descended, grabbing branches and saplings to balance myself.

When I reached the upended wreck, I had to kick a purchase in the dirt to keep from falling down into the brush. I could see that the grade steepened below and became almost vertical. I steadied myself and crouched to peer into the narrow slot still remaining in the shattered driver's window. An airbag had exploded, but I saw no indication it had saved the driver. A streak of blood was painted over the remaining chips of glass in the window, and I could see just a brief swath of dark skin, perhaps a forearm. Lennox Suggs had been crushed to death. Chances of survival, zero.

I tried to open the driver's door, but it was dented badly and jammed shut. I looked through the scrub to where Cody stood on the shoulder peering down.

"Can't get to the driver," I said.

"What about the shooter?"

I slowly traversed to the passenger side. The roof was not as deeply crushed there, and though I could look clearly into the interior, there was nothing to see except the blood-soaked pants of the driver. No one was in the passenger seat. I snaked my arm inside and tried to reach where Suggs's wallet might be, but it was too tight.

I stood and attempted to open the rear passenger door. The surrounding metal had folded in, the paint peeling off the creases. The door wouldn't budge. I stepped back and looked at the destroyed rig. Then I heard a sound from within.

"He's trying to come out the back!" Cody yelled.

I took Cody's pistol from my coat pocket and scrambled up to where I could look down at the rear doors of the SUV. But before I got there, I heard a grunt and a sprinkling of glass falling, then I saw a black man's face appear, looking down from where his torso hung out the broken rear window.

The man's face was coated with blood, which ran freely from an empty eye socket and a thick gash in his scalp. He looked at me with his remaining eye but seemed oblivious to my presence. Then he reached out with a muscular arm and slowly pushed himself farther out the window. Bubbles of blood formed on his lips. I trained the automatic at him and watched as he maneuvered out the window.

He leaned his weight out, holding the window ledge until he could grasp the rear bumper. Then he pulled, and his lower body followed, and he meant to hold on, but he was too weak, and fell in a heap into the mangled brush. As soon as he hit the ground, I heard a loud crack, and the GMC began falling toward me. I leaped away but tripped over a tangle of deadfall. I heard metal shrieking, bark tearing, and the snap of dry wood as I rolled away and tumbled downward for a second before grabbing a stout branch. The wreckage slammed down not two feet from where I lay and began sliding down the slope on its side. It slid through the scrub, leaving a scoured path, flattening small trees, picking up speed until it hit a large boulder jutting from the hillside. The vehicle flipped up with the impact, and a ray of sun penetrating the trees glinted off the twisted metal. Then the wreckage barrel-rolled and tumbled free of the hill and cartwheeled into the void until it reached somewhere unseen with a final, thunderous crash.

"Fucking Christ!" Cody shouted.

I pushed myself to my feet and made my way to where the man had fallen. I didn't know if he'd still be there. But he was, or what remained of him. The SUV had fallen over his body and crushed his legs. I knelt and put my ear to his mouth. A faint wheeze came from his lips.

"Who are you?" I said.

I felt a weak hiss of air in my ear. His breath was dank, like rotting fruit in a pool of stagnant water. "Two, seven, six, four..." he whispered.

"What?" I said. But when I pulled away and looked at him, his eye was fixed, and he breathed no more.

He wore jeans and a camo tank top. I checked his front pockets, and when I turned him onto his stomach, I saw a tattoo on his shoulder, a grinning skull resting on a pair of automatic rifles as crossbones. "Semper Fi," was scrolled below. I found a thin wallet in his back pocket.

"Time to boogie, Dirt," Cody called out. "Sirens coming, cops must have been nearby."

I scrambled through the brush up to where Cody sat in the Toyota. He put the car in gear and U-turned, and we headed back the way we'd come.

"Dismantle that piece of junk," he said. "Throw the pieces out."

I released the clip from Cody's automatic, ejected the bullets, and tossed them one by one off the side of the road. The sirens were getting louder. We came around a bend, and I chucked the slide deep into a clump of manzanita. We drove for another couple minutes before Cody turned onto a side road.

"This ain't gonna take us back to the highway," I said.

"I know. But I don't want to get spotted. Best we wait them out."

"Might take hours before the police clear out."

"You want to get questioned for this? With a fresh bullet hole in the door?"

The road turned to dirt and dead-ended at a hilltop lot that looked like it had been cleared some years ago but was never built upon. We stopped, and Cody took a day pack from his trunk, then we hiked through the dry grass to the apex of the lot. Before us lay a series of forested valleys that turned from green to shades of blue and purple. The hills rose and fell to the west until we could see where the Pacific Ocean merged with the sky.

We stood for a moment, taking it in. Amid other circumstances, I'm sure I would have enjoyed the splendid view. But I could still feel the adrenalin in my blood, and my lips were clenched tight against my teeth.

"Hey, don't look at me that way," Cody said. "I didn't plan this."

"You insisted on shooting at them."

"Right, and so what did we learn? A guy with a Marine Corps tattoo tried to take us out with an assault rifle. Now we know more about who we're dealing with."

"Bullshit," I said. "We should have pulled over, seen what they had to say."

"And risk getting shot? You're kidding, right?"

I threw up my hands. "You assume they were out to kill us. I don't."

Cody raised his eyebrows, an incredulous expression on his face. "Yeah, they probably just wanted sit down for tea and crumpets."

"I don't take dead bodies, lightly, Cody. We weren't exactly acting in self-defense."

"And we ain't exactly responsible for their fate. They shot at us with an assault rifle, and drove off the road on their own."

I spit into the weeds. "We might have been able to learn a lot more about this damn case if we could question them."

Cody made a huffing sound. "I doubt that."

I looked away from him at the panorama of color before us, the natural beauty of the view utterly incongruous with the day's events. I heard him unzip his pack.

"Here," he said. He tossed a pint bottle of Jim Beam my way. I snatched it out of the air. "You always like getting drunk when someone dies, right?"

I shook my head. "That's usually at the end of a case," I replied. But I twisted the cap and hit off the bottle anyway, the whiskey bitter in my throat. And then I took another small swig before I lobbed the bottle back to him.

"Good man." Cody winked and tilted the bottle to his mouth. He stood looking out over the ridges, then he stomped a patch of dry grass and sat and lit a cigarette. After a minute I heard the gurgle of whiskey again.

"Hey," I said.

"What?"

I sat and held out my hand. "Quit hogging the bottle."

·   ·   ·

Two hours later we drove back to the highway and into Los Gatos. I had dozed off while we were killing time, and dreamt that the black man with the missing eye and crushed legs had spoken to me before floating away in a wheelchair. The dream was short and vivid and not something born of deep sleep; really it was more like a vision that hovered just beneath my consciousness. But I couldn't remember what the man was trying to tell me.

It was six o'clock, and we stopped at a bar and grill in a strip mall at the end of University Avenue. The place had changed names since I'd last been there, but inside it hadn't changed. The bar was U-shaped under a low ceiling, and there were no windows. The lighting was minimal, as if welcoming day drinkers to an environment where it was always night, always time to drink. I had spent a Christmas Eve here during my divorce.

We took a table in the back, near a row of electronic dartboards, and ordered food from a young, tattooed waitress with torn jeans and a slender waist. When she leaned down, her loose, low-cut shirt hung from her shoulders, and her small breasts were fully visible, the nipples just touching the cloth. I looked away and pulled from my pocket the wallet I'd taken from the dead man. There was no driver's license, but a gym membership card identified him as Ahmad Jones.

"That's the recent trend in dive bars around here," Cody said when the waitress left. "Hire nubile bimbos to keep the boozers interested."

"Works for you, huh?" I said.

"Sure. I'm a sportsman."

"If whoring's a sport, you're a champ, all right."

"Well, not everyone is destined for domestic bliss." He tried to sound flippant, but there was a flicker of hurt and indignation in his eyes.

I sighed. I was still angry with Cody over the death of the two men in the SUV, which was a situation that never should have happened. I was angry at him not only because he goaded them into the altercation but also because it was likely they'd identified him because of his foolish indiscretion with Shanice Tucker. Regardless, I felt a stab of guilt over my remarks. "I didn't mean anything," I said.

"Don't worry about it."

I rubbed at the stubble on my jaw. I wished I didn't have to concern myself with Cody's personal life, which was akin to worrying about global warming, or perhaps the AIDS epidemic in Africa. But it was clear his sexual habits had become a professional liability. His affair with his SJPD boss's wife was only the tip of the iceberg. A couple years ago, we worked a case together, each of us separately hired by a woman who seduced Cody early on. Our search for her stepson, who'd won the lottery, left a number of people dead (including the stepson), and she walked away with his fortune while we barely escaped with our lives. And in a more recent episode, Cody had shown up in South Lake Tahoe with an outrageously dressed bimbo, who created a scene and stormed out of the fancy restaurant where Candi and I had joined them for dinner on New Year's Eve. The woman was found dead the next day. The chaos that ensued left me seriously considering a different line of work.

The waitress brought Cody a schooner of beer, while I sipped a cup of black coffee that no doubt had been aging since morning. Cody's impulsive and jeopardous actions made it easy to blame him for the events of the afternoon. But blaming him entirely would be to ignore my own actions. I had been the one who broke into Farid Insaf's residence and hogtied Duante Tucker. No doubt that had influenced the agenda of the men who followed us. Given that perspective, maybe Cody was right; maybe they did plan on killing us. So taking the offensive may have been the right move. But that didn't make me any happier with the outcome.

Bottom line: Farid Insaf now knew who we were and had determined we needed to be discouraged, or worse. We'd have to factor that into our tactics moving forward.

•   •   •

We ate dinner at the bar and drove back to Cody's house. At eight o'clock my cell rang. It was General Raymond Horvachek.

"I've spent the last couple hours reviewing Lawrence Tucker's history," he said. "I've got to hand it to you, Reno. You've picked an interesting subject."

"How so?"

"I'll start at the beginning. Tucker came out of the projects in Compton and enlisted in the marines in 1980. His record was exemplary for ten years, pretty impressive for a ghetto kid. By 1990 he'd been promoted to gunnery sergeant. In August 1990 he was deployed to Saudi Arabia, one of the first squads sent over for the Gulf War. When ground assaults began in January 1991, Tucker had fourteen confirmed kills before he was wounded, shot in the shoulder, a minor injury. A month later he was back with his unit, but by that time hostilities were winding down, and a cease-fire was declared."

"Okay, so we know where the Purple Heart came from," I said.

"Correct, but then Tucker went AWOL."

"In the Mideast?"

"Yes. He vanished in Kuwait, assumed to have deserted."

"Why would any sane American want to stay in the Mideast?" I asked.

"That's a good question, and here's where it gets murky. Some of the marines in Tucker's squad voiced suspicion he'd become friendly with locals in Saudi Arabia. The MP investigated and came up empty but conjectured that Tucker potentially posed a threat to US interests. So they forwarded the case to the CIA."

"What kind of threat?"

"The initial assumption involved opium trafficking, which in itself is not enough to concern the CIA. But the Taliban and al-Qaida rely heavily on heroin revenue to fund their organizations."

"So the CIA thought Tucker was involved with al-Qaida?" I asked.

"They had suspicions because some of the Saudis he knew were linked to the Taliban in Afghanistan. Understand, Afghanistan is a nightmare for us. Our troops are trying to eradicate the Taliban, but we can't do it without the support of the rural tribes. If the tribes side with the terrorists, we're screwed; we can never win. So we try to make nice with the tribes, who are not much more than a ragtag group of millions of poor farmers living in places you or I wouldn't use for a latrine. Guess what crop makes up the biggest portion of the tribe's income?"

"Opium."

"You got it. I'll tell you, we'd like nothing more than to burn every poppy field in that godforsaken region and screw al-Qaida's revenue stream. But in the long term, that would be a losing strategy because if we turn those tribes against us, al-Qaida will have a safe haven, one protected by the majority of the Afghan population."

"How does Lawrence Tucker fit into all this?"

"Be patient," Horvachek said. "I'll get to that. You might ask, so do we just let the Afghans harvest their poppy crops and allow it be processed into heroin and distributed? No, we don't. Our strategy today is to let the famers sell their crops and then we intercept the heroin before the money finds its way to the terrorists."

"How successful have we been?"

"Somewhat," he answered. "But here's where Tucker comes in. In 1997, CIA operatives in Pakistan identified Tucker in a video clip they'd acquired. Tucker was spotted with a group of unsavory Arabs, all objects of US interest. We're talking brothers of political bigwigs, oil rich sheiks suspected of kidnapping American women to staff their harems, and two known terrorists who had ties to Bin Laden. This was the first surfacing of Tucker since he deserted."

"So he'd been living over there the whole time?"

"Apparently. He was bearded and wearing a turban and robes. They only discovered it was him when they used facial recognition software."

"You said 1997," I mused. "That was one year after Lamar Tucker was killed."

"Who?" asked Horvachek.

"Is there any record of Lawrence Tucker's family?" I asked. "Siblings?"

I heard the rustling of papers. "Yes," the general replied. "Lamar Tucker, younger brother. Was he in the service?"

I paused for a self-congratulatory moment, then said, "I don't think so. He also grew up in Compton, dealt drugs with the Crips until he was sent to jail and murdered by the Aryan Brotherhood."

"Sounds like drug trafficking runs in the family. Anyway, in 1998 the DEA boarded a freighter as it approached the Port of Oakland, and seized eighty kilos of pure heroin. The CIA linked the shipment back to an Afghani drug lord. Lawrence Tucker allegedly brokered the deal."

"Was Tucker arrested?"

"By who, the Afghani police? Not a chance. But he did drop off the radar after that for a number of years. His whereabouts were unknown until 2004, after we'd invaded Iraq and captured Saddam Hussein. I spent two years in Iraq during that time, and the entire region was a massive cluster-fuck. Iraq was teetering on civil war, various factions of Shiites and Sunnis were fighting for power, suicide bombings happened daily, and a new brand of ultraviolent al-Qaida emerged in Iraq. Despite heavy US military presence, to say Iraq was lawless would be an understatement.

During this mayhem, the CIA was monitoring a senior al-Qaida member's e-mail. There were repeated references to an individual they called Black Dog. He was involved in training al-Qaida soldiers for pay. In one of the e-mails, he was referred to as an American ex-soldier loyal to radical Islamic causes."

"Meaning terrorism?" I asked.

"Right," said Horvachek. "But he was also called greedy and not a true Muslim, so it seemed his relationship with the fundamentalists was somewhat tenuous. Anyway, the CIA confirmed this man was Lawrence Tucker, and we tried to take him out in a drone attack at a terrorist training camp in Afghanistan.

"Unsuccessful, I take it?"

"His death was considered likely but was never verified."

"And?"

"That was the last we've heard of him."

I rose from my chair at the kitchen table. Cody was sitting on his couch, the television on mute, his eyes staring at me. "I've got another name I'd like you to check," I said. "A marine, or ex-marine. Ahmad Jones. Black male. Thirty years old."

"He's connected to Lawrence Tucker?" Horvachek asked.

"Maybe," I said, and paused long enough for him to say, "Yes?"

"General," I said, "I believe Lawrence Tucker is alive and is in the US."

"How do you know this?" he demanded.

"Would the CIA still like to get their hands on him?"

"He's a deserter who's cavorted with the Taliban. What do you think?"

"I need a little more time to confirm it's him. I'll update you when you get the G-2 on Ahmad Jones."

"Reno, Lawrence Tucker is considered an enemy of the people. If you have information to his whereabouts, you need to report it immediately."

"I hear you," I said.

You mess with the CIA, you're in over your head, son."

"What else is new?" I replied.

• • •

"Jesus Christ," Cody said. "Lawrence of Arabia, what a piece of work. Ditches the marines, sets up shop peddling opium in camel jockey land, and on the side trains suicidal ragheads who'd like nothing more than to pull off an encore to nine-eleven." He paced around his living room. "Two bricks of C-4 in his closet, and who knows how much more he has?"

"We report him, the CIA will grab him, and we'll never see him again."

"So what?"

"Lawrence Tucker is the key to the case, Cody. He's the one who hired the attorney. He's the one who paid off someone to disappear the evidence. He's the one who went to a lot of trouble to make sure Duante Tucker wasn't prosecuted."

"How do you reach those conclusions?"

"He's got money, and he's spent the last twenty years surviving in the most hostile region on the planet, in a place where he could be killed simply because he's an American. This is a guy who knows how to operate and thrive in the underworld, where rules and laws and allegiances change without warning. He's a special kind of guy. He's also Duante Tucker's uncle."

"Fine, but why would he go to the trouble to free the shitbag?"

"Don't know yet," I admitted.

"Dirt, we got other angles to play here. I just got e-mailed updated audio files from Suggs's house."

"Suggs is dead," I reminded him.

"Yeah, that's a shame," he said. "But I'd like to hear what he was talking about before he bit the dust, wouldn't you?"

"Yeah, I would. What about the bugs from the Skyscape?"

"Nothing yet. Should get an e-mail tomorrow."

"How about Shanice Tucker's mobile phone?"

"Haven't heard from the encryption dude." Cody sat on a chair across from me. "I'll call him."

"Let's keep our eye on the ball, all right?" I said. "Ryan Addison hired us to uncover who was behind Duante skating on the rape charge. He also wants justice done—he wants Duante to pay for the crime."

"One way or another."

"We find out how that evidence disappeared, maybe Duante will be retried. Maybe—"

Cody laughed. "You're dreaming. First, he's protected by double jeopardy, and second, even if we could find the DNA evidence, it would be tainted. Any defense attorney would tear it apart. Sorry, Dirt, it ain't gonna happen that way."

I felt my face twist in a grimace. I got up and went to Cody's refrigerator, but I wasn't hungry or thirsty. When I came back to the couch, I said, "Whatever Lawrence Tucker's up to, he's gonna be extra cautious now."

"Extra cautious? Or maybe extra motivated to take us out."

I grunted and bent down to tie my shoelace. A flash of light panned the room through the partially drawn drapes on the big window overlooking Cody's front yard. I looked up in time to see a car creeping along. It wasn't just one car; two sedans had stopped across the street. I peered out, watching as the four car windows facing us simultaneously lowered. I froze for a second when I saw the glint off a rifle barrel, then I yelled, "Take cover!" and dove to the floor. An instant later the front window exploded in a shower of glass. A row of bullets tore into the couch above me. Cody flipped backward in his recliner just before a series of rounds stitched the bottom of the chair and blew chunks of wood into the air.

The staccato clatter of automatic weapons fire continued. At least two shooters, I estimated. Bullets ripped through the house, shattering the television screen, reducing a potted plant to a pile of dirt and clay fragments, and blasting large chips out of the tile counters in Cody's kitchen.

"I'm hit," Cody said. I was pressed flat to the carpet. I looked up and saw blood soaking through the thigh of his jeans. "I can't fucking believe this," he said.

I pulled my belt out of its loops and shimmied on my stomach to where he lay. "Stay flat," I said, and tied the belt above the wound. Then I crawled on my stomach toward the laundry room, where I had set my gear bag next to a door to the side yard.

The hail of bullets paused. I pulled my Beretta .40 semiauto from the bag and stuck an extra eleven-round clip in my pocket. Crouching low, I turned the light off, opened the side door, and stepped onto a strip of baked dirt. The side yard was fenced in by seven-foot-tall wood planks. I ducked under the branches of a large tree growing near the front of the strip. Then I stepped up on the utility meter, wedged one foot against the tree, and looked over the fence. A slice of moon lit the clear night. The two cars idled across the street. The trailing car was a Chevy sedan. From its rear seat, a black man got out and brought a small weapon with a large clip to his shoulder. An Uzi, or a similar piece. I put him in the Beretta's sights and pulled the trigger just as he took a step forward. At about sixty feet, the Beretta was a sure thing. The slug hit the man in the center of the chest, and he bounced off the car and fell flat on his face.

In a fluid motion I turned my pistol on the car in front, a Ford four-door. I fired six shots, blowing out the windows, the lead punching through the doors, and then I fired twice more at a dark figure moving in the front seat. Each pull of the trigger jolted my arm with a force of an eighteen-pound sledge hitting a railroad tie.

What happened next I would later think of as a microcosmic culmination of two hundred years of racial prejudice and a resulting culture that inspired poor black teenagers to become ghetto thugs. I would think in context of a race brought across an ocean to serve as slaves and winning their freedom, only to be relegated to the lowest strata of society. I would think of single mothers, abusive or imprisoned fathers, tenement apartments without heat, hungry children, desperate financial predicaments, and a criminal element that recruited innocent youngsters and taught them that not only was gangsta life the sole path to material comfort, but also that there was nothing wrong with dying young, if only one could enjoy a few good years. I would think these thoughts with an underlying of sadness before reminding myself that many of the people I came across had choices but, being evil at heart, chose evil.

The rear door of the lead car opened on the side opposite me. A man came around the front of the car, pointing his handgun my direction, palm down. His clothes were oversize, from his floppy beanie to his T-shirt and baggy jeans. He was festooned with silver and gold necklaces and sported matching rings and grill work.

"Come get some a dis, bitch!" he yelled, walking forward, the moonlight glinting off the silver on his front teeth. He raised his hand and started shooting. The first round passed over my head, and the second hit the tree a couple feet to my right. Before he could fire again I squeezed the trigger, but my aim was imperfect. The slug hit him in the crotch, and he went down with a squeal and started writhing on the pavement.

The driver of the Chevy sedan reacted by shifting into reverse, but he must have slammed the gas pedal to the floor, because the single rear tire shrieked and spun futilely, spitting gutter water, and the vehicle barely moved. I fired twice through the windshield, and the howl of the motor ceased. The car began rolling backward, billows of smoke rising from the wheel well. I ejected the spent clip and jammed in a fresh magazine. A man tried to jump out of the still-moving sedan, but I shot him before he could fully exit, and his torso folded under the chassis, his legs caught inside, and then he came free and the right front tire rolled up on him, stopping the car. The weight of the vehicle would have crushed him to death, but I was pretty sure he didn't feel a thing, because I'd seen my round exit the side of his head.

From my perch I methodically fired seven more shots into the Chevy. I targeted carefully, aiming low in the windows. With three rounds remaining, I pulled myself up and jumped over the fence. Both cars sat still. I walked to where the man I wounded lay curled on the asphalt. His breath came in tortured wheezes, but when he saw me he didn't plea for help or mercy. Instead, he raised his gun, a final glimmer of hate still burning in his pupils. I shot first, and the light instantly went out of his eyes, and then blood spilled from the hole in his forehead.

"Life would have sucked with your balls blown off anyway," I said.

•   •   •

After checking the cars and seeing nothing but dead bodies, I rushed inside and found Cody sitting upright and pulling on the tourniquet around his thigh.

"There goes the neighborhood," he said, trying to smile. "Sounded like fucking World War Three."

I became aware of sirens, the volume increasing. "I'm calling an ambulance," I said. "You hurt bad?"

"You ever hear of anyone hurt good?"

I looked at his blood-soaked pants and the stain on the carpet. "The paramedics will be here in a couple minutes."

"It didn't hit bone. But the bullet's still in there."

"I'll get you some water. You look a little pale."

"Make it a can of Coors and pour me a shot of Beam, too."

I brought him his drinks, then took the ends of my belt and worked the tourniquet. And that's the way the San Jose PD found us when they stormed into Cody's house a few minutes later.

• • •

The uniforms were followed closely by four plainclothesmen, then the ambulances pulled up, along with a medical examiner. They closed off the street, and more cops arrived to keep the neighbors at bay. Within five minutes there were more than a dozen vehicles on the street, half with blue and red lights swirling atop their roofs. I stood on the front lawn surrounded by policemen, as if I was the main attraction at some sort of macabre carnival.

I ignored their questions until I saw that Cody was loaded in an ambulance. Then two plainclothesmen took me aside and asked what had happened.

"A drive-by shooting. Except they took their time, which gave me the chance to defend myself."

"Defend yourself? There's six dead bodies out there!" The detective was a stocky Hispanic man with cocked eyebrows and a round chin.

"They didn't expect anyone to return fire. They were on their way into the house to finish us off."

"Why would someone want to kill you?" The second detective was a woman in her forties. Her face looked leached of moisture, the skin dry and wrinkled, and her frown looked so permanent I wondered how much muscular energy she'd have to expend to muster a smile.

"I'm a licensed investigator and bounty hunter. I also have a license to carry the firearm." I took my wallet from my back pocket and handed the woman my ID cards.

"What, you think this grants you some kind of immunity?"

"Immunity from what?" I asked.

"I wouldn't even know where to start," she said.

"Come on, we're heading downtown," the other cop said. He put his hand on my arm and began toward his car.

"Do I need to call my lawyer?"

"I don't know," she said. "Do you?"

• • •

The next three hours were exactly what I expected—intense questioning broken by spells of boredom, followed by different questions from different detectives, followed by more alone time in an interrogation room. The tedium finally played itself out at one in the morning, when the Hispanic cop said I was free to go as long as I promised to return at ten a.m., when the DA would determine whether or not to file charges.

"Six men dead, a neighborhood shot to hell, and your story is pretty damn thin," he said. "There's a lot you're not telling us."

"I'd like a ride over to Valley Medical," I said.

"Call a cab. And don't be late tomorrow, or I'll issue a warrant."

I went through the checkout process and collected my belongings, except for my Berretta, which was being held as evidence. Ten minutes later I walked into the nearby hospital and was told Cody had undergone a minor surgery to remove the slug from his leg, and was asleep. I rubbed my eyes and wondered briefly about a hotel, then I took a cab back to Cody's house.

Crime scene tape was stretched from the side yard fence across the street to where the two bullet-pocked cars were still parked. The tape was routed along the cars and around a tree and then back to the other side of Cody's house. Near the cars, white chalk outlined the shapes of the three men who'd died on the street. A single squad car was parked perpendicular in the middle of the road. I got out of the cab and walked over to the cruiser, where two patrolmen sat sipping from coffee cups.

"I'm gonna spend the night here," I said. "Okay?"

"No problem," said a cop. "The detectives are done inside." He yawned.

"Hey," his partner said, leaning forward so I could see his ruddy complexion. "Got to hand it to you, you sure took it to those spooks. You used to be a Green Beret or something?"

"Nope. Just lucky."

"Lucky, my ass. We ought to turn you loose at Story and King."

"Not me, fellas. I'm just trying to make a living."

"Amen, brother," the cop said, and gave me the thumbs-up.

I went inside. Broken glass and tufts of cotton filling from the couches were scattered about the living room. A hanging lamp had fallen and lay shattered on the kitchen table, which was splintered down the middle by a row of bullet holes. More holes patterned the walls, the paint chipped around the edges, and I could see where the detectives had dug a pair of slugs out of the sheetrock. I walked to the adjoining laundry room and saw my bag was where I'd left it. The contents appeared unmolested. I double-checked the gear, placed the bag in Cody's guest room, and went out the back door to where my truck was parked outside his garage. I got in the driver's seat and turned off the dome light. With my fingernails I pried up the molded storage compartment in the center console and yanked free the Hi-Point 380 ACP subcompact I'd taped to the transmission tunnel. I'd acquired the piece from a Mexican citizen at the time of his death, and I knew for a fact that it was untraceable.

I returned to the bedroom and checked the safety before putting the gun under my pillow. Then I lay down, put my arm over my eyes, and focused on pushing my thoughts aside. On the periphery of my consciousness, I sensed a growing swarm of images, all charged with negative energy, recriminatory and accusing, but I was exhausted, and within a minute I was asleep.

I woke at five a.m. with a case of what I call the night dreads, something that haunted me on a regular basis back in the days when I was trying to deconstruct myself with whiskey, vodka highballs, and ice-cold beer for breakfast. My mouth was dry, and the moonlight shining through the window was like a spike through my eyelids. I got up, gulped water from the bathroom faucet, then closed the shade and got back in bed. A lump had formed in my stomach, and I took deep breaths, hoping to stem a wave of nausea. Beads of sweat broke out on my forehead and my hands were clammy. I lay on my back and tried to meditate myself back to sleep. Eventually my stomach calmed, and I entered a state of semislumber. The dialogue that then commenced in my head was attended by a variety of voices: those of men I'd killed, my father's, Candi's, and that of a prosecutor who'd once tried to convict me of murder. Their condemnations were serpentine and mercurial in nature, which made it impossible to articulate an effective defense. But it was pointless to try, as their verdicts were foregone and rendered me something less than human.

After perhaps an hour, the voices subsided and were replaced by a dream in which a condemned man was put against a wall to be shot. His heinous crimes were unspoken, but there was no denying his guilt. The firing squad, comprised of men dressed in seventeenth-century French Colonial soldier uniforms, became unavailable at the last moment. I found myself recruited for the task and faced the convict, my pistol cocked.

"Have you any last words?" I asked.

"Yeah. I did what I did because it suited me." He was white, his face unshaven and grizzled.

"You'll burn in hell for it."

"I stole and raped and murdered whole families. No one could stop me."

"I'll stop you now."

He smirked, and then I realized the man was Hubert Sheridan, the psychotic degenerate who'd ambushed my father and ended his life with a shotgun blast.

I fired, and the bullet hit him square between the eyes. He raised his finger, dabbed at a small drop of blood, and smiled at me. I pulled the trigger again and again, but he remained standing.

I woke with a jolt. It was seven o'clock. I walked out to Cody's kitchen like a zombie and looked for his coffee maker. A bullet had shattered the pot and pierced the stainless steel body.

"Ah, shit," I said.

• • •

I pulled into Valley Medical at nine, showered, wearing fresh clothes, and alert after breakfast and three strong cups at a local diner. In the light of day, the remorse lurking in my subconscious was gone, replaced by the cold hard logic that I'd killed men who were trying to murder both Cody and me. A person not familiar with combat situations might claim I could have shot fewer than six and perhaps allowed some of them a chance to surrender. Following that tactic would have surely increased my chances of getting shot, and that was a risk I was unwilling to take. The six men had thrown all in when they chose to attack at night, with superior numbers and firepower and without warning. In hindsight, they were clearly amateurs, gangbangers with no practical training. As assassins, they might be effective in close quarters against unsuspecting targets, but they probably botched those jobs half the time. But there was no way I could have known that in the heat of battle, and I probably wouldn't have reacted differently even if I did.

When I walked into Cody's room, he was sitting upright in the hospital bed. He put down the newspaper he was reading and said, "What's that?"

"I got you breakfast at Denny's." I set two Styrofoam cartons on the table next to the bed. He opened a container and set it on his lap.

"You are a saint." Cody picked up a piece of bacon with his fingers and began eating.

"You said it, not me," I said. "How's the leg?"

"Not bad, considering. I'll limp for a while, but it was just a flesh wound. There's the round." He nodded toward the table, where a small piece of lead sat in a plastic cup. I dumped it into my palm and held it up to the light.

"They worked me over pretty good at the station last night," I said.

"Six stiffs, what do you expect? Pass me those paper towels, would you?"

"I've got to be back there in a few minutes for another round of interrogation."

"Listen," he said, "if Landers questions you—and he probably will— get him alone if he starts acting like an asshole. He'll probably try to turn the screws on you if he knows I'm involved. Tell him about the pictures we got of him and the black whore."

"All right."

"Have you called the general yet?"

"No," I replied. "I was waiting for him to call with the G-2 on Ahmad Jones."

Cody swallowed and put down his plastic silverware. "Give me his number," he said.

"Don't worry, I'll talk to him."

"I'm in the hospital, my house shot to shit, you just cooled out six homeboys, and you want to slow-play this? Do you not think Lawrence Tucker put the hit on us?"

"I said I'd talk to him—"

"Dirt, listen to me. We'll take care of our obligation to Ryan Addison. But we're dealing with something bigger now. The general calls the CIA, they'll take Tucker off at the knees, and then we can do our job."

"We're on the same page, Cody. I'll call him as soon as I get done with SJPD."

"Call him now," he said. "I've been thinking about that C-4 and Tucker's phony Arab name and his history with the carpet pilots."

"I hear you," I said.

"You didn't say anything to SJPD about Lawrence Tucker, did you?"

"Nope."

"Good. Because Landers is probably getting paid off by someone linked to the case. And even if he's not, what good is SJPD gonna do in investigating Tucker? Most of their detectives are bozos, and their bureaucracy is a fucking joke."

A nurse pushed aside the curtain and walked in.

"It's time to check out, Mr. Gibbons," she said, clipboard in hand.

"Call me as soon as you get done," Cody said, pointing his finger at me.

• • •

After clearing the scanning machine and undergoing a thorough pat down from a rookie cop doing his best tough guy imitation, I sat on a plastic chair in the police lobby. The minutes ticked by, and I pondered the parade of disparate characters involved in the case. Duante Tucker, violent rapist; Darrian Bannon, high-flying attorney on the downside of his luck; and Shanice Tucker, a beautiful hooker who just happened to be turning tricks with police captain Russ Landers. Throw in hapless South Lake Tahoe prosecutor Tim Cook, Lindsey Addison and her temporary friends, and eight dead black men, and the possibilities were endless.

Or were they?

Cody Gibbons was a man of unquenchable appetites who often acted irresponsibly, and sometimes I felt he was unwilling to invest himself fully in the particular drudgeries that come with investigative work. The stakeouts, the interviews, the paperwork—it was usually me driving these activities when we worked together. So what did Cody bring to the table, aside from his cavalier approach to violence? He possessed an attribute that some may call intangible, but after years of working with him, I'd learned to not discount it; Cody had gut criminal instinct. He brought this to his job from day one, as a cop and then as a private investigator, and he'd once summed it up succinctly by telling me, "When you assume anything but the worst from a criminal, you do exactly what they want you to do."

Lawrence Tucker, by virtue of his background, seemed a man capable of almost any crime. Ahmad Jones, who died along with Lennox Suggs, was a marine, unless he chose to be inscribed with a misleading tattoo. That meant that Lawrence Tucker's crew consisted of both gang members and individuals with a military background. Cody wanted to sic the CIA on him, and the FBI and Homeland Security Department would probably join the party, too. My hesitation was based on a desire to keep Lawrence Tucker in the game until we could discover his connection to Duante Tucker. But Cody viewed the situation with a fair amount of urgency, and that was something I couldn't ignore. I don't like to admit it, but Cody sometimes sees things more clearly than I do. Particularly when it involves the most nefarious aspects of criminal behavior.

The door on the far side of the lobby buzzed, and the dour-faced female detective stood in the doorway and crooked her finger at me. I followed her down a hallway to the same cement-walled room where I'd been held until one a.m. the night before. I took a seat at the metal table, and she looked toward the opaque window covering one wall. Then she sat on the edge of the table, her hip nearly touching my hand. I looked up at her. There were black hairs growing from her nostrils and two moles trapped in the folds of skin under her jawline.

"We need to review everything you said last night," she said.

"You've got it all in writing. You taped it, too."

"Forget about that. Let's start from the beginning."

"You're kidding, right?"

"Do I look like I'm kidding?"

"We did this last night. For three hours. You have my statement."

She lowered her face, and I raised my eyes to meet hers. "You're saying you won't cooperate?" she said.

"I'm saying I already have."

"You see, that's the problem. We're not buying your bullshit." She got off the table and walked to the side opposite me, put her hands on the table, and leaned in until her face was six inches from mine. "Six dead bodies, and all you can say is they must be friends of Duante Tucker?"

"That sums it up, Detective."

"You know, I'm really tempted to slap that smirk right off your mouth."

"I came here voluntarily, and this is what I get? If you were going to arrest me, you already would have, so get out of my face."

She shot me a withering glare, then walked out of the room, the steel door clanging behind her. I looked into the window and shrugged my shoulders.

It was five minutes before Russ Landers came through the door. He wore black slacks, polished wing tips, and a sky-blue button-down shirt that looked painted to his barrel-shaped torso. A perfectly knotted necktie rested against his bulk, and his sports coat was gray with patches on the elbows.

"So you're Cody Gibbons's running buddy," he said. He sat across from me. His hair was jet black and hair-sprayed in place.

"That's right."

"What are you doing in San Jose?" He probably had once been handsome, but the flesh on his face had turned meaty with booze and middle age. His nose was small and pitted, and his chin was split by a vertical crease running down from the center of his lower lip.

I sighed. "Like I told your detectives last night, I'm investigating Duante Tucker, who was acquitted of a rape in South Lake Tahoe after the evidence disappeared from the police locker."

"What have you found out so far?" He spoke quickly, the words quiet and clipped.

"There's no doubt Tucker committed the rape, and he also impaled the victim with a twelve-inch screwdriver. He's a sadist and a world-class degenerate."

Landers shook his head. "You're not answering my question."

"All right, Captain. I've also found out Tucker used to live in Compton and grew up in gangs, and has probably killed people and dealt drugs. Other than that, I haven't learned anything that's been helpful to my investigation."

"If you keep lying, we can hold you indefinitely." His upper lip jerked when he spoke.

"I call my lawyer, I'll be out of here in an hour."

"You think so, huh?" He glowered at me, brow furrowed, his eyes lighted with an anger that seemed inappropriate and a little too sudden.

I stared back at him. Landers was a career cop who had risen through the ranks and was probably a competent detective and administrator. He had also successfully worked the system, taking dirty money and living in a home far more expensive than one affordable on a police captain's salary. His ability to line his pockets while avoiding consequences meant he was a savvy crook. It also indicated a police organization that allowed graft to exist, as long as crime rates stayed low and the corruption was invisible to the general populace. But those were tricky caveats.

"Let's take a walk, Captain," I said.

"What?" he replied.

"It's a beautiful morning. Let's go get some fresh air."

"You're either a moron, or you've lost your mind. Which one is it?"

"Neither."

Landers eyed me warily, then his countenance turned contemplative. After a moment, he said, "Okay, PI. You want to walk, we'll walk."

When we left the room, I recognized the assistant DA, a woman named Anisa Clark. I caught an exasperated expression on her face before she turned on her heel and walked away from the one-way glass window. She was probably annoyed at wasting her time listening to the detectives futilely try to badger me into a self-incriminating remark. Or maybe her irritation was directed more specifically at Landers.

We went outside and strolled up the street toward the court building on Hedding. It was sunny and the rays reflected in bursts off the patrol cars that drove in and out of the parking lot ahead of us. To our left, traffic flowed on a raised section of Guadalupe Parkway. When we stopped at a traffic light, Landers turned toward me.

"All right, Reno. Say what you gotta say."

I stood looking at him. There was a hard glint in his eyes, cocksure and defiant, but beneath it I could tell he was at full alert, trying to anticipate my play, trying to guess what angle I might have. I think I surprised him.

"You're shoveling the coals to a black prostitute who looks like she could be in a Miss Universe pageant. I've got pictures and a recording of your voice, calling her 'Mama' and moaning about her sweet ass. Sound familiar?"

I saw the blood rise in his face. "You son of a bitch," he said.

"I suspect you're busting my balls because you and Cody Gibbons got bad history. But I don't have time for your bullshit. Your DA's already determined my shooting was self-defense, so this little time-wasting exercise is over."

Landers face flushed red, and when he spoke, spittle flew from his lips. "You got all the answers, huh?"

"I'm gonna split now, Landers. You can keep you dick in your pants or not—I don't give a rat's ass. But fuck with me or Gibbons, and I'll send the pictures and tape to everyone you know, including your wife."

"That sounds like blackmail to me."

"Call it whatever you want. Cody Gibbons was a good cop, probably the best investigator SJPD ever had. He left the force because assholes like you were taking payoffs from the worst criminals in San Jose, and Cody would have no part of it. You railroaded him out of a job because he was an honest cop."

"Get the hell out of my city, you scumbag."

The light turned, and I began crossing the street. But before I made it two steps, Landers said, "I better never see those pictures."

I looked back over my shoulder. "Get back to your minions, Captain. They await your example."

I caught a brief glimpse of Landers expression as it changed from anger to something less certain. Then he turned and stolidly paced back to the police headquarters.

· · ·

I drove toward Cody's house but pulled over as soon as I got off the parkway. I parked at the curb in a residential neighborhood and dialed the number for General Horvachek. He answered after a single ring.

"I was just about to call you," he said. "Where are we on Lawrence Tucker?"

"He's living at the Skyscape high-rise in San Jose under the assumed name of Farid Insaf. Sixteenth floor, number 1602."

"You're a hundred percent sure it's him?"

"As sure as I can be," I said. "And that's where I saw the C-4."

"You were in his home? How'd that happen?"

"Don't ask."

"Okay, I won't. But as soon as we hang up, I'm calling the CIA."

"Do me a favor and leave my name out of it, all right?"

"Sorry, no can do. Best I can do is vouch for you."

"Hmm. They'll want to talk to me, I imagine."

"Count on it."

I stared out my windshield. Most of the homes had large trees growing in their front yards, a mix of weeping willows, maples, and elms. The lawns were shaded, but the sun was high, and the street was bright and warm. Up the street two teenagers were running pass patterns and throwing a football, the ball spiraling through the air and bouncing off the pavement. A couple walking a dog waved at a trio of little girls jumping rope on the sidewalk. Through my closed window, I could hear the girl's laughter and a singsong rhyme they chanted.

The scene struck me as profoundly Californian: the well-kept middleclass homes, happy children, and friendly neighbors suggesting an American dream that was alive and well and immune to the crime and violence that plagued other countries, or other cities, or just simply other nameless people. I looked out at the street and then realized with a surprised pang of nostalgia that my perceptions were from my childhood, a flashback to the innocent, cheery times before my father was killed.

"Reno?" said the general.

"Did you find anything on Ahmad Jones?" I asked.

"Yes. He was a lance corporal, Marine Corps. Deployed in Afghanistan, fought the Taliban in the Korangal Valley. Went MIA during a battle in December 2009. Likely captured and presumed dead.

"You might tell the marines to check with the Santa Clara County coroner's office," I said.

"Why?"

"Ahmad Jones didn't die in Afghanistan."

The line went silent. When the general spoke again, his voice was subdued and edged with suspicion. "Care to comment further on that?"

"Yeah. Jones was likely working for Tucker. Find the connection, and that might explain what Tucker's up to."

"What I meant was, how do you know Jones is dead?"

"Call it a strong rumor."

• • •

The cars had been towed and the crime scene tape removed from the front of Cody's house. When I looked through the busted front window, I saw Cody sitting in his recliner, his leg outstretched, a pair of crutches propped against the wall. "Come on in, the water's warm," he said. I went through the front door and surveyed the mess, then found a broom and dustpan and began sweeping the broken glass in his living room.

"A glassman is coming out. I got to get a new TV."

"Will insurance cover it?" I asked.

He laughed. "Yeah, right."

"I talked with Landers," I said.

"What'd my old buddy have to say?"

"Not much, after I told him we got pictures."

"Wish I could have been there for that." Cody smiled, then held his leg and grimaced. "My meds must be wearing off. You called the general, right?"

"Yeah. I suspect CIA agents will be showing up at the Skyscape any minute."

"Good. Maybe they'll haul Lawrence Tucker off to a local version of Guantanamo Bay."

"We'll see." I finished with the broom and looked around. A bottle of prescription pills sat on the table next to the recliner. Cody tilted the bottle to his mouth and drank from a plastic glass.

"We should get caught up on the bugs," I said.

"Bring me my computer."

After Cody e-mailed me the updated audio files from the Skyscape and Lennox Suggs's house, we settled in, headphones on. I'd already drawn the conclusion that Lawrence Tucker was responsible for putting the hit on us and also was behind the Duante Tucker case. But these were assumptions without any substantive evidence.

An hour into the process I came across an interesting section. It was time stamped 7:38 a.m. Tuesday morning at the Skyscape, which was roughly thirty hours ago.

Sound of front door opening, keys jangling, footfalls.

Male voice: "What the..."

Ripping sounds (I assumed to be duct tape being removed from Duante Tucker's eyes and mouth).

Second male voice (Duante Tucker): "Motherfucker. My arms—cut me free."

Male voice: "What the hell happened?"

Two distinct snaps (I assumed the plastic ties binding Duante Tucker's wrists to his feet being cut).

A prolonged groan of relief. "I got up to piss in the middle of the night. Someone was here."

"Who?"

"He caught me unaware, choked me unconscious."

"What did he look like?"

"White. Dark hair. Wearing black. Over six feet."

"Not the big bearded one Shanice described."

"No."

"His partner, maybe."

"Could be. How could anyone get in here? You said this place was secure as Fort Knox."

An unintelligible grumble, then, "How long have you been tied up?"

"About four fucking hours."

"Are you okay, Duante?"

At that point I paused the recording and replayed it. The tone of the conversation between Duante Tucker and the man I assumed was Lawrence Tucker had been relatively emotionless until the last sentence. I replayed it three more times. There seemed to a genuine concern expressed by Lawrence for Duante, who was probably still sitting naked on the floor. Maybe Duante was showing some sign of physical stress, the result of being hogtied for hours. But the degree of sympathy in Lawrence's voice seemed odd, not only because both men came from violent backgrounds but also because Lawrence had supposedly spent most of the last twenty years outside the United States, which made it unlikely he'd formed much of a relationship with his nephew. I thought about that for a minute, then continued the playback.

"I'll be all right when I get my hands on that motherfucker."

"Go get yourself cleaned up."

"Does this change our plans?"

"I'll let you know."

The file skipped past five minutes of silence, then resumed.

Lawrence Tucker's voice, loudly: "Duante, my box is gone. Did you see him take anything?"

"I couldn't see anything through the goddamn duct tape."

"This changes things."

"Why?"

"Because now they'll know who I am."

"What do we do?"

"Find out who has my box. Then we'll fix it."

"Right on."

"Get some rest. I need you sharp."

After fifteen minutes of silence, the tape began again. It was 8:00 a.m.

"Duante?" (the voice a whisper)

"What?" (voice groggy with sleep)

"Don't say anything. I found a bug."

"A what?"

"A listening device. Shut up and help me search the house."

The remainder of the audio file was blank. It hadn't taken Lawrence Tucker long to discover his home had been bugged, and he wasted no time in neutralizing the tactic. I shouldn't have been surprised. He was a man who'd spent years dodging our government's ultramodern electronic surveillance efforts and he'd been able to slip into the United States undetected. He'd also assumed a new identity and was no doubt involved in felonious activity, and had, until now, avoided the scrutiny of police and government agencies. It probably took him all of five minutes to find the bugs once he decided to search.

"Lunch break?" Cody said, when I got up from his kitchen table.

"Hold on," I said, and walked into the guest bedroom. I knelt down and looked under the bed where I'd left the metal box I'd taken from unit 1602 at the Skyscape. I slowly returned to my feet and walked back to where Cody sat. "You didn't happen to move Lawrence Tucker's box of memorabilia, did you?" I asked.

Cody removed his headphones. "No. I don't even know where you put it."

"It was under the bed."

"So?"

"Now it's gone."

"What?"

"It was here last night when I went to sleep."

"Wait a minute. Maybe the cops took it."

"No." I sat on the couch and watched a glass repair company truck stop at the curb. "Lawrence Tucker did. Must have done it this morning after I left."

"That son of a bitch was in my house?"

"Him or one of his boys. Maybe he sent Duante."

Cody's face looked like a ripe melon, the skin taut as an overfilled volleyball.

"I'm gonna search for bugs," I said.

"Do me a favor, would you, Dan? Go in my closet and bring me my sawed-off Remington."

•　•　•

It was midafternoon before we finished with the audio files. The recordings from Lennox Suggs's residence had terminated at 8:15 a.m. yesterday, right after the bugs went silent at the Skyscape. Obviously, the Tuckers must have called and alerted Suggs. The same phone call probably instructed Suggs to put a tail on us, but there was no record of either conversation. But there were a couple interesting conversations from the previous day.

In two separate phone calls, Suggs repeatedly spoke of "D-Day," and he also made references to an eagle landing. In one sequence, he said, "After the eagle has landed, it's gonna be fat city for us. You ain't got to ask those questions, the details is my business. All you gotta know is, I'll put you in diamonds, know what I'm sayin'?"

I played the sections for Cody, and he said, "They're not very creative with their code words, are they?"

I looked up at him. "Drug dealers have been saying 'the eagle has landed' for years," he said. "It means a shipment has come in. They got it from some old movie, I think."

"What about D-Day?" I said.

"The invasion of Normandy. The American forces landing in hostile territory to kick ass on the Nazis. The liberation of France and the rest of Europe. The beginning of the end for Hitler."

"Thanks for the junior high history lesson. You got any idea what it means to the case?"

Cody rested his hand on the butt of his shotgun. "Not really. But you're the deep thinker, I'm sure you'll come up with something."

I stuck my hands in my back pockets and stared vacantly out the new sheet of glass in Cody's front window. It was a still, languid afternoon, silent except for the random chirping of birds from the treetops along the street. There was no hint of the mayhem that occurred the night before. The neighborhood seemed serene and undisturbed, as if the residents had chosen to be oblivious to the fact that something evil had invaded their domain. A car drove by, a white family, the parents in the front seat, two teenagers in the back. They did not gawk as I suspected they might, even though I recognized the car from a few houses away and knew they must have been aware of the shooting.

"You know what?" I said. "You're right about Lawrence Tucker. He'll have his hands full with the CIA. Fuck him. I want to find Duante. It's time to nail his balls to the wall."

"Oh, really?" Cody said, a sleepy grin beginning on his face.

"What are those pills you're taking?"

"Oxycodone."

"Take it easy on that stuff," I told him. "It's addicting."

"Okay, doctor."

I started to say something else, but my cell rang. It was Candi. I'd not spoken to her since the crash in the Santa Cruz Mountains and the drive-by shooting. In all honesty, I'd been too busy to call her. I also had not invested any thought into how I'd tell her about my involvement in the death of eight men.

"Hi, Candi."

"Hi, my guy."

"How's everything at home?"

"Just fine," she said. "I did notice something weird, though."

"Like what?"

"I went out to the supermarket, and when I came back, I passed a car parked on Alma, facing our house. There were two guys sitting in the car, and one had binoculars."

"Looking at our house?"

"Yes, that's the way they're facing."

"Describe them," I said.

"I didn't get a chance to study them, Dan. They're about a hundred yards away."

"They're still there?"

"Wait a minute," she said. "Yeah, I can see the car from the kitchen window."

"Step back from the window, Candi. Don't let them see you."

"Okay. They have dark skin, dark hair."

"Black guys?"

"No, they're not black. Maybe from the Mideast somewhere. Iranian, maybe? But they're clean-shaven."

I felt my scalp tighten against my skull. "Give me just a sec," I said. I waved nonchalantly at Cody and walked outside and went to where my truck was parked in front of Cody's garage.

"Is Tim next door home?" I said.

"I don't know. He works nights, so probably."

"I'm gonna call him and check. Make sure the doors are locked and the alarm system is on. I'll call you right back."

I hung up and called my neighbor. Tim was a cook at one of the casinos. He'd lived alone in the small cabin next to my house since before I moved in, and I felt I could trust him to perform a relatively simple task. He answered his phone, and I described what I'd pay him a hundred dollars to do. Then I had him repeat it back to me. As soon as we hung up, I redialed Candi's cell.

"Candi, I need you to listen carefully and follow these instructions. I'm gonna leave in a minute and drive back home, and I'll call you from the road. But first you need to do what I say."

"Okay. What is it?"

"Pack an overnight bag right now. Then go out the back door and go around to Tim's back door. He'll be waiting for you there. Get in his truck and duck down as low as you can, so there's no way anyone can see you. Tim is going to drive you to Harrah's. I want you to check into a room."

"But—" she began.

"Listen, doll, this is for your safety. I can answer questions later, but now we need to get you to a hotel room, Okay?"

"Okay, I got it."

"Call me as soon as you're checked in."

We hung up, and I went back inside. Cody had a can of beer in his hand, and the shotgun rested across his lap.

"I think Tucker's sent someone to watch my house. I'm gonna drive back to Tahoe and see what I can do about it. You gonna be okay here?"

"Why wouldn't I be?"

"Because you're shot and doped up and drinking, for starters."

Cody laughed. "I do my best work in this condition." He pointed the cut-down barrel at the window. "Anyone has an issue with me, they can talk to *Señor* Remington."

"You best keep your wits about you," I said.

"What about putting the cleats to Duante?"

"It'll have to wait until I get back."

Cody raised his eyebrows. "We'll see," he said.

I collected my clothes and assorted items and stuffed them into my canvas duffel bags. In two minutes I was backing down Cody's driveway. I waved at his front window, then gunned it down the street and out to the freeway. It was 3:30 and I knew the thick of the rush hour traffic lurked ahead. But as long as Candi was safely out of the house, there was no need to hurry. Still, cruising at an easy seventy-five, I could feel the anger and frustration building in my chest, and the old arguments began to play themselves out in my mind.

This was not the first time Candi's safety had been put at risk as a result of my career. Each time it happened, I swore I'd not let it happen again. But it was an empty promise. Because if I turned down every case that included the potential for seriously unhappy criminals, I wouldn't make much of a living. And I was goddamned committed to bringing home a good income so I could provide a comfortable life for Candi…and maybe even for a couple kids one day.

My father had busted his ass all his life, from law school to passing the bar exam, and then in his career as a district attorney and later in a successful private practice that abruptly ended just as he finished a major case. The money from that case had sustained my mother for many years. Of course, it was little consolation for his death, but it sure as hell made things less difficult for her, and for my sister and me too.

I used to wonder, if my father had been less adamant and more relenting on certain issues, might he still be alive? The answer could well be yes, but then he would have been a different man than he was. Particular traits are hardwired, and there's no changing that. But despite his staunch ethics and appetite for confrontation, I always saw my old man as a lighthearted, happy person.

As for the miscreants I deal with, their ethics defy any definition of human decency. They live in a world where crimes ranging from petty to deplorable are the currency of the day. As individuals they are usually greedy and sadistic, often sexually retarded, and live within bizarre mental frameworks they've constructed to justify their antisocial behavior. Some are quite intelligent and resourceful, which makes them even more dangerous than the typical psychopaths that populate our state and federal penitentiaries.

I had no doubt Lawrence Tucker was among the intelligent, resourceful class, and that was probably an understatement. His criminal background was the most impressive I could recall. A product of the Compton ghettos, he'd been steadily promoted in the marines. Somewhere along the line, he learned to speak Arabic and had become familiar with Islamic culture and customs to the extent that he could operate as a heroin broker and terrorist trainer in the Middle East. Hunted by the CIA, he'd survived a drone attack and had managed to change his name and sneak back into the US. Actually, it was beyond impressive—it was amazing.

And now two Mideastern-looking men were casing my house. That led me to three conclusions: One, Lawrence Tucker had sent them; two, they planned to kidnap Candi and use her as leverage to get me to back off; and three, I had not the slightest doubt that, given the chance, they would rape Candi and kill us both.

And it was those thoughts that kept me occupied through the stretches of commuter gridlock, past Sacramento and up into the rolling Sierra

Nevada foothills, until the road narrowed to two lanes and finally led over Echo Summit and dropped through the corkscrew turns above Lake Tahoe, where the sun was just settling behind the granite ridges west of the lake, glowing like a jagged chunk of white-hot steel against the hard blue of the sky.

9

I PARKED AROUND THE corner from my house and walked through the dusk across a vacant lot that provided access to the meadow behind my back fence. The dirt trail that ran along the fence line was hard packed, and the air smelled of deadfall, dry weeds, and the wildflowers that stayed in bloom through the heat of the summer. I followed the trail for a minute until I reached a loose board in the fencing. I pried it free and wedged myself between the boards and into my yard. Then I pulled my duffel bags through, unlocked the backdoor, and went inside.

The lights were off, which meant that if the two men Candi described were still parked down the street, they wouldn't be able to see much, even with binoculars. I crawled along an area that would be in their line of sight, then went up the stairs to the loft above my living room. From there I could look through the slats of a ventilation screen straight down the street that ran perpendicular to mine.

The area was tight with boxes stacked on old furniture. I moved a box and fit a pocket-sized telescope between the slats. I immediately spotted a green Honda hatchback with two occupants parked at the curb. The license plate frame advertised a rental car company. It was too dark to make out much detail on the pair behind the windshield other than their tenebrous complexions.

It was 8:30 p.m. and would be full dark soon. I took a variety of items from one of my bags, as I had planned during the drive from San Jose. Then I went back downstairs, drew the curtains, and turned on the living room light. After that, it was a matter of waiting.

They disappointed me. I'd hoped they'd come as soon as the last hint of blue faded from the horizon. But they waited until an hour after I turned off the lights at ten o'clock.

From the chair I'd placed behind the kitchen counter, I heard them creep across my lawn, past my deck, and around to the back of the house. When they reached the unlocked back door, I was waiting in the darkness.

The first man came through the door and whispered something in a foreign language. His partner, carrying a black leather bag, came stealthily behind him and eased the door shut. I waited until they took another step into the house before I pounced, my stun baton in my left hand, my Taser in my right. I jabbed the baton into the gut of the first man and simultaneously shot the second with the Taser, almost point blank. They both seized up, their arms splayed at unnatural angles, their facial skin quivering as if caught in hurricane force winds. After a second they both collapsed, jerking and shuddering, to the floor.

The younger of the two lay faceup, blinking rapidly while his teeth chattered so hard I wondered if he'd break a molar. He was rail thin, and his face was shaped like a scythe, the nose long, the chin pointed. The second man was shorter and barrel-shaped. He had powerful, rounded shoulders and a neck like a fire hydrant. The stubble on his face was gray, and one of his eyes was twisted shut. The other eye was locked open, the black pupil vacant and still. He would be the leader.

In thirty seconds I had their hands and feet zip-tied and their eyes and mouths wrapped with duct tape. After searching their pockets and finding nothing, I grabbed them by the feet and pulled them through the house and into my garage, their heads clunking off the concrete steps. Two blue plastic tarps lay spread on the floor. I dragged the taller man onto a tarp, rolled the plastic around him, and wrapped him with rope, cinching the knots tight. I did the same to the heavier man, who tried to make it difficult by bucking and rolling. I put a stop to that with a kick to his gut. Then I went outside, jogged down the street, and returned in my truck, backing it up my driveway and into the garage.

They squirmed when I hoisted them into the truck bed, but they were securely mummified. I slammed the tailgate shut and placed their black bag on the passenger seat next to me. Then I wheeled down my driveway and out to Pioneer Trail toward the mountains.

I turned onto Black Diamond Boulevard, then onto a steep street that bordered the ski resort, climbing until the road turned from pavement to dirt. The track was rutted, the switchbacks tight. I drove slowly, my chassis and suspension straining against the uneven terrain. After ten minutes, the road dead-ended in a flat clearing above a deep, forested valley.

I turned off the engine, unzipped their black bag, and went through the contents. Duct tape, handcuffs, a ball of twine, a hypodermic needle in a plastic case, and a fillet knife, the kind hunters used for slicing meat neatly away from the bone. Also, at the bottom of the bag, a black dildo. It was molded in the shape of a human phallus, but the size was exaggerated, like something that might be found on a mule or a bull.

There was another item in the bag that gave me pause. Beneath the dildo was what appeared to be a pornographic magazine. But when I flipped through the pages, the photos all depicted various acts of bondage.

I closed the magazine and got out of my truck. At the side of the clearing, the lip of a granite headwall rose a few feet over the dirt. I knelt and looked over the ledge. A sheer face fell about two hundred feet into a sea of broken boulders. The moon was bright, and I could clearly see the jagged edges of the granite scree below.

The face was known by local rock climbers as Quarter Dome. They called it this in deference to Half Dome, the geologic wonder in Yosemite National Park that had attracted extreme mountaineers since the 1800s. The vertical face of Half Dome is over 1300 feet. Quarter Dome offered only a 200-foot face, but it was no less deadly if one were to fall.

I eased my truck forward until the bumper was within ten feet of the rock. Then I took my climbing rope from behind my seat and pulled a full ski mask over my head, an old-fashioned variety that had holes only for the eyes. I tied the rope around my front bumper and walked to the back of the truck. The men were lying motionless.

I untied the rope binding the younger man and rolled him off the tailgate. He hit the ground with a thud. I ripped the tape from his mouth and then from his eyes. He stared into my hooded face as I looped my climbing rope around his ankles and tied a double knot. "What ad you doing?" he said. His accent was thick, his voice high-pitched.

I dragged him to the outcropping and pulled his shoulders over the ledge so he was looking straight down the face.

"Allah akbar!" he exclaimed.

"That means god is great, right?" I said. "Isn't that what your suicide bombers yell when they go into a crowded market and kill a bunch of women and children?"

"Allah akbar," he yelled again.

"Keep telling yourself that, pal." I grabbed his belt and jerked him farther over the edge until he teetered on the brink of falling. I could hear him panting and could smell his fear in the sour stench that rose from his clothes.

"I'm going to ask you some questions, my friend. If your answers are right, you get to live. Lie to me, and you'll find yourself up close and personal with those rocks down there. They'll have to scrape up what's left of you with a putty knife."

He made a sound like something was tearing loose in his throat. "Something else to keep in mind," I said. "I'm gonna question your fat friend, too. He better give me the same answers, or you'll both take the big dive."

"I—I can't contdol what he say," he rasped.

"You just concentrate on telling the truth. Maybe your god will save you."

He started replying in a different language. "Hey," I said. "Speak English. I don't want to hear any of your foreign gibberish. Who hired you to break into my house?"

"I not knew his t-due name," he stammered.

"What name do you know?"

He hesitated, and I grabbed his feet and pushed. "No!" he screamed. The weight of his upper body broke free from the rock, and then he was falling. He dropped a few feet down the face before the rope snapped taught.

"Oh god, no," he moaned.

I leaned my head over the wall. "The name?"

"Black Doog. He go by Black Doog."

"Think hard now, or I'll cut the rope. What other name does he have?"

"Fadid, I heard Fadid. I don't know more zan zat, I swear it."

"Why did Farid hire you? What's he up to?"

"He not said anyzing about why. He not tell detail."

"Do you really believe forty virgins will be waiting for you in the afterlife?"

"What?"

"Because I think you're about to find out for real." I held my knife up so he could see it.

"Don't! He waging *jihad* in San Jose!"

"He's planning terrorist acts?"

"Yes, yes!" he cried. "But you musd believe me, I don't know detail."

"What about heroin? What's Farid's plans for heroin?"

"He a smuggler."

"No shit. Is he bringing a shipment into this country?"

"I don't know. But smuggling his business."

I heard my cell ring in the cab of my truck. I ignored it and looked down at the man dangling at the end of the rope. His face was sweaty and shinning in the moonlight. There were black stains on his teeth, and the crotch of his jeans was soaked dark and I could smell the odor of urine.

"What's your name?" I said.

"Me? I'm Basel. Bull me up, blease?"

"What does Basel mean in Arabic?" I asked.

"Brave one."

"Really. Okay, Basel, what role is Duante Tucker playing?"

"Who?"

"Farid's nephew."

"I don't know nephew."

"Black man, about your age."

"I don't know anyone like zat. I swear it."

"I'm going to give you one last chance, Basel. I want you to tell me everything you know about Farid Insaf. You're working for him, so don't pretend you don't know exactly what he's up to. Otherwise you're gonna learn to fly the hard way. So let's see how brave you are."

He started whimpering and spewing forth random comments and pleas. I tried to focus on his words, but his ramblings quickly became incoherent. I stood and began toward my truck. Even if I could understand his mishmash of English and Arabic, I doubted there was much value in what he was blubbering. I believed he was truly terrified and had reached the point where he'd say anything to relieve the fear that I'd cut him loose and send him plummeting to his death.

I climbed into my cab and backed up until I saw him pop over the ledge and onto the dirt. I untied the rope from his ankles and taped his eyes and mouth again and dragged him to where the blue tarp lay on the ground. After wrapping and binding him in the tarp, I yanked the larger, older man out of the truck bed.

When I tore the duct tape from his eyes and mouth, his face showed no fear or concern.

"You can take off your mask," he said. "I know who you are and everything about you." His accent was far less pronounced than his counterpart's.

"You know a lot? That's good to hear. I'd hate to be wasting my time."

"Too bad I'm not in a talkative mood."

"We'll see what we can do about that," I said.

"A tough guy, eh? Am I supposed to get all fearful?" He smirked and spat a wad of phlegm at my feet.

I tied the rope around his ankles. "Let me guess," I said. "You've been through all sorts of grim stuff, maybe in the Mideast or Africa, seen men dismembered, seen women and children sodomized and tortured, maybe even participated yourself, probably enjoyed it. Am I on the right track here?"

"Not really. But let your imagination run wild, if that's what gets you off."

I dragged him to the ledge. "Heights bother you?" I asked.

"It's a nice view. I wish it was daylight, so I could see better." He lay on his front, looking down the face.

"Let's see if we can improve your angle." I gauged the slack in the rope, then I jammed my heel in his buttocks and shoved him over. He fell a couple feet before the rope caught his weight.

"Comfortable?" I asked.

"Fuck you," he grunted.

"How much effort you think it would take for me to snip the ties on your hands and feet and cut this rope? They'd find you in a couple days, your bones protruding from your skin, your head split open, your brains like scrambled eggs frying on the rocks. They'll assume it was a suicide or an accident. They'll scoop what's left of you and take you to the morgue in a plastic garbage bag. You'll be declared a John Doe. Nobody will call about you, nobody will invest much in trying to learn who you are. They'll leave you in a freezer for a while until someone decides you're no longer worth the space. Then they'll cremate you and toss your ashes in a Dumpster full of dirty diapers and rotting food."

"You really love the sound of your own voice, don't you?" he said.

"You get one chance to walk out of this. What's Farid Insaf up to, and what does Duante Tucker have to do with it?"

The man chuckled. "You're a funny guy. You ever consider stand-up?"

"I'm glad I'm entertaining you. Wait until we get to the punch line."

"I'm on a need to know basis with Farid Insaf, you fool. That means he tells me only what I need to know. That's how the business works."

"How did Insaf arrange for Duante Tucker to get off on the rape charge?"

"I have no idea what you're talking about."

I stood and looked around. To my right, the moonlight glinted off a distant steel tower high on a hillside in the closed ski resort. A cable looped from the tower into the darkness. I turned around and gazed past the valley, down toward the lake. A section of Highway 50 was visible, right at the state line. Through the trees, the lights of the casino hotels looked like sparks in the forest. I imagined Candi was lying in bed in one of those hotel rooms, probably sleepless and worrying and wondering about our life together.

I knelt back down over the ledge. I could see the man's face was flushed with blood from hanging upside down. But when he looked up at me, he smiled. "Are we done here?" he said.

"Just another question or two. I won't take much more of your time, I promise."

"What, then?" he asked.

"That big, black dildo in your bag. How does that fit into your routine?"

He didn't say anything for a second. "That's Basel's."

"And the S&M skin mag? His too?"

"You got it."

"You were just going to sit and watch while he tormented the woman you intended to abduct from my house?"

"That's his thing, not mine."

"Sorry, that doesn't flush. I think you work as a team."

"You don't know shit."

My stun baton was a foot and a half long. I made sure it was set on maximum voltage, then I held onto a crack in the rock, reached down, and extended my arm. I jabbed the baton into where his testicles hung between his legs. "Your equipment may not work so well after this, but let's consider it a social service," I said. Then I pushed the button and sent eight hundred thousand volts into his genitals.

His body jerked violently, saliva sprayed from his mouth, and the curly hair around his ears stood straight out. The rope scraped and bounced against the rock, and a wisp of smoke rose from his crotch.

I waited until he stopped shaking. "Tell me about Farid Insaf and Duante Tucker," I said.

"I don't know any Duante," he said, his voice a labored hiss.

"Round two," I said, and reached down again. When the current coursed through his body, he bucked so hard his head slammed against the rock wall. His breath came in heaves, and a loop of yellow snot lay across his cheek.

"All right, buddy," I said pleasantly. "I zap you again, your nuts are gonna look like raisins and be about as functional. So you get to dictate your fate here."

When he spoke, agony and the beginnings of panic were plain in his tone. "Three days," he moaned. "He said hold her for three days, then we could do anything we want with her."

"Farid Insaf said this?"

"Yes. And I never heard of Duante Tucker. I don't know who that is."

"What did Farid mean by three days?" I asked. "What's he up to?"

"He said he'll be leaving in three days, but he'll wire me payment."

"Leaving to where?"

"Pakistan, Syria, maybe Qatar. He didn't tell me."

"Is he involved in jihad?"

He groaned in pain and squeezed his eyes shut. "He's involved in whatever pays the most. That's all I know. I think I'm going to puke. Please, that's all I know."

. . .

Once the kidnappers were secure in my truck bed, I checked my cell and saw I had missed a call from an unknown number beginning with a Sacramento area code. I began to drive down the rutted road, then stopped and returned the call.

"Dan Reno?" said the voice on the other end.

"Yeah?"

"Greg Stillman, Central Intelligence Agency. I'd like to speak with you regarding Lawrence Tucker."

"Ask away."

"Do you have information as to his whereabouts?"

"You don't have him in custody?"

"Answer the question, please."

"Skyscape building in San Jose, unit 1602. That's where he lives."

"That unit is vacant. Scrubbed clean, not even a fingerprint."

I turned off my motor and set the e-brake. "One of his associates, Lennox Suggs, was renting a dump in east San Jose. I'll text you the address."

"You think Suggs is there?"

"No. He's recently deceased, victim of an automobile accident. But it's possible you might find Duante Tucker there."

"Who's he?"

"Lawrence's nephew. He's involved up to his eyebrows."

"Involved in what?"

"Whatever Lawrence Tucker is planning, which at a minimum is bringing heroin into the US. I also think it's likely he's involved in terrorist activities."

The line went silent for a moment. When Stillman spoke, his voice was precise, the words clipped. "How do you know this?"

"I've been investigating Duante Tucker. I've also got two Arabs in the back of my truck, men hired by Farid Insaf, which is Lawrence Tucker's alias. They broke into my home and intended to kidnap my girlfriend. They told me Tucker is planning jihad."

"You have these men in custody?"

"That's right. I'm making a citizen's arrest, and I'm pressing charges, too. I'm taking them to the police station here in South Lake Tahoe."

"Are these men secured? They can't escape?"

"Not a chance."

Another pause, then he said, "You seem quite resourceful. I'm getting on a helicopter. I'll meet you at the police station in forty-five minutes. Please confirm you'll wait for me there."

"I always cooperate with the authorities, Mr. Stillman."

"I hope you're not being sarcastic."

"Nope, that's straight up," I told him.

"Good," he said. "I look forward to meeting you."

· · ·

Marcus Grier reacted exactly as I anticipated when I called him. It was midnight, and he was groggy, angry, and confused, in that order.

"Just meet me at the station, Marcus. A CIA guy named Stillman is on the way from Sacramento."

"This is related to Duante Tucker?" he sputtered.

"Right. You better get dressed. I'll be there in about ten minutes."

He started to protest, but I interrupted him. "We'll talk when I see you," I said, and disconnected the call.

· · ·

When Grier pulled into the police parking lot, I was standing next to my truck. He looked in the bed where the two men were still wrapped in the plastic tarps.

"They're mercenaries, terrorists, hired henchmen—call them whatever you want," I said. "I caught them breaking and entering my home. They intended to kidnap Candi. I doubt they're US citizens, and they're probably here illegally. Lock them up. I'm pressing charges, but that might be a moot point once the CIA gets their hands on them."

Grier went inside the complex and returned with two patrolmen. They untied the Arabs, cuffed them, and took them to a cell. Then Grier and I went to his office.

"Those guys looked in pretty sorry shape. Things get a little rough?" Grier sat at his desk and closed his eyes tightly, then opened them wide and blinked a few times.

"For them it did," I replied.

"You really think they're mercenaries?"

"They're pros, especially the older one. But they got lazy and underestimated the situation."

Grier grunted and fixed his bloodshot eyes on me. "You make them talk?"

I nodded. "I think they told me all they know about Lawrence Tucker, aka Farid Insaf."

"Anything about Duante?"

"Nope."

"Did you learn anything that could help solve the case?" he asked.

I sighed and shook my head. "Not really."

Grier leaned forward and sat with his palms pressed to his forehead. "I'm tired, Dan. I'm tired of being questioned by internal affairs, and I'm tired of lie detector tests and newspaper articles accusing my force of being corrupt. And I'm tired of not being able to walk past a cop or even a goddamned clerk without wondering if they were the ones who took that evidence."

"Hang in there," I said.

"I don't need your sympathy," he said, his voice rising, but his anger quickly tailed off. "I just want to find out what happened and put this mess behind us."

"Cody and I are still working some leads. But he's laid up for now."

"Laid up?"

"Took a bullet to the leg. Not serious."

"Shot, again?" Grier exclaimed. "That Gibbons is a magnet for lead."

"He's a big target."

"That he is. Tell him to get well soon."

"I'll do that."

•   •   •

Twenty minutes later we heard the thumping slap of the helicopter blades. The chopper landed in the parking lot, and two figures in army fatigues jumped out, their assault rifles slung over their shoulders. They were followed by two men wearing suits and ties. They ducked low and ran to the entrance of the building, where Grier and I stood waiting.

One of the suits had gray around the temples and wore wire-rimmed glasses. He asked to be taken to the cell holding the two men. The soldiers went with him, leaving Grier and me with a tall, hollow-cheeked man with piercing blue eyes that seemed mismatched with his pitted complexion.

"Greg Stillman," he said. "Let's go to a room." Grier led us to his office, but when he got there, Stillman said, "I'm sorry, Sheriff Grier. I need to interview this man in private. I hope you don't mind." I caught a brief glimpse of Grier's expression, surprised and offended, before Stillman shut the door.

Stillman turned on a recorder, and I was true to my word with the CIA agent. I told him everything I knew about the Tucker clan and their associates. Aside from avoiding any detail that would implicate me in a crime, I gave a full recounting of my investigation into Duante Tucker's rape of Lindsey Addison. As I expected, he had little interest in the rape case. He was only interested in the auxiliary characters to the extent that they could lead him to Lawrence Tucker.

"I'd bring in Abdul Talwar," I said. "He owns a restaurant in Fremont, and he's likely partnered up with Tucker in the heroin business."

"What about Duante Tucker? Why do you think he might be complicit in a terrorist plot?"

"Because I think Lawrence Tucker somehow arranged to get him off the rape charge. That wasn't easy or cheap. So whatever Lawrence is up to, Duante's involved."

"And the sister, Shanice?"

"I'd consider her a person of interest. She's been to the Skyscape, visited Tucker there. And here's a line of questioning you might pursue; she's a prostitute, and one of her johns is Russ Landers, captain at SJPD."

Stillman raised his eyes, considered that for a moment, then changed direction. "Do you have any ideas where the plastic explosives you saw came from?"

"Ahmad Jones died with Lennox Suggs in a car crash. Jones was a marine. I think Tucker still has contacts in the marines, working with him—or for him."

Stillman looked away, his blue eyes cold, his jaw set. He nodded briefly, as if I'd confirmed something he hoped wasn't true.

• • •

At three in the morning I left the police complex, right after the helicopter took off with the two men I'd dangled over a cliff and tortured. They would no doubt be subjected to rigorous interrogation at the hands of the CIA, but it would probably seem mild compared to what I had put them through. In hindsight, I didn't feel the slightest remorse over how I treated them. They crossed a line when they entered my home, and their intentions were of a nature I did not wish to dwell upon. Simply stated, they belonged to an unfortunate human subspecies that, by their actions, forgo any claim to leniency or mercy. Their pain and suffering is by their own design.

When I left, Marcus Grier was asleep on a couch in the squad room. I didn't bother waking him. My mind was unsettled, but I was dead tired and could barely keep my eyes open as I drove to Harrah's.

I called Candi's cell and told her I was coming, and when I knocked, she was waiting at the door without the nightshirt or panties she usually wore to bed. Her naked body was luminescent in the moonlight that shone through the twentieth floor window. She came to me, and we fell into bed together. Her eyes were full of questions and concern, but we did not make love or have conversation, because I was asleep before I could remove my clothes.

10

W E WERE HAVING BREAKFAST in the coffee shop the next morning when my cell rang. It was ten o'clock, and I was still tired and really not ready to begin the day. That thought was compounded when I saw who was calling.

"Are you going to answer that?" Candi asked.

"It's Ryan Addison," I said. "I'll call him back."

"Dan, you look exhausted. I can see it in your face."

"The last couple days have been pretty busy."

"Let's go home," she said. "I think you should take the day off."

"That's a nice thought."

"How much longer you think you'll be working this case?"

I rubbed my unshaven jaw. "Maybe three days. Hopefully, not more than that."

"Come on, stud. Let's go back to our house."

We left the restaurant, and I drove us through my neighborhood and down the street where the would-be kidnappers' green rental car had been parked. It was no longer there, probably towed to the police impound yard. I pulled into my garage, and after Candi went inside, I removed the tarps and rope from my truck bed and put them away. Then I went inside and mopped the area where the kidnappers had entered my home, and then I mopped the path where I had dragged them to the garage.

When I was done, I showered and turned the water as hot as I could stand it and let the torrent beat on my neck until the bathroom was thick with steam. Afterward I put on shorts and flip-flops and went outside to the deck and sat at my picnic table in the sun. I looked past the back fence and the grasslands to where the mountains rose against a sky flecked with tiny wisps of clouds. I stared at the sky for a long time. It was a warm, beautiful morning, and the natural elements—the sun, the trees, the earth—all seemed in peaceful harmony. It was so quiet I could hear the gurgle of the stream in the meadow.

I sat there and tried to appreciate and absorb the tranquility of the moment. I told myself that benevolent forces would once again rule the day, and that the violence and evil that had been visited upon me was of my own choosing, and I could also choose for it to be temporary. I told myself that the CIA would no doubt find Lawrence Tucker and halt whatever nefarious schemes he had hatched. I also told myself that Duante Tucker would likely be picked up by the feds and would be jailed once his complicity with Lawrence Tucker was revealed. In that scenario, my investigation could be brought to a premature conclusion. If the Tuckers were incarcerated, it might effectively end any chance of uncovering the story behind the disappearance of the DNA evidence.

When my cell rang, I was hoping it was Cody. No such luck—it was Ryan Addison calling back. I pinched the bridge of my nose with my thumbs.

"Investigations."

"Hi Dan, thought I'd check in…for an update." His voice was quiet and sounded morose and distracted.

"I'll work on my report and send it to you this afternoon," I said.

"Thank you," he mumbled. "Have you made much progress?"

"It depends how you look at it."

"That doesn't sound encouraging. Listen, you should know, Lindsey's been hospitalized."

"What for?"

"She had a breakdown two days ago. She became hysterical, and we couldn't stop her screaming. They have her medicated now, so…"

"I'm sorry to hear that, Mr. Addison."

"I thought I could deal with this. I really did."

"I think you're doing everything a parent can do."

He was silent for a moment, then I heard him sniffle. "She's my daughter, my little baby." His voice began to crack. "I just want her back."

"You have to give her more time."

"I know. I hope you're right. God, why did this have to happen? What kind of world is this?"

"You're asking the wrong guy," I said.

"She said she dreams of the rape every night. It's like a horror movie in her head that she can't turn off. She said she wants to ram a screwdriver up his ass and see how he likes it."

"I don't know what to tell you, Mr. Addison."

"You know what you could tell me?" he said, his voice rising. "That the creep is dead. That he's in a hole in the ground, worms burrowing in his flesh. That he died violently and suffered first. How about that?"

"You really think that would make a difference to your daughter?"

I heard him suck his breath in. "You really don't understand what we're going through, do you, Reno? Yes, it would make a fucking difference. Don't try to play dumb, because I ain't buying it. This is about retribution—is that simple enough? It's about payback, an eye for an eye. There will be no rest until this is righted, and by that I mean Duante Tucker must suffer ten times worse than Lindsey, and then he must die, hear me, motherfucker, and die badly, pleading for mercy like a coward until the pain alone kills him and sends him to hell!"

"Those are pleasant thoughts," I said. "Is that all?"

"I'll be waiting for your goddamned report," he said. "So get on it."

I hung up and watched a gopher poke his head up from a hole near my back fence. Candi came outside and joined me at the table. She was wearing short shorts and a sleeveless shirt. Her hair was wet, and I could smell her tropical perfume.

"Ryan Addison?" she asked.

"Yeah."

"What did he want?"

"More than I can give him."

"He's just going to have to live with that. You can't let his grief become yours."

I looked up at her, then pulled her onto my lap. "I like the way you think," I said.

• • •

We spent almost two hours in bed, and during that time my head was quiet and uncluttered, almost like part of my mind had gone into a deep sleep. I became totally immersed in Candi and her body, and our sex opened a door to a dimension that felt natural and true and completely detached from my normal consciousness. In comparison, everything I'd experienced in the last week seemed unreal and almost trivial. In this blissful state, I made love to Candi, and the events of the Tucker case seemed like an evanescent obscurity that carried no more gravity than the prospect of a household chore.

My serenity lasted into the afternoon, and I was committed to hold onto it as long as I could. Like Candi said, I deserved a day off.

Then Cody Gibbons called.

I walked outside and onto my lawn. The air smelled of rosemary and pine, and I could hear the fading drone of a small airplane heading across the mountaintops.

"What happened with the guys watching your house?" he asked.

I gave him a recap of my interrogation and the intervention of the CIA agent, Greg Stillman. When I was done, Cody grunted his approval. "Zapped his balls, you say?"

"It made him talk."

"You're hardcore, Dirt. Don't let anyone tell you different. So, Lawrence Tucker boogied from the Skyscape?"

"Stillman said the place was cleaned out—not even a fingerprint."

"And the guy who looked like Yasser Arafat said Tucker was planning to leave for the sand dunes in three days?"

"That's what he said. But I doubt Tucker can leave the country. Not with the CIA looking for him."

"Be almost impossible to get on a commercial flight," Cody said. "But he's a resourceful son of a bitch."

"I told Stillman to check the dump where Suggs was staying," I said.

"You did? I was thinking of taking a spin by there myself."

"How's the leg feeling?"

"I can hobble around."

"You think Duante might be staying there?" I asked.

"He's got to stay someplace," said Cody.

"Or, he's hiding out with Lawrence Tucker, who could be anywhere."

"Sure, but Lawrence wants to split the US, and I don't think he could bring Duante with him."

"Probably not."

I heard Cody take a long swallow, then he belched. "Ryan Addison called me. He put me on the phone with Lindsey."

"He what?"

"Put me on the phone with Lindsey. She was very calm and collected."

I exhaled through my teeth. "Amazing. What did she say?"

"She asked if Duante Tucker would be brought to justice. She said it just like that."

"And?"

"I told her, yes, he'd pay for what he did. She asked me if I could guarantee it. I said, yeah, you can take it to the bank. She got all giddy and thanked me over and over."

"Pretty bold prediction, don't you think?" I said.

"Huh? You mean predicting we're gonna do our job, what we're paid to do? No, I don't see that as bold at all."

"I'm glad you're so confident."

Cody took another hit off whatever he was drinking. "Dirt, Dirt, you overthink things. That's a benefit and a liability. Look, this isn't all that complicated. We find Duante Tucker, chat with him, and we'll put this case to bed. It's that simple."

"He'll come clean with a full confession, huh? Why didn't I think of that?"

Cody's laugh was genuine and mirthful. "You told me just yesterday you wanted to nail his balls to the wall," he guffawed. "And, you *are* the expert on interrogation. I'll talk to you later."

"Wonderful," I said, but he'd already hung up.

I put on my sweats, loaded a twenty-pound pack, and headed out to the meadow to jog. An afternoon breeze rustled through the trees, but the sun was still hot and bright. I followed the trail into the woods and couldn't help thinking that maybe Cody was right; maybe I thought too much, overanalyzed, got myself needlessly wrapped around the axle. On the other hand, he tended to oversimplify things and take irresponsible and dangerous shortcuts. Maybe it was the contradictions in our mental approaches that made us a good team.

Whatever the case, it seemed clear that Lawrence Tucker had a three-day window, which was now down to two days, to conduct his business and flee the country. If we could find Duante Tucker in the next forty-eight hours, that could get us somewhere. If not, I couldn't predict what might happen.

Vowing to not invest any more brain cells on the matter for the time being, I finished the five-mile loop and returned home. I washed the sweat from my face with the garden hose and stripped off my pack and drenched T-shirt. When I went inside, I saw I had missed a call from Cody. I pushed the callback button.

"What's up?" I asked.

"I just picked up Shanice Tucker's phone from the encryption guy. I'm still parked in front of his house."

"Anything interesting?"

"I'm going through her text history. There's a bunch to a Lake Tahoe area code. But there's no listing of that number in her address book."

"What do the texts say?"

"Dates, times, and responses with hotel room numbers. Not much else."

"Sounds like she has a john in Tahoe," I said.

"That, or something. Write down the cell number, see if you can trace it. I'm on my way to Suggs's."

"Let me know what you find there," I said. I went to my desk to type the phone number into an online reverse directory. It would be easy to put a name to the number as long as it was a registered cell phone. But the number came up untraceable. That meant it was probably for a prepaid phone, which were typically used by someone who didn't have an account with a cellular provider, or someone who wished to keep his activity anonymous.

I crossed my arms. Shanice wouldn't travel four hours to Tahoe to turn a trick unless the money made it worthwhile. So her john had money but was using a prepaid phone to text her, which would be the smart thing to do if he was married, or otherwise wanted to make sure he couldn't be linked to the text messages. There were plenty of semiretired executive types who summered in vacation homes around the lake. A smart businessman would certainly want to keep his sexual habits discreet, especially if it included regular patronage of a prostitute.

I thought back to an incident a few years ago, when a popular British actor—young, handsome, rich—was dating a well-known, high-society actress. The actor seemed to lead a charmed life, but then he was caught with a black streetwalker who called herself Divine Brown. The tabloids had a field day, and the public was greatly amused and titillated by the incident. The actor, obviously embarrassed and in big trouble with his girlfriend, did not try to explain why, having his pick of willing women, he chose a hooker with a ghetto background.

I didn't think Shanice Tucker had much in common with Divine Brown, who cashed in on the talk show circuit and became a minor celebrity. For starters, I doubted Shanice had any interest in public scrutiny. Given her involvement with her brother and uncle, and also Russ Landers, she would definitely want to keep a low profile. At a minimum, her associations made her suspect. Factor in the link to Lake Tahoe, and her role could be something beyond what I had previously considered.

An hour later it was happy hour, but I didn't feel like a drink, and I was wondering when Cody would call. When he finally did, I was heating vegetable soup on the stove.

"Suggs's pit is cleaned out," he said. "No dogs, either. I walked right in the front door. The safe in the closet was wide open and empty. The only thing left is some ratty furniture."

"Duante would have emptied the safe. Any sign the authorities have been there?"

"Not that I could tell."

"Are you at home?"

"No, I'm driving."

"Those text messages Shanice sent to the five-three-zero area code—were any hotels named?"

"Yeah. Harrah's, Pistol Pete's, and a couple others."

"I need you to read me off the dates and times."

"Why?"

"Because the cell number is untraceable. I want to see if I can get a look at the casino security tapes, find out who she was meeting."

"All right. I'll call you when I get home."

Twenty minutes later Cody read me information for five different meetings, dating back two months. Each was at a different hotel, and three were at the casinos.

The times were all in the late afternoon, during the week. It would be simple enough to get the check-in information from the reservations desk, but it was possible that whoever booked the room used an assumed name.

I knew people at the casinos and had enough ruses up my sleeve to get the reservation data on my own. I might even convince certain people to provide access to surveillance discs. But the clock was ticking, and I didn't want to risk any delays. I needed to get Marcus Grier involved. I glanced at my watch and called Grier's cell.

"I just got home," he said. "I slept at the station last night, and not well, either. Please tell me this is something quick and easy."

"Just need you to make a single phone call. To the chief of security at Harrah's."

"To Joan Wallace? What do you want me to say to the iron maiden?"

"Duante Tucker's sister has been turning tricks in Tahoe since the beginning of the Tucker trial. I want to know who Shanice Tucker's been seeing. I have a specific date and time she met someone in a room at Harrah's."

The line went silent. I waited for him to say something, and after a moment I thought he we might have been disconnected, although my screen still showed the call was active.

"Are you there?" I said. "Hello?" He didn't reply, and then a thought that seemed both bizarre and ominous struck me. Could Grier be Shanice's john? If so, the implications for him would be disastrous. I thought about his wife and his two daughters and felt a queasy unease in my gut.

"Sorry about that," he said a second later. "What do you want me to say to her?"

"Tell her I'll call in a few minutes, and I'll need access to reservation info and maybe video surveillance."

"Tell me the room number and the date. I'll get the info."

I paused. "All right," I said. "Room 18227. May 12."

"I'll let you know," he said.

"If we don't recognize the name, I need to go to Harrah's tonight to look at video surveillance and try to identify the guest. Can you set it up for me?"

"I suppose," he said. "But if it comes to that, I'll go with you."

"If that's what you want," I said.

"I'll call you back."

"Marcus?"

"What?"

"Nothing."

"I'll call her after I have dinner," he said. "Is that soon enough for you?"

After we hung up, I hiked my foot up on my desk. The day was getting late, and I wanted to call Grier back and tell him time was critical and to ignore his stomach and call Joan Wallace immediately. But first I needed to dismiss the idea that Grier had anything to do with Shanice Tucker. My suspicion had no factual basis other than Grier's silence on the phone when I mentioned her name. It probably meant nothing at all. He could have just muted his phone while he spoke to his wife or daughters. Of all the flimsy what-ifs I'd come up with over the course of my investigation, the notion of Grier fornicating with Shanice Tucker had to be the most baseless.

I closed my eyes and rubbed my temples. Maybe my sudden suspicion was simply a neurotic extension of my own repressed sexual desire. Projection, shrinks call it. Or maybe it was just the stress getting to me.

"This is ridiculous," I said out loud. In the years I'd known Grier, I'd never seen any evidence of character deficit. He was a devout family man and an honest sheriff who hadn't showed the slightest indication he could be corrupted by the lure of money or sex. I had never known Grier to make a crude or suggestive remark or to even cast a sideways glance at a provocatively dressed woman. More important, I knew he had turned down bribes and was considered a clean cop by his underlings and superiors alike.

But how stalwart were his ethics? I hoped the worst he could be accused of was ignoring petty or moderate graft. I didn't think he was willing to leap into the grief pit that would result if he tried to make his department squeaky clean. He was a career man, and his priority was providing for his family. That meant he valued job security and stability. Cops who choose to fight for moral imperatives are loved by the public but often end up in the soup line.

Conclusion? Grier was a good cop—but not infallible. But did I really believe he could be involved with Shanice Tucker and, by extension, Duante Tucker? No, I didn't, and I felt like an asshole for even entertaining the thought. Grier and I had been through a lot together. He was my friend and ally.

With a shake of my head, I redialed Grier's cell, but he didn't pick up. I paced around my office for a minute, then I texted him: "Urgent we get Harrah's G2 tonight."

It wasn't until eight o'clock that he called me back. Candi and I were sitting out on the deck, watching the low clouds turn orange and pink as the sun fell behind the ridgeline. She was smoking her nightly peace pipe, and I had made a whiskey seven, but after a sip I'd set it aside, and the ice cubes had melted.

"The registered guest for room 18227 was Nate Forrest," Grier said. "No idea who he is."

"Did he leave a credit card number?" I asked.

"No, checked in with a cash deposit."

"Figures."

"Since there's no credit card, there's no time stamp showing the exact check-in time. She said she'd call her on-duty manager and have him prepare video for the time range they allow check-ins."

"I wonder how much viewing that'll take."

"Wallace said we can head over now."

"I'll meet you at the security office," I said.

• • •

Joan Wallace had been head of security at Harrah's for as long as anyone I knew could remember. She was an androgynous black woman nearing sixty with dusty skin, sharp eyes, and a body that showed no curves under the canvas pants and long-sleeved shirts she wore regardless of season. On the occasions I'd met her, she'd made it plain that her time was valuable, and she would not allow it to be wasted. On one occasion Cody had tried to turn on the charm, and her response prompted him to nickname her the "iron maiden." The name had apparently circulated and stuck, because I'd heard individuals I'd never met, a few of them cops, call her the same.

It was a Friday night, and Harrah's was packed with gamblers. They crowded three deep around the card tables and jostled for seats like a swarm of cars searching for spots in a full parking lot. The slot machine aisles were also crammed, the ceaseless electronic cadences like a manic chatter. Grier was wearing street clothes, and we stood at the security booth until a middle-aged woman with curly brown hair finished a phone call. She hung up and looked down at us from her tall perch.

"We have an appointment with Joan Wallace," I said.

"And you are?"

"Marcus Grier, sheriff," Grier said. "Tell her I'm here."

She gave a little raise of an eyebrow and picked up the phone. Then she said, "Chris Davies will come get you."

Within a minute, a slim, athletic-looking man with a suntan and lank blond hair came down a set of stairs. I'd met him on a previous case, and he'd been cooperative and helpful, unlike a couple of his surly counterparts.

"Dan Reno, right?" he said.

I nodded. "Chris, this is Sheriff Grier, South Lake PD."

"Hi, Sheriff. Follow me, gentlemen."

We went to the upstairs room where Harrah's managed its surveillance operations. Above a corner desk, a double row of screens was set in the wall. Along another wall, a long counter had been installed with computer monitors and chairs every few feet. Two of the chairs were occupied by men studying screens.

"I had our tech burn CDs from the reservation desk camera and the camera in the elevator lobby. I covered from noon to five p.m. You can set up over here." He pointed to two empty chairs. "Dan, do you remember how the program works?"

"Could use a refresher," I said.

"Sure. Hit F4 to pause, F5 to rewind, F6 to fast forward, and F9 to enlarge. Very simple. Call my mobile number if you need anything. I'll be on the floor."

Grier and I sat, and we each inserted a CD into our terminals. I had the reservation desk. After watching a few transactions, I realized I was at a big disadvantage. The problem was, I no longer considered it likely the room guest was an innocent businessman. If my hunch was right, Shanice

Tucker's john was a policeman. But I only knew a few of the local plain-clothesmen or patrolmen well enough to recognize them. The majority would be anonymous faces to me.

I reset the disc to the beginning, but this time, when a new person approached the reservation clerk, I leaned over and said, "Hey, Marcus. Recognize this dude?" Grier would then pause his disc and scoot his chair over and peer into my screen. In this manner we worked for a solid hour and a half until Grier said, "I'm done. I've got to get some sleep."

"I'll meet you here tomorrow morning," I said.

"No, I'm taking the CDs with me. I'll finish up at the station."

"You want me to come by in the morning and help you?"

He reached over and ejected my disk and slid it into his shirt pocket. "What for? You probably wouldn't know the suspect even if you saw him."

I stuck my thumbs in my belt loops. "Are you gonna get anyone to help you?"

"Don't worry about it." He started toward the exit. "Are you coming, or are you going to hang out here all night?"

The other two employees, who had largely ignored us, were now shooting glances our way. I didn't say anything and followed Grier downstairs and through the casino. When we got to the parking lot, the night had cooled, and the air had a bite to it. Grier walked to his car like a man determined to put the day behind him. But I stopped him before he could unlock his door.

"Listen, I busted my ass on this case," I said.

He unlocked the door and lowered himself into the driver's seat. "What's your point, Dan?"

"I think whoever was banging Shanice Tucker is your prime suspect. Those discs are the key to the case, the answer to who is crooked in your department."

"I'll keep that in mind," he said. "You ought to get some sleep. You look like death warmed over."

"Don't let me down, Sheriff," I said, but he was already closing his door, and then he backed up and pulled away, his tires rolling over a shoulder and flattening the grass alongside the pavement.

• • •

When I got home, I made a stiff drink and finished it in two swallows. Then I went to my desk and ran a people search on Nate Forrest, a name that meant nothing to me and almost certainly was not the real name of the person who reserved the room at Harrah's. After looking at over thirty hits, none of whom lived in California or Nevada, I tried a different tact. I typed the name into Google and found a biography on a Confederate war hero named Nathan Bedford Forrest.

He was a slave trader, a riverboat gambler, a Ku Klux Klan grand wizard, and a lieutenant general in the Civil War. He was accused of war crimes for the slaughter of black union soldiers and praised for his fierce energy and brute courage. An uneducated man, he killed at an early age and earned a fortune as a planter and real estate investor before the war. No less than thirty-two historical markers bear his name in his home state of Tennessee, including a bust at the Tennessee state capitol building. An army base is named after him, as are two high schools.

He seemed an interesting character, a symbol of Southern culture: tough, unrelenting, a self-made man of wealth and power. Apparently his history as a Klan wizard and slave trader made little difference to the people who revered and memorialized him. What kind of person would identify with this type of man? Someone from the deep south or, more specifically, from Tennessee. Someone who had no problem with discrimination against blacks. And maybe someone who, despite his prejudices, had a particular lust for black women.

Or someone could have selected the name for no reason other than it sounded ordinary and would not be recognized or remembered by most people in this part of the country.

I sipped at the watery dregs of my cocktail. The Tennessee angle bore further scrutiny. In the morning, I'd call Marcus Grier and ask if anyone employed by South Lake Tahoe PD had any background in Tennessee.

• • •

I'd been asleep for about an hour when my cell phone rang. It was midnight.

"Hello?" I croaked.

"Sorry to wake you," Cody said." But there's been a development."

Candi murmured something, and I got out of bed and walked out to the hallway.

"What?"

"I didn't find much else useful on Shanice's phone. So I drove over to her apartment. I've been parked down the street for the last few hours. Guess who just showed up?"

"Landers?"

"Good guess, but no. It's our boy, Duante. Has a suitcase with him. Looks like he's spending the night."

I walked out to the family room and sat on the arm of the couch. "What do you want to do?" I asked.

"I want to be here at eight tomorrow morning and see what Duante does with his day. Can you make it?"

"I guess I better set my alarm."

"Get some sleep. Tomorrow could be interesting."

"Thanks for the advice," I said.

11

IT WAS SPRINKLING WHEN I left my house at four thirty the next morning. The odd summer shower had dampened the roads just enough to bring translucent streaks of oil to the surface. A thin white cloud cover cast an eerie illumination over the mountains. I drove in silence over Echo Pass, my tires squeaking on the slippery asphalt. There was no radio reception, and the metronome of my wiper blades had an almost hypnotic effect.

The dawn began to break as I descended out of the foothills above Sacramento. When the first burst of sunlight flared on the horizon north of the city, the clouds turned silver and blood red and began to break up like a sheet of glass shattering in slow motion. By the time I reached the flatlands, a rainbow arced over the valley, and mist rose from the pavement. In the distance, the sun's reflection off the gold towers of the Sacramento Bridge was so bright I had to shade my eyes.

I was right on time when I exited the freeway in San Jose and turned down the street where Shanice Tucker lived. It was a Saturday, and there was no commuter traffic; I had made the drive in three and a half hours. I spotted Cody's maroon Toyota a half block from Shanice's apartment.

"Good morning," Cody said when I opened his passenger door. "All quiet so far."

I tossed my bag into his backseat. "You sure Duante's still there?"

"No. But I stayed here until two a.m., and he didn't leave. And Shanice's car is still in the parking lot. I got you a coffee."

I leaned my head back and shut my eyes.

"Here's an article you should read," he said, handing me a section of the *San Jose Mercury*. "The one about US aid to Egypt."

I yawned and blew the steam from the cup of gas station coffee I took from Cody's console. "Why?" I asked.

"Because it's interesting."

I closed my eyes again and tried to sip from the cup, but the contents were scalding hot. I set the cup down, crossed my arms, and let my chin fall on my chest.

"All right, because it will provide great clarity and illumination to our international affairs and the intractable problems we face," Cody said.

"Intractable, huh?"

"Yeah. It means fucked up beyond repair."

"I know what it means," I said. "I read the dictionary."

"You're no doubt a great scholar." He reached over and the tapped the newspaper. "Read it."

The article was written by a *Washington Post* columnist. It described how, despite our huge federal deficit, the US secretary of state had just gifted $250 million to Egypt. The newly elected president of Egypt gladly accepted the funds, which would help stave off the looming collapse of the Egyptian economy. The new president had been elected during the series of Mideast revolutions known as the Arab Spring. The people of Egypt had overthrown the prior authoritarian regime and elected into office a Muslin Brotherhood leader who was lobbying for the release of terrorists convicted of killing Americans. The president also urged his countrymen to teach their children and grandchildren that Jews were "the descendants of apes and pigs" and thus forever should be hated and, if at all possible, exterminated.

The rationale for our financial aid was misguided and murky, claimed the writer. He posed the question: why would we spend our taxpayers' money to support regimes that endorse terrorism and cannot even offer us oil in exchange?

I handed the paper back to Cody. "Intractable seems to sum it up," I said.

"Our politicians are funding the same pukes they claim to be protecting us from. They need to pull their heads out of their asses."

"If they did, they wouldn't be politicians."

"Buckle up," Cody said. My eyes snapped to the windshield. Shanice Tucker's Ford Taurus had just turned out of the alley aside the apartment building. I caught a brief glimpse the car's sole occupant. A tall black man.

"Duante?" Cody asked.

"Looks like him."

"Let's go see if we can contribute to the greater good, eh, Dirt?"

"I always say, if you're not part of the solution, you're part of the problem."

"Hey, a line of your own. Not bad."

The Taurus drove out toward the freeway. We followed south on 101 to the Guadalupe Parkway off-ramp. The driver drove the speed limit and took the Saint James exit. There was little traffic downtown, and to keep a safe distance, we had to drive slowly. But after the first turn, it was clear where the driver was headed.

"The Skyscape," Cody said.

"The CIA man told me unit 1602 was empty, cleaned out."

We pulled over at the corner adjacent to the ascending black windows of the Skyscape. The Taurus continued forward, past the main entrance, and turned the corner, out of our view. We followed but did not turn down the street where the Ford had gone. Instead, we passed through the intersection, and when I looked I saw the Taurus had pulled over and parked behind an older-model BMW, opposite the Skyscape.

Cody hung a U-turn, and we crept up to the corner. I grabbed my bag, got out of the car, and walked to where a hedge of shrubs lined the perimeter of the building on the same side of the street the two cars were parked. I shimmied under the hedge at the corner, lay in the dirt, and peered down the street through a small telescope.

Duante Tucker stood talking to two men sitting in the BMW. Tucker wore shiny blue sweat pants with red strips down the side and a white V-neck T-shirt. His cheeks were unshaven and looked hollow, and his eyes roved up and down the avenue. He stepped back from the BMW, and the driver stuck his head out the window and craned his neck, looking upward. Then he nodded, and Tucker walked back to the Taurus and got inside.

The BMW's driver continued looking up at the Skyscape. He wore wire-rimmed spectacles, and the scraggly beard covering his face was uneven and reminded me of the coat of a mangy dog. The hair on his head was equally ratty and looked matted, as if he had been wearing a close-fitting hat.

I looked up in time to see a car pass through the intersection down the block. It was a black Ford, a Crown Vic, a car that for years had been the most popular choice of government agencies.

I looked back at the BMW. The driver was still staring out the window, his neck twisted diagonally. I couldn't be sure, but I thought he was likely the man Cody had photographed at the Arabic restaurant in Fremont.

For a long moment, nothing happened. The dirt where I lay was moist, and I could feel the damp cold through my clothes. An insect landed on my knuckle, and I shook it free. Then, within that instant of distraction, the ground shook with a concussive force, and my ears felt the atmospheric pressure change as a massive explosion erupted from above. For a second

I froze in shock, then I looked up to see a ball of fire balloon from the sixteenth floor of the Skyscape.

I scrambled to my feet. Burning glass and metal rained down, and the concrete balcony of unit 1602 dangled by a few strands of rebar. Dense gray smoke poured from a gaping hole in the structure, and flames curled outward and lapped at exposed iron girders. The balcony swayed for a moment before breaking loose and plummeting downward. It crashed into the sidewalk with a thunderous boom.

The man in the BMW hadn't moved. He continued staring upward. The Taurus also hadn't moved, and when I brought the telescope to my eye, I saw Duante Tucker furiously jabbing at his cell phone.

I heard the screech of Cody's tires as he pulled to the curb near me. "Let's go!" he shouted. He held his .357 revolver in his right hand. I jumped into the passenger seat, he dumped the clutch, and we burned rubber around the corner. Cody's souped-up Camry fishtailed, and as we straightened, the Taurus launched forward, steering around the BMW. We roared in pursuit, and when we passed by the BMW, the man was still staring upward, as if he was in a trance, or perhaps waiting for a secondary event.

When we reached the end of the block, Tucker took the corner without braking, and the Taurus went wide into oncoming traffic. A pickup truck jumped the curb to avoid a head-on and smashed into a fire hydrant. A jet of water blasted skyward, and I saw the black Crown Vic come from the opposite direction and turn away from us. Its tires squealing, it raced toward where the BMW was parked.

Cody handled the corner in a neat four-wheel drift, and we rapidly gained on the Taurus. We were nearly on its bumper when Tucker veered again into the opposing lanes and used every bit of the roadway to manage a seventy-MPH left-hand turn. Cody downshifted, and we narrowly avoided a minivan pulling from the curb.

"He's going to fucking kill someone," Cody said. He mashed his foot to the floor, and we roared down San Fernando Boulevard. Tucker blew through a red light, and we had to slam the brakes to avoid T-boning a box truck. Cody skidded sideways and corrected and the Taurus had gained on us and was probably going close to a hundred MPH. We passed under Guadalupe Parkway and away from the downtown grid. We were in an industrial part of town that was largely deserted on a Saturday morning. The Taurus roared through another stoplight, and then Tucker hit the brakes and tried to turn left onto a side street, but his tries locked, and the car spun in a 360. He regained control and turned right down a street lined with warehouses and cabinet and flooring shops.

Cody had to slow to avoid a collision at the stoplight. Then he worked the gearbox, his left foot jabbing the clutch in a flurry of motion. The ugly Toyota that he called the hellfire hooptie flew ahead, hitting 120, then we slowed faster than I thought possible, and Cody skidded around a corner, all four tires squealing loudly. I saw the Taurus ahead just before it turned left behind a weathered building with stained stucco and blacked-out windows.

I could hear sirens in the background, but they were distant and probably all heading toward the Skyscape. We came around the corner, and the Taurus was accelerating down a long straightaway. Up ahead the road ended in a T, where a long, windowless, single-story structure ran along the street.

Cody's foot never left the floor, and we were gaining on the Taurus.

"He'll never make it," I said as we neared the end of the street. A second later the Taurus's brake lights flashed, and Tucker tried to make a right turn. The tires howled in protest and the car slid sideways, leaving black stripes of rubber on the road. I could see Tucker hunched over and fighting the wheel. But the steering was not responding, and the Taurus slammed hard against the curb and jolted into the air. It landed on the sidewalk, the tires smoking, both left side rims folded under the chassis.

As we came up from behind, Tucker jumped from the car and began sprinting down the street. Cody hit the gas, but before we could cut him off, Tucker bolted through a doorway into the building on our left.

I grabbed my bag from the backseat and found my backup piece, the Hi-Point 380 subcompact.

"I'll come around the block," Cody said.

I got out of the Toyota and ran to the door. Inside, the room was cool and cavernous. It was a granite slab warehouse. Row after row of eight-foot-tall slabs stored on steel frames stretched across a floor nearly the size of a football field. To the left was a counter where a woman drank coffee and studied a mobile device. She didn't look up at me.

"Stay down," I yelled. Her head jerked up, her eyes wide and startled.

I sidestepped past each aisle in a crouch. Tucker could have been hiding behind any of the vertically stacked slabs. Or he could have headed for an exit across the floor. I made it to the end of the building without any sign of him. I jogged along the perimeter and down a center aisle, my eyes darting to each row.

A shot rang out, and a bullet powdered a chunk of granite an inch from my face. I ducked and saw Tucker peering from around a slab, taking aim. I returned fire while diving for cover. When I peeked out, I didn't see him.

I held the Hi-Point in a two-fisted grip and ran to where Tucker had been. When I came to the end of his aisle, a slug punched a hole in the loose material of my jeans behind the knee. Tucker was kneeling forty feet away, pointing a revolver.

He shot again as I leapt behind a stack of granite. I reached out, took quick aim, and jerked the trigger. The short-barreled gun bucked, and I saw my slug tear a trench in a shiny green slab above Tucker's head. He fired once more and ducked out of my sight.

I ran at his position, then saw him running toward an exit sign. "Freeze!" I yelled and fired a round over his head. He somersaulted, twisted in the air, and fired. It was a prayer and shouldn't have been close, but his slug grazed my shoulder, and little spots of blood appeared on my sleeve. I shot back just as he slid behind a forklift twenty feet from the door.

My arm stung like it had been burned, but I ignored it and kept my weapon trained on the forklift. Five long seconds passed until Tucker dashed for the door, firing as he ran. I put him in the sights and shot at his legs, but my shot was wide, and I cursed because the Hi-Point was a cheap weapon, and the aim wasn't true. Tucker would have been down if I had my Beretta, which was still being held by SJPD. I took another shot, aiming wide to compensate, but Tucker yanked open the door just as my bullet hit the wall near his calf, and then he was gone.

I sprinted for the door. Tucker had fired six shots, and it was possible he was reloading. But it only took a few seconds for me to cross the roughly sixty feet, and I was betting he was not practiced enough with a revolver to reload that quickly. I yanked the door open. Tucker had crossed the deserted street and was at a dead run, on his toes, his knees pumping high, leaning forward as if stretching for a finish line.

For a brief second I considered whether to give chase or fire. I don't lose many footraces, but Tucker was flying, and I doubted I could run him down. Instead I took aim. But then Cody came around the far corner in his Toyota and skidded to a stop, the car perpendicular to the curb. His window was down, and I could see his great head of shaggy hair and the glossy black of his .357 revolver. He straightened his arm and was no more than fifty feet from Tucker, and the big bore of the Magnum was pointed and promised an irrevocable outcome. But Tucker shoulder-rolled and tried forcing open the door to a closed roofing supply outlet.

The door was stout, and I was sure that Tucker, out of bullets and trapped, would surrender. He turned toward Cody, and when he tossed his revolver to the pavement, I lowered my gun.

But to assume Duante Tucker would concede at this point was not only wrong, it was foolish. Surely I knew better, because even though I believe that in the human heart there is a great capacity for kindness and compassion, for some, that space is consumed by hatred. It's a process that begins in the womb and grows with each year of life until the heart turns wholly black. And then one day, the realization sets in that no amount of misdeed is enough, and after that it's only a matter of time before the hatred turns inward and the soul devours itself.

If that moment had arrived for Duante Tucker, I can't truly say. Maybe he thought the journeys of his black heart were just beginning, and the party was not yet in full swing. Or maybe he was just a desperate, sadistic son of a bitch whose blood lust wouldn't be denied.

In a fluid, athletic motion, Tucker pulled a small automatic from the back of his sweat pants, let off a shot at Cody, and spun to face me. For an instant he had me dead in his sights, and I raised my gun but knew I was too late. Then I heard the thunderous boom of Cody's .357, followed by the sharp crack of Tucker's automatic.

Tucker threw his arms up as if praising the heavens, knees bent, back arched, his mouth wide in a silent scream. Then his legs buckled, and he fell to the ground as if his bones had been liquefied.

I turned and saw where Tucker's shot had split the wood molding on the building behind me. The small round was embedded in the stucco next to a sealed window. I looked back to the street and watched Cody climb from his car, the smoking pistol dangling from his hand. He dropped it in his window and began limping toward Tucker. There was a bullet hole in the Toyota's back door.

We met at Tucker's body. Cody knelt with a grimace and said, "He's still alive."

Tucker lay facedown, his shirt soaked with blood. The .357 round had hit him dead center in the middle of the back. I had automatically assumed the shot was lethal. If you've ever shot a .357 Magnum, you know what I'm talking about; the pistol is like a handheld cannon, and it's difficult to imagine anyone surviving a wound to the torso.

I leaned down and looked at Tucker. His face was against the asphalt, and a bloody foam dribbled from his lips with each breath. I looked into one of his eyes. He blinked and the skin around the socket grew tight.

"Can you hear me?" I asked.

He made a sound like you might hear from a mentally retarded person or an individual with a severe speech impediment.

"He's not dead," I said. "But I don't think he's having a very good day."

"That's too bad," Cody said. "Maybe tomorrow will be better."

We stood looking at him. His arm shuddered, and his wrist curled inward, the fingers splayed and twisted.

"Maybe not," I said.

"That's the breaks. Hey, I got a new place we should try for lunch today. They make real New Orleans style po' boy sandwiches."

The distant sirens were getting closer. The lazy blue sky was split with a dirty plume of dark smoke rising high above downtown San Jose. I wondered if the Skyscape was burning down, or if further explosions had occurred, or if the authorities had apprehended the occupants of the BMW. I also wondered if the CIA had found Lawrence Tucker.

The cops who showed up a minute later didn't seem preoccupied with those uncertainties. They didn't even interview us long enough to see the paramedics get Duante Tucker in an ambulance. They were still tending to him when we were cuffed from behind and stuck in separate squad cars.

• • •

I sat in the same interview room at SJPD that I'd been in two days ago. They left my cuffs on, and I waited for thirty minutes until Russ Landers came through the door. He wore a brown suit jacket over a white shirt that looked too tight around his fleshy neck.

"Am I under arrest?" I asked.

"I'll let you know. Describe what happened this morning."

"Cody and I followed Duante Tucker from his sister's apartment. You know, your friend, Shanice."

"Actually, I don't know who you're talking about. But we'll come back to that. Go on."

"Tucker parked in front of the Skyscape building and spoke with two men in a BMW. Then Tucker went back to his car, and a moment later an explosion occurred on the sixteenth floor. I think Tucker activated a charge from his cell phone."

"What next?"

"We drove toward Tucker, and he took off."

"You followed him at a high rate of speed, causing two accidents." Landers put his hands on the table and leaned his weight forward. His eyes were small and dark and unblinking.

"After Tucker wrecked his car, he took off on foot," I said. "I followed him inside a granite warehouse, and he shot at me. We exchanged shots, then he left the building and sprinted away. But Cody came around in his car and ordered Tucker to stop. But he pulled a second gun on us."

"Did he fire?"

"Yeah, twice. One round hit Cody's car, and the other hit the building behind me. Cody shot him to save my life."

"In the back." Landers smiled and rubbed his hands together.

"Tucker had me in his sights. I'd be dead if Cody hadn't shot him. Tucker was trying to kill us, if that's not obvious to you."

"I don't consider it obvious. I also don't know where you get off thinking you can provoke a car chase, endanger citizens, and engage in a shoot-out, all under the authority of a PI badge any two-bit chump can get."

"Tucker had just committed a terrorist act. I'm an American citizen. I wasn't about to let him drive away."

Landers came back to the table and leaned into my face. "Our prosecutor is gonna eat you alive, you prick. You're under arrest." He read me my rights.

"What are the charges?" I asked.

"It will be a long list," he said. "How about attempted murder, to start?"

"It won't stick, and you know it."

"Oh, I think it will. And one more thing. We may add blackmail to the list. With today's digital technology, any criminal can create phony pictures and audio files. So you can shitcan the threats you've made to me. How does fifteen years in San Quentin sound?"

"I need to make a phone call."

"You've been watching too many movies."

"My Miranda rights say I can contact counsel. If you don't let me use the phone, they'll throw your case out. So you decide."

"Maybe they'll let you and Gibbons be bunkies," he said, a happy smirk on his face. Then he left the room, and a minute later, two uniforms came for me.

•   •   •

It wasn't until they completed the entire booking process that I was allowed access to a phone. For three hours I had waited, while they took my mug shot, collected my property, fingerprinted me, conducted a full body search, and took X-rays and a blood sample. It's in this initial stage that an arrested individual realizes his time is no longer his own. Minutes blur into hours, and there's never any hurry, because there's nowhere to go and nothing to do, at least nothing you decide on your own.

For someone new to prison, the booking is probably among the most benign of institutionalized experiences. The rude awakening usually occurs when the fresh convict is introduced to his cellmates and understands that he has entered a predatory world where the weak are raped and forced into servitude, and even the strong are shanked and die gruesome deaths on a regular basis. The realization there is no escape from this hellish world for the duration of the sentence drives some to suicide early on. More commonly though, the convicts join prison gangs, which affords them some protection, but the price is mandatory participation in a variety of crimes, including murder.

I stood at the end of a dirty hallway where a pay phone was mounted to the wall, and called my attorney, who didn't answer. I left him a detailed message, then dialed the cell number for Greg Stillman. He answered on the first ring.

"Stillman."

"Greg, it's Dan Reno. I was at the Skyscape this morning when the bomb went off in unit 1602. I assume you're aware of it?"

"Go on."

"I think your boys were there too, maybe swooped in on a couple dudes in a BMW, maybe Abdul Talwar and one of his cousins. While your agents were going after the BMW, Cody Gibbons and I chased down Duante Tucker, who was there talking to the guys in the BMW."

"I heard something about it."

"Tucker ended up shot. He's probably over at Valley Medical, if he's still alive. I think Tucker was the one who set off the bomb. I also think there was possibly more than one bomb that was meant to go off."

"Why do you think that?"

"Because after the explosion, the BMW's driver sat staring up at the building, and I got the impression he was waiting for something else to happen. And Tucker kept dialing his cell phone, and then he took off in a big hurry."

"Thanks for the tip," Stillman said. "Are you still in San Jose?"

"I'm calling from the jailhouse phone at San Jose PD. They arrested me and my partner Cody Gibbons for the attempted murder of Duante Tucker. It's a bullshit charge brought on by Russ Landers at SJPD. He's the cop who was in the sack with Lawrence Tucker's niece."

"That's unfortunate."

"You're damn right it is. How about helping me out here?"

"I'm sorry, Mr. Reno. This is a particularly busy time for my team."

I took a deep breath and fought a surge of anger rising from my chest. "There're a few more interesting facts I've uncovered that I'd like to share with you, Mr. Stillman. That is, if you have the time."

"Go ahead."

"Not on the phone. Get me out of here, and we'll talk."

The phone went silent. Then he said, "I'll see what I can do," and hung up.

The jailer, a mustachioed middle-aged man with a stomach that hung over his belt, crooked his finger at me. "Times up," he said. He took me through a steel door that opened with a wave of his electronic key. The door clanged shut behind us, and he steered me to the holding cell, a large, barred room with cots on the wall and a toilet in one corner. A half dozen men were in the room. Cody sat in the corner furthest from the toilet, hunched on a cot and studying his fingernails. He looked up, along with each of the men, when I joined the unfortunate group. Saturday lockup meant a weekend stay. Even the dimmest among them understood there would be no arraignment until Monday.

I sat next to Cody. "Did Landers interview you?" I asked.

"He was very professional about it, even polite," Cody said quietly. "I think he was putting on a show for the DA. He sees this as his chance to fuck me over for the count." Cody raised his head and stared down a tattooed Mexican who was watching us.

"You get ahold of your lawyer?" I asked.

"Mine doesn't work weekends. How about yours?"

"Left him a message."

"I'm sorry about this, Dan. We're here because of my beef with Landers. But it's my deal. You shouldn't have to suffer for it."

"No need to apologize. Your enemies are my enemies, partner. Besides, I told Landers to go fuck himself the other day, so I made my own bed."

"We'll beat this thing. Anisa Clark is a practical DA, and she also knows Landers is dirty. She'll be the one to decide whether to prosecute, and I doubt she was even here today. It was probably an assistant watching when Landers interrogated me."

We fell silent. Neither of us wanted to discuss the possibilities if our case went to trial. Ask anyone accused of a felony about his or her experience with the court system. An overzealous prosecutor, a biased judge, a lost or fabricated piece of evidence, a false testimony. All it takes is one of the above to queer a jury and result in a conviction. But often trials don't get that far. Once the momentum swings far enough in the prosecution's favor, they typically offer the defendants a chance to plead out. In our case, that might mean three to five instead of ten to fifteen years.

But my attorney was rock solid, one of the best, I told myself. He wouldn't let me down. I expected he'd call back before the day was out. I'd ask him to contact Anisa Clark, who was probably at home enjoying her weekend, and explain to her that Cody and I were acting in self-defense and should never have been arrested.

I suddenly felt a great weariness descend over me. I was sitting on the edge of the thin mattress, and despite my reservations, I pushed myself back to the darker middle section and leaned against the wall. I'd not slept enough last night, and a throbbing headache had settled in behind my eyes. My face felt oily to the touch and I wondered if I could sleep sitting upright, and I tried but was interrupted when the jailer brought lunch. I was hungry, but the smell of the baloney sandwiches and mashed potatoes made me nauseous. I repressed a gag and closed my eyes again.

Sometime later Cody shook my shoulder. "Wake up," he said. "Someone's here for you."

I rubbed a kink in my neck and looked up at where the jailer stood at the barred doorway. "You have a visitor," he said.

Cody and I exchanged glances, then I got up and the cop opened the door and took me back down the long hallway. We went out the steel door and past the interrogation room and entered a small office where two men sat. The jailer left, and I stood looking at the men, one of whom rose from behind a desk.

"I'm David Cohen, assistant DA," he said. He was a short man in a blue business suit. He had thick eyebrows, and when he looked at me his eyes were very still.

The other man didn't stand. He also wore a suit and was handsome in a way, but the skin on his forehead and around his eyes looked unnaturally creased, as if he spent long, unrelieved hours in deep concentration. He stuck his square hand out for me to shake. "Matt Royce, CIA," he said. "Take a seat."

I took the chair next to Royce, and he turned and uncrossed his legs. "I was told you had information you'd like to share regarding the bombing at the Skyscape."

"I told Greg Stillman I'd be happy to share everything I know, once the bogus charges against me are dropped. And that goes for Cody Gibbons, too."

I shifted my eyes to the DA, but he made no gesture or comment.

"Do we have a deal, Mr. Cohen?" I said.

When he didn't respond, Royce said, "That depends if you have something of value to offer."

"That sounds pretty arbitrary to me."

"It's as good as it's going to get," Cohen said.

I stared at the two men for a long moment. "All right," I said. "Since I last spoke with Stillman, and delivered to him two men hired by Lawrence Tucker, I've learned that Tucker's niece, Shanice, a known prostitute, had been frequenting South Lake Tahoe before Duante Tucker's trial. I think she was likely meeting someone from the police department there, and influenced the disappearance of the evidence against Duante Tucker. I think Lawrence Tucker put her up to this, because he needed Duante Tucker's help in his scheme to blow up the Skyscape."

"Any suspicions who Shanice Tucker was meeting?" Royce said.

"No. But here's something to consider. Shanice was also turning tricks with none other than Russ Landers. I doubt that's a coincidence."

"Elaborate on that," Cohen said. His face was impassive but he had leaned forward, his elbows on his desk.

"Landers was probably taking heroin money from Tucker or his associates," I said. "He's been crooked for a long time."

Cohen didn't blink, but I caught a tiny nod of his head, a brief tightening of his lips.

"Why would Lawrence Tucker want to bomb the Skyscape building?" Royce said. His tone had turned aggressive, a hard edge to his voice. He sat upright in his chair, and it struck me that he was about my age and my size. For a moment I wondered if our similarities posed us as adversaries in his mind.

"There's one theory that occurred to me," I said. "Lawrence Tucker cut a deal with al-Qaida. In exchange for heroin, he offered to blow up a building in San Jose. Kind of like a small-scale nine-eleven. Maybe al-Qaida liked the idea of sending a message that no city is safe."

"But the building didn't go down," Royce said. "Not even close."

"I think Tucker had to hurry his plans. Cody Gibbons and I were closing in on him."

The creases in Royce's forehead grew deeper. He stared past me for a long moment. Then he picked up his briefcase and stood.

"If there's nothing else, we're done for now," he said. "But don't be surprised if we contact you down the road."

"My charges are dropped, and Gibbons too, right?"

He tilted his head and looked at his watch. "Greg Stillman asked me to relay a message, Mr. Reno. He says he considers you a patriot. Between you and me, I'd consider that a high compliment." He nodded at the DA, then turned and left the room.

I sat there silently until Cohen sighed and said, "It's been quite a Saturday." He picked up the phone, and I heard him give instructions to release Cody and me without delay. "They'll have your property at the desk," he said after he hung up.

"My Beretta, too. That was taken earlier this week."

"Yes, I'm aware. You can have it."

"Good. See you later, then."

"Let's hope not," he said.

· · ·

The sunlight assaulted my eyes when Cody and I walked out of the police station. The white steps to the street glared blindingly, and silver bursts ricocheted off the steel fence poles at the impound yard where we picked up Cody's Camry. I put on my sunglasses and waited for a cop, who was clearly in no hurry, to process the release of the automobile. When we finally drove off, it was almost five o'clock.

"Where are we headed?" I asked.

"Today's been a long, weird day," Cody said. "I'm starving and thirsty, and I'd say it's time to celebrate."

"Celebrate what?"

"Huh? Snap out of it, Dirt. We're free and clear, and Duante Tucker is off the playing field."

"Our work's not done," I reminded him. "Ryan Addison hired us to find out who stole the evidence."

"Fine. Call Grier and see what he's found on the CDs. But as your friend and spiritual advisor, I strongly recommend you partake in strong drink beforehand."

"Why?"

"Because you look like you're ready to have a brain hemorrhage. You'll feel like a new man after a couple pops. Trust me."

Cody took the Lark avenue exit and drove us to the lounge I used to know as Gerhard's Garden Room. We sat at the bar and ordered burgers from Lana, the tall, sultry bartender. Cody also instructed her to mix us whiskey-seven highballs in pint beer glasses. "Make 'em fifty-fifty, Lana," he said.

On the television above the bar, newscasters were reporting on the explosion at the Skyscape. The reporter at the scene said the police suspected it was caused by a gas leak, but other possibilities were being investigated, and federal authorities had become involved. The camera zoomed in on the jagged hole where unit 1602 had been.

"Let me tell you, there's nothing that tastes better on a hot summer day," Cody said when Lana placed the tall cocktails in front of us. "Drink it down and tell me I'm wrong. We're getting ripped tonight."

"You heard him, Dirty Dan," Lana said with a wink.

It was against my better judgment, like many things Cody pre-
scribed during our long friendship, but I raised the glass to my lips
anyway. Then I ate two cheeseburgers and drained two more drinks.
Afterward, I checked my watch a couple times and decided the call to
Marcus Grier could wait. We moved to a table near the jukebox, and
when Cody went to the restroom, Lana came over, flashed me her freckled breasts, and said her shift was ending soon. I declined as politely as
I could and called Candi and told her I'd drive home in the morning
and take her to dinner. That, unlike many of the events of the evening,
I remember specifically.

By the time the sun went down, we had moved on to another bar—
for a nightcap, Cody said—and I lost count of drinks. A strange woman
wearing star-and-crescent necklaces and turquois bracelets came in with
a man who disappeared shortly afterward. She moved next to me at the
bar, touched my hand, and offered to tell my fortune. I don't remember
what she said, but after a while, it occurred to me she had been reading my palm for too long. I looked around for Cody but couldn't find
him, and then he came from a hallway with a curly haired blond woman
who looked tiny next to his frame. I vaguely recall an introduction being
made.

I don't know what time it was when we made it back to Cody's house.
I woke up on his couch, and sun filtered around his curtains and lit the
room with a fuzzy warmth. I had been dreaming I was in a diner with
my parents, and realized it had been prompted by the smell of bacon and
potatoes frying nearby. I blinked the dream away, then heard a woman's
voice and sat up and saw Cody in the kitchen with someone.

I rested my head on my palms and noted the bottle of aspirin and a
half-full plastic water bottle on the coffee table. I was dazed but in no hor-
rible pain, and for that I was thankful. It had been months since I'd been
drunk to oblivion.

"Up from the dead, Pegasus rises and flies to the sun!" Cody exclaimed when he looked over. He held a glass in his hand. "Bloody?" he asked.

"Breakfast of champions," the lady added. She was grinning and drank from a straw. Her jeans were tight and low on her hips, and she was petite except for heavy breasts, which swayed unencumbered beneath her blouse.

"Put your shirt on and get some grub," Cody said.

"What time is it?" I mumbled.

"It's Sunday, kemosabe, time for love and libations and libidinal excursions and livin', man!"

The woman laughed merrily, her pretty smile framed by locks of blond hair that fell on her cheeks. "What a life!" she exclaimed.

I think I tried to smile, but the best I could manage was a parting of the lips and a hollow-eyed stare.

●　　●　　●

There's a particular virtue to hangovers. The alcoholic fog dulls the mind, thoughts slow to a crawl, and details blur into smudges. Yesterday's problems become insignificant, as if they were part of some fabricated and unnecessary illusion. In a numbed stupor, there's no energy left for worry or action. A good hangover is not always a bad thing, especially if you need a day off from your life. The trick, though, is to resist the temptation to drink your way out of it.

Although I felt far from great as I drove home, at least my heavy head was quiet. I was still a little drunk, and in this whiskey-induced peace I drove automatically, slumped in my seat. I didn't think of talking to Marcus Grier or reporting the recent developments to Ryan Addison. I also didn't think of what would become of Lawrence Tucker or Russ Landers. If anything, my thoughts were of getting home to Candi and immediately taking her to our bedroom. My brain cells may have been deadened, but I was horny as a two-peckered billy goat. Another by-product of a hangover, I suppose.

When I got home, I undressed Candi and our lovemaking was raucous and exhilarating, and her fervor nearly matched my own. Afterward, I was sated and tired and sat on the couch for most of the afternoon and didn't do a shred of work. In the evening I finally snapped out of it after drinking two vodka tonics, strictly for medicinal purposes. When Candi and I got back from dinner, we watched television and by ten o'clock I was asleep. And it was not the sleep of the damned either, like I half expected. I didn't wake up for ten solid hours.

12

THE NEXT MORNING I assembled all my notes on the case and began working on an update for Ryan Addison. I was almost done by nine o'clock, which was when I called Marcus.

"Did you figure out who Shanice's john was?" I asked.

"Maybe. I need you to send me the other hotel dates and times you said you have."

"Who's the suspect?"

"We need collaborating evidence, so send it over."

"Who is it, Marcus?" I persisted.

"I'll let you know when I'm good and ready. Like after we make an arrest."

"I need to know as soon as you do. Don't forget, you wouldn't be onto him if it wasn't for me."

"I doubt you'd let me forget that for half a minute. I'll be waiting for your e-mail."

After we hung up I added a few sentences to my case report, then called Ryan Addison.

"Hey, what's happenin', No Problemo Reno?"

"I'm about to send you an update, Mr. Addison."

"Good. But no hurry, I'm on the road. Cody called me yesterday."

"What'd he say?"

"He said he shot Duante Tucker in the spine, and the scumbag is paralyzed, and they got him on tubes. His mind is fully functioning, but he's a slug, and his chances of surviving the next six months are maybe fifty-fifty. Right on, huh?"

"Are you in town?" I asked.

"No, I'm driving to San Jose. Lindsey's with me, too. We're going to pay Duante a visit, just to say hello, you know? I think it might be very therapeutic."

"You sure that's what you want to do?"

"You know, Dan, nothing against you, I think you're a pretty good guy, but there's something we never quite synced up on," he said.

"What's that?"

"Have you ever had a family member badly fucked over? If you have, you might understand where I'm coming from. But my guess is you've never had that experience."

"You guessed wrong," I said.

"Really? Well, maybe we've been on the same page all along. Could that be the case? Whatever, I'm pleased with the outcome, my man. You might even say, tickled pink."

"The investigation's not over yet. But we're getting close to identifying who stole the evidence."

"Glad to hear it. They better prosecute the son of a bitch."

"I think South Lake PD has every intention of that."

"They better. If they screw up again, don't be surprised if your phone rings."

• • •

Three days went by. I left two messages for Greg Stillman, and he didn't respond. I also left Marcus a message asking for an update. He didn't return my call, either.

During that time, the national news media ran daily stories reporting that the Skyscape explosion was not the result of a faulty gas valve, as local authorities had suggested. Anonymous sources had leaked that not only was the blast caused by plastic explosives, but federal investigators had discovered enough C2 planted in the stairwells to bring the entire building down.

That afternoon I called General Horvachek.

"Did you talk to the media?" he asked abruptly.

"No, why?"

"If anyone from any news agency contacts you, hang up on them. I'm serious about that. Don't say a word, just hang up."

"What's the issue?" I asked.

"People get the idea that al-Qaida tried to blow up a building in a city like San Jose, it creates problems. It's bad for the economy, bad for politicians. Our government doesn't want the public in a panic."

"Best to keep the civilians blissfully ignorant, huh?"

"I'll let you draw your own conclusions on that."

"How about Lawrence Tucker, General? Did the CIA find him?"

"He's in their custody."

"I suspected he was scheming to bring a shipment of heroin into the US. Any perspective on that?"

"He was apprehended in a trawler approaching a containership eighty miles east of the Golden Gate," said Horvachek. "That's all I can tell you."

"Will he be charged with a crime?"

"The military has first shot at him, for desertion and treason."

"I know this is a stretch, but any way I can talk to him?"

The general laughed. "Not a chance."

• • •

I waited until just before five o'clock that afternoon before calling Marcus's office number. I told the receptionist I was a detective from the county seat in Placerville, and she put me through.

"Sheriff Grier."

"Talk to me, Marcus."

"Representing yourself as a law officer is a crime," he said.

"Tell me something I don't know. Like who hijacked the evidence against Duante Tucker."

He blew out a long breath. "It will be announced tomorrow. But I suppose you don't want to wait until then."

"You suppose right. Who was it, Marcus?"

"Christian Wayne Sawyer. *Judge* Christian Wayne Sawyer. He presided over the case."

"The *judge?*"

"Yes, sir."

"Did he confess?"

"No, but we know he was dallying with Shanice Tucker," said Grier. "And she's cut a deal to testify against him."

"What kind of deal?"

"He claims she was blackmailing him. But she says he was infatuated with her and offered to get her brother off in return for an ongoing relationship."

"With a prostitute? He put himself at that risk for freebies?"

"She says she recorded every conversation they had. She's got it all on tape. He's done."

"She skates, I take it?" I asked.

"What would we charge her with, besides prostitution?" he replied.

"How about aiding and abetting a criminal act?"

"Not part of the deal."

I was silent for a moment. Actually, I didn't know what to say. Christian Wayne Sawyer was a well-known member of Lake Tahoe's uppercrust. It was not uncommon to see his name and picture in the local newspaper, as he participated in charity events and lake conservation politics. He was a man in his midfifties with a full head of silver hair and a florid face, and I knew he was married because I remembered seeing his wife posing with him in newspaper photos. She was a fit woman of at least his age who had multiple cosmetic surgeries and was known to wear expensive jewelry and clothes. I imagined she worked very hard to maintain her fitness and sex appeal. Apparently that hadn't been enough to keep her husband faithful.

"There's something else I should tell you," Marcus said. "I asked the CIA agent if he would provide Lawrence Tucker's DNA sample to help us resolve the Duante Tucker case. I received it last night."

"What use is Lawrence Tucker's DNA?"

"After we found out Duante's father died in prison, I was curious why Lawrence would be motivated to spring Duante. After all, Lawrence Tucker seemed to have a lot of resources, right? Ex-soldiers, gangbangers—so why would he need Duante?"

"Because he could trust him?" I said.

"It was more than that. I had DNA samples from Duante that were not part of the court case. Our lab compared Duante's DNA to Lawrence Tucker's. They sent me the results. Duante Tucker is Lawrence Tucker's son."

"How could that be?"

"Lawrence was sleeping with his brother Lamar's wife."

"The results are that definitive?"

"There's no doubt. I spoke to Shanice earlier today, and she confirmed it."

"How would she know?" I asked.

"She said it went on for years, before Lamar went to prison and after, when Lawrence was on leave from the marines."

"I wonder if Duante knows he's Lawrence's son."

"Shanice said he did," Grier replied.

I held the phone away and shook my head. Then I said, "Hey, Marcus?"

"Yeah?"

"Nice work, figuring that out."

"And you think I just sit around on my fat ass all day long."

. . .

The next morning a news story broke on the Internet. The DEA had seized one hundred kilos of pure heroin from a freighter churning toward the Port of Oakland. A group of men on a nearby deep-sea fishing vessel had been arrested in conjunction. The heroin was reportedly from Afghanistan, where the wholesale price was around $5,000 per kilo. The retail value of one hundred kilos in the US market, after being cut and packaged for street level sale, was over $30 million.

Later in the morning, I uncovered my barbeque and lit a bag of charcoal. When the coals were whitehot, I threw on a couple of chicken breasts I'd been soaking in barbeque sauce. While Candy made a salad, I sat at my picnic bench in the shade and scanned news sites on the Internet. I was looking for information on Christian Wayne Sawyer. I wanted to send Ryan Addison my final case report, and I hoped to include a confirmation that Sawyer had been taken into custody.

There was no report of Sawyer's arrest, but I did find a brief bio on him. As a young man he had worked as a policeman in Tennessee and Alabama. He put himself through law school and became an attorney and a magistrate. Before moving out west, he'd run for public office and at one point had served as a zoning commissioner. His family roots extended deep into southern history. Among his predecessors were plantation owners, real estate barons, mayors, and bankers. I didn't expend any effort in researching him further. I guessed his lusts and motivations probably stemmed from a cultural upbringing that reinforced particular entitlements. He chose to release a black rapist and to sleep with his sister because he thought he had the power to do so, as if it was part of some natural order. I imagined he was outraged and, on some level, shocked that he would be prosecuted for what he'd done.

The day grew late, and I busied myself with yard work. Then I lifted weights in my garage and responded to an e-mail from a restaurant owner who suspected his employees of theft. At five thirty, my cell rang. It was Marcus Grier.

"Sawyer's not going to jail," he said.

"What?"

"Half of the force is at his house. His wife shot him, then killed herself. A murder-suicide. A first for South Lake Tahoe, I think."

"Are you there?"

"No. Plainclothes is handling it. I'm at home, and that's where I'm staying tonight. This is over, thank god."

"That's too bad," I said slowly. "I was looking forward to going to the trial."

"Really? Well, if you're such a glutton for punishment, you can go to his funeral instead."

After Grier hung up, I sat at my picnic bench and stared out at the landscape. I don't know how long I sat there. Finally, when the sun dropped from its high perch in the sky and fell behind a band of clouds along the ridgeline, I went inside and finished my final report and bill for Ryan Addison. I double-checked the math and spent a few minutes scanning over the case details. Then I mixed a drink and finished it before I went back to my desk and hit the "send" button.

EPILOGUE

CODY CALLED THE FOLLOWING afternoon. "Sorry I've been off the air for a bit," he said. "I've been on a roll, and I just picked up my liver from the lost and found at the Last Call."

"You dried out yet?" I asked.

"Oh, yeah. Back in training, nothing but good, clean living for me. Listen, I just had lunch with Ryan Addison and Lindsey. Ryan's broad, Ramona, the one with the big knockers, was also there."

"What'd they have to say?"

"They seem like one happy family. Lindsey says she thinks she's worked all the negative emotion out of her system, and she's ready to start dating and move on with her life."

"That's good to hear. What are the Addisons still doing in San Jose?"

"They've been visiting Duante the last four days. Addison told the hospital they were there to pray for him. He claimed the only way they could cleanse themselves was to forgive Duante."

I laughed out loud. "Do you believe that?"

"I may be a drunk, but I'm not an idiot. It's a moot point anyway, because Duante Tucker expired this morning. The Addisons were in his room when he died."

"You don't think—"

"That they killed him?" said Cody. "No, not that anyone could prove. I doubt their words provided him much comfort, though."

"They probably threatened to torture him to death after his release," I said.

"Or something like that. Anyway, I got your share of the money from Addison."

"What money?"

"The hundred grand cash he offered if Tucker ended up dead."

"I told him I wanted nothing to do with that, Cody."

"Yeah, I know, you're a pillar of ethics. You want me to keep it all? I'll probably booze myself six feet under with all that dough, and it will be on you."

"That's the dumbest rationale I've ever heard."

"I've got your share in a briefcase in a safe deposit box at the bank down the street from my office. You can pick it up when you're in town next. Forty-five grand."

"I thought it was fifty."

"That was before I put aside five to cover a week vacation at a luxury resort down in Cabo. I hooked up again with Heidi-ho. You remember her, right? We want to go next week. Tell Candi to pack her bags."

"How did this all come about?"

"It was the result of deep contemplation. Like, I worked hard and got shot and finished a case, and now I deserve a vacation. Profound, huh?"

"Did you hear anything on Landers?" I asked.

"Oh, yeah, my good buddy," Cody said. "He's on unpaid leave, and the FBI is building condos in his colon. I doubt he can talk his way out this time. He's circling the drain."

"I guess that's another reason to celebrate."

"Fuckin'-A, brother. We'll see you in Mexico."

. . .

And that's how things worked out that summer in California. I may have had some brief illusion that the world was a better place with people like Duante Tucker, Lawrence Tucker, and Russ Landers either dead or out of commission. But one look at the evening news put that farce to rest. Suicide bombings were still a daily event in Iraq, Iran was moving forward with plans to develop nuclear weapons, civil war was raging in Syria, and with the departure of US troops, opium cultivation in Afghanistan had flourished to the point that the country had become "the world's first true narco-state."

But those problems are on the other side of the globe, right? It's easy to think the strife that exists in underdeveloped countries doesn't apply to the United States. Until you turn on the television and learn that two young Russian immigrants detonated bombs at the Boston Marathon finish line and killed three (including two eight-year-old children) and maimed scores more. There was no evidence the bombers were connected to any known domestic right-wing terrorist organizations. No affiliation to neo-Nazi militias or White Nationalist or Holocaust Denial groups. Nor were they linked to black separatists, gay hate, or racist skinhead factions. For twenty-four hours, the nation wondered what could have possibly motivated two young men to commit such an atrocity. The authorities then announced they'd linked the bombers to a radical brand of Islam. All indications were the pair had become radicalized without any direct support from al-Qaida; instead, they'd acted independently, planning and executing the bombings on their own.

And that's the way it is these days. Even though I live in a country where the most grievous crimes seem trivial compared to the genocide and mass killings commonplace in less fortunate regions of the world, there's no shortage of evil here. There will always exist a percentage of people who are driven by greed or hate or insanity or some diabolical combination of those traits. These individuals cause most of the world's grief, and in doing so, they provide me both a paycheck and job security.

If in some small way I contribute to the greater good, then I'm glad for that. I've read the human mind will eventually evolve into a form that universally embraces peace and rejects all things evil. The projected time frame for that process is thousands of years. In the meantime, I don't see any shortage of work on the horizon.

Regardless, I wake every day and walk out my front door and gaze over a landscape that I consider as beautiful as any on this planet. The cool, clean mountain air fills my lungs, and in those moments, I never think about anything except how lucky I am to be alive.

Overall, I'd say that's a pretty good deal. So why complain?

ABOUT THE AUTHOR

Born in Detroit, Michigan, in 1960, Dave Stanton moved to Northern California in 1961. He attended San Jose State University and received a BA in journalism in 1983. Over the years, he worked as a bartender, newspaper advertising salesman, furniture mover, debt collector, and technology salesman. He has two children, Austin and Haley. He and his wife, Heidi, live in San Jose, California.

Stanton is the author of five novels, all featuring private investigator Dan Reno and his ex-cop buddy, Cody Gibbons.

To learn more, visit the author's website at

http://danrenonovels.com/

If you enjoyed *Hard Prejudice*, please don't hesitate to leave a review at:

http://bit.ly/DaveStantonAmazon

To contact Dave Stanton or subscribe to his newsletter, go to:

http://danrenonovels.com/contact/

More Dan Reno Novels:

STATELINE

Cancel the wedding—the groom is dead.

When a tycoon's son is murdered the night before his wedding, the enraged and grief-stricken father offers investigator Dan Reno (that's *Reno,* as in *no problemo)*, a life-changing bounty to find the killer. Reno, nearly broke, figures he's finally landed in the right place at the right time. It's a nice thought, but when a band of crooked cops get involved, Reno finds himself not only earning every penny of his paycheck, but also fighting for his life.

Who committed the murder, and why? And what of the dark sexual deviations that keep surfacing? Haunted by his murdered father and a violent, hard drinking past, Reno wants no more blood on his hands. But a man's got to make a living, and backing off is not in his DNA. Traversing the snowy alpine winter in the Sierras and the lonely deserts of Nevada, Reno must revert to his old ways to survive. Because the fat bounty won't do him much good if he's dead…

Available on Amazon.com: http://bit.ly/Stateline-Amazon

Dying for the Highlife

Jimmy Homestead's glory days as a high school stud were a distant memory. His adulthood had amounted to little more than temporary jobs, cheap boarding houses, and discount whiskey. But he always felt he was special, and winning a $43 million lottery proved it.

With all that money, everything is great for Jimmy—until people from his past start coming out of the woodwork. First, his sexy stepmother, who seduced him as a teenager. Then his uncle, just released from Folsom after a five-year jolt for securities fraud, a crime that bankrupted Jimmy's father. Mix in a broke ex-stripper and a down-on-his luck drug dealer, both seeking payback over transgressions Jimmy thought were long forgotten.

Caught in the middle are investigator Dan Reno and his good buddy Cody Gibbons, two guys just trying to make an honest paycheck. Reno, straining to keep his home out of foreclosure, thinks that's his biggest problem. But his priorities change when Gibbons and Jimmy are kidnapped by a gang of cartel thugs out for a big score. Fighting to save his friend's life, Reno is drawn into a mess that leaves dead bodies scattered all over northern Nevada.

Available on Amazon.com: http://bit.ly/TheHighlife

Speed Metal Blues

Bounty hunter Dan Reno never thought he'd be the prey.

It's a two-for-one deal when a pair of accused rapists from a New Jersey-based gang surface in South Lake Tahoe. The first is easy to catch, but the second, a Satanist suspected of a string of murders, is an adversary unlike any Reno has faced. After escaping Reno's clutches in the desert outside of Carson City, the target vanishes. That is, until he makes it clear he intends to settle the score.

To make matters worse, the criminal takes an interest in a teenage boy and his talented sister, both friends of Reno's. Wading through a drug-dealing turf war and a deadly feud between mobsters running a local casino, Reno can't figure out how his target fits in with the new outlaws in town. He only knows he's hunting for a ghost-like adversary calling all the shots.

The more Reno learns more about his target, the more he's convinced that mayhem is inevitable unless he can capture him quickly. He'd prefer to do it clean, without further bloodshed. But sometimes that ain't in the cards, especially when Reno's partner Cody Gibbons decides it's time for payback.

Available on Amazon.com: http://bit.ly/SpeedMetalBlues

Dark Ice

Two murdered girls, and no motive…

While skiing deep in Lake Tahoe's backcountry, Private Eye Dan Reno finds the first naked body, buried under fresh snow. Reno's contacted by the grieving father, who wants to know who murdered his daughter, and why? And how could the body end up in such a remote, mountainous location? The questions become murkier when a second body is found. Is there a serial killer stalking promiscuous young women in South Lake Tahoe? Or are the murders linked to a different criminal agenda?

Searching for answers, Reno is accosted by a gang of racist bikers with a score to settle. He also must deal with his pal, Cody Gibbons, who the police consider a suspect. The clues lead to the owner of a strip club and a womanizing police captain, but is either the killer?

The bikers up the ante, but are unaware that Cody Gibbons has Reno's back at any cost. Meanwhile, the police won't tolerate Reno's continued involvement in the case. But Reno knows he's getting close. And the most critical clue comes from the last person he'd suspect…

Available on Amazon.com: http://bit.ly/DarkIce

Made in the USA
Monee, IL
23 June 2021